God's Country

By Charles F. Trafford

Clarkia
I hope you like reading it
as much as I liked
writing it
Love and peace —
Charles

ISBN 1-4116-4747-5

To Deb, with love
Without your support this book would have never been written.

Contents

In the Beginning

It was the summer of nineteen eighty-three – arguably the best four months of my life - everything was right. I had just been admitted to university for the next fall and I was pretty proud of myself. I figured that it was no small task considering that I had been hauled down to my counselor's office in my junior year of high school. I was told that I wasn't college material and should think about dropping out to go to trade school. I had no hard feelings about it. Frankly - and understandably - I think that my advisor just wanted to get rid of me.

I was also six months out of a three-year relationship with a woman who had all of the emotional warmth of Hermann Goring. She was the kind of person who would readily cry at sappy movies but was totally unmoved when she crushed people's hearts for real. I thought that was a pretty bizarre character trait. I didn't miss it.

I was desperately in love with my fresh new girlfriend, Althea. Sometimes she spelled her name Altheah, Altheia, Althya, Althe-aaah, or whatever other variation came into her head. She was a beautiful young woman with full lips and curly light golden blond hair that fell in broad ringlets past her shoulders. Her positive attitude was infectious and I found it hard to ever be in a bad mood when I was around her. She was the kind of person who could find joy even in good dental hygiene. Every so often she would enthusiastically jut her head forward, grin and remind me, "I don't have a single filling!" Hell, I hadn't been excited about that since I was eight years old.

One of her most prominent features was her neck. Althea was sure, although it had never been confirmed medically, that she had an extra vertebra. Regardless of the fact that it accentuated her beauty, just the thought that God had blessed her with an extra bone made her feel pretty special. In elementary school kids had made fun of her, but as an adult she had a gracefulness not unlike a gazelle. Althea was an artist - a painter. She loved to get up early in the morning; it was her favorite time to work. She would get out of bed, put some coffee on, staple a canvas to the wall, and stand there stark naked, painting like mad.

It was a warm summer day in mid-August. The low morning sun shone through the new leaves of the paper birch outside our window and cast the entire bedroom in green. I stared up at the ceiling drinking in the color and the light rhythmic snoring of Althea next to me. I rolled over and looked at the clock. It was 7:15 and I was awake in spite of the two bottles of Gato Negro that we had consumed the night before over a wine and cards version of strip gin rummy.

Today was the day that my friend Leonard and I were going to go look at a 1960 Bug that I had sniffed out yakking it up with the Czechoslovakian VW mechanic down the road. We needed a car for the road trip that Leonard and I were going to take this summer. We had planned the trip for months and I had exactly one thousand dollars to get us a car. I figured that I could probably drive the Bug away for that.

I got up, put on some coffee, and lit a cigarette to pass the time while I was waiting for it to brew. I looked at the clock - 7:25. What the hell. I picked up the phone and dialed up Leonard. After the fifth ring (I was questioning my judgment after the third), the line clicked. For a few seconds there was nothing but rustling on the other end. I broke the silence.

"Hello? - Hey, Leonard, wake up, man."

Leonard croaked out, "It's seven fucking fifteen in the fucking morning."

I corrected him, "No, it's seven fucking thirty. And hey, since you're awake already why don't you come on over. I'll make you some coffee and we'll run over and take a look at that Bug."

"Jesus." The line clicked again, then dial tone.

Two more cigarettes, another cup of coffee, and a half hour later there was a knock at the door - Leonard.

"Hey, man. Sorry about waking you up but I don't want someone else buying the Bug out from underneath us." Leonard stood there for a moment and stared at me through moderately bloodshot eyes then walked expressionlessly past me into the apartment.

Leonard was Native American – but I didn't know what tribe – I never did know. I'd asked him a couple of times but somehow we always got off the subject before he could, or would, tell me. He was six foot two - a calm and strong person, with a cutting and frequently ironic sense of humor. His hair probably reached to his butt but it was impossible to tell because he habitually wove it into a single thick black rope braid tied at the end with a rawhide leather lashing. It was cool, and in high school it made me a little jealous. I knew if I had tried to grow my own hair that long I would have ended up looking like a pathetic white imitation of Super Fly.

Leonard's eyes were probably his most striking feature. They were a light crystalline blue, and were even more extraordinary set against his dark complexion. They had the kind of depth and intensity that made people either want to turn away or gaze into them forever.

We had met in high school while smoking pot out behind the portables and been friends ever since. I remember one day after getting thoroughly stoned on what was allegedly "Panama Red," I asked him, thinking it was a pretty deep question, if he had been named after Leonard Peltier.

He told me, "No, I was named after my father. What about you, Carl, were you named after Carl Bjorgen?" My Norwegian history wasn't that good, so I had no idea who Carl Bjorgen was, but I was fairly certain that I hadn't been named after him. I got the point.

As I was pouring the cup of coffee that I had promised him I heard movement from the direction of the bedroom.

"Hi Leonard," said Althea cheerfully. She was standing in the doorway in nothing but my shirt, which was fully unbuttoned, leaving nothing to anyone's imagination.

"Hey Althea, how ya doin'?" Leonard replied with slightly more expression than he had given me. He was unshaken by her frank display of nudity. He, I, and everyone else knew that for Althea there was nothing sexual in displaying her body to friends – it just was.

"We gotta get going here, Althea – we're going over to the mechanic's to take a look at the Bug," I said. "We should be back in a couple of hours or so."

"Okay," she said and then planted a kiss on me like we weren't going to see each other for a year.

It was 9:15 by the time we got to the shop. The Czechoslovakian mechanics had been hard at work since 7:00 a.m. and were now sitting around the garage on break smoking cigarettes and drinking coffee.

"Hey, Jim." I always thought that it was a pretty unlikely name for a Czechoslovakian but what the hell, I didn't name him. "We came by to look at the Bug."

"Ya, I got the Bug out back but ya know I was talking with my wife last night and told her that you were going to take the car on a trip. She suggested that maybe you want to look at this other one that I got – I had forgotten about it – might be better for you - a Van."

Leonard nudged me and said "Gimme a cigarette – I'm out." I gave him a Camel and he promptly busted the filter off muttering "cigarettes with diapers."

"Yeah, okay let's look at both of 'em,'" I said.

We went around back to the storage building behind the garage. Jim opened the door and there was the Bug. What a beauty – totally restored, with a fresh coat of salmon pink paint.

"Ya, this was stock color for that year. The engine she is rebuilt too – 36 horsepower – that's all. Takes a while but you get where you are going." He smiled as he opened the hood.

Leonard wasn't paying any attention to Jim's spiel about the Bug.

"Hey Carl, look over here."

"Ya, that is the van I was talking about. I am teaching my son to be a mechanic and we put that van together." I looked over toward Leonard and saw the van. It took me a second to adjust. The van was two-tone – matte black over red.

"That one is a 1964."

There was a six-foot CB antenna that stuck up over the center of the cab that made the van look like it might be radio-controlled. Behind the antenna there was a fabric sunroof, which was about four feet by six feet and covered a good portion of the roof. I looked at the tires. They were a few sizes bigger than the original equipment and gave the van a more imposing presence.

"Ya, we had to put bigger tires on when we replaced the motor. Too much power, not enough rubber. The old motor was shot when we got it so we put in a two-liter Porsche motor. It goes like heck now." I opened the driver's door and got in – the smell of pine-scented Christmas tree air freshener overwhelmed me. Incidentally, that smell never left the van the entire time I owned it, even though I was dead certain I had found every air freshener in there … (and I found eight of them).

"It even got the gas heater. It was in Montana and this guy found it in a field. He bought it, and brought it back to Mount Vernon to have us fix it. Too many things wrong so he sold it to us." The Bug that I came for was now completely forgotten.

"How much you want for it?" I asked.

"Well, it has new motor, new brakes ... how about $900?"

"Can I take it for a drive first?" I said.

"Ya, keys are in it – go ahead."

Leonard climbed into the passenger seat beside me. "Shit, Carl, this is one cool van."

"Yeah ..." I said, abruptly cut off as the engine roared to life. We both just looked at each other – it didn't sound like any VW van that I had ever heard. I stuck it in first, let out the clutch, and promptly, but inadvertently, left 500 miles worth of rubber on the storage building floor. I shut the motor off and opened the door.

"How about $800?" Jim paused for a second and looked at the ground as if his answer were in the concrete. "Ya, sold."

We went back to the shop and drew up the paperwork. I gave him a check for eight hundred dollars and he handed me a fistful of keys – there were six of them, one for the ignition and one for each door on the van.

"Congratulations, you now own the limp 757" said Jim, smiling and pointing to the license plate – LMP-757.

"Hey, Althea," I hollered up at the apartment, "come on down and check out my new car." A few seconds later Althea came bounding down the stairs – this time she was fully dressed. She got two-thirds of the way down the outside stairs when she stopped, an ambiguous expression of surprise on her face. She approached me and the van with intentional steps, and with each step her face brightened. By the time she got to me she had a broad smile. I followed her as she methodically walked around the van.

"This is perfect," she repeated over and over. Judging from her reaction, you would have thought that I had brought home a brand-new Lincoln Mark Five. Finally she got to the side wing doors, grabbed the handle, and swung both doors open. She took a few steps back as if to get a better perspective on the seven-passenger interior, put both hands on her hips, and with a huge smile on her face proclaimed, "We could fill this thing full of kids!" I should have seen it coming - she was proud of her full hips and regularly reminded me that they were made specifically for childbearing. I wasn't sure that I was ready to find out.

X played on the portable tape deck that I had just bought from Chubby and Tubby for our trip (we ended up forgetting to bring it) while Leonard and I packed the van in preparation for leaving the next morning. I was looking forward to it, but we were going to be gone for at least two weeks and I knew that I would miss Althea as well.

It was mid-August and it had been a cloudless hot summer. I had made money by hammering nails for a local contractor. As a result, I was in great physical shape, especially for a pseudo-beatnik. Althea and I had taken full advantage of the heat by running down to a nearby lake whenever we could to lie in the sun and swim. We were young, tan, and inseparably in love. Some nights when it was too hot to sleep in the apartment we would grab a bottle of Ouzo from the liquor store. The state had seized a warehouse full of the stuff earlier in the year in a tax foreclosure and they were selling it off for six bucks a bottle. It was perfect for our purposes. We would go down to the lake and go skinny-dipping half-drunk in the moonlight. There was something both sensuous and mystical about all of it. It was a good way to be twenty-five.

Upstairs in the apartment Althea stood half-naked in the kitchen (she claimed it was the heat – we both knew that was an excuse) baking her fourth batch of chocolate chip cookies. The scent of the cookies wafted down to the van in the still afternoon air. If nothing else, Leonard and I would have a fair sugar high for a good portion of the trip.

"What the hell are you doing?" said Leonard. Startled, I turned around. I had been in deep concentration arranging the multiple religious icons on the dashboard of the van.

"Insurance," I said. I had never been affiliated with any particular religious denomination despite of my parents' efforts to bathe me at a young age in the teachings of Presbyterianism. "Some of this seems to work for some folks and not for others, but none of it works for everybody," I explained. "This way, I figure we're covered." I pointed to each one, "We have Christ, Mary, Shiva, Vishnu, Buddha, Asadu, and some dirt in a box from a new age church in New Mexico where folks get faith healed. Check this out – we're even covered at night - the rosary glows in the dark."

Leonard just stood there straight-faced and looked at me, then shook his head. "Don't act so high." He went back to rearranging supplies in the aft compartment. We spent the next four hours packing every conceivable thing that we thought that we might need for the next three weeks, including two and a half ounces of very moderate pot that Leonard had grown under a fluorescent light in his closet over the summer.

Althea and I stayed up most of that night as if the more we made love the less we would miss each other over the next three weeks. I don't think that either one of us thought that it would really work but it was sure worth a try.

I woke up the next morning at 7:15 after about three hours of sleep to heavy pounding on the door.

"Hey, wake the fuck up, Carl. Time to hit the road."

"What's wrong with you? It's seven fucking fifteen in the fucking morning," I said.

"That's right, it's seven fucking fifteen in the fucking morning," Leonard agreed. "Let's go." I extracted myself out of a tangle of arms, legs, sheets and pillows, knocking over a half-spent glass of Ouzo and an incense holder in the process. I opened the door.

"Hey, since you're awake, why don't I make you a cup of coffee and we'll hit the road," said Leonard, half-smiling. I got the point.

After two cups of coffee, a couple of cigarettes, and a package of Hostess powdered Donettes that Leonard had thoughtfully brought for breakfast, we were out the door. Althea and I planted a volley of I-ain't-gonna-see-you-for–two-and-a-half-weeks kisses on each other while Leonard, shaking his head, went down to warm up the van.

I looked deeply into Althea's eyes. "I love you baby ... I'll see you in a little over two weeks," I said quietly as I cupped her face in my hand.

"You sure will," Althea smiled. "I love you too." A yellow-red spark of love lightning flashed between us, and we kissed passionately one last time.

Exodus

We had driven south on Interstate 5 from Mount Vernon, picked up Interstate 90, and were now exactly seventeen miles outside of Seattle headed east. Leonard had been juggling the map, our schedule, and a cup of coffee since we had left. He finally gave up and dumped the whole pile, minus the coffee, onto the floor of the van and got out a pipe. Leonard saw me looking at him questioningly.

"Hey, don't give me that look; it's a tool, not recreation. It'll help me figure out where we're going," said Leonard. "See, you need to be in the same state of mind reading these things as when you wrote them," he said philosophically, lightly tapping pot into the pipe.

He may have had a point. We had drawn the schedule up over the last two months over copious beers at the local tavern, The Humpie (named after the pink salmon that ran in the nearby Skagit River). Half, and sometimes fully drunk, we had religiously sat at the bar and laid out a map of the western United States. Through smoke and beer, we followed the roads that we thought were most interesting at the time with a precision cartography mileage counter that my cousin from Norway had sent to me, God knows why, for my birthday. Even at the time I had a hunch that the beer maybe altered the calibration of that fine tool - but probably not by much.

Leonard stifled a cough as he handed me the pipe. "Here, this will help you get us there."

Four hours later we were just getting out of the mountains. By our schedule it should have taken us two - hmm. Now, there are two factors when considering speed -

one is power and the other is control. With a two liter Porsche motor in it, the van had plenty of power, but with a chassis designed for a forty horsepower engine it lacked a fair amount of control. It was a bit like strapping a Saturn Five rocket motor to a piece of plywood – oh, you could go as fast as you wanted – you just couldn't always control which direction.

It had only been raining for a few minutes. "Hey, Carl, we're taking on water aft." I turned around and saw two geysers shooting up from in front of the rear wheel wells and water was sloshing back and forth on the rubber mat in the passenger compartment.

"Well, shit, get back there and see what you can do," I told Leonard.

"Arrrrh matey," Leonard replied, making a pirate hook with his forefinger.

"Quit being an asshole, man, this is serious stuff. We're sinking."

As Leonard was trying to shore up the flood by packing a Hefty bag into one of the melon-sized holes in the rusted-out floorboard, I saw a blue highway sign ahead. From previous road trips I knew that blue highway signs were good. It was a rest area a quarter mile up ahead: "Traveler's Rest - Free Coffee." Free anything is good.

Nearly missing the exit in the rain, I had to jam the van into a hard turn, killing a few road turtles and sending the van into a momentary fishtail in the process. I pulled into a parking space, turned off the motor, and went back to see if Leonard had found a solution to the water issue.

"Problem solved," said Leonard. "I crammed two plastic bags in the holes in the floor. I think we should be okay for at least a few thousand miles."

I agreed. "Cool, let's go get us some free coffee."

By then the rain had let up and from the rest area, which was at the top of a foothill, we were able to see a sweeping view of the flatlands of eastern Washington. We grabbed a cup of weak coffee from a couple of old guys at a folding table that had a sign that said "VFW Outpost 104." I don't know if they had noticed Leonard's Che Guevara pin on his jacket or not, but they gave us both an "I didn't fight the communists for people like you" look when we didn't drop any money in the donation can. Leonard looked at both of them expressionlessly and said, "Hey, the sign says free."

Leonard and I wandered over to the edge of the rest area with our coffee to take in the view and relax some after our near-sinking. A few feet away two German-looking tourists, a man and a woman in their late twenties, talked enthusiastically in some Bavarian dialect and pointed at a couple of remnant clouds hanging in the sky off in the distance.

"What the hell are they so excited about?" said Leonard, looking at the sky where they were pointing.

"Hell if I know, I'm Norwegian, not German. Language ain't genetic." Leonard just looked at me.

They were a good-looking pair, tall, blond and perfectly Teutonic – they could have been extras from the movie "Heidi." They both had that sort of rosy complexion that reflected a sausage and potato-based diet. The woman was about five foot ten and statuesque. She had obligatory blonde hair and blue eyes and a pleasing physical robustness. Without being crass, her children would never go hungry. The man was similarly tall, maybe six foot two, with light blue eyes that were the color of cool, clean water. His hair was cropped short and was so sun-bleached that it was nearly white. He had the physique of a man who could take on the job of repopulating the world if he had to, and there probably wasn't a woman alive who would mind if he did.

Leonard and I stood there for five or ten minutes sipping the acrid watery coffee and looking out at the clouds the German couple were still pointing at. Even looking hard, I saw nothing other than clouds.

"What the hell *are* they looking at?" I said, more to myself than to Leonard.

"No sense in standing here wondering. Let's go ask," said Leonard. I shrugged and followed him.

Leonard and I wandered over to the couple, who were by this time even more excited than when we had first observed them.

"Hey, how you guys doin'? My name's Leonard and this is my friend Carl."

"Hello, please to meet you. My name is Dieter and this is my girlfriend Marta." Marta smiled warmly. "We are from Germany and are vacationing here in America. We came here to see what you call God's Country," said Dieter in a subtle, clean German accent.

"Really? Germany?" I tried to make it sound as if I was surprised. The Germans didn't catch my sarcasm and just smiled.

"So, my friend and I here have been looking out at those clouds that you have been pointing to for the past few minutes. Pretty, aren't they?" said Leonard, innocently probing.

"Oh, yes, the clouds they are very beautiful. There is one - look there," said Marta pointing again excitedly, "You can see the Virgin."

"What?" Leonard and I said nearly in unison.

"Yes, look at the big one just above the others - there she is, the Virgin," said Dieter.

Leonard and I stood there looking up into the cloud trying to grasp exactly what they were talking about. The pair took our stares as comprehension.

"Ah, then you see her too," said Marta, with an air of tranquil conviction.

Either Leonard didn't want to hurt their feelings or all of a sudden had a vision that he wasn't telling me about. "Well ... sort of..." The Germans both smiled and nodded at us, as if we had a mutual secret holy understanding.

"Well, look, we gotta get going here, we have a long way to go," I said. "Maybe we'll run into you again."

"Yes, it was nice to meet you," Dieter said, smiling, and they turned their attention back to the cloud. We waved as we walked away.

When we were a few feet away, Leonard leaned over to me and half-whispered (I don't think he wanted to hurt their feelings), "Ya know, I'm a little bit stoned and I still don't see anything up there but clouds."

"I do," I said. Leonard stopped and stared at me. "That one, over there," I pointed. "I think it looks a little like Woody

Allen." We both stifled a laugh as we walked back
van.

We were back on the road and were now he
southeast on US 97 toward Oregon. Leonard turne
"Wow, man, was that some seriously weird stuff back there, or what?"

"Whaddya mean, the Virgin in the sky stuff with the Germans?"

"Oh duh, Carl, what do ya think I'm fucking talking about? I mean, are those two Germans freaks or something?"

I couldn't help but laugh a little at the way he said "freaks." I pondered his question a little more deeply for a moment then said, "Yes, Leonard, I suppose that you *could* call them freaks. On the other hand though, maybe they're just full of holy conviction."

"Yeah, sure, Carl, you just call it whatever you want. I still think they're German freaks."

"Yeah ok, but I don't think that it really has anything to do with 'em being Germans. Folks who are wound up that way are, as you call it, freaky no matter where they come from."

"Yeah, maybe, but it made it just that much weirder when they said that stuff with a German accent."

"Yeah, I'll have to give you that."

"And what was that shit about 'God's Country?' Jesus, are they going to go all the way across the whole fucking United States doing that I-see-shit-in-the-clouds stuff?"

"Maybe ..."

"Well it sounds like a pretty fucked-up vacation if you ask me." We both busted up.

A few minutes later, after our laughter had subsided, I stared out at the road ahead and thought. On one hand, I had to agree with Leonard. I thought that they were probably both crazy, but on the other hand there was something eerily convincing in their conviction of having seen the Virgin in that cloud.

Icons

We drove on. It was late afternoon and Leonard was snoring quietly as his forehead bounced lightly against the side window. How the hell he could nap above all of the racket inside the van was beyond me. The Porsche motor, combined with an extractor muffler, made being inside of the van at freeway speed a little like being a test monkey inside of a big tin box being beaten with a jackhammer. As the trip went on, we would find that after driving for three or four hours, we would get out and yell at each other for at least fifteen minutes before our hearing would return to somewhere near normal.

As I drove on through the Umtanum Mountains just north of Yakima my thoughts began to drift - I thought of Althea. Although it had been less than twelve hours since I had last seen her, I already missed her like crazy. I knew that she missed me too. It had been such a time – an amazing time since we had met. My life had taken on a whole new excitement. Every day was colored in exaggerated hues and my world had come into a clear focus of definition and meaning – starkly contrary to the dark days of my not-so-distant previous girlfriend.

That old relationship had been a difficult one – three years of difficult. Since the day that we had first met, it was clear that we were polar opposites. Why we ever dated I'll never know. She was a serious woman with her feelings buried deep inside of her. She chose not to share her feelings except in the safety of the media. The only time that she ever cried was at the movies. Hell, she didn't even shed a tear the day that she came home and coldly announced to me that "she had to go find herself." Translation: I am already sleeping with someone else and seeing you is making me feel guilty about it. When she told me she needed to "find herself," I had a tremendous urge to drive her to the local mall and find one of those maps that say "you are here" and point at it – still I don't think that it would have resolved the issue. It probably would have just pissed her off. On top of it, her break-up timing was poor – she dumped me on my birthday. I suppose that in itself was just one more subtle clue about her inability to display empathy for another human being.

In the time between the breakup and meeting Althea I had languished for a few months in an alcoholic stupor of self-loathing and depression. The old relationship had been doomed for some time. For at least two of the three years of our relationship, both of us had lied to ourselves and to each other whenever either of us said, "I love you." Still, the whole breakup hurt.

Thank God for Leonard – he had stuck with me through all of it. He patiently watched me night after night obliterate myself and my feelings in any one of a number of local taverns. He would let me go, but only so far – and knew when to gently cut me off. He was better than any therapist would have been – he was a true friend. His approach had worked, and when I finally met Althea I had grown tired of alcohol and self-loathing and was on the upswing.

Leonard was getting restless and was in a state somewhere between asleep and awake when we rounded a curve just outside of Selah. It was now early evening and the sun was lying low on the hills around the highway painting them in a golden orange. I always liked this time of day - it was a spiritual time. It was a time when deep things seemed to happen.

About a hundred yards off in the distance on the opposite side of the highway there was a road sign. At the base of it there were what appeared to be bouquets of flowers – probably close to a hundred bouquets. As we neared, I could see that in addition to the flowers, there were at least an equal number of candles. Some were in makeshift holders of various cans and bottles. Others were melted into the sandy soil at the base of the sign creating amorphous blobs of candle-sand-flower-and-whatever-else-fell-in.

I pulled the van over onto what shoulder there was. The van skidded to a stop in the sand and listed at a good twenty-five degrees at the side of the road.

"What the hell are you doing?" said Leonard. "Are you practicing suicide?"

"Oh, hey Leonard, I didn't know that you were awake," I said.

"Well, I am. I decided to wake up so I could experience my own death," said Leonard.

"Hey, this is important stuff, take a look over there," I said, as I pointed to the roadside altar beneath the sign.

"Where the hell are we, and what the hell is all that," said Leonard, as he looked out at the desert landscape. "Did you drive us to Mexico while I was asleep?"

"No, I didn't drive us to Mexico, I drove us to fifteen miles outside of Selah," I said as I got out of the van and walked across the highway towards the road sign. Leonard nearly fell out of the van, with the twenty-five degree list and all, and followed me.

We both stood there silently looking at the conglomeration of liquor bottles, beer cans and baby food jar candleholders mixed in with the few hundred homemade flower bouquets. A number of the candles were still burning – someone must have been there fairly recently. There were a few scorch marks in the earth - remnants of spent emergency road flares. Interspersed amongst all of it were hundreds of crosses of various sizes, shapes and ornamentation. There was one that was large and hand-carved of wood – it looked like it took years to make. Another one that was spray painted Day-Glo orange was made out of Popsicle sticks with dried macaroni pasta glued to it.

"Man, someone who was either really loved or who was really important must have died here," said Leonard.
"Yeah, no lie, just look at all of this stuff," I said as a semi tanker truck with a "Drink-a-mug-a-milk-a-day" sign and a picture of winking cow on the back of it screamed by at

breaking-the-law speed. "I think I have an idea of how they died. Let's get out of here before they make one of these shrines for us."

"Hey, hang on for a second, Carl. Take a look up over there," said Leonard. Leonard had stepped back from the sign about twenty feet and was looking intently at the back of it. I went back to where Leonard was standing and looked up to where he was looking.

"Do you see what I see?" said Leonard. I stood there looking at what seemed to be a rainbow-colored heat image in the back of the sign. It was as if someone had taken a blowtorch to the sheet metal, but somehow I thought it unlikely that anyone had. There it was - it was unmistakable - a clear and perfect image of Jesus on the cross heat-embossed into the sign.

"If you see Jesus in the back of that road sign, then yes, I do see what you see," I said.

"Well," said Leonard, "as a matter of fact, I do see Jesus in the back of the road sign, and a matter of fact I would like to get the hell out of here because this is all just a little bit too weird." Leonard started to head back towards the van. I followed. Halfway across the highway I turned around and looked back at the other side of the sign. It was a blue one. "Rest Area - 93 miles."

We blazed on through the Umtanum Mountains, past Selah, and through Yakima. By now the sun had gone down and it was dark – not just regular dark – it was dark dark. There wasn't a whole hell of a lot on that eighty-mile lonely strip of highway south of Yakima. To the west stretched arid foothills that make up the Yakima Indian reservation. From a cursory glance they got robbed ... again. To the east was the Yakima Firing Center, a place where the military conducted practice maneuvers and tried out its newfangled ordinance on the critters of the desert.

Every once in a while though, some of those critters got back at the army. I remember reading a few months earlier about some poor infantry grunt who was running around out there with his unit playing war. Without looking he threw himself down behind a small hill to take cover. Unfortunately it was an anthill - fire ants. I had personally had the experience of having been bitten by fire ants, and it was a few degrees less than enjoyable. The newspaper article that reported on the incident said that he was "bitten repeatedly in the abdomen," and that "only by quick action of his fellow soldiers who stripped him naked to remove the ants" did he survive. When I had read the article, I speculated that the word "abdomen" was used in place of "genitalia," in order to get the story printed. The thought made me wince.

We had been driving through the area for over an hour and both Leonard and I stared out past the van's headlights at the darkness. It was so dark that it was impossible to get our bearings - it was even hard to tell which way was up. If we'd had a compass I was sure that it would have been spinning wildly.

Every so often, eyes would reflect back off of the headlights. At first when it happened, either Leonard or I would say "deer" or "raccoon" or some other benign animal. Now, though, it was getting surreal, and the shapes and sizes of the animals that those eyes were attached to began to be blurred by our imaginations.

"Did you see that ... what the hell was that?" said Leonard anxiously.

"Oh, hell, it was probably another deer," I answered unconvincingly.

"Bullshit if that was a deer. Deer do not have eyes the size of pie plates, they sure as hell do not reflect back red, and they sure as hell don't have teeth like that."

"What the hell are you talking about? You didn't see any teeth back there."

"Hell if I didn't," Leonard said emphatically. "Whatever that was back there, it had big fucking teeth." Then he narrowed his eyes and added, "Whatever you do Carl, don't you stop this fucking van... not for fucking anything."

"Yeah, well, what if one of us has to pee?"

"Tough, we wet our pants. It's better than being mutilated by one of those things out there."

The rest of the drive pretty much went like that until we got to Goldendale forty-five minutes later. Incidentally, I did not wet my pants but I did have to pee so badly that by the time we got to Fred's Texaco in Goldendale I squealed into the parking lot, bounced the van against the concrete parking barriers, and ran into the bathroom inside. In the bathroom I nearly wet my pants when the third button on my 501's hung up momentarily. The woman behind the register gave me a pretty weird look when I came out. She must have overheard my feverish dialogue in the bathroom: "Let go, you fucker – have to pee, goddamn it." Leonard, who was buying a package of Hostess Snowballs and a couple of Mountain Dews, didn't help the situation when he said loudly and seriously after I came out, "Is he okay?"

On the road again, Leonard was peeling the marshmallow coconougat vulcanized icing off of a Snowball.

"Good Lord, why don't they sell just this icing stuff? The cake part is disgusting," he said as he threw the cake center out of the van window. "You know, I hate to be detail-oriented and all, Carl, but exactly where the heck are we spending the night tonight ... or were you just planning on driving forever?" He was right. It was nearly ten-thirty and we probably should have pulled over and found a place to stay about four hours ago.

"Well, pull out the map and take a look at what is around here," I said. Leonard fumbled with the map, which stuck to his Snowball covered fingers.

"Exactly where the hell is 'around here,' because as far as I can tell we are exactly six miles south of nowhere."

"Well, Leonard, we're still on Route 97 going south from Goldendale which *is* somewhere. I'm not a whiz at Washington State geography but I think that we are going to run out of road pretty soon and run into the Columbia River. Maybe you could take a break from your Snowball and Mountain Dew snackathon over there and find us a place to camp." Leonard acted like he hadn't heard me and continued to study the map.

"Damn it, I can hardly see a fucking thing," said Leonard, squinting in the dim dome light. "Wait, hang on, I think I see a place on the map down by the river. Yeah, it looks like there is a park – Maryhill State Park. It looks like it's maybe twenty minutes or so from here."

By the time we pulled into the park it was close to eleven-thirty. The entire campground was completely dark – no one was awake. I tried to drive the van into the campground as quietly as possible, but when I let off of the accelerator and dropped it into first it backfired so hard that I saw the campground light up in my rearview mirror from the flash from the tailpipe. If anyone had been asleep they sure as hell weren't anymore.

"Jesus Christ, Carl, what the hell are you doing? You scared the shit out of me."

"Yeah, well, get tough, pal, and start looking for an open spot."

There were few other campers there, and after circling around once, we settled on a campsite at the far end of the park. Only after I switched off the motor and turned off the lights did I realize how incredibly quiet and dark it was. We got out of the van.

Leonard half-whispered, "Man, it's so quiet here it's almost creepy ... Shit ... Huh!" In the darkness Leonard had fallen over a fire-grate.

"Are you okay?"

"Yes, I am okay. Jesus, it's so friggin' dark I can't see a fucking thing. How in the hell do you propose that we set up our camp?"

"Screw it, let's just stay in the van tonight."

"Oh, that's a brilliant idea, Carl. Maybe you could have come up with that before I nearly broke something important."

Back in the van we dined on a nutritious combination of leftover Mountain Dew, tortilla chips, salsa, and carrots. Althea had insisted that we take ten pounds of these on the trip. One of her favorite food mantras was, "carrots make you smart!" I had always been told that they made you see better, but what the hell. For dessert we shared a healthy pipe-full of marijuana and a dozen or so chocolate chip cookies. Our conversation rambled until we finally came to the issue of our itinerary.

"So, I think that we should talk about where the hell we're headed tomorrow, Carl. It seems that currently we are just a little bit off our schedule." Leonard was right. Apparently the copious amounts of beer that we had drunk while we had created our timetable had had somewhat of a negative impact on the reality of the road. Still, on day one I wasn't ready to let go of our itinerary.

"Well, Leonard, according to our schedule we *are* supposed to be in Pendleton, Oregon right now. And I agree that since Pendleton is about two hundred miles from here that does put us about three hours behind schedule. But I think that if we get up early and stick to it we can probably make up that time tomorrow."

"You're delusional, Carl. First, the likelihood that I am getting up early tomorrow is zero. Second, according to our plan here we already have a twelve-hour drive ahead of us if we are going to get to Devil's Tower in Wyoming. The possibility of making that - again, zero."

"Well, then what do you ..."

I was cut off by a noise outside of the van. *Ahummmm dum da la dummmmm ...*

"What the fuck is that, Leonard?" *Ahummmm dum da la dummmm da da ...*

"Shit, Carl, I don't know what the hell it is. It sounds like some kind of fucking chanting." *Ahummmm dum da la dummmm ...* I opened up the door of the van to see if I could get a better bearing on where the sound was coming from.

"What the hell are you doing, Carl? Close that door! Did you ever consider that maybe those are friggin' cannibalistic pygmies out there and they're preparing some twisted ritual that involves eating tourists?"

"Jesus Christ, Leonard, calm the hell down. You're being high. There aren't cannibalistic pygmies in this part of the country. I'm sure of it." *Ahummmm dum da la dummmm da da ...*

I studied the sounds further. "Whoever the hell it is, it sounds like there's a bunch of them. They sound like they're close, but they don't sound like they're coming any closer." I tried to sound reassuring. Leonard and I continued to speculate on the source, location, and reason for the chanting long after it stopped fifteen minutes later. Neither one of us ever came up with any solid answers but we did a good job of completely freaking ourselves out with bizarre theories until we finally fell asleep.

The Pagans

When I woke up I had no concept of what time it was, and since we had come into the campground under cover of darkness I really had no comprehension of our surroundings. Leonard was still asleep and every so often let out a muffled snore. I lay there with my feet up on the rear seat. Apparently I had put them up there sometime in the night to compensate for the lack of room on the floor of the van. Leonard on the other hand had compensated for it by wedging his head in the tiny walkway between the front seats. I lay there in the silence staring up at the sun coming through the van windows and thinking about Althea. I was in love – really in love. Even without her there I could feel her presence, and I was sure that wherever, or whatever she was doing, she felt mine too. This awareness, I was told, is something that only a few people who are deeply in love feel. It is a feeling of knowing that there is another person in the world with whom they share a place. That person, no matter where they are on the planet, is always with them. It was a rare and precious thing. I lay there and savored the feeling.

A while later, as I was lying there I heard it. It came softly at first, *Ahummmm dum da la dummmm ... Ahummmm dum da la dummmm ...* Then it got louder and louder, *Ahummmm dum da la dummmm ... Ahummmm dum da la dummmm ...* It was the same chanting that we had heard the night before. This time, though, it sounded closer. Much closer.

"What the hell is going on, Carl?" Leonard had woken up. "Oh no, it's those goddamn cannibalistic pygmies again," he croaked.

"Yeah, you might be right, Leonard, and you know what, I think they are closer than they were last night ... a lot closer." I got up and cracked the curtains on the van window to see if I could see what was going on while Leonard fumbled in his sleeping bag to get his pants on. "Oh, Jesus, Leonard, you have to see this."

"What?"

"No, you just have to see this for yourself ... oh man."

Leonard, who finally had his pants on, looked out the window next to mine. "Oh Carl, Carl, Carl – this is too weird, weird, weird. Who the hell are those people, druids?" We both stared out the window at about forty people not more than seventy-five feet from the van. They were walking slowly single-file in a circle and chanting. Every one of them was wearing long brown, hooded robes that had what appeared to be a small white egg embossed on the left side of the chest. *Ahummmm dum da la dummmm ... Ahummmm dum da la dummmm ...*

In an open field a couple of hundred yards behind them was a huge circle of monolithic stones shaped like what appeared to be Stonehenge.

"Man, do you see that, Leonard? I think that's frickin' Stonehenge."

"Yes, I see that. Where the hell did you drive us to last night, Carl – the United Kingdom?"

"No, I couldn't have. The land bridge between here and Europe hasn't existed for some time now."

"Quit being a smart-ass, Carl. This is serious stuff. I know something about these druids. Last year I read an article in National Geographic about them. It said that druids were into human sacrifice. I bet that's what that altar in the center of that Stonehenge thing is for, friggin' human sacrifice. Since I don't see anyone else around here, and my guess is that they don't sacrifice each other, and we are probably it."

"Bullshit, Leonard, these druid guys aren't into the human sacrifice thing - that shit's ancient history. They're just a bunch of earth-loving witches."

Leonard immediately turned and looked at me with a somewhat panicked look on his face. "Witches! Are you insane, Carl? Man, that's even worse! Witches do the capture your soul, torture-you-for-eternity, mind-screw thing."

BANG, BANG, BANG. Leonard and I both jumped as the interior of van reverberated with a knock on the van's cargo doors behind us. "Oh sweet Jesus Christ – this is it – they're here for us!"

"Calm the hell down, Leonard, my God, you are paranoid."

Leonard looked at me and said seriously, "Don't open those doors, Carl. I swear you will be so fucking sorry if you do." I put my hand on the door handle anyway. "Wait, Carl. You know what else?"

"What?"

"If they burn us at the stake, I'll doing a big fucking I-told-you-so."

"I'll take my chances, Leonard."

Despite Leonard's vehement warning I opened the van doors to see who was there. In front of us stood a smiling young woman, maybe twenty-five years old or so. She was dressed in a druid robe. Even through the thick fabric of that robe, it was apparent that she was a shapely full-breasted woman. Her hood was down, and revealed curly dark brown hair that fell past her shoulders. She had lovely warm hazel eyes that smiled. She was extremely beautiful. Leonard and I just sat there with the van doors open, speechless. She finally broke the silence.

"Hi," she said. "My name is Gwendolyn." Her voice broke the trance that I was experiencing looking into her eyes. Leonard, who was also apparently half-hypnotized, just sat there staring at her.

I hesitated for a moment, then said, "Hi, my name is Carl and this is Leonard. It's nice to meet you."

"It's nice to meet you, too," she smiled in response. Leonard continued to stare.

I went on, "So ... what can we do for you?"

"Well, my friends and I were wondering if you would like to come and have breakfast with us. We heard you come in very late last night and thought that you probably didn't have dinner. We thought you might be hungry."

"Well, that's very nice of you to offer." I turned to Leonard. "What do you think?" Leonard said nothing. He just nodded, and kept staring.

"Fine ... well, just come over to our camp whenever you are ready." She motioned towards the camp behind her.

"We will." She turned around, flipping her hair slightly, and walked away.

Leonard's speechlessness left with her. "My God, Carl, did you see that woman? I don't think that I have ever seen a more beautiful woman in my entire life."

"Yeah, I have to agree with you there, she is beautiful ... but ya know what, Leonard, she's probably a witch."

"Who the hell cares what she is? Shit, I can only hope that I'll get my soul captured for eternity by that woman."

Twenty minutes later we were walking into their camp. By that time everyone had changed out of their hooded robes. They now looked more like just a bunch of hippies in a Dead show parking lot. Gwendolyn had seen us coming. She half-walked and half-skipped to greet us. She showed us around, and introduced us to everyone. In the center of the camp a man and a woman were preparing a breakfast of granola and fruit. Everywhere the mixed smell of patchouli oil and marijuana filled the air.

After touring the camp we sat down near the center of the gathering with Gwendolyn and a couple of her friends, a woman and a man, on a large hand-woven woolen blanket. They both smilingly introduced themselves.

"My name is Mark and this is April. Welcome." They were both somewhere in their mid-twenties. In spite of being a few pounds overweight Mark was handsome. He had reddish hair that was cut roughly, and a patchy beard. It made him look like a Viking. April was his girlfriend, and was a blond, blue-eyed version of Gwendolyn. They could have been sisters. As it turned out, they were.

After we settled in a bit and ate some breakfast I asked him bluntly, "So, do you mind if I ask you a couple of questions?"

Mark smiled, "No, not at all ... please."

"Well first, if you don't mind me asking, what the heck were you guys doing last night and this morning with the robe chanting thing? My friend Leonard here says that you guys are druids. I say you're witches. Second, where the heck are we?" Leonard stared at me in horror. I think that he was afraid that I had offended them, thereby blowing any designs that he had on Gwendolyn. Everyone immediately began laughing at my question. Mark in particular laughed so hard that tears came to his eyes. It actually took him a couple of minutes to compose himself.

When he did he said, "We're neither druids nor witches, at least in the traditional sense. Although you are closer in calling us witches. We call ourselves Wiccans. We worship the earth, the trees, the sky ... basically all of nature. Our religion springs from our kinship with the earth. We practice ritual rites to attune ourselves to the natural rhythms of life forces. Unlike most people's concept of witches we do not worship Satan or the forces of evil that would harm others. To answer your second question, you are at a place called Stonehenge." Leonard nudged me. "Of course it isn't the Stonehenge in England, but rather a half-scale replication of it, accurate in every way but in its size. We created this monument many years ago for our seasonal rituals. Last night and today was our ritual of the passing of the last full moon of summer. Although we don't recognize an organized hierarchy, in our coven I am considered an elder teacher of our practices. We openly welcome all to our group as brothers and sisters. I invite both of you to stay with us and experience our celebration today." He paused and smiled, "I hope that I have answered your questions."

"You have," I replied. "Unfortunately, we have to be..."

Before I could finish I was cut off by Leonard who had by now made a comfortable place next to Gwendolyn, "Thank you, we would be honored to attend your celebration." At this

Gwendolyn inched herself a little closer to Leonard and smiled at him.

After we finished breakfast I managed to pry Leonard away from Gwendolyn and we returned to the van to clean up and prepare for the day's festivities.

"Jesus, Leonard, what's the deal with signing us up for the pagan love-fest? I thought that you were scared as hell of druids and witches. And you know what else? According to our itinerary we're supposed to be at Devil's Tower tonight."

"Well, Carl, the deal with me signing us up for the pagan love-fest is that I happen to really, really like pagan love-fests. Oh, sure I'm still scared as hell of druids and witches, but these people aren't druids or witches, Carl, they're *pagans* – it's a big difference, buddy. Oh, and about the itinerary – screw it. We wouldn't have made it to Devil's Tower today anyway. And one more thing ... you, my dear friend, happen to have a girlfriend. And, she, I'm sure, satisfies certain natural urges that you have. I, on the other hand, do not have a girlfriend and must do what I can to have those same urges met. If I have to dress up like a fucking minotaur and dance around half-naked in order to have my carnal desires with Gwendolyn met, then that is exactly what I am going do." There was no fighting it. Leonard had a good point – actually two good points. We would have never made it to Devil's Tower that day, and Gwendolyn was indisputably beautiful and attracted to him.

The festivities with the Wiccans continued throughout the day and long into the evening. I spent much of my time talking about pagan philosophy with Mark while smoking grass and drinking copious amounts of a powerful home-brewed mead-like concoction. As the evening went on, our conversation became less focused and I was often swept up in the merriment and danced like a fiend with the rest of the Wiccans. In the moonlight the tribe celebrated at a fevered pitch fueled by mead, grass, psychedelic mushrooms, and the continuous beat of drums. At one point later in the evening, Leonard did in fact get dressed up like a minotaur, and to the delight of the Wiccans danced around closer to full than half naked while playing the Pan-flute. Not surprisingly, in the end he hooked up with Gwendolyn.

I woke up the next morning lying flat on my back in the middle of a field. The sun was already high enough to be warm and when I tried to open my eyes the glare nearly burned my retinas. When I finally mustered enough energy to hoist myself up I felt as if I had an anvil on the back of my skull. My mouth tasted like honeybees had made a nest in it the night before. It was an unpleasant sensation. I was just outside the camp, which by now had begun stirring with life. I quickly scanned the camp - Leonard was nowhere to be seen. I suspected that if I found Gwendolyn, Leonard would be somewhere nearby. I looked at my watch. It was ten twenty. We should have been on the road hours ago.

I wandered amidst the tents searching for Leonard. I found Mark. He had just crawled out of his tent and was sitting cross-legged on the ground drinking a large mug of tea, which gave off a strong odor that smelled like a mixture of rotting leaves and horse manure.

"Hang-over cure - want some?" He motioned with a mug as I approached.

"No, thanks. What I could use, though, is my friend Leonard. Have any idea where he might be in all of this?" Mark had the same theory that I did about his proximity to Gwendolyn and pointed to a camp a few feet away.

"Gwendolyn's tent is that one over there. It's the one with the 'If this truck's a' rocking don't come a knocking bumper sticker on it." I thought to myself that even though the sticker was on a tent, the message still applied.

Even from some distance it was apparent that someone inside was awake. As if to live up to the bumper sticker pasted on it, the tent shook with intermittent tremors. I wondered to myself what this small seismic phenomenon would measure on the Richter scale.

"Hey, Leonard, are you in there?"

The tent gave one last shake, a pause, then, "Yeah, I'm in here – why?" Giggling erupted from the tent.

I sighed, shook my head and smiled. "Hey, it's already ten forty-five. We need to get going here." There was more giggling accompanied by a rustling. After a few moments the door of the tent opened up and a pair of heads popped out – one Leonard's, the other Gwendolyn's. They both had sort of wild, dazed looks in their eyes and broad grins on their faces. Leonard's hair had at some point in the evening been liberated from its usual single thick black rope braiding and now was a complete tangled mass erupting from his head.

"I'll be out in a few minutes, Carl."

"Well, I'll be over talking to Mark. Come on over when you're ready." I knew what "a few minutes" really meant, and I wasn't going to stand there listening to it. I already missed Althea and I didn't need Leonard's help.

I was on my second mug of tea, which tasted exactly like it smelled, but true to Mark's claim seemed to offer some restorative powers, when Leonard finally arrived.

"Mornin' sunshine."

"Afternoon, Leonard."

"Oh really ... so it is," he said with a wry smile as he glanced up at the sun and then at me. Then he observed, "Wow, Carl, you look like heck."

"Yeah, well, I feel like heck. How about you? You want some tea? It helps."

"Heck, no – I feeeel grrrrreat."

At this Mark began laughing, "Oh man ... that's Tony the Tiger, right? Oh man, that's funny." It really wasn't that funny. I think that he only thought it was because he was still a little drunk from the night before.

I turned back to Leonard, "Well, Mr. Tiger, we need to be on our way here. And since you are feeling so 'grrrrreat' you can drive." I tossed him the van keys. I turned to Mark, who was still chuckling a bit.

"Hey, thank you for your hospitality."

"You are welcome, Carl – you and Leonard are always welcome here." By now those who were awake had gathered around the campsite. This included Gwendolyn who had wrapped her arms around Leonard and was hugging him tightly.

"Before you go ..." Mark leaned back and into his tent. He produced a large basket whose contents were covered with a blanket and handed it to me. "Please accept this. It is our way to give aid to travelers ... the seekers of the world. We have collected some things among us that will be of help to you on your journey."

I took the basket from him. "Thank you again, Mark. You - all of you -have been very kind to us." We spent the next ten minutes saying our good-byes to everyone. In the end I had to nearly pry Leonard and Gwendolyn apart to get Leonard to leave.

Leonard was still talking about Gwendolyn when he fired up the van.

"Oh my God, what a fine pagan woman, Carl. I still don't understand why we're leaving so soon."

"We are leaving so soon, Leonard, because we are on a road trip and were supposed to be on the road hours ago."

"Well, Carl, we are also on vacation, and to me a part of any good vacation is getting laid by a fine pagan woman."

"Good, then can I assume that you are having a good vacation, Leonard?"

"Yes, you can," said Leonard who smiled a wry knowing smile that comes to those who have just had sex.

The campground and the Wiccans behind us, we followed US 97 across the Columbia River into Oregon. From there we got on Interstate 84 and followed the high cliffs along the river east toward Pendleton. According to our well-thought-out plans we were supposed to be at Devil's Tower in Wyoming yesterday. According to the mileage markers on the map that was a distance of roughly eleven hundred miles. I thought it unlikely that we would be able to do that today, especially leaving after noon.

As Leonard drove on, I dug through the straw packing in the basket the Wiccans had given us and tried to identify the contents.

"So, what the hell all is in there, Carl?"

"It's a little hard to tell exactly what everything is. Looks like we have a couple of loaves of bread, some apples, onions, carrots, oh... and here are a couple of jars of I think jam. Hey, look here, we have some sticks of incense, too." I held them up for Leonard to see, then went back into the basket.

"Hmm ... and here is a little bag of..." I opened it up and sniffed to make sure, "... grass – nice Wiccans. Oh, and we have another bag here with some brown dried-up something in it." I sniffed that one too to see if its odor would aid in identification. It smelled like dirt. "I have no idea what the hell this is." I passed the bag over to Leonard to see if he could identify it. He did.

"Those are dried mushrooms, Carl – but I can't tell you what kind," and handed them back.

"Thanks for the identification, Leonard. We'll save those for later." I put them back in the basket. "Let's see here, what else do we have ... hey, they gave us a bottle of mead, oh boy, just what I want right now. And, wait, one more thing here at the bottom." I put my hand on what felt like a bunch of sticks lashed together and pulled it out of the basket.

"Well, what is it, Carl?"

"Well, it's a little man made out of sticks woven together with bark. It's kind of weird, but not weird - weird, ya know what I mean?" Leonard glanced over to take a look.

"Well, stick him up on the dashboard with the rest of your icons. Maybe he can give us a little extra insurance." I agreed with Leonard that the dashboard was a good place for the little man. I propped him in a spot between the bronze Vishnu and the magnetized glow-in-the-dark crucifix. He fit perfectly.

We drove on through the afternoon alternating between talking and snacking on Wiccan bread and what was in fact jam - blackberry. For most of the day Leonard couldn't contain himself about Gwendolyn and by the time we had passed through Pendleton and LaGrande, he had shared a full and graphic picture of what happened the night before. It was erotically entertaining but it made me miss Althea. I was determined to call her later. By late afternoon, we had covered nearly two hundred miles of road. Still, it was far short of the eleven hundred miles to Devil's Tower.

As we neared Baker City, and with a call to Althea in mind, I thought it best to start looking for a place to stay for the night. I pulled out the map.

"Hey, Leonard?"

"Yeah?"

"So, you probably know this by now, but there is no way in hell that we are going to make it anywhere near Devil's Tower, let alone the state of Wyoming today."

"Yes, Carl, I am clear about that. So what do you suggest?"

"Well, I suggest that we start looking around for a place to stay for the night."

"Good suggestion. Do you see anything on the map nearby?" I looked intently at the map trying to get some sense of what might be an interesting place to stay not too far off of the main Interstate.

"Hmm, I see a bunch of those little tent symbols all over the map around here, but nothing too ... wait, it looks like there's a campground near the John Day Fossil Beds National Monument. Yeah, it's called the Kam Wah Chung State Campground and it is off of Route 26 about forty-five miles west of here. It's a little out of our way, and about in central fucking nowhere, but since we are way off our itinerary anyway, what the hell." Leonard slammed hard on the brakes and with squealing rubber caught the off-ramp for westbound Route 26.

"Jesus, Carl - fuck the itinerary. That thing was useless the second we left Mount Vernon. Learn to loosen up a bit and just go with it."

"Yeah, well, I thought that we had a plan, Leonard."

"We did." And with that he smiled, grabbed the itinerary off of the floor of the van, and casually chucked it out the window. I turned around and watched the papers dance in the slipstream of the van across the highway and then out into the eastern Oregon desert. "Now we don't, Carl."

"What the hell did you do that for?"

"Like I said, Carl - fuck the itinerary."

Oasis

Finally after driving for well over an hour across a desert that showed no sign of human existence, we arrived at the campground. It was six forty-five.

"Here it is."

"Here it is, you're right - more like *what* it is," replied Leonard. Leonard stopped the van at the entrance to the campground and we both stared at the random insanity of it. Spanning the road to the park entrance was an enormous pagoda-like red archway maybe twenty-five feet tall. The archway was meticulously carved with dragons, snakes and warriors - some intricate scene from an ancient Chinese tale - maybe the Ming Dynasty period ... then again maybe not. On top of it each figure was painstakingly painted and gilded down to the minutest detail. Below the carving in bold flowing Chinese styled letters were the words "Kam Wah Chung State Park." The whole thing had to have taken someone years to create - it literally was a work of art.

Even more strange was that right next to the park entrance was a building of equal enormity, opulence and insanity, especially given that its location was in the middle of the Oregon desert. It too was of Chinese architecture. It had a pagoda-like red tiled roof that rose close to two stories above a structure made of large handcrafted wood beams. At the entrance there were sweeping stone stairs leading up to a pair of eight-foot doors that were painted deep red. All around the building, just under the eaves, there was a bead of red neon which cast a glow down onto the rest of the building. In front of the building, near the highway, on a steel pole that was nearly as tall as the roof there was a neon sign that was probably twenty feet wide and fifteen feet high. On it there was a huge green neon dragon with flashing red eyes. Underneath it, in red lettering, it said "Kam Wah Chung Chinese Restaurant." Since there wasn't another light bulb for sixty miles in any direction I'm sure that you could have read the sign from an orbiting spacecraft. I wondered if they did takeout.

Leonard and I sat in the van, speechless. Leonard broke the silence.

"Hey, Carl."

"Yeah, Leonard?" I said without breaking my stare.

"Are you high?"

"No, Leonard, are you?"

"No, but I am getting a contact high from the weirdness of all of this weirdness."

"Yeah, me too. This is weird. Very weird."

"Yes, Carl, it is." With that Leonard put the van in gear and we drove into the park to look for a place to set up our camp. The campground was as unremarkable as the landscape around it – flat, treeless, sagebrush covered desert. Although the campground was nearly full, picking from the spots that were left wasn't a challenge. There must have been a hundred sites and every one of them looked exactly the same: a picnic table, a fire pit, and a clear spot to pitch a tent. I felt like we had entered the suburbs of campgrounds. I hoped that if we really did get high later, and had to go to the bathroom, I would be able to find my way back to our tent.

We pulled into one of two empty spots, which were next to each other. "Hey, Leonard, I don't know which one I like more this spot or the one next to it. What do you think?"

I caught him - Leonard stared at the two identical spots as if studying them, then realized what he was doing and said, "Oh, screw you, Carl. Jesus, what an asshole."

After sharing a small bowl of grass that the Wiccans had given us, which incidentally was a couple of steps better than Leonard's closet weed, we proceeded to set up our tent without incident - although it did take us forty–five minutes. Even though we had set up the tent countless times before, this time for some reason the task seemed inordinately complex, and we found that we had to keep referring back to the directions.

After the tent was finally up, we decided to take a walk and survey the rest of the campground. The campground was packed. From what I could tell we had gotten one of the last of three or four open sites in the entire park. As we walked along the road, we noticed that among the predominantly Washington and Oregon plates there were a few license plates from all over the country, and a few from Canada as well. Road-tripping, America's favorite pastime.

"Hey, Leonard, check out where all of these people are from. There is someone from Georgia over there, and back there there was one from Minnesota."

"Yeah, and there's one from New Hampshire, 'Live Free or Die,'" Leonard pointed, "How monomaniacal is that?"

I stopped walking and looked at him, "Monoma what?"

"Monomaniacal, Carl. It means being obsessed with one idea, man. It's kind of like when you were all obsessed with the itinerary..." he said sarcastically, then grinned. I could sense where this was going. We were heading into one of our "high" conversations. That could go on forever. I ignored his comment, and his sarcasm, and got us back to the subject.

"Whatever, Leonard ... so what do you think is the deal with all of these people coming way the hell out here in the middle of fucking nowhere to this less-than-remarkable state park?"

"To tell you the truth, Carl, I have no idea. But I'll tell you what, though – I did notice that there isn't a single fucking human being in this fucking park – not a one. Have you seen, or do you see anyone around here at all? " He was right. In spite of all the cars and all the tents and all the RV's, there wasn't a soul in sight. I felt like we were walking through a tourist ghost town.

"Oh, shit, Leonard – you're right, there isn't a single fucking person here." All of a sudden I felt a shiver and said in an almost-whisper, "Oh man, this is too spooky ... where the hell did everyone go?"

We were both teetering on the verge of a major freak-out. I all of a sudden wished that I weren't high anymore. Then, as we stood there staring at each other trying to think of any plausible explanation for the disappearances, an amazing and familiar aroma began filling the evening air. It was so pervasive and remarkable that it immediately caught our attention and brought us back to terra firma.

"You smell that, Leonard? Chinese food, man."

"Hell yes, I smell that."

"My God, does it smell good or what?"

"Yes it does ... come on." Our desire to satisfy our munchies immediately replaced any kind of freaky thoughts that we were beginning to have about the campground situation, and we headed back toward the restaurant that we had seen when we drove into the park.

It took us less than ten minutes to walk to the restaurant, but by the time we got there our hunger was at near-panic proportions, in part because along the way we rehearsed exactly what we were going to order when we got there. We walked up the stairs to the entrance. Leonard grabbed a hold of the brass bamboo–shaped door handle and pulled open the red lacquer eight–foot-high door. As soon as he opened it, we were immediately overwhelmed with a flood of noise, lights, and aromas. For a few moments we just stood speechless in the foyer of the lobby and took it all in. The restaurant was as huge on the inside as it was on the outside. The vaulted ceiling rose up to the same height as the roof above it – nearly two stories. It was held up by massive beams that were intricately carved and gilded – clearly done by the same artisan who had created the park entrance sign. From these beams hung equally ornate brass chandeliers. Each one was probably five feet across and had six brass warrior horsemen that radiated from the center. Each warrior held a different weapon – a spear, a bow and arrow, a mace, an axe ... and at the end of each of those different weapons was a socket with a light bulb in it. Although the interior was massive, it didn't seem so – in part because the walls too were painted a deep red color.

Both of us were so distracted by our surroundings that we didn't even see the maitre-de approach.

"May I help you? Two for dinner?"

Startled, we both turned. Facing us was a genteel-looking Chinese gentleman. He was dressed in a light gray two-piece suit, which was obviously - although I don't even remotely consider myself a fashionologist - made of silk. His shirt was made of fine tight-weave cotton and was open at the collar. His shoes, which looked like they were probably custom-made for him, were of some sort of dark colored exotic leather. The whole ensemble must have cost close to five hundred dollars. He made me feel slightly underdressed in my jeans, cowboy boots and T-shirt. I guessed him to be about 50ish, but his healthy looks and pleasant demeanor didn't give up his age.

"Yes, please, two for dinner," I answered.

The Chinese man smiled warmly. "I believe that I have one table left, sir. Let me check. I will be back in a moment."

"Jesus, Carl, there must be a hundred tables in this place."

"Yeah, and nearly every one of them is filled. I think we just solved the mystery of where everyone from the campground went." After a few moments, the man returned and from a few feet away he smiled, nodded, and motioned for us to follow him.

He seated us and handed us menus. "Please, enjoy your meal."

"Thank you, I'm sure we will," replied Leonard.

By the time the waitress appeared with our water and utensils our munchies were at crisis levels. Leonard and I, while fumbling through our menus, managed to order enough food to feed a bowling team. After she left, I noticed across from our table there was an older couple who were dressed from head to toe in forest green. On each of their shoulders was an official looking patch. It had an embossed picture of a deer and a jumping trout. Underneath it read "Oregon Parks Department." The man was talking wildly at the woman and waved a pair of chopstick at her when he emphasized particular points. The woman, who silently picked at some chow foon and fried rice on her plate, looked like she was either not listening at all, which I thought nearly impossible, or simply didn't care. From the bits and pieces that I could overhear, the one-sided conversation had something to do with dinosaurs. Leonard noticed the pair as well.

"What the fuck is that guy's problem, Carl? What, is he having some sort of seizure?"

"Maybe ... I think it might be some sort of spasmodic allergic reaction to MSG." Both of us erupted into an uncontrollable fit of laughter that was refueled every time Leonard and I made eye contact with each other. Even at the time I was aware that my comment wasn't really that funny, but we were both still fairly stoned.

After nearly five minutes of laughing so hard that we were crying (Leonard even laughed so hard that he farted loudly a couple of times – which only made things worse), people at the tables around us grew somewhat irritated and began to stare at us. Everyone except the parks department couple at the next table, who looked at us with genuine concern.

Finally the man leaned over and asked sincerely, "Are you fellas okay?" Leonard took a couple of deep breaths, and after a few moments managed to compose himself enough to talk.

He looked right at the man and said rather seriously, "No."

This brought on another fit of laughter, which only ended a few minutes later when both Leonard and I finally realized that the man was truly concerned.

Leonard again composed himself and leaned over to the couple and said, "Sorry about that, folks. My friend and I here just got a little carried away on a joke."

"Oh, no, perfectly fine. My wife and I here were just a little worried about you. I know that lots of folks have funny reactions to that monosodium glutamate that they put in the food here. Myself, I get a little tired." The grass must have been wearing off because, although we both laughed at his monosodium glutamate comment, our laughter was a bit more appropriate and neither one of us launched into another spasm.

"Let me introduce myself." He put out is hand. "My name is Henry, and this is my wife Doris."

"Leonard and Carl," I replied, "Nice to meet both of you."

"So what brings you fellas all the way out to this neck of the woods? Did ya get roped on that park deal next door?"

"What do you mean, roped?" I replied. Before Henry could answer we were interrupted by the arrival of our food. The waitress had to make two trips to bring everything and politely announced each dish as she set them the table. By the time she was done we barely had room for our plates.

As we served ourselves up and started to eat, Henry began. "So, ya don't know about that park deal, huh?" We both shook our heads and grunted through mouthfuls of food.

"Ya just ended up here on yer own?" He was surprised. We both nodded in response. "Well, I'll tell you what, us four is probably the only people in this here restaurant that ain't been roped. See me and my wife here come on in about once a week fer a lovely meal. We is rangers about an hour up the road at the John Day Fossil Beds. Say ... you fellas like fossils?"

I managed to shove my mouthful of potted mountain goat and rice to one side of my mouth so I could talk. "Yeah, fossils are cool, but what about this park thing?"

Henry got back on track and continued. "Well, the feller who owns this establishment is a man by the name of Kam Wah Chung. That ring a bell?" He looked at us, squinting one eye.

"Yeah, that's the name of the restaurant, too," said Leonard, who was beginning to slow down to a more normal eating pace.

"Well, Mr. Wah Chung had a grand idea few years back. He purchased the land that both the restaurant and the park are now on. He then donated four acres of it to the state for a park – even donated the sign for it. The parks department was so happy about it they didn't care what the hell he named it. Then after they put the park in he built this here restaurant.

Folks all around the county thought that he was crazy. After all, the nearest town is at least sixty miles away, and who the hell is going to drive sixty miles for Chinese food? Well, Mr. Wah Chung had that all figured out. He made sure that a hyped-up description of the park was published in every destination travel brochure about Oregon. He even pulled big ads all about it in a bunch of them destination travel magazines. As you can see there is plenty of folks who's been roped." He made a sweeping motion with his hand. "This here restaurant's been packed nearly every night, nearly every summer for the past fifteen years or so. Heck, look at this country, once folks are here ain't nothin' else to do 'cept eat." He chuckled a little. "Yep, I gotta hand it to that Mr. Wah Chung, he sure has made hisself a fortune on the tourists who he trapped here. Darn good Chinese food, though." By the time that Henry had finished the story Leonard and I had slowed down considerably on the food. Leonard let out a belch.

"Oh God – I'm as full as a tick."

"That's disgusting, Leonard."

"It's not if you're a tick." Leonard smiled.

I turned again to Henry. I had been fascinated with fossils as a kid so I asked. I didn't know it then, but I was going to be sorry that I did.

"So, Henry, tell me a bit about this fossil thing. How'd you folks end up being park rangers all the way out here at the John Day Fossil Beds?" Henry looked up from the table and straight at me. His expression changed from the more calm, relaxed air that he had had while telling his last story to something more intense. It was the same concentrated fanatical look I had seen on his face when he had been talking at his wife earlier. Behind him his wife shot me a look that translated loosely to "Jesus God Mother of Mercy, you know not what you have done."

"So ... you fellas *do* like fossils," Henry said slowly and intentionally.

The whole feeling of the table had changed so dramatically that I paused for a moment, then said tentatively, "Well, yeah, I kind of got into them a bit when I was a kid."

Leonard apparently had also picked up on the new feeling at our little spot in the restaurant, and settled back in his seat on the other side of the table to watch the entertainment.

Henry continued, "Well, I've been studying fossils for..." he turned to his wife, "what is it, Doris, 52 years?" Without looking back at him, Doris nodded passively. "I got one of the most complete collections of trilobites in the Western Hemisphere - twenty-seven thousand four hundred and ninety three to be exact. And I'm adding more to my collection every day. Folks, I know my stuff. I'm a trilobite expert. Why, folks write me from all over the world to identify all sorts of trilobites. As a matter of fact, five years ago I found this trilobite way out up 'bout four miles in around Dry Creek..." He stopped and narrowed his eyes suspiciously, "Hey, you fellas ain't gonna tell no one, are ya?" I immediately shook my head no. Leonard also said that he wouldn't and emphasized his point by raising his right hand to swear it.

Henry, satisfied with our promise, continued. "Good ... there's plenty of people out there who want to get a piece of the fame. They want to know where I find my fossils. Well, I ain't going to tell them, and they ain't going to find out on their own neither. Anyway, 'bout five years ago I find this trilobite - beautiful specimen, and big too - maybe three feet long. Well it ain't like no trilobite that I ever seen before, and I tell you what, I *am* an expert on trilobites. I knew that I had discovered a new species. So I take a picture of it, give it a full description, and send it into the folks at the Smithsonian to get my credit. I even named it, too - Trilobiteis-Henryis - that's Latin." Leonard yawned, but Henry ignored him and kept going. "Well, I don't hear from those folks for months so I write them again. I still don't hear from them, so I write them again. Finally, about three months after that I get this snotty letter from a Dr. - oh, hell, what's his name ..." Henry stopped, reached into his right breast pocket, and produced a somewhat worn-looking envelope and pulled out the letter inside. "Here it is, Dr. Fitzmartin." He cleared his throat and read,

'Dear Mr. Ulum,
I am writing to you in regard to your latest 'new' trilobite discovery. We have assessed your picture, and your description, and have determined that what you have in fact found is again a rather mediocre example of Olenoides Serratus. We do appreciate you sending us your many 'new' discoveries, but again remind you that there are already 15,000 identified species of trilobites. Although new trilobites are unearthed and described every year by professional paleontologists, you have yet to send us any 'new' species of trilobite yourself. Further, Mr. Ulum, I would like to remind you that trilobites were one of the most plentiful ectoskelectic creatures to ever inhabit the earth as they were here for over 300 million years – ample time to create many, many fossils. Although we appreciate your willingness to donate your finds to the institute, the institute has many, many fine examples of this and other species you have sent us. Finally, while your many 'scientific discoveries' are I'm sure very interesting for you they are of absolutely no value to the academic scientific community. Good luck on your amateur fossilizing. My staff and I look forward to hearing from you again in the near future, as it is very entertaining for us.
Sincerely,
Dr. Fitzmartin, Director, Fossil Studies,
The Smithsonian Institute.

By the time Henry got done reading the letter aloud he looked like he was going to have a stroke. His face was flushed and little froths of spittle had formed in the corners of his mouth. I looked at Leonard to see what his reaction to all of this was. He rolled his eyes and swirled his index finger around the side of his head to indicate that he thought that Henry was completely crazy. Inside, I felt the spasmodic laughter rising again, and had to look away.

Henry, with shaking hands, folded the letter up and stuck it back in his breast pocket. It took another minute after that for him to compose himself enough to speak.

Finally he said, "That Dr. Fitzmartin is a bastard, isn't he, Doris? He talks to me like I'm some sort of crackpot. Why,

I'm a doctor, too. I used to be a veterinary neuropsychologist... probably the best this side of the Mississippi ... self-trained. Practiced right out of Baker City I did. Good practice I had ... I was respected in that community. Only reason I quit was to give me time to dedicate myself to my fossil research ... trying to do something for humanity you know. Maybe I don't have no formal education like them fancy Ivy League boys back east, but damn it I'm a doctor too!" He took a couple of deep breaths and leaned into the table, "I'll tell you what, though, one day they'll be sorry, oh they'll be sorry alright that they mocked Henry Ulum. I'll make them all look like the fools that they ..."

Leonard could feel the gravitational pull of the one-sided conversation and stopped him mid-sentence, "I hate to interrupt you in the middle of your fascinating story, but my friend and I have been traveling most of the day and I think that we are going to get going back to our camp here."

Henry looked stunned and a bit hurt at Leonard's words. As crazy as he was, I felt a little sorry for him so I added, "but maybe we can pick this up again tomorrow before we leave." Of course I was only being polite. I assumed that since they were rangers they would be going back to the park that evening after dinner and we would never see him again or have the privilege of hearing the end of his story. Later I would find out how wrong I was.

My ploy worked, and Henry graciously accepted our excuse. Without any further ranting he bid us goodnight as we left the table. His wife Doris also wished us a good night, which was accompanied by another look that Leonard interpreted on the way to the cashier as, "For the love of God, please tell someone ... I'm being held fossil hostage."

We paid our tab, which came to a total of $36.57. Not bad for stuffing ourselves stupid. As we walked out the restaurant door I spotted a telephone booth at the far end of the parking lot. It felt like had been days since I had talked with Althea, and I was missing her like mad.

"Hey, Leonard."

"Yeah?"

"I'm going to give Althea a ring here before I head back to camp. I'll meet you back there in a while."

Leonard nodded and said, "Yeah, well don't be on the phone all night there, 'Mr. We-Have-A-Schedule-To-Keep.' Remember, we were supposed to be at Devil's Tower yesterday, today, tomorrow, or the day after that."

"You're such an asshole, Leonard."

"Yes I am, Carl ... and may I remind you, that makes you friend-of-asshole."

I smiled back at him, "I suppose it does. Gosh, what a warm fuzzy feeling ... I'll see you in a while."

Inside the phone booth it was warm, quiet and intimate. The red and green glow of the restaurant's neon sign bathed the now emptying parking lot. Beyond that the eastern Oregon desert was utterly black. Under the light of the phone booth I fumbled for change. Having none, I picked up the handset and dialed "O." I shook a Camel out of the pack in my shirt pocket and lit it. As I listened to the distant ring I watched the smoke curl up around the light at the top of the phone booth. After two rings the operator came on. "Operator, may I help you?" Her voice sounded like she had spent the past forty years smoking Pall-Malls and drinking Greyhounds.

"Yes ma'am, you can. I would like to make this a collect call."

"May I say who is calling?"

"Yes, say it's from 'your man.'"

"My man, sir?"

"No, me - I'm calling my girlfriend, and I'm her man."

The operator laughed a hoarse laugh, "Oh I know, honey - I'm just funnin' with ya." She put the call through. In the receiver I could hear the phone ringing ... two, three ...

"Hello?"

"This is the operator. Will you accept a collect call from your man?"

"Hell yes, operator ... Carl!" Althea shouted on the phone.

"Hey, Althea."

"Oh baby, where are you? I miss you so much." It was good to hear her voice. I closed my eyes and fell. Here in the closeness of the phone booth I could almost feel her presence, smell her scent. I opened my eyes.

"Althea, I miss you too ... I miss you bad. We're out here in eastern Oregon in the middle of outer fucking nowhere, at this place called Kam Wah Chung State Park. It's a pretty weird. I'll tell you more about it when we get back, but we're having a great time."

"Oh Carl, it feels like you are so far away. It feels like you've been gone forever."

"I know, Althea, I know."

"I wish you were here right now, Carl, I would eat you up." It was her tribal cannibalistic way of saying "I love you," and I could think of no better way of dying. "You've only been gone for three days ... I can't believe that you're going to be gone for two weeks – I'll go crazy by then."

I tried to comfort her with my own "I love you and I miss you," but I felt the same way. I wanted to be on this trip with Leonard, but talking with Althea made me wish that I had never left. In that phone booth in the parking lot in the middle of the lonely Oregon desert I could think of nothing better than lying in bed intertwined with Althea.

Our conversation went back and forth for over a half an hour – little snippets of what each of us had been doing the past few days in between telling how much we missed and loved each other. At last, though I didn't want to, I knew that I had to go and get back to the camp and to Leonard.

"Althea ... I have to go. It's getting late and we have to be on the road early tomorrow. We're headed to Devil's Tower. That's a long drive from here." There was a pause. Sometimes when Althea got frustrated or sad she could be difficult. I wondered if this was going to be one of those times.

Then quietly she said, "I understand, Carl. You better go and get back to Leonard. I love you Carl."

"I love you too, Althea."

"Promise that you will call me again as soon as you can."

"I will, Althea."

"Promise me – Rama, Rama, Carl."

Rama, Rama, was a mantra that Althea demanded I say when I made an unbreakable promise to her. The entire chant went, "Hare Krishna, Hare Krishna, Krishna Krishna, Hare Hare, Hare Rama, Hare Rama, Rama Rama, Hare Hare." At the end Althea would put her forefinger to her lips and say "shusssh." I didn't have to do that part. I wasn't entirely sure what it all meant. She said it had something to do with George Harrison being spiritual and cool. I just thought that it sounded kind of nice. I did it.

"I'll call you as soon as we get to Devil's Tower. I have to go now. I'll call you in a couple of days."

"Okay, Carl, sweet dreams." Reluctantly we hung up.

The parking lot was now completely empty with the exception of a single black newer model Mercedes Benz near the restaurant entrance. It didn't take much imagination to guess that its owner was probably Mr. Wah Chung. I walked across the gravel lot towards the campground, my boots making a loud crunch with each step in the silence.

The campground was almost totally dark aside from a few camp lanterns. I looked at my watch. It was only a little after ten-thirty. I figured that the population must have succumbed to the Kung Pao Chicken that had been on special at the restaurant and lapsed into a tryptophanic coma. As I approached our campground I could see that Leonard was still awake and was sitting at the picnic table. Two other people were there with him.

"Hey Carl, is that you?" Leonard must have heard my steps.

"Yeah, Leonard, it's me." I walked into the camp.

"Hey, look who's camping next door to us." Sitting at the table directly across from Leonard, and grinning like crazy, were Dieter and Marta.

Dieter rose to greet me and extended a hand like we were old friends, "Hello, it is good to see you again."

"Yes, ah ..." I was taken a little by surprise at seeing the pair and fumbled for a second, "... it's good to see you as well."

"Isn't it, how do you say in English ... mmm ... what is that word ... when you see someone in a place you do not know."

Leonard helped him out, "Ironic?"

"Ya, that is the word ... funny word, ironic."

"Yes I agree, it's a bit odd that we should run into each other again way out here," I added.

"Ya and that we should find the campsite next to yours too ... ironic." He grinned at his own use of the word.

"Ironic ..." Leonard repeated. The way he said it I could tell he had gotten slightly stoned again while I had been gone. I sat down at the table with them.

"So, exactly what brings you all the way out here?" I asked.

"We are taking a vacation in America. We want to see all that is part of 'God's Country.' In the morning we will go see the fossils."

"Oh ... so you folks like fossils?" Leonard inquired, intentionally trying to sound like Henry.

"Ya, the fossil beds." Dieter said enthusiastically. As soon as he said 'fossil beds,' Marta giggled just a bit. I theorized that her somewhat embarrassed response was probably due to some linguistic chasm in their translation book. Probably neither Dieter nor Marta was really completely clear what "fossil beds" really were.

I tactfully glanced at my watch – it was after eleven. "I hate to be rude but we have a very long drive ahead of us tomorrow and we should get some sleep here."

"Yeah, we're driving to Devil's Tower tomorrow," Leonard added with particular emphasis on "Devil's." As expected, at the mention of anything vaguely having to do with Satan, Dieter and Marta's eyes widened some and their expressions turned from innocent curiosity to genuine theological consternation.

"Devil's Tower?!" They echoed in unison, with an audible unease in their voices. Then Marta said pensively, "It is so ironic that this place that you call Devil's Tower would be found in God's Country. Why would you want to go there?"

Since Leonard had started all of this, I figured I'd let him answer. I shouldn't have. He looked at them intently and seriously, leaned across the table, and then replied softly,

"Well... it is one of the most popular vacation places in all of America."

I looked over at Dieter and Marta. They both looked utterly confused. Gently, Dieter took Marta's hand in his and they stood up. They didn't ask anything more about Devil's Tower.

Dieter said somberly, "We must be going now. We let you sleep."

The way that he said it made me feel sad for them. I thought that Leonard had probably done enough emotional damage for one evening, so I stood up, and tried to leave them with lighter thoughts.

"Hey, it was nice seeing both of you. I'm sure that we'll see you in the morning before we leave. Maybe we can have coffee together." They both seemed a little bit relieved by my benign words.

"Yes, that would be nice ... coffee. Thank you ... we see you in the morning." And with that Dieter and Marta headed back towards their campsite.

When they were halfway to their camp Leonard called after them, "Sweet dreams." As soon as he said it, Marta turned and looked at him. Even in the darkness I could see the intensity in her eyes. She gave him a look as if she knew exactly why he would want to go to a place called "Devil's Tower."

After they were out of earshot I whispered, "Jesus Christ, was that last part about 'sweet dreams' really necessary, Leonard?"

"Oh, shit, Carl, lighten up. Those two are just a little bit too full of holy innocence for me. A few paradoxes in their lives are good for them."

"Yeah, well, I don't think that they need to lose sleep over it, though."

In the background I could hear them at their camp feverishly talking in their native tongue. Although I couldn't understand a word that they were saying, the seriousness and the message of their conversation was clear. I sincerely doubted that they would get a good night's sleep.

I figured that I had made my point and there was no reason to go on about it with Leonard. I let the whole thing drop and changed the subject.

"You know, if we are planning to make it to Devil's Tower tomorrow we should probably turn in."

Leonard sat opposite me intently packing a light load of grass into the pipe. "Yeah, you're right, man ..." He put a match to the pipe, inhaled deeply, and looked directly into my eyes as he passed it to me.

"Here, this will help you have sweet dreams too." He smiled. I took the pipe from him and smiled back. The weed tasted good. Then Leonard said quietly, "As I was saying, I think you're right, man ... I was too hard on those two." He was serious, and seemed slightly ashamed at his own harshness. We looked at each other.

I nodded slightly and exhaled. "Yeah ... let's go get some sleep."

Within a couple of minutes Leonard was asleep. I, on the other hand, lay in my sleeping bag staring at the tent ceiling listening to the rhythm of his breathing. My conversation with Althea earlier, no doubt intensified by the weed, made my mind wander. I followed. I closed my eyes and thought that she must be in bed by now as well. I let my mind go. I felt her next to me, not there in the tent, not there at home, but somewhere else - somewhere that is no particular place. We kissed and held each another until our bodies melted into oneness. I told her again that I loved her and inside our oneness her voice echoed back the same. Indeed, I did have very sweet dreams.

The Heretic and The Missionaries

"Knock, knock." I was in a dead sleep. At first I thought I was dreaming, then I heard the voice again,

"Knock, knock! – Good morning! – Rise and shine!" I opened my eyes. I rolled over and looked at my watch to try and see what time it was but the radium dial had long since lost its glow from the day before, and it was still far too dark to see the face otherwise. Leonard was now awake as well.

"Who the fuck is that? It's the middle of the fucking night."

"How the hell should I know who the fuck it is?"

"Who the fuck is it?" Leonard repeated the question, this time directing it at the voice outside the tent.

There was a pause, then the voice outside the tent said, "Are you talking to me?"

"Yes I am fucking talking to you. Who in the hell else do you think I am talking to? Everyone else in the campground is fucking asleep."

"Oh ..."

I could tell this was going exactly nowhere, so I unzipped the tent to see who the mystery person was. Standing directly in front of the tent door, looking a little perplexed but grinning nonetheless, was Henry. His wife, who I'm sure was happy to be rid of him for a while, was not with him.

"Hi," I said.

"Hi," said Henry.

"Who the hell is it, Carl?" came Leonard's voice from inside the tent.

"It's Henry."

"Ask him what the fuck he is doing here waking my ass up at whatever unnatural fucking time it is."

"Well ... you heard the man, Henry," I tried to be as polite as I could in spite of having been woken up. "So what can we do for you?"

"Oh, it's not what you can do for me, Carl, it's what I can do for you ... fossils, my friend, fossils." He straightened himself proudly. "I am here to offer my services as a guide. As the park ranger for the John Day Fossil Beds I can show you fossils that you never dreamed of."

I yawned, "Henry, do you have any idea what time it is?"

"Why, yes, Carl. I left the ranger station at four and..." He glanced at his watch, "it is an hour or so drive here so ... yes, it is five o'clock." He seemed proud of his calculations. It was apparent that he was oblivious to what was a socially acceptable time to wake up near strangers at campgrounds.

"So, what the hell does he want?" Leonard asked from inside the tent.

"He wants to show us the fossils up at John Day." Leonard popped his head out of the tent,

"Oh shit ... you have to be kidding."

I was already putting my pants on. I knew that there was no way that Henry was going to let us escape from going on his expedition.

As I crawled out of the tent I called back at Leonard, "I'll make the coffee." Leonard rolled back over in his sleeping bag and groaned.

I fired up the stove and put on the coffee to brew. All the while Henry jabbered on about trilobites and his secret trilobite fossil beds, "... yer never going to see fossils like this in a museum, my friend – no sir-ee." By the time the coffee was done brewing Leonard was up. We stood there hunched over in the cold of the morning downing our coffee, both to warm up as well as to catch up with Henry's frenetic spirit.

The campground was still totally devoid of any human activity, with the exception of some subtle stirring from the campsite directly next to us.

"Hey, Carl?"

"Yeah?"

"Hey, isn't that the Germans' campsite over there?" Just as I turned to look to where Leonard was nodding, Dieter and Marta emerged freshly out of a Volkswagen van parked in the spot next to us.

They both grinned and waved, "Good morning," Dieter called. I waved back. Apparently the pair had resolved whatever issues had arisen from our discussion the night before.

"Ach, I smell coffee." Leonard motioned them over.

Their van was considerably newer than ours was – probably only two or three years old. It was a Westphalia Camper model, a restrained desert beige color that Leonard later identified as "poo." Judging from all of the vents and hookups that stuck out from the side of it, it appeared to have every convenience that the boys in Stuttgart could think of.

As I was busy examining their van, Dieter had noticed ours.

He said enthusiastically, "Ah, you have a van too!" He shook his head, "There is that word again – ironic." He was proud of that word.

Leonard handed both of them a cup of coffee and said apologetically and sincerely, "Hey, I hope that we didn't wake you."

"No, we have been up early to go to the fossil's beds." At the phrase Marta blushed ever so slightly again and smiled warmly. She was apparently over the trauma from the night before. I was glad for that.

Henry launched, "Fossils? Did you say you're going up to see the fossil beds?!" Without letting either one of them answer, he continued, "Let me introduce myself, Henry, Henry Ulum." He stuck his hand out. "Why, I'm the park ranger up at John Day. As a matter of fact, my friends and I here were just heading up there ourselves to look for trilobites. We sure would be honored if you would join us."

Leonard rolled his eyes, leaned over to me and whispered in a Henry-like voice, "trilobites."

"Yes, we would be delighted," Dieter said. Marta nodded in agreement.

"Fine, then let's be off ... we're wasting valuable daylight."

Unlike the night before, we had no difficulties with the tent, and it only took us ten minutes to break it down and get ready to leave. The Germans were so excited that they already had their van idling.

When we finished, Leonard turned to Henry and said convincingly, "We'll follow you."

Henry grinned with excitement. "Fine." He jogged back to his pickup truck, hopped in, and our little caravan was off.

We followed Henry toward the park entrance. We were last in the caravan. When we got there, Henry, Dieter, and Marta went to the left. Leonard, who was at the wheel, had a different plan. He punched the accelerator hard and hung a right.

"What the hell are you doing, Leonard?"

"What the hell do you think I'm doing? I'm saving us from becoming fossil hostages."

"Oh, come on, I think that the least that we can do is follow him out to the fossil beds for at least part of the day. Heck, the guy got up at four o'clock in the morning to come down here and get us for his little expedition." Leonard slammed on the brakes hard, sending the van into a dramatic four-wheel lock-up in the gravel on the shoulder of the road. He leaned over the steering wheel and turned to me.

"Jesus, Carl. I thought that you were the one who was all compulsive about this schedule thing."

"Yeah, I was. But hey, to quote a great man, 'fuck the itinerary.'" Leonard raised one eyebrow, cracked a smirk, stuck the van in gear, and wheeled a U-turn across the highway back toward Henry's direction,

"Yeah, sure, Carl, to quote a great man."

The half-light of dawn gave way to the summer sun and it came crashing over the desert highway. Kam Wah

Chung State Park was far behind us now. We drove on for over an hour across the arid landscape following Henry and the Germans. Early in the drive Leonard brought the conversation back to Gwendolyn the Wiccan. He punctuated nearly every vignette of their meteoric twenty-four hour relationship with, "My God, what a fine pagan woman." Apparently it was not an experience that he was going to be forgetting anytime soon. I was glad that we had left the Wiccans when we did. The more he talked, the more I was convinced that had Leonard spent any more time with Gwendolyn, he would have fully succumbed to whatever spell she put on him and that would have been the end of our trip.

At last we arrived at the John Day Fossil Beds State Park. As we approached the park entrance, Henry waved his arm wildly from his truck window motioning us to keep following him and not go into the park. We drove on for a few more minutes until Henry again waved his arm wildly for us to follow him. We turned off onto what was a barely discernible dirt road and headed off into no-man's-land. Being at the end of the caravan, we were continually covered in a plume of dust and could hardly see where we were going. From what we *could* see, the "road" was a barely passable Jeep track, which was traversed by Grand Canyon–like ruts. Leonard tried to keep the van on the ridges of the ruts to avoid high-centering us. I tried to help him as much as I could by leaning my head outside of the passenger window and calling in coordinates. The whole time we could hear the shrieking scrape of sagebrush as it raked the sides of our van. After about ten minutes we came to a stop – or rather Leonard nearly drove into the back end of the Germans as their stopped van suddenly appeared out of the dust in front of us.

"Shit!" Leonard shouted as we came to another wheel-locking halt, literally inches from the Germans. We both stiffly exited the van.

When I got out I noticed an acute pain at my sides. My kidneys were so sore from the brief but rough ride, I probably would be urinating blood later in the day.

"My God, where has this maniac taken us?" Leonard commented as he scanned the vast wasteland. My own attention was turned toward a somewhat stunned Marta and Dieter, who were standing there looking at the thousands of scratches that the scrub-brush had inflicted on the sides of their van. Dieter, who said nothing, seemed to take the cosmetic damage a little better, or at least more quietly, than Marta, who stared at the scratches and repeated over and over again softly, "Mein Vestphalia, mein poor Vestphalia." I glanced at the sides of our own van and discovered that we had suffered similar if less extreme damage. Apparently the matte finish had some sort of remarkable capacity to absorb the majority of the scratches. What was visible I thought only added character to the van's already utilitarian looks. Leonard saw me examining it.

"Beauty marks, man."

Henry, who was completely single-minded, was oblivious to anyone's vehicular concerns and yelled over to us, "Alright, everybody ready to see trilobites that no human has ever laid eyes on before?" He stood by his truck geared up in full expedition wear. Hanging over both shoulders was a pair of canteens. In his right hand was a massive pick that must have weighed a good fifteen pounds. Around his waist he wore a web canvas utility belt that had a ton of stuff hanging from it – a knife, a smaller pick, a flashlight, two paintbrushes, a toothbrush, a dental probe, and a number of other pouches whose contents was a complete mystery. Batman would have been jealous. To top his look off, he wore an Australian safari hat, the kind with one side of the brim snapped up. Henry was ready. There was more, though, and we were needed to carry it.

"Don't just stand there, come on over and grab some equipment." As we neared, Henry motioned to the bed of his truck. "I can't carry all of this myself." In the bed were a pair of picks, a pair of shovels, a screen, and a box of what appeared to be road flares. Henry pointed to Dieter and Marta, "You two carry the shovels and that screen." He then turned to us, "You two carry those picks and grab about a half a dozen of those sticks from the box – and for heaven's sake be gentle with them." Leonard stood there motionless staring at him in disbelief. Henry looked both perplexed and annoyed. "What?"

"Are you crazy, Henry? I am not going to carry any fucking dynamite. What the hell do we need fucking dynamite for anyway? I thought that we were going on a happy little fossil walk."

"Oh hell, it's harmless till you put a match to it."

"Yeah, well, if it's so harmless maybe you can put a few sticks in your own pockets."

I had to agree with Leonard - dynamite just wasn't the sort of thing that I was used to carrying around. As a kid I had seen an episode of Bonanza where Hoss was driving a whole wagonload full of the stuff. The entire time that he was driving that wagon he was so scared he looked like he was going to soil his britches. Hell, I figured that if a big bad guy like Hoss was scared of the stuff then I guess I was too. That episode was my dynamite lesson and it stuck with me.

Henry leaned into the bed, impatiently grabbed the sticks and put them in his rear pockets. "Oh hell, I'll do it myself."

We followed Henry and the Germans across the scabland, although at Leonard's recommendation from a bit of a distance. Leonard must have seen the same Bonanza episode. He said that if Henry happened to trip and fall on his ass he didn't want us to be blown up with him.

After about twenty minutes of walking and a half a dozen "come on fellas," from Henry, we arrived at our secret destination. Henry stood proud, "Well, here we are, folks."

"Wow ... impressive," Leonard replied sarcastically, as we all stood on the rim of a deep blast-scarred depression in the ground. I nearly laughed aloud. Dieter and Marta, who seemed somewhat perplexed by it all, just stood there. Henry didn't detect the sarcasm in Leonard's voice,

"Yes, it is impressive, my friend ... yes it is. I'm going to run down there and loosen up some rock for us. You folks stay here. I'll be up in a minute." And with that he half-ran, half-slid down the steep side of the pit.

Less than two minutes after he reached the bottom, he started frantically scrambling back up, slipping and falling on the loose rock that covered the sides. About a hundred feet from the top he pantingly yelled, "Fire–In–The-Hole!"

"Oh, shit," Leonard and I said in unison. Reflexively we both ran back about fifty feet beyond the rim and laid our bodies flat to the ground. As we lay there I looked back at the rim of the pit. The Germans, who had missed the critical danger in the translation, were standing there innocently looking into the pit watching Henry.

I waved my arm and hollered at the pair, "Hey, over here ... get your asses over here." At first they blinked at us with confusion, but then complied. Maybe they didn't understand why, but they sensed the urgency in my voice.

They strolled over and we pulled them down to the ground. Lying next to me, Dieter said smiling unsuspectingly, "What are you doing? What is this 'fire in the hole'? I see no fire down there." Before I could answer his question, a huge explosion reverberated from the pit. Henry, who we later learned was caught just short of the safety of the rim when the dynamite detonated, was launched over us by the blast. We watched him soar above our heads with a surprised look on his face. He harmlessly landed in a large creosote bush twenty feet behind us. After he passed, small rocks and gravel showered down on us as the echo of the explosion faded off across the desert.

I looked over at Leonard. "Jesus Christ ... what the fuck, he must have set all of those sticks off at once." Leonard just lay there and shook his head in disbelief. Then he began laughing. It was infectious - I started to laugh too. The whole situation was totally absurd – trilobites and dynamite.

Leonard made it even worse and asked, "Do you think that happens every time he comes out here?" We both were laughing so hard that we had tears in our eyes.

After a couple of minutes we got a grip on ourselves. As our laughter subsided, I was able to turn my attention to the Germans

Marta was so upset she was on the verge of crying. She said, her voice shaking, "It's ... it's so, so horrible ... who is this man?"

As if to answer her question, Henry, who had extracted himself from the creosote bush, walked up to us. He was covered from head to toe in dust. Other than slight powder burns on his lower pant legs and a few scratches, he looked no worse for the trip.

"Don't worry, folks, just a slight miscalculation in the length of the fuse." He saw that Marta had been crying, "There, there, young lady, don't you worry none, Henry Ulum is just fine." As usual Henry egocentrically misread the situation - Marta was not particularly concerned about his well-being. "Well, no sense in crying over spilled milk ... let's go see what we loosened up down there."

Dieter was confused, "Milk?"

I nudged his arm, "Never mind, Dieter, come on. Let's go."

The four of us followed Henry over the rim of the pit and began our decent. This time it was the Germans who cautiously took up the rear. Before anyone else had reached the bottom, Henry was maniacally beating on a half-cracked boulder with his larger pick.

"Yeah, I can smell it - yer in there, yes-sir-ee, yer in there, all right." By the ninth or tenth blow the boulder he was beating on gave up and split in two. "Oh yeah, there you are. Thought you could hide from Henry, did you? Well, I guess you were mistaken. Oh, you are a fine one, aren't you." He motioned to us. "Come on over here, folks, and look what we have here. We got us a might-tee-fine trilobite ... fat one too."

Leonard and I walked over to see what Henry had found. The Germans followed us tentatively. He pointed at the rock, "Look there, that's what you call a perfect specimen." Leonard and I looked down at the rock. Embedded in the slab was a distinct raised outline of what appeared to be a twelve to fifteen inch beetle-like critter.

"Wow, looks like a bug," Leonard commented blankly. I knew that Leonard's unenthusiastic comment was going to enrage Henry.

I tried to cut him off at the pass, "Leonard, it isn't a bug, man, it's a *trilobite*."

"Well, I don't care what kind of Latin name you give it, Carl, in my opinion it looks like a bug in a rock." Henry stared at him blinking. I cringed inside for what was going to follow.

Then Henry began, "A bug, huh?" He paused and thought about it. "Well ... I suppose in a sense you're right. Trilobites were a kind of bug ... water bugs. But now the only thing that would make them different from insects would be..."

While Henry continued on, I turned my attention to Dieter and Marta, who were now standing beside us. The pair looked down at the rock in amazement.

"Pretty neat, huh? So, is this the first fossil that you've ever seen?" Neither one of them seemed to have heard a word that I said, and they continued to stare in amazement down at the slab.

Then finally Dieter spoke, but not to me. "It is beautiful, is it not?"

"Ya, it *is* beautiful," Marta replied, without taking her eyes from the rock.

Dieter went on, "This must be another reason why they call this God's Country." They looked at each other and smiled knowingly.

Seeing the Germans' intense interest in the fossil, Henry abandoned Leonard for the time being. "Well, what do you folks think? Pretty fine trilobite, ain't she?"

"Ya, he is magnificent," said Dieter.

"He ... did you say he?" Henry replied, "Oh, no my friend, that one is clearly a female. You can tell by the rounded carapace towards ..."

Henry was cut off by Marta who seriously observed, "He looks so ... so full of sorrow." Dieter nodded in agreement,

"Ya, like the weight of the sins of the world is upon him."

Henry was totally perplexed. "What the hell are you people talking about? I'm looking at a trilobite – what are you looking at?"

Dieter looked right at him and said with surprise, "Christ." At the mention of his name, Marta knelt down and touched the impression in the rock tenderly with just the tips of her fingers as if it were some holy artifact.

Henry was stunned, "What did you say ... Christ?"

"Yes, do you not see him there?" Dieter replied sincerely.

"No, I do not see him there. Are you people crazy? That there is a trilobite, not Christ."

Since both Leonard and I had had previous experience with the Germans' divine perception of the environment, neither of us was particularly surprised by their interpretation of the petrified organism.

Dieter knelt down. "His image is clear," and gently traced his finger over the artifact, "Here is his body ... and here... here the cross." He continued, "And look at his ... his ... how you say ..."

I helped him out, "Expression?"

"Ya, this is the word ... expression ... he peacefully carry the sins of the repenters."

By this point, Henry was outraged, "Why, you people are insane! There ain't nothin' there but a trilobite. Hell, this trilobite here is probably 300 million years old, give or take a half a million years. Jesus wasn't even a good idea when these things were alive."

Now it was Dieter and Marta who looked at Henry in disbelief. Marta spoke first, "Your words are of an unbeliever."

Dieter agreed, "Ya, the words of the doubter."

"Oh, for the love of ..." Henry stopped and corrected himself before he said it, "... for the love of Sam. I'm no heathen, I believe in Christ just as much as the next person. All I'm saying is that this here is a trilobite. Why, ain't you folks ever heard of evolution?"

Dieter and Marta were shocked and looked at him as if he spoke the language of the antichrist. I turned to Leonard, who was by now smiling at the confrontation. We both instinctively took a few steps back from the trio so as to avoid becoming part of the conflict. Marta narrowed her eyes with a serious intensity. She was so upset her words caught in her throat as she spoke, "He ... he is a heretic." Dieter's reaction was similar. He fixed his body solidly, as a warrior about to set out on a holy war. I didn't envy Henry – Dieter was going to eat him alive. Leonard and I took another couple of steps back.

If Henry was going to be hit by lightning, neither one of us wanted to be too close to him.

Dieter started in on him. "Sir, it is you who are the lunatic. You come and you scar the country of the creator, and then when you are shown the way you speak with the tongue of the heretic. You are an unstable and dangerous man, Mr. Ulum, and you frightened my wife very much and nearly made her cry. We will be going now."

Henry looked madder than when he had read the letter in the restaurant the night before. His face was so flushed that it looked like he had opened the door to a nuclear reactor and stuck his head in to take a peek.

I leaned over to Leonard. "I think that we should take this as our cue to make an exit."

"No, man, wait ... this is just getting good. Let's stay and see who comes out of this alive."

"Come on, Leonard, I'm serious, let's get out of here. I don't want to get caught in the middle of any divine intervention." Reluctantly, Leonard agreed with me. Neither Henry, nor Dieter, nor Marta noticed as we quietly backed our way out of the pit.

We made our way back across the desert in the direction of the van. For a good portion of the way we could hear in the distance the fevered argument between Dieter and Henry. At one point I questioned my decision to leave.

"My God, Leonard, I think those guys are going to kill each other. Maybe we should have stayed with them for a while longer just to prevent a homicide."

"Nah, those guys are harmless. Who knows, maybe they'll learn something from each other."

When we got back to the van I looked at my watch. It was 11:15.

"Hey, look at that, Leonard, it's not even noon yet."

"Oh boy, what a surprise, Carl. I would have thought that it was later than that considering that we slept in so late."

"Come on, Leonard, it was worth it, wasn't it?"

"Not as worth it as the Wiccans." I shook my head and stepped up into the driver's seat of the van. "I'll take the first shift driving us out of here." Leonard got into the passenger seat beside me.

"Do you have an extra cigarette?"

I pulled one out of my pack and passed it to him. He, as he always did, promptly broke off the filter before putting a match to it. "Well, let's see if you can get us out of here."

Since there was no one in front of us, and we could actually see where we were going, the drive out to the highway wasn't nearly as bad as when we had come in. It only took us only a few minutes.

Back on the highway, Leonard got the road atlas out from underneath the seat. He quietly studied it, flipping back and forth between pages.

After a few minutes I asked him, "So, navigator, where are we heading?" He looked at me with a twisted smile and said simply, "East."

"Yes, I know that we are headed east, asshole. What I meant was, what is our destination? Obviously we're not going to drive all the way to Wyoming today."

Leonard agreed, "No, probably not."

"Well?"

"Well, keep your pants on, I'm looking." He went back to the atlas. "Hmmm, hmmm ... maybe, well, or ... hmmm, yeah, here we go."

At last he came up with a plan. "Okay, here it is, Carl. The way I read it is this - I think that we can make it pretty easily to a place called Craters of the Moon National Monument. It's in Idaho, it's in the right direction, it doesn't take us too far off the main highway, and here's the best part ... it sounds like it's weird."

"Sounds good to me. Plot me a course, Mr. Spock." I laughed out loud. Leonard glared at me.

"Fuck you, Carl." Leonard never seemed to fully appreciate the humor in the fact that he and the actor who played Mr. Spock on "Star Trek" shared the same first name. I, on the other hand, thought it was tremendously funny and reminded him of this fact every so often. I figured the humor value in it was well worth getting him a little pissed off at me from time to time.

"Sorry, man, I just couldn't help myself," I lied.

Leonard knew it. "Bullshit. You say that every time. Ya know what, Carl? I'm beginning to think that you have some kind of disorder." He said it so deadpan I almost thought that he wasn't kidding.

"Are you serious, man?" He looked back at me gravely, like one of those TV doctors who is about to tell you that you have a fatal disease and only two weeks to live. He strung me along for a few moments, then burst out laughing.

"Jesus, Carl, sometimes this is too easy." He continued to laugh and went back to studying the map. Finally he looked up, turned to me and said in his best Mr. Spock voice, "Mr. Jerkov, Highway 26 - warp factor three."

Idaho

We continued on US 26 for nearly three hours until we came to a sign that had a waving anthropomorphized potato named "Spuddy Buddy" on it. Coming out of the side of his mouth was a big callout that said, "Welcome to Idaho – Famous Potatoes."

Leonard observed philosophically, "Ya know, Carl, I think that it's just a little more than sort of sad that the people of Idaho can't think of anything better about their state than their potatoes."

I agreed, "Yes, it is rather sad, isn't it."

Shortly after crossing the border, we picked up Interstate 84 and headed south towards Boise. After only twenty minutes in Idaho, I realized why the Idahoians were so proud of their potatoes – there was nothing else. The country was harsh. Unlike the subtle stark beauty of the eastern Oregon desert, the landscape of Idaho offered, well ... nothing. It was flat, featureless, and desolate. It made me think that folks who lived here probably were pretty proud that they could grow anything on the land.

"Wow, what is the deal with this state? Man, that sign back there should have said 'Welcome to God forsaken shit country – enjoy your stay if you can.'" We both laughed, but only a little. There was something about the land - something emotional. It was almost as if there was a profound sadness about it, and both Leonard and I felt it. Half-depressed from being in Idaho, and half-asleep from being woken at five AM, we silently stared out of the van window as we ate up the lonely miles on the interstate.

We passed through Caldwell, Nampa and Boise. At four-thirty we approached Mountain Home, and the cut-off from the interstate to Route 20. We hadn't spoken for so long that I was startled by Leonard's voice,

"Hey Carl, this is where you want to turn off."

"Christ, don't sneak up on me like that, partner."

"I hardly think giving you directions from all the way over here in the passenger seat constitutes sneaking up on you, Carl. You know what?"

"What?"

"I think that this whole Idaho thing has us both in the bad funk. And you know what else?"

"What?"

"I think that I have a remedy for it." I knew exactly what he was talking about but I played along anyway,

"Really, and what might that be?" Leonard already had the pipe out and was loading it up with some of the weed that the Wiccans had given us. He put a match to the bowl, took a long drag, and lay back in the van seat with his eyes closed. He let the smoke out slowly, and as he did, he gradually opened his eyes. "Nice Wiccans." He handed me the pipe, which was still smoldering a bit.

"Here, I think you're going to need a little bit more fire on that," and he handed me a book of matches. I tried to juggle the steering wheel, the pipe and the matches but was unsuccessful with any of it. Leonard reached over and took the steering wheel.

"Thanks, man."

"No problemo."

With hands now free I took a long drag on the pipe. I held the smoke for a few seconds. I felt better already. After I let the smoke out, I handed the pipe back to Leonard.

"Man, no foolin' ... Nice Wiccans."

We passed the pipe back and forth three times before there was nothing left but ashes. By the time we were done we both felt remarkably better.

"Man, Leonard, you were right, that was the cure. You know what? You should be a doctor."

Leonard deepened his voice like a radio announcer and said, "Funny you should say that, Carl. In real life I'm not really a doctor but I like to play one on vacation."

It wasn't that funny. Hell, it didn't even really make sense, but it made us erupt into a gale of pot giggles for a few minutes. I snapped out of my laughing fit abruptly when I momentarily forgot that I was actually driving a vehicle and narrowly missed clipping a guardrail.

"Fuck, Carl, watch it! What are you, some kind of maniac?"

"Whoa, sorry, man," I thought that I would fuck with him a little more. "For a minute there I thought that you were driving."

Leonard glared at me straight-faced and said, "Don't act so high."

Somewhat back in reality, we noticed that our surroundings had changed. While we were busily getting high, without noticing we had driven into the foothills of the Sawtooth Mountains. Gone was the lifeless, barren landscape of the Idaho flatlands. Before us lay rugged mountains covered in fragrant pine forest. I saw a road sign for the exit to Ketchum - this was Hemingway country. This was the kind of country where real men do real men things like drink bourbon, fish in mountain streams, and shoot big game. It was also the kind of country where desperate men do desperate things, like commit suicide as Hemingway did. It made me wonder ... maybe if had Hemingway indulged in a little grass himself, he might have avoided some of the crushing depression that the state of Idaho seemed to generate.

"So what is our ETA there, Leonard?"

"Well, it looks from the map here like we are about forty-five miles or so from our destination." I glanced at my watch; it was just before six-o'clock.

"Hey, we might actually make it to the campground before dark ... kind of novel, huh?"

"Yeah, well considering that we've been up for twelve hours already ..."

Leonard was cut off mid-sentence by the sudden appearance of a semi truck careening around the corner ahead of us. The truck had obviously taken the corner far too fast. His tires were shrieking, he was halfway over into our lane, and he was doing at least eighty. Thick gray smoke was pouring from his wheels ... something was bad wrong.

I took evasive action and turned the van as close as I possibly could to the guardrail to give him room. The truck kept coming.

"Oh, sweet Jesus, that guy's going to cream us!" Leonard yelled. I couldn't say anything – I was scared shitless. Just as his grill passed our front end a deafening "Bang!" resonated inside of the van. I was sure that he had hit us, and my mind raced in those few slow-motion microseconds that horrific accidents create. I braced myself to be either flung over the guardrail, ground up under his wheels, or pinballed across the highway in little van pieces. But nothing happened, and the rest of the rig shot past us harmlessly. I slammed on the brakes, came to a stop, and turned around just quickly enough to catch the sign on the back of his truck. In big red letters it read "Danger – Show Chickens." The truck disappeared around the next curve, wheels smoking.

We both stepped out of the van by the side of the road to calm down and do a damage assessment. A haze of burning brake pad smoke hung over the highway. The whole incident had happened so fast that it kept replaying in my mind over and over and over again. It wasn't until I tried to pull a cigarette out of my shirt pocket that realized I was shaking like mad. Finally I managed to get one out, but I went through three matches before I got the thing lit.

I came around to Leonard who was visibly shaken as well.

"Gimme one of those things, Carl." I handed him the pack and he continued, "Oh man, oh man, that was so close ..."

I was almost stuttering, "... that was so fucking close. I thought we were road-critters for sure."

"No shit. I think that I soiled myself."

Leonard had the same shaking problem that I did but only went through two matches before he got his cigarette lit.

"So what the hell was that big bang that I heard in the van?"

"Fuck if I know." We walked around the van for five minutes looking for any signs of damage – we found none.

"I don't see anything here, Carl."

"Yeah, I don't either. Maybe the guy was breaking the sound barrier and what we heard was a sonic boom." Leonard looked at me like I was an idiot,

"Yeah, Carl, I bet that's exactly what it was ... So are you driving or do you want me to take over?"

"No, I think I can handle it."

Leonard opened the passenger door and got in as I walked around the other side of the van. I opened the driver's door, hoisted myself up into the seat, and fired it up. Instinctively I looked into the side-view mirror as I put the van in gear. All that I saw was chrome.

"Hey Leonard, I think I know what that bang was."

"Does it have to do with Chuck Yeager?"

"No it does not ... look at the side-view mirror." Leonard leaned over to get a better view of the outside mirror, which was flattened against the side of the van.

"Jesus Christ, Carl – two inches ... just two inches closer."

I opened the window to see what the extent of the damage was. Gently I folded the mirror back on its hinges to its proper place. To our surprise, it remarkably hadn't broken.

Leonard commented with amazement, "Whoa, that's a trip. He didn't even bust it."

"Yeah, well, now you know why I have all of these icons on the dashboard ... insurance, man, insurance." Leonard didn't reply, but I could tell that he was thinking about it.

I stuck the van in gear and pulled back onto the highway.

"Hey Leonard, what do you think happened to that guy?"

"What, the guy in the truck?"

"Yeah, maybe we should backtrack and make sure that he didn't fly off the road down there somewhere."

"Nah, he only had a few miles left of these foothills before Idaho levels off for a few hundred miles ... he'll be okay." I shrugged my shoulders. Leonard was probably right. We drove on.

Once we were back up to highway speed, detailed bits and pieces of the incident came back to me. One in particular perplexed me. I shared it with Leonard.

"So, did you see the sign on the back of the truck?"

"No, I was too busy preparing to die – what did it say?"

I looked over at Leonard, "It said, 'Danger – Show Chickens.'"

"What?!"

"Yeah, 'Danger – Show Chickens.'"

"What in the fuck is that supposed to mean?"

"Hell if I know, I didn't write it on there. Maybe they're stunt chickens."

"Oh yeah, Carl, like Evil Kneivel."

"Yeah, exactly ... except they're chickens."

"Fuck, Carl, don't be such an idiot ... Jesus, chicken stunt drivers, that is one of the stupidest things I have ever heard."

"Yeah, well, did you see the driver?"

"No, did you?"

"No, but you know what?"

"What?"

"I bet it was a fucking chicken."

Leonard was getting genuinely impatient. "Oh my God, why am I in this conversation?! What bullshit ... there is no such thing as a driving chicken."

"Exactly, that's my point." In light of our near brush with death, I thought that my theory was funny as hell. Leonard just glared at me. The absurdity of my hypothesis wasn't even remotely humorous to him – it was just annoying. I guess he took his near-death experiences seriously.

We drove on and made the last leg of the day's journey without further incident. As we approached our destination, the terrain again changed dramatically. We quickly dropped out of the high country into a vast valley. Amazingly, there was even less vegetation here than there had been in the flatlands leading up to the foothills.

It was just after seven when we rolled into Craters of the Moon National Monument. There was really no mystery as to how the park had gotten its name.

"Man, Carl, this place is so ... so ... lunar."

"Yeah, it sure is. I don't see a sign anywhere - I wonder where you're supposed to camp."

"I think what we're supposed to do is radio back to Houston for a radar fix and have them guide us in." With that he jokingly picked up the handset of the CB radio that had lain dormant since the day I had bought the van.

"Do you have any idea how that thing works, Leonard?"

"Well, Carl, it's pretty complicated. I don't know if I can figure it out," he said sarcastically. "Oooh ... look here, a knob that says on/off. I wonder if that does anything." I rolled my eyes. He switched the radio on.

"Come on, man, quit fucking around. Turn that thing off and help me find a place to dock the van."

He ignored me and pressed the button on the side of the handset. "Ah, mission control Houston, this is Apollo – do you read me – over?" He released the button - the radio crackled with static, "kkkkkkkkkk." Leonard turned to me as the radio hissed. "Sorry ... I just couldn't help myself." He reached down to turn off the radio. Just as he was switching it off, very, very faintly the static was interrupted, "kkkkkkkkkkk ... read you."

"What the fuck - did you hear that?" He fumbled with the radio, quickly turning it back on again. The radio hissed static but nothing else. "Shit – did you hear that? - somebody answered me."

"Don't get so jacked up, you probably just picked up part of someone else's conversation. Hell, it's so flat out here you could probably pick up a signal from Nebraska." Leonard looked at me skeptically, half-accepted my explanation, then turned the radio back off.

"Well ... somebody *could* have answered me."

"Yeah – sure, Leonard."

We continued to follow what seemed like an unlikely ribbon of blacktop heading to nowhere. A few minutes later we came to a sign that simply said, "Camping."

"Here we go." I turned the van into the parking lot.

"Here we go what, Carl? There isn't anything here."

"Yeah, well, the sign says 'camping.'"

I switched the van off and got out. I stood in the middle of the gravel parking lot and surveyed our surroundings. Leonard got out to join me. When he closed the van's door it seemed unnaturally loud. The only other sound was the whispered moan of the wind across the miles of lava rock. The scenery around us was extraterrestrial - lava rock for as far as the eye could see. I half-expected that when the sun went down the earth would rise up over the horizon rather than the moon.

"Wow, a whole lot of nothing."

"Yeah, no shit, not regular nothing ... this is nothing - nothing."

We set up our tent on a sandy, flat spot near the edge of a bluff. From the door of the tent we had a sweeping view of the valley. Since there were no picnic tables at the campsite, we found a medium-sized, flat piece of shale nearby and carried it back to our camp to serve as a table. We got our box of food, the stove, and the Coleman lantern from the van. Leonard dug through the box of supplies to rustle up some dinner while I farted around with the Coleman lantern. There was probably only an hour or so left of daylight and I didn't want to be screwing around with the thing in the dark.

Leonard held a can in each hand and said formally, "Can I tell you about the special tonight, sir?"

"Please do."

"Tonight, we have on the menu a wonderful full-bodied chili con carne. It comes with a side of corn tortillas and as many cold carrots as you can eat."

"Mmmmm, sounds delicious."

"Very good," Leonard put down the cans and picked up a beer out of the six-pack in the box.

"Might I recommend a beverage, sir?"

"Why, yes." Leonard held the beer across his arm like he was a wine steward.

"Might I recommend this lovely domestic beverage? It is crisp and light in body, yet boasts subtle hints of hops and malt. Its refreshing clarity goes exceptionally well with spicy dishes such as chili."

I examined the Henry's label seriously. "Yes, that sounds superb ... thank you." Leonard twisted off the cap, handed me the bottle, then reached into the six-pack for one for himself. We both laughed while we heated up dinner over the stove.

We had just finished dinner as the sun began to dip below the horizon. The vast sky exploded into a pallet of red and orange and bathed the valley below in its sentimental colors. We took the lantern with us and walked a bit further up the bluff for a better view. As we sat there watching the sunset, the warm desert air blew its fragrance of sage around us.

Leonard pulled out the pipe, "Dessert?"

"Excellent idea." We smoked. The weed's smell seemed at home in our surroundings.

We watched silently in awe as the last colors left the sky and were gradually replaced by stars.

Leonard broke our quiet. "This is good, man ... this is really good."

I paused, "Yeah, it is."

"You know, Carl, there is something about this," he swept his arm in front of him, palm out, "that makes me feel whole inside."

"Yeah, I know what you mean. I can't really describe it... I just feel like I understand."

"Yeah, it's like, like there's meaning." We were quiet again. After a few minutes Leonard said, "Maybe that's what we are all looking for ... this meaning, connection ... understanding. Like those Wiccans, they do that earth worship thing trying to connect with all of this."

I nodded and added, "Yeah, and Dieter and Marta, they're looking for it too in the same place, just a different path." We paused again.

Then Leonard pensively said, “I suppose we’re doing it too.” As he spoke I felt a glow grow around him. The wind took away his words and it was quiet again.

We continued to talk for another two hours. Under the night sky our conversation meandered from the meaning of life to our relationships with women to our own friendship. We both knew that it was a high conversation, but it was a good one, and in the end we both felt closer to understanding everything.

Eventually the effects of the grass wore off and our conversation became less profound. We deemed that it was time to wander back to the tent and crash. In the dark the sameness of the landscape was confusing. In spite of having the lantern with us, and being only a few hundred feet from our camp, we got completely lost.

“Fuck, Carl, where the hell is the camp?”

“Over here ... no wait ... yeah, this way.”

“Oh, shut up, Carl, you don’t have any idea where it is either. Wait, hang on, I think I see it over there ... fuck, no that’s not it either, it’s a goddamn rock.”

I figured that a little humor might lighten the situation. “Hey, Leonard?”

“What?” he said sharply.

“Why did the chicken cross the road?”

“Oh, shut the fuck up, Carl.”

“Oooh, good answer, but *not* what I was after ... the answer is - to try and kill us.”

“You know what, Carl?” He didn’t wait for me to answer. “One more story, joke, comment, or theory about chickens and I am going into the first novelty shop that I find, buying a fucking rubber chicken, and beating you out of my misery with it.”

I shut up.

Twenty minutes and at least fifty expletives later, we found our camp. It had been a long day, and we were both exhausted. We were in the tent and in our sleeping bags in a flash. I was almost asleep when Leonard said, “Hey, Carl?”

“Yeah?”

"Do me a favor and take a flashlight if you have to go pee. I don't want to have to go look for you tomorrow morning." I smiled but was so tired that I fell asleep before I had a chance to laugh.

When I woke up it was probably over a hundred degrees in the tent. This explained why I was having an elaborate dream that I was an extra in the film "Samson and Delilah," starring Victor Mature. In my dream I was a slave and was right in the middle of being squished by a large stone from a pyramid that I, and a cast of thousands, was building. Fortunately, I woke up. I thought it was ironic that the near-death experience in the dream probably saved me from being baked alive in the tent.

I rolled over and looked at my watch – it was only seven-thirty. The intensity of the late summer sun combined with the reflective qualities of the nylon tent turned it into a solar oven. As I struggled with the zipper of the door I looked over at Leonard. Sweat was pouring off of his forehead – he looked about roasted. I got the tent door open. The warm wind outside felt refreshing compared with the stagnant sweat-filled air of the tent.

"Hey, Leonard, wake up, man."

"Mmmm ... oh Jesus, what the ... oh my God it must be a hundred degrees in here."

"Yeah, we should have brought some potatoes to bed with us last night so that we could have had hash browns for breakfast."

We both groggily crawled out of the tent. I put on some coffee and while we waited for it to brew we shared a quart of plain water.

"Man, I think that I'm seriously dehydrated," Leonard said after taking a long drink.

"Yeah, me too." He handed the bottle to me.

"Note to self – pitch the tent in a place with shade."

After a breakfast consisting of a couple of cups of coffee and a half a dozen or so cookies, we were ready for the road. We broke down the tent and packed up the van.

"So Leonard, do you want to take the first shift?"

"Sure. Hell, you drove all day yesterday." Leonard fired up the van's motor as I climbed into the passenger seat. "Well, Carl, how do we get out of here?"

I picked up the map from the floor of the van. "It looks like we need to drive back on the road we came in on and then pick up Route 93 going east." Leonard put the van in gear, punched the accelerator, and fishtailed out of the parking lot, a hail of gravel spewing behind us. "Do you really have to do that every time we leave anywhere?"

"Yes I do, Carl. I think that it's dramatic and it makes me feel like I'm in an episode of 'The Rockford Files.' Those things are very important to me." I didn't comment. I just shook my head.

The Plague

I studied the map as we blazed across the Idaho moonscape. As I tried to plot our course for the day, I kept hearing intermittent little metallic whacks reverberate on the sheet metal of the front of the van. After the twentieth or thirtieth whack I asked Leonard, "What the hell is that?"

"Oh, it's just the big ol' grasshoppers that I keep hitting." I looked up and out of the van's window to see if I could see one come on in.

"Jesus, they must be huge."

"Oh yeah ... they're big boys all right ... yeah, here comes one now." Leonard was smiling.

"Where?"

"Over there, just on the left." He pointed somewhere out towards the shoulder of the road ahead. I squinted hard, then saw what he was talking about.

"No shit, those things are huge. My God, it looks like a small bird."

Leonard continued to smile, "Oh yeah, come to papa ... come on, that's it, yeah, yeah ..." WHACK! The grasshopper exploded against the front of the van.

"Man, that's disgusting!"

Leonard turned to me with a big manic grin on his face, nodded enthusiastically, and said, "Yeah ... it is, isn't it."

"You know what, Leonard?"

"What?"

"I think that you're taking just a little bit too much pleasure in this."

"Oh hell, I'm not doing anything, they're just flying into us," he said innocently.

"Bullshit, I saw you swerve to clip that one."

He kept grinning, and said with a little shine in his eye, "Well ... maybe just a little."

I tried to go back to the map but the whacks kept steadily increasing, making it impossible to concentrate. "Would you knock it off, Leonard, I'm trying to read the map."

"Shit, I'm not doing anything, really ... these things are everywhere."

"Bullshit, you even admitted that ..." WHACK! I was interrupted by an especially large grasshopper that hit the windshield directly in front of me. A burst of radiating color covered the passenger windshield. "Oh God ..." I reached over and turned on the windshield wipers, which only smeared the remains across the window. I tried the windshield sprayer – it helped, but only a little. WHACK, WHACK! "Man, no shit, Leonard, these things are everywhere."

"Yeah," Leonard agreed. He was no longer smiling.

We both continued to look out of the van's windshield as grasshoppers hurtled themselves into the front of the van. As I watched I noticed a darkening in the sky a few miles up ahead.

"I don't think that we are going to have to put up with this too much longer, Leonard."

Leonard stared straight ahead, and said flatly, "Why?"

"Look up ahead ... I think that's rain." Leonard looked beyond the carnage that was occurring directly in front of us and saw the darkening in the sky as well.

"Yeah, I believe you're right ... that's rain. Hell, these things won't be airborne in a downpour."

Leonard stayed courageously calm at the wheel as we approached the cloud. "Oh, this is getting bad ... man I wish we would get to that storm."

"Yeah, me too." Gradually it came closer and we both felt a certain degree of relief knowing that soon we would be in rain and out of the hail of insects.

I turned to Leonard, "Hang in there, buddy, we're almost there."

"Yeah, I think so too ..."

Just after he said it the sky darkened dramatically. WHACK, WHACK, WHACK, WHACK, WHACK, WHACK, WHACK, WHACK! It wasn't rain at all; it was the main body of a huge swarm of grasshoppers. Up until now we had apparently only been on the edge of it. The windshield was instantly covered in a mass of exploded grasshoppers, and the interior of the van resonated with the sound of thousands of bodies hitting it. It was like being inside of a sick entomological snare drum. Both Leonard and I were completely unprepared for it.

"Jesus Christ, what the fuck!" Leonard screamed. I felt the van decelerate hard as he slammed on the brakes. The combination of crushed insects on the windshield and just being in the thick swarm reduced visibility to near zero. I turned to Leonard. He was clearly disturbed by the experience. He clutched the steering wheel hard with both hands and leaned forward to try to see the roadway.

"Maybe we should pull over and wait it out," I suggested.

"Are you insane! What if they start getting into the cab... did you think about that? They could strip us to bone in minutes!" I hadn't thought of it.

By now we were crawling along at twenty miles an hour. Even so, it seemed a little fast for the conditions. I tried to offer some solace.

"Ya know, Leonard, I think that grasshoppers are vegetarians."

He looked at me with a shocked expression on his face. "Think? Think? - You *think* that grasshoppers are vegetarians! But are you sure? Are you willing to risk a hideously slow munching death on it? I'm not." He snapped his attention back to the road.

I wasn't entirely certain about the vegetarian thing, and the way that Leonard put it I really wasn't willing to risk such a fate. I too just stared silently out the window helplessly at the horde and the resulting slaughter on the windshield.

Ten tense minutes passed in what seemed like hours. Gradually the mass began to thin and we could see the sun again. Leonard increased the van's speed as the insects began to diminish. In spite of the still-reduced visibility because of the smeared windshield, I didn't object. I wanted as much distance between them and us as possible.

Progressively the whacks became fewer and fewer till a full five minutes passed and we heard nothing. It seemed safe to talk again.

"Wow, Leonard ... I've never really seen anything like that before in my life."

"Man, no shit, I haven't either. If it wasn't for these smashed insects all over the front of the van, I would say that we just shared a bad flashback."

"Yeah ... bad is right. Maybe we should stop and take a picture of the van so people will believe us later."

Leonard decelerated and pulled off the highway. "I have to pee. You do whatever you want, Carl."

"I got so scared I already did." Leonard smiled, but only a little.

Leonard relieved himself by the side of the road while I grabbed my camera out of the back seat. I got out and came around to the front of the van. I probably should have thought my decision to photographically document the event through a little more. On an already nervous stomach, the nose of the van was almost more than I could take. I immediately began to feel nauseous. Leonard must have seen me weaving light-headedly as I tried to focus the camera.

"You okay over there, Carl?"

"Ah, no, I don't think so ... I'm a little nauseous."

"Well, take the fucking picture and get back in the van before you hurl."

I took his advice and got on with it. I managed to click three pictures before I felt seriously in danger of succumbing to my natural gastric reflexes. I got back in the van.

"Whew, man ... that was rough."

"I wouldn't know, Carl, I have too much sense myself to get anywhere near all of that."

"Thank you so much for your support, Leonard."

"You're welcome, Carl."

After chewing a couple of Tums that I dug out of our supplies, we were back on the road again. Leonard turned to me, "So, what's the cutoff that I'm looking for here, Carl?"

"Well, we should be turning right at a junction onto US 26. Thing is, in that mess back there, I have no idea if we passed it or not. Looking at the map here, at that junction you can either take 93 north, US 22 northeast, or US 26 east." I thought that I would test his nerves. Casually I said, "Maybe we should turn around and backtrack a few miles to see if we can get our bearings."

Leonard whipped around, "What brand of lunatic are you, Carl?"

I cut him off before he could really launch into it, "Hey, easy there buddy ... just testing you."

"Asshole."

"Friend of asshole."

We drove on in what appeared to be roughly an easterly direction. A couple of minutes later we were reassured of our course when I spotted a blue road sign that read "Route 26 – Butte City, Atomic City - Next Right."

"Who would want to live in a place called 'Butt City'?"

"It's not 'Butt City,' you knob, Carl ... it's 'Butte City,' you know, like 'mesa.' And to answer your question, I for one would not mind living in a place called 'Butt City.' As long as it was short for its more formal name of 'Fine Butt City.' Now... if it were short for 'Big Butt City,' or "Broad Butt City,' or even 'Ciudad Butto Extremo,' I would definitely not want to live there."

"Ah, yeah ..." I shook my head. "Hey, here we go, Leonard, it's coming up here." As we passed by, what I saw out of the van's window was a bleak conglomeration of run-down buildings that served as the center of the town. It was surrounded by equally run-down trailers. The whole scene had that "burned-out mining town" look about it. Probably the only people who were left there were miners from a former booming gold, silver or copper industry. They had been made half-idiots from years of heavy metal exposure, and they now spent their days attempting to scratch out a living on the tailings of the former lode.

Leonard beat me to the observation, "Well ... this is definitely not 'Fine Butt City.' I actually think that this is 'Stinky Butt City."

"Really, are you sure? Maybe you should pull off the highway and ask one of the residents just to make sure."

"Maybe you should give yourself an enema, Carl." We both burst out laughing – butt humor is always funny. We kept driving.

Ghosts

"We should be coming up on Atomic City here pretty quickly. It looks like only about twenty minutes down the road. Maybe we should pull over, fuel up, and see if we can get some lunch somewhere."

Leonard glanced down at the gas gauge. "Yeah, we've only got about a quarter of a tank left. Good plan - God knows when we'll see a gas station out here again. Besides, I could use a little food myself. Amazingly, I'm starting to get my appetite back."

A few minutes later, just around the bend in the highway, we came upon Atomic City. Probably a more appropriate name for it would have been Atomic *Town*, but it just didn't have the same ring to it.

"Can you see from here if there is anywhere to get gas? I don't want to get off the highway for nothing."

"No, I don't see anything but I saw a road sign back there that said 'Gas.'"

"Yeah, well, don't believe everything you read, Carl."

In spite of his doubts, Leonard took the next exit. We drove into the town. It wasn't much, but at least it didn't exude the same feeling of desperation that Butte City had.

"Over there up on the right." I pointed out the window.

"I see it," said Leonard, and he pulled the van into the gas station.

Before we could get out of the van an attendant was at Leonard's window. He was a young man dressed in a white mechanic's jumpsuit that had grease spots all over it and an embroidered "Tim" over the left breast. He wore his dark, short hair slicked back with some type of grease-based styling product. I hoped it wasn't motor oil. It made him look older than I think he actually was.

"Can I help you fellas?"

Leonard leaned out the window and said as friendly as he could, "Sure Tim ... hey, could you fill 'er up with regular?"

"Be happy to. Name's not Tim though, name's Bob."

While our misnamed attendant filled the tank I noticed a troublesome phenomenon beginning to occur around the front of the van.

"Leonard, check out all of these yellow-jackets buzzing all over the front of the van."

Leonard looked out the window and curled his lip some. "Jesus Christ ... that's disgusting. They're feeding on the slaughtered bodies of the grasshoppers. Opportunistic little vermin."

Before we could get too panicked about it, Tim-Bob came over with squeegee in hand to wash the windshield.

Leonard tried to warn him. "Hey Tim-Bob, I'd watch yourself there." Tim-Bob nodded from outside the window.

"Appreciate the concern ... got it covered," he said calmly. Out of a deep pocket in the right side of his jumpsuit he produced a can of Raid brand Wasp and Hornet Killer. He calmly stepped back from the van about ten feet and said, "Might want to roll your windows up, fellas."

We just barely got the side windows up when he let fly with a high-pressure chemical stream, hitting both sides of the front window squarely. Every yellow jacket that had been on the window instantly dropped to the ground. They stung at the air in a dance of death as they writhed in agony from the caustic attack.

I turned to Leonard and said, "Good Lord, I thought that stuff was outlawed at the Geneva Convention."

The hornet danger now dealt with, Tim-Bob walked back to the van and casually whistled as he cleaned the windows. Leonard rolled the side window back down. "So, Tim-Bob, just a guess on my part, but it looks like you maybe have had to deal with this situation before."

The attendant stopped washing and looked seriously and directly at Leonard. It was the first time that he had made full eye contact with either one of us since we had stopped.

He said slowly, "You see all sorts of weird things out here. Why those grasshoppers ... that happens regular round here." The way he said "weird things" kind of gave me the chills. He went back to work.

After finishing with the window, Tim-Bob topped up the tank and came around to the cab.

"That'll be eight seventy-five. Oh, and you might want to take a look at that right rear tire. It's pretty thin and losing air." I got out, handed him a ten, and asked him to show me what the tire business was all about. Tim-Bob and I walked back to the rear of the van. With the authority of an automotive engineer, he knelt down next to the tire in question. I joined him. He took a pressure gauge out of his pocket, as if to emphasize the fact that air pressure was the issue here, and used it as a pointer to show me what he believed to be the problem.

Sticking out of the tire was a one-inch by four-inch flap of woven fabric-like metal. I am no expert on the construction of tires, but I assumed that it was part of the radial. I examined it with him for a few moments and then said, "So how far do you think that I can get on that?"

Tim-Bob took the question seriously, "Well, where are you heading to?"

I gave him a rough itinerary, "We're heading out through Wyoming and maybe out to South and North Dakota. We'll come back through Montana and Idaho on our way back to Mount Vernon, Washington - that's where we're from." Tim-Bob patiently studied me and the situation while I rattled on.

When I finished he stared at me deadpan and simply said, "You might make it three or four miles."

I wasn't really budgeted for a tire, but Tim-Bob's warning seemed real. Heck, I wasn't even sure that we had a spare. When I had bought the van I really didn't consider tires to be essential to the actual mechanical function of the vehicle, therefore I didn't bother with them. Sure, they were all bald, and sure we were taking a long road trip, but they held air – that's all that mattered.

I studied the tire for a few moments, as if considering my many options. Then I said to him, "Do you have one that will fit?"

"Maybe – I'll go check ... Let's see, that's a 165-75 R15." I had no idea what he was talking about. He went back into the shop to check on his stock and I went over to Leonard who was still sitting in the cab.

"What's the story there, Carl?"

"Looks like we need a new tire. The one on there's pretty shot. It's losing air."

"Does he have one that'll fit?"

"No clue – he's checking on it now."

Tim-Bob returned. "Yeah, I got one that'll fit. Only one problem."

"What's that?"

"It's a whitewall, it ain't going to match them other tires, but it's the only thing I got."

"How much?"

"Fifty bucks – mounted."

"Sound fair. Besides, I don't think we have a choice."

He motioned towards the garage. "Go ahead and pull yer rig in the bay there. It'll take me 'bout fifteen minutes."

Leonard started the van and pulled it into the shop. "Sounds good ... say, is there a place 'round here where we can get some lunch?"

"Yeah, The Beehive Diner, two blocks down, on yer right."

"Thanks. We'll be back."

Leonard and I left the van with Tim-Bob and headed for the diner. In spite of it being ten-thirty in the morning, the streets were totally vacant. The town was clean and well kept. Obviously the citizens, whoever or wherever they were, had a sense of civic pride. It was so quiet that our footsteps echoed slightly off of the surrounding building as we walked down the deserted street.

"Is this a ghost town or what?"

"I don't think so, Carl, we already saw a human being."

"Yeah, but maybe that was it, maybe he's the only person here. You just wait, you're going to freak out if we walk into that diner and he's behind the counter."

Leonard looked at me blankly. "You are correct, Carl, I will freak out if that happens." We kept walking.

A block and a half after leaving the gas station we saw another sign of life ... sort of. In the doorway of a western shop that had a giant cowboy boot hanging above it stood an old man. He must have been close to a hundred and twenty-five years old. He leaned against the doorway and slowly smoked the short butt of a Camel straight as he watched us approach.

"Howdy fellers," he said, looking us over. His voice sounded a hundred and twenty-five years old as well.

"Hi, how ya doin'," Leonard answered.

I nodded, "Hi."

He looked down at my feet. "Nice boots."

"Thanks."

"How 'bout a shine?"

"Thanks, but we're just headed down to The Beehive to get some chow."

"Man's got to take care of his boots, sir. Come on in, won't take a minute. It's on the house." He pitched his cigarette butt into the gutter and headed into the shop as if the decision had already been made. I shrugged my shoulders at Leonard and followed the old man in.

Inside, the shop was like any other western store I had been in: work wear, boots, and tack. Hung up on the wall there were posters advertising familiar brands like Wrangler, Carhartt, and Stetson. One poster advertising Nocona boots showed a giant cowboy boot holding a pissed-off rattlesnake to the ground while a hand with a glistening hunting knife prepared to slay it. I wasn't entirely sure why that would make me want to buy their product.

"Have a seat." The old man motioned over to a chair against the wall.

"Thanks." I sat down. The old man produced a wooden box full of boot care products and proceeded to rub down each of my boots with polish. In the meantime, Leonard busied himself by wandering around the store grazing through everything that it had to offer.

When the old man finished rubbing in the polish, he reached into his shirt pocket for a pack of cigarettes.

"Best to wait for the polish to dry up nice an' hard." He shook a Camel straight out and put it in his mouth. Then he shook one my direction. "Cigarette?"

"Thanks," I took one. Out of the same pocket he produced a Zippo and offered a light to me. I lit my cigarette from his shaking hand, then he lit his.

The straights were considerably stronger than the filters that I had been accustomed to smoking. The first drag made me dizzy. It was like my first cigarette all over. The old man, on the other hand, seemed completely unaffected by his. He let his cigarette hang from his mouth as he got a boot brush from the box.

The cigarette bounced as he talked. "This'll put a shine on 'em." He brushed with speed and finesse. Halfway through brushing up the first boot he stopped. He took the cigarette from his mouth, turned his head away, and coughed hard. When he was done he turned back to the boot he had been working, leaned towards it, spat on it, and went on brushing.

"That really brings the shine on." I was more fascinated than disgusted by the ritual. When he was done my boots had a shine on them that was better than when I had bought them two years ago.

"What do I owe you?"

"Nothin' – like I said this one's on the house." Then he looked right into my eyes deeply and added slowly, seriously, and emphatically, "Just remember this ... man's got to take care of his boots for the journey ahead."

His words sent a tingle along the back of my head. I nodded back at him as if having received a profound message, and quietly said, "Yes sir, I understand." He nodded back, smiled, and winked, assured that I had understood him. I wasn't sure what it had all been about, but I was sure that there was something more in what he had said to me than just boot care.

I got up to leave. "Hey Leonard, ya ready for some lunch?"

"Yeah, let's get a move on."

"Hey, thanks again, Mister."

"You bet."

We headed for the door. Just as we were leaving he said, "You fellas having lunch at the diner?"

"Yeah."

"Might I personally recommend the chicken-fried steak."

"Thanks. We'll try it."

The diner was just around the corner. It was hard to miss. Hanging from the corner of the building there was a giant sign in the shape of a beehive. Below the hive there was a waving bee that said, "Buzz on In Honey."

"Hmmm, just a guess, but this must be it."

"Good guess, Leonard."

We walked in and were greeted by a woman in her fifties who had her red hair done up, not surprisingly, in a beehive.

"Hi, Honey." Given the restaurant's theme, I should have heard it coming. Twenty years ago she had probably been a good-looking woman with a fine figure. Since then her flesh had settled and she had grown tired. She wore a yellow and black striped dress with a white apron. She matched the interior of the diner.

"You boys here for lunch?"

"Yes, ma'am," I answered.

"Well, you're here before the lunch rush. Go ahead and seat yourself where you like." She swept her hand with a motion like a pageant queen. There wasn't another soul in the restaurant.

"Thanks." We took at seat by the front window.

She produced a pair of menus and handed them to us. "Coffee?"

"Please."

After she left the table Leonard leaned over and said in a whispered voice, "Good thing we missed that lunch rush; we would've never gotten a seat." We both laughed.

Moments later she produced a couple of cups of coffee. "You boys know what you want?" I hadn't touched the menu, but I had already decided.

I ordered for both of us, "We'll take the chicken-fried steak."

"Fine choice, it's a house special. You boys want gravy with that?"

"Is there any other way?"

She smiled approvingly, "Not in my book. That'll be just a few minutes." She left.

"Thanks for ordering for me there, Carl. I wouldn't have wanted to have made a mistake and gotten something healthy."

"Ah, but Leonard, chicken-fried steak is healthy."

"Oh really ... and how do you figure that?"

I leaned forward. "Does chicken-fried steak make you happy?"

"Yes."

"And would you agree that happiness is an essential part of one's mental health?"

"Yes."

I leaned back in my chair. "I rest my case."

"Yeah, well, I'll put it on your headstone after you have a heart attack at forty. 'He Loved Chicken-Fried Steak.'"

Leonard and I talked and drank coffee while we waited for our food. As we talked, I thought in the back of my mind about the trip. It seemed that every day we had been blown slightly off course by some unforeseen event, and we were now essentially only vaguely sticking to any previously planned destination. Optimistically, we had thought that we could cover up to six hundred miles a day. In reality we were covering little more than half that. We needed another plan.

After two warm-ups of coffee, lunch arrived. Over our artery-clogging meal I brought up our travel plans for the day.

"You know, Leonard, it's after eleven already."

"Yeah," Leonard said through a mouthful of food. In spite of his previous condemnation of my menu choice Leonard appeared to be enjoying the meal.

"So, I am thinking ..."

"You are?"

I ignored his sarcasm, "I am thinking that Wyoming is a very big state."

"Yes it is, Carl."

"I am also thinking that Devil's Tower is located on the very eastern side of the state and that we are way over on the west side."

"Yes, we are."

"Please tell me if I'm wrong, but I think that it will probably take us a very, very long time to drive across Wyoming."

"Yes, it will ... and your point is what?"

"My point is this, I think that we should forget going to Devil's Tower for a couple of days and head on up to Yellowstone. It's about three hours from here."

Leonard put down his knife and fork, took a drink of coffee, and looked at me from across the table. "Now you're talking, Carl. That's good - you're loosening up a bit. You're starting to go with the flow."

"Thank you for your approval." I cut off another piece of steak.

Leonard ignored the sarcasm in my comment and simply said, "No problem. To quote a famous bumper sticker, 'Not All Who Wander are Lost.'"

I swallowed my bite. "Oh, Jesus Christ, Leonard, don't go hippie on me. I hate that fucking bumper sticker. You always see it on some fucking VW van with some aimless hippie at the wheel. They stick that saying on there as if it justifies their pointless existence."

Leonard landed on me. "Oh really, Carl? And what are you driving?" He stared at me. I stared back. He was right - I shut up. He continued, "I agree with you that the saying might be a little trite, but I think that you have to agree with me that it does have some merit. Sometimes you just have to go with the flow and see what you find."

I nodded a little reluctantly. "Yeah ... I suppose you're right."

When we finished our meal Leonard got up went to go to the restroom. "Got to make room for the steak."

"Thanks for sharing." While I waited for him I had another cup of coffee and a cigarette for desert. I watched the smoke curl up toward the ceiling into the stagnant air of the diner. I wondered if I would get to be a hundred and twenty-five years old, or at least look like it, if I kept smoking these and eating chicken-fried steak.

When Leonard came back we went up to the register to pay our bill. Our waitress put down a six-month-old copy of People she had been reading. "How was it, boys?"

"Good, really good ... probably one of the finest chicken-fried steaks that I've had in my life."

She smiled. "We aim to please. Let's see here, that'll be eleven ninety-two." Leonard reached for his wallet.

"Forget it, Leonard, I've got it. I owe you for a philosophy lesson." Leonard casually looked around the restaurant while I paid the tab. On the way back from leaving a tip at the table I found him intensely looking towards the direction of the kitchen. "What's up?"

"Shit, Carl, I saw him," he whispered.

"Saw who?"

"Saw Tim-Bob."

"Quit fucking with me."

"No man, I'm serious, I fucking saw Tim-Bob, he's the fucking cook."

"No he's not ... you are so full of shit. I'm not going to bite on this one."

Leonard looked at me seriously. "No, I am really not shitting you, he is the fucking cook here. Look over at the kitchen." I entertained him and skeptically looked towards the kitchen. A few moments later a face briefly appeared at the order-up counter between the kitchen and the dining area.

"You're not shitting me, that is him!"

"See?!"

We were still staring in the direction of the kitchen when our waitress returned from clearing our table. "Can I help you boys with anything else?"

"Yes ma'am, maybe you can answer a question for us," Leonard said.

"Shoot."

"That guy back there in the kitchen, does he work anywhere else?"

"Why, yes he does, sometimes he works down at the gas station." We both stared at her.

"What's wrong, boys, you're lookin' mighty confused."

"How often does he work there?"

"Well I don't know, pretty regular, I suppose. Why?"

"We left our van down at the gas station with a guy that looks just like him."

"Oh, that's probably Tim. They look pretty much the same. Dark hair, same height and all ... that's probably it."

"What's this guys name, if you don't mind me asking?"

"What, that's Bob back there." We both continued to stare at her. I she could tell that we were suffering from total confusion. "Maybe if you met him that would help." She turned and hollered in the direction of the kitchen, "Hey Bob, come on up here ... got a couple of fellers want to meet you." No one answered. "Oh, damn it, I bet he went out back to have a cigarette. Maybe on yer way out step behind the restaurant here, that's where he'll be."

"Thank you, ma'am, we'll do that."

We walked out of the restaurant and went out behind the building to see if we could meet Bob and settle the whole thing. He wasn't there.

"Man, that's freaky ..."

"Oh, don't get all worked up about it, Leonard. He probably just finished his cigarette and went on back in. Come on, let's get back to the van and get back on the road." Leonard nodded.

As we approached the gas station we could see Tim-Bob, or whatever the hell his name was, sitting in the office reading a newspaper. He looked like he had been sitting there for a while. He must have seen us coming out of the corner of his eye. He put down the paper and came out.

"Got the tire on ... boy, that other one was pretty bad, just about fell apart when I took it off. Come on into the bay and I'll show you." We followed him into the garage.

I'm sure that he sensed that we were both looking at him kind of weird, but he acted like there was nothing out of the ordinary. Neither one of us mentioned our restaurant experience. "Look here, nothing left." He nodded in the direction of the old tire. We came over and looked at it. He was right. The radial was trashed. As I stood next to him examining the tire, I thought that I detected the faint odor of chicken-fried steak on him, but it was impossible to tell for sure. There were too many other smells in the garage, like gasoline and oil. Also, I was looking for it. I probably just imagined it.

"So what do I owe you?"

"Like I said before, fifty bucks ought to cover it." I reached into my wallet and pulled out a pair of twenties and a ten.

"Thanks for pointing out that tire for us. We could have been left in a bad spot."

"Yes sir, we aim to please."

We got in the van. Leonard fired it up and we backed it out of the garage. "I don't know, Carl, there is something mighty weird about Tim-Bob. I still think that it was him back at the diner."

"Oh, I think that's probably pretty unlikely. Hell, when we came back here to get the van he looked like he'd been sitting here doing nothing for about forty-five minutes. "

"Yeah, you're probably right." Leonard put the van into gear and pulled out onto the street. I looked back at the gas station as we drove away.

"Hey, hang on, Leonard – stop the van." Leonard immediately pulled over to the curb.

"What?"

"Look over there behind the gas station," I motioned with my hand.

Walking at a fast pace from the rear of the gas station in the direction of the diner was Tim-Bob. He was unzipping the front of his jumpsuit and looking around as if to make sure that no one was watching him. He stopped for a moment to fumble with the zipper. When he looked up again he spotted us and broke into a dead run behind the building across the street.

Leonard turned to me, "See, I told you that Tim-Bob was Bob-Tim, didn't I?"

"Yeah, I guess you did, but it was just too fucking weird to believe."

"Yeah, it is too fucking weird ... what the fuck is the deal with that? Does this guy just run back and fourth between the gas station and the diner working two jobs under two different names and no one in this little nothing town knows anything about it? Is that the deal?"

I thought about Leonard's question for a moment, then said, "Yeah ... I guess that's the deal. Come on, let's hit the road."

Still shaking his head in disbelief and confusion, Leonard punched the gas hard and swung the van into a tire-squealing, fish-tailing, U-turn in the middle of the street.

"Goddamn it, Leonard, that's a brand new tire!"

He grinned at me. "Not anymore."

For the next half an hour, until we hooked up with Interstate 15, we explored a number of theories as to who else in the town Tim-Bob/Bob-Tim might have been. These included both the waitress and the old man, since they were the only other people we had seen. Leonard kept insisting that we had never seen any of them together and that it was completely possible that the real reason that we never saw anyone else in the town was that there was in fact only one citizen – Tim-Bob/Bob-Tim. It seemed unlikely to me, but I didn't argue with him. I suppose anything's possible.

Yellowstone – The Sentinel

We got to the junction with Interstate 15 and headed north toward Yellowstone. I looked at the map again to see exactly how far it would be.

"It looks like we are about a hundred and twenty miles away from the park entrance, a couple of hours or so."

"I don't think so, Carl. I think that we are actually hundred and thirty-seven miles away from the park entrance."

"Oh really, Mr. Distance Estimation guy ... I'm the one with the map."

"Well, Carl, I'm the one with the eyes, and I just saw a road sign back there that said 'Yellowstone 137 miles.'"

"Oh ..."

The closer we got to Yellowstone, the more pleasing the terrain became. Trees replaced the sagebrush, and the flatlands were replaced by the foothills of the Rocky Mountains. I was going to be happy to have a change of scenery, something more familiar.

I had found Idaho to be a sad and unpleasant place, at least what we had seen of it, and I wasn't going to miss it. By my estimation the state was the leftovers of what Washington, Montana and Oregon didn't want. Sitting there for the taking, it seemed that a few rough individuals who didn't want to be bothered by crowds had moved in and made it home.

We made pretty good time, but not as good as either of us had imagined. In spite of the strong horsepower that the van had, Leonard was not able to bring our speed up to much above sixty.

"I don't know what the deal is with the van, Carl. I have this thing nearly floored and I can't get anything more out of it than this. Did you put regular or super in it back there?"

"I had him fill it up with regular. That's what I've always put in it."

"I don't know, maybe you should have put super in instead."

I started to feel a pit of concern. "Does it feel like there's something wrong with it?"

"Nah, it doesn't feel like there's anything wrong with it... I mean, it sounds fine, it just doesn't have any power."

"Well, hell, it sounds like it's running fine to me too. Let's try not to worry about it, we'll just fill it up with super next time."

At around four-thirty we arrived at the west entrance to Yellowstone. Leonard slowed the van, pulled into a parking spot at the ranger station, and switched off the motor. We got out. The quiet of the woods was welcome after four hours of the echoed drone of the engine inside the van. I stretched and took a deep breath. The sent of pine and fir permeated the clean air. The buzz of crickets floated on the light wind. It was good to be in the mountains.

I stretched my legs and wandered over to the information board near the ranger station. In big letters at the top of the board it said, "Welcome to Yellowstone National Park – West Entrance – Elevation 7,772 feet." I called back to Leonard who was doing leg and back stretches against the side of the van.

"Hey, Leonard?"

"Yeah?"

"I think I know why you weren't getting any power out of the van."

"How's that?"

I nodded over towards the sign. "We've been driving uphill ever since we left Atomic City."

He rolled his eyes like we were both idiots. "Let's go in and talk with the ranger and find out where we can camp around here."

"Good plan. I'd like to just set up camp, hang out and relax for a while."

We went into the ranger station. Behind the counter was a big, handsome, dark-haired guy of around thirty. He was dressed from head to toe in an official green ranger uniform much like the one that Henry had worn. Unlike Henry, he looked like he'd been pressed into it, with light starch, that morning. On his head he wore a traditional hard-brimmed Smokey the Bear ranger's hat. On his left breast was a shiny gold badge that simply said "Federal Ranger" across the top of it. He was an impressive, strapping fellow who looked like he had been raised since birth on a strict diet of red meat. I was glad that he was on our side.

His rugged, direct voice matched his looks.

"Good afternoon, gentlemen. Welcome to Yellowstone. What can I do for you today?"

Leonard and I stepped up closer to the counter. I handled it. "Hi, I am wondering if you could point us to a good place to camp around here."

"Yes I can," he said firmly and confidently. He reached under the counter and produced a fistful of maps and brochures about the park. On top of the pile was a map of Yellowstone. He opened it up and spread it roughly across the counter. He then leaned over the map like he was field officer in a battle room somewhere in France – circa 1944.

"Gentlemen - you are here." He circled our location with a red pen. "Now, you have a choice. If you want, there is camping right here, about four hundred yards up the road," he indicated the location with the pen, and motioned the direction with his hand. "I wouldn't do that, though, if I were you. I would go on deeper into the park. Right here," he highlighted the map again, "about fifteen miles in, there is another campground – Madison. Here you have a choice: stay there, go north another ten miles to Norris, or go southeast forty-five miles to Lake Village." He looked at us from under the brim of his hat with a searching and demanding expression that said, "Well, soldiers – what is your field strategy? Can I count on you to take the bridge?"

Leonard and I studied our options on the map. The ranger stared at us waiting for an answer. I said, "I think that we'll stay at Madison ... what do you think, Leonard?"

"Sure, looks good to me."

The ranger quickly folded up the map and thrust it at me along with a half a dozen or so other brochures. "Excellent, men. One more thing." He slapped down on the counter an official looking pamphlet. Across the top of it, it said "Bears and You" in bold letters. Under it was a picture of a man-eating grizzly rearing up on his hind legs with teeth bared. This was the enemy. I wondered if we should have volunteered for the mission.

"Gentleman, this is a bear. Let me warn you, the park is full of them. These animals are powerful, quick, and cunning. They will take every opportunity to infiltrate your bivouac in search of food. Do not underestimate them. They can, and will, tear open a vehicle like it is a tuna can if they think there is a meal inside. But if you keep your rations sealed and your camp clean you should have no problem." Then he paused and narrowed his eyes. "Gentleman, let me remind you, these are wild animals. Under no circumstances are you to approach them."

Then he produced a black three-inch thick binder from under the counter. "Every year someone in the park is horridly mauled because they failed to heed my warning." He opened the binder. On the first page was a Polaroid picture of a balding middle-aged man in Bermuda shorts and a Hawaiian shirt. He looked stunned. His face was badly scratched and his shirt was torn to shreds.

"Summer, nineteen eighty-two: this man tried to feed a bear a piece of beef jerky."

He turned the page. There was another Polaroid picture. This time it was of a woman in a blue and white striped dress. She too looked traumatized. Her hair was disheveled, and the lower right half of her dress was torn badly. Her right arm, which was in a sling, was totally bandaged from the shoulder down.

"Spring, nineteen eighty-three: this woman, I believe she was from Iowa, tried to shoo a bear away from her potato salad." The ranger paused before turning to the next page, and said emphatically, "Do you need to see more?"

I answered, "No, sir. I think we get your point, sir."

He handed me the pamphlet. "Good." He shook each of our hands firmly. "Enjoy your stay, men, and good luck."

As soon as we got out the door of the ranger station, Leonard turned to me. "Wow, Ranger Hunk-Meat. I bet every married woman who comes through here on vacation questions her wedding vows the moment she meets that guy."

"Yeah, I think that guy was an extra in 'Pork Chop Hill.' You know what else?"

"What?"

"If I were married, I'd question my wedding vows too." I batted my eyes and pretended to swoon a bit.

Leonard looked at me blankly. "I'm not even going to dignify that with a comment."

Twenty-five minutes later we rolled into the Madison campground. The campground was only about half-full and we had no problem finding a good private spot off in the trees away from the other campers. We set up the tent and rolled out our sleeping bags. Leonard went and got a couple of beers from the cooler. Fortunately he'd had the foresight to pull over at a convenience store back in Idaho Falls and replenish our dwindling beer supply, along with a few other items.

"Here you go, Carl."

"Thanks, Leonard." I took a long drink. The cold beer tasted good. "Man, it's damn good to get out of that van and relax."

"Yeah, it's been a long day. I was starting to go a little road-nuts there."

"Yeah, me too."

Leonard stretched his arms over his head, yawned, then lay back against the picnic table and surveyed the surroundings. "Nice forest ... that Ranger Hunk-Meat steered us to a pretty good spot here." Then he sniffed the air. "A pretty good spot with the exception of the odor of brimstone."

"Yeah, I smelled that too when we pulled in. What's the deal? Did Mr. Ranger just happen to forget to tell us that we would be camping near the Gates of Hell?"

"Don't be a knob, Carl, that's the smell of the hot springs that are around here ... ya know, geysers and stuff like that. Here."

He dug through the pile of pamphlets on the table that we had gotten back at the ranger's station. He handed me one that said "Geothermal Phenomena of Yellowstone National Park." I took it from him and opened it up.

"Oh, man ... yeah, I remember this stuff from when I was a kid. My folks took me through here on vacation when I was about four. I remember my favorite thing was the bubbling mud."

"Oh, and I bet that you have changed a lot since you were four," Leonard said sarcastically.

"Come on man, this is totally cool." I put the pamphlet down. "What we should do is get stoned out of our marbles and go and check out some of this stuff. It'll be a trip."

Leonard managed to nod his head in approval while he took another long drink from his beer. When he was done he said, "I'll tell you one thing, though ..."

"What's that?"

"You just hope that Dieter and Marta aren't planning on coming here. They won't even ask about smell, they'll just exorcise the place and it'll never be the same."

We whittled the late afternoon and early evening away drinking beer and figuring out what geothermal sights we were going to see the next day. At the top of the geo-phenomenon list was Old Faithful and my personal favorite (even though Leonard said that it was pathetic), the bubbling mud. When we exhausted that topic, we talked about our girlfriends. We were both slightly drunk by then.

In spite of the briefness of their encounter, in Leonard's mind, Gwendolyn had been elevated to the status of "girlfriend." I understood his fascination with her. Hell, I'd had a few fixations of my own he'd talked me through. I owed him one. I tried to reason with him that merely sleeping with Gwendolyn once hardly made her a girlfriend.

"How can you fucking call her a girlfriend, man? I always had the impression that a girlfriend was someone that you saw on a regular basis. You don't even know how to get a hold of her. Even if you did know how to, she probably lives in fucking California, and even I know that you're not going to go to fucking California. Shit, she's miles away now ... out there somewhere, Leonard." I waved my hand. "Let it go as a good memory. Man, I'm not trying to be rough on you, but you'll probably never see her again."

His obsession was deep, though, and he was hardly swayed by my attempts at instilling him with rational thought.

He countered, "I'll call her my girlfriend if I want to, you asshole. She and I shared a spiritual connection back there. Those kinds of connections that span both time and space. Hell, you above all people ought to know that ... you and Althea have it. And you know what else? I didn't sleep with her 'just once,' I slept with her five times."

His argument was good. I did know exactly what he was talking about with the connection thing. I guess that I was just being selfish in thinking that Althea and I were the only ones on earth who had the privilege of feeling that. Leonard had also made my antlers feel a little small. In spite of Althea's and my deeply passionate and sexual relationship, I myself had not approached 'five times.' I thought it best that I apologize to him and then shut the hell up.

"Hey, I'm sorry Leonard. I had no cause to say that stuff to you. You know, just trying to be a friend ... I'll blame it on the beer."

Leonard nodded. "It's okay man ... I know, I'm watching out for you, too."

After our conversation, we both agreed that maybe eating something would sober us up a bit. It was dinnertime and neither one of us had eaten anything since the chicken fried steak that morning. The combination of our "it-will-take-you-a-week-to-fully-digest-it" breakfast and the fine domestic lager that we had been drinking that afternoon left us only moderately hungry. We rummaged through the box of food and the cooler in search of dinner. The ice in the cooler was nearly totally melted so we agreed to eat what was in there first. We decided that bacon and egg sandwiches would be the best way to use up as many perishables as possible.

It was almost dark when we got dinner on the table. I lit the lamp and we sat down to eat. I was mid-bite when Leonard said, "Yum. Fried embryos and squealer flesh ... just like mom used to make." I chewed a couple more times then swallowed hard.

"Oh man, that's revolting, Leonard. You don't have to be so literal. Why don't we just be nice and stick to calling it bacon and eggs?"

"Nah, I think that it's better if everyone keeps in mind exactly what it is and where it comes from, because remember, Carl, " He raised his eyebrows, cocked his head and grinned like a psycho, "You are what you eat."

By the time we had finished dinner it was dark and had started to rain ... hard. We got the cooler and the box of food back into the van.

"You know, Leonard, we should do these dishes before we crash."

"Oh shit, they'll wait 'til the morning. I don't really feel like getting my ass soaked in the middle of the night trying to wash 'em. Pour some soap over 'em and let the rain do it." The rain was really coming down now.

"I don't think that's such a good idea, Leonard. That ranger was pretty adamant about us keeping the camp clean. Do you have any idea where there's a water spigot around here?"

Leonard looked up at the sky. "Come on man, forget it, you're going to get soaked. Shit, it's raining so hard every bear in the park is holed up in a cave somewhere."

"I already am soaked." I grabbed the lantern, the dishes, the soap, and the scritcher pad and headed out in search of a spigot.

After fifteen minutes of wandering around in a deluge, and no success in finding a spigot, I decided that the dishes would just have to wait. When I finally got back to the camp I was, as Leonard had predicted, completely soaked. Leonard was messing around with the flashlight inside the van. I opened the side door. He was laying out our sleeping bags inside the van.

"What the fuck are you doing?"

"It's raining so hard that I decided that it would be a good idea if I started rounding up pairs of animals ... what the hell does it look like I'm doing? By the way, you're soaked."

"It looks like you are laying our sleeping bags out on the floor of the van. Oh, and by the way, yes, I am soaked."

"That's right, Carl, that's exactly what I am doing. I thought that you probably didn't want to sleep in a water bed tonight."

"What's wrong with the tent? It's waterproof."

"I would say that 'waterproof' is a relative term. We pitched the thing in a slight dip. When I went over there to stow a few things, the bottom of it was sitting in about two inches of water. It wasn't wet inside yet, but I bet it will be soaked by morning. By the way, did you get those dishes done?"

"No."

"Let me guess, you couldn't find any water."

"No, I could not, and don't do an I-told-you-so."

"I won't." He looked at me. He didn't say anything but his eyes were laughing hysterically.

"Knock it off ... you're thinking it."

"Yes I am, Carl ... yes I am."

I dumped the pile of dishes in the middle of the picnic table and squirted a fair amount of "New Dawn – Now with Lemon" all over them. Under the driving rain, they started foaming immediately. Leonard had had a good suggestion. I should have taken it before I got soaked.

I abandoned the dishes and climbed into the van with Leonard. It was starting to get surprisingly cold outside. I was shivering. When I got in the van, Leonard used his best midwestern grandmother voice, complete with lisp.

"Now you get out of those wet things this instant before you catch your death of cold, young man." I was too wet and cold to give him any shit back.

While I was changing, Leonard loaded up the pipe with a little Wiccan weed. When I finished changing he lit it and inhaled.

"Here, buddy, this will warm you up."

I took it from him and took a deep drag. "Thanks."

I held my breath and patiently let the marijuana charge into my system. I could hear the rain drumming hard against the steel roof of the van. It was a comforting sound. I was glad, though, that we weren't staying in the tent. I exhaled and handed the pipe back to Leonard.

"Man, you were right about staying in the van tonight. Shit, if we had stayed in the tent we would have died of hypothermia by morning." Leonard, who was holding his breath, nodded in agreement and handed the pipe back to me. I took another hit.

Leonard exhaled. "Yeah, well then, I suppose that I saved your life. You owe me."

I exhaled. "Well, I promise to save you when the bears come in the night."

We finished the pipe and lay back on our sleeping bags listening to the rain. I don't know if it was my heightened sense of hearing because of the weed or if it was real, but the rain seemed to be coming down even harder. While I listened, I stared up at the windows and watched the raindrops appear, hang for a moment, and then zip quickly down, only to be replaced by another. It made a pattern, a complex one. I felt like if I stared at it long enough I would understand.

After probably an hour of silently lying on our backs and listening to the rain, we decided to blow out the candle and get some sleep.

"See you in the morning, Leonard."

"Goodnight, John-Boy."

A couple of minutes after Leonard blew out the candle I reached over to the side of the van and scratched it with my fingernails. At the same time I half covered my mouth and made a low sniffing grunting noise. I caught Leonard off guard – he was almost asleep.

He sat up quickly, "What the fuck was that?"

"Huh?" I pretended to be asleep myself.

"Did you hear that?"

"Hear what?"

"I think I heard a fucking bear outside of the van."

"Oh, man, you probably just dreamed it." I could hardly see Leonard in the darkness, but I could tell that he was listening intently for more signs of bear. "Come on man, you're tripping, there's nothing out there ... go back to sleep."

"Shhhhh, I'm fucking listening."

"Whatever, Leonard, I'm going to get some sleep." I turned over in my sleeping bag and smiled – my work was done.

We were both in a dead sleep when we were suddenly awakened by someone shrieking a few campsites down from us. "Ahhhhhhhhhh!" We were both up in an instant.

"Jesus Christ, Mother of mercy, what the fuck was that!?"

"Shit - it sounded like somebody was getting eaten by a fucking bear!"

I had fucked with Leonard earlier about the prospect of bears hypothetically attacking us. At the time the possibility seemed totally remote – that's what had made it funny. Now I wasn't so sure. It sounded like someone was being disemboweled in the campground. Before either one of us could say anything we heard it again, "Ahhhhhhhhhhhhh!" This time immediately after the screaming there was a metallic crash right outside of our van followed by the sound of heavy feet running and brush breaking.

"Fuck, it is bears! They ate someone and now they're right outside of our fucking van! Fuck, fuck, fuck, fuck, fuck," Leonard kind of hysterically sang the expletives, "They're coming for us next!"

I tried to be reassuring, "Shit, calm down ... we're in the van, it's metal. Whoever just got eaten was probably in a tent."

"Oh, fuck, that's a huge relief, Carl. As I recall, Mr. Ranger Big Nuts told us that bears could open up a vehicle like it was a tuna can!"

I couldn't argue with him about that. I tried another tack. "I think I heard them running away."

Leonard didn't respond right away. He was intensely listening for anything that would give us any indication of what was going to happen next. Finally he said, "Fuck if they ran away. Those things have had a taste of human flesh, they won't ever be satisfied by peanut butter and jelly sandwiches again." We went back to listening. At first all we could hear was rain.

We listened hard, then finally, almost imperceptibly, through the sound of the rain we heard crying. Then we heard voices, a man and a woman. I couldn't tell what they were saying. We talked in whispers.

"You hear that, Carl?"

"Yeah, it sounds like someone crying a little bit, maybe a kid."

"Yeah, maybe the bears didn't kill him after all ... maybe they only maimed him."

"Maybe we should go out and see if they need any help."

"Maybe we shouldn't. Maybe we should wait until it's light."

I looked at my watch. It was a quarter to six. "The sun should be up pretty soon."

"Yeah, we'll wait till we can see something. The only heroes I know are dead people. I don't want to be a hero that badly."

Fifteen minutes later there was enough light in the sky to be able to see clearly. The clouds were clearing as well and the rain had tapered off to only a few intermittent sprinkles. Tentatively, we poked our heads up to the van windows. I think that we were both half-expecting to see a scene of carnage, a bloodied shredded tent tangled in human viscera. For the most part, we saw nothing.

We both scanned the campground. The only thing that was out of the ordinary were the pots, pans, and dishes from the night before. The bears had certainly been here. The dishes were strewn all over the ground around the picnic table. Covering them, the picnic table, and the ground was a thick layer of foam. Even through the walls of the van, the campground smelled pungently lemony.

"Gee, Carl do you think that you put enough soap on those dishes last night?"

"Oh, screw you, Leonard, it was your idea. You see any bears?"

"No, do you?"

"No."

"Do you think that it's safe to go out there?"

"No."

"Well, we have to go out there sometime. We can't just drive off and leave all of our shit."

"Yes we can."

I put my hand on the door of the van, "I'll go first."

"If you get eaten, Carl, I promise that I'll go for help."

"Thanks, Leonard, you're a real friend."

"I know."

I cautiously opened the van door. It had totally stopped raining and the sun was starting to come out. The campground was completely quiet with the exception of a pair of voices coming from the direction of the early-morning incident. I looked around. "I think that it's safe, Leonard. The only thing I hear is a couple of voice coming from a few spots down."

Leonard joined me outside the van. Every one of his, as well as my, senses scanned the campground for any sign of danger. We were still whispering.

"I don't see or hear anything."

"No, I don't either."

"Let's head on down to that campsite and see if they need any help."

"Yeah, I'm with you."

We quietly made our way toward the direction of the voices. With each step we scanned the area for bears. We saw none. Part way there, though, we did find more evidence of their presence the night before. By the side of the road there was a twisted trashcan that had clearly been on the wrong end of an encounter. Leonard whispered behind me, "Shit, did you see what they did to that fucking can? I know that metal is thicker than the metal of the van." I nodded.

We approached the campsite where the voices had been coming from. Sitting at the picnic table was a woman in her mid-thirties and a boy of about seven or so. The boy was busily stuffing his face on scrambled eggs and sausage links. Nearby, dad was tending another round over a Coleman stove. I glanced over at their avocado green Pontiac station wagon in the drive - they were from Minnesota. They appeared as if nothing was wrong at all. They were just one happy little family, on a happy little vacation, having their happy little eggs and sausages.

"Hi," I said half whispering. The entire family jumped a bit. We had apparently approached their campsite unnoticed and I had startled them. The dad spoke.

"Morning fellas, you startled us a bit, didn't even hear you come up there. Something we can do for you? How about a cup of coffee?"

I still half whispered, "Sure, a cup of coffee would be nice." His wife smiled pleasantly and poured a couple of cups from the pot sitting at the table and handed them to us.

"Do you take cream or sugar?"

"No, thank you, black is fine. So is everything okay over here? We heard some screaming a bit ago from the direction of your camp and with all the warnings about the bears around here and all we were ... well, frankly, a little worried." The mom continued to smile pleasantly, and the boy continued to stuff his face with a hunk of sausage.

The dad chuckled a bit, "Oh, that ... huh, huh, huh ... sorry if he woke you up. We've gotten so that it's just a routine with us anymore."

The mom broke in, "What Father is trying to say is that our son suffers from night-scares. He's had the same terrible recurring nightmare the past three years or so – ever since he saw a National Geographic special on marsupials."

I looked at Leonard. He had an expression on his face that was a mixture of relief, bewilderment, and annoyance. I'm sure that I had the same expression on my face.

The mom continued, "You see, our son has the same frightful dream every few nights that he is being chased by a duck-billed platypus." At the word platypus the boy stopped chewing and his lip began to tremble. His mother put her arm around him comfortingly, "There, there, it's okay, son, there aren't any platypuses here in Yellowstone." Then she put her other hand on the coffeepot and turned to us, "Would you fellas care for a warm-up?"

"Thanks, no, just glad to hear that you folks are okay," I said as pleasantly as possible, trying not to show my annoyance.

Leonard took a final sip of coffee, set the mug on the table, and calmly said, "No ma'am, I'm fine too ... we should get going here. I would like to ask you folks a question, though."

This time the dad answered, "Certainly, what's that?"

"I'm just wondering if you ever thought about getting your kid into therapy. He sounds like he is a little fucked up."

Back at the campsite I collected the dishes that had been strewn around the night before by the bears. Leonard fired up the stove and put on some coffee of our own.

"Man, those folks looked a little shocked when you suggested that their kid needed therapy."

"Oh, shit, I think that the Cleavers can handle it. You want a cup of coffee?"

"Yeah, I think that I'm going to make us a little breakfast, too. We should eat up the rest of the eggs."

"Are you sure it's safe to cook, Carl? Maybe before you make breakfast you should hose yourself down with some bear pheromone spray and sashay around the campground just to make sure there aren't any more bears around."

"Yeah ... or maybe not."

I had just served up breakfast when a light green forest service pickup came tearing into the campground. It was the ranger. He stopped the truck at the vacant campsite next to ours and jumped out of the cab. In his right hand he was holding an enormous rifle. It looked like something that you would use to take down an elephant. He was all business.

"Morning. You men see any bears around here?"

"No sir, we heard some come through our camp last night, but we haven't seen any this morning. Why?"

He scanned our site for bear evidence. "I had a report this morning from a couple from Nebraska. Said that they saw a bear run across the road near here. They said that he looked pretty panicked and he was foaming at the mouth. He's probably rabid."

"Sounds serious," Leonard said.

"It is serious – deadly serious. I'll have to take him out before he hurts somebody. In the meantime I'm closing this campground. I suggest that you men pack up as soon as you can and move on. Oh, and if you see anything make sure that you contact me ASAP."

I nodded that I understood and added, "Roger – will do." He jogged double-time back to his truck, jumped in and was off.

I turned off the stove and began to clean things up. Leonard didn't move. "What the hell are you doing, Carl?"

"Packing up our camp like the ranger said. What are you doing?"

"Enjoying my breakfast." In the background I could hear the ranger circling the campground. He was leaning out of the window of his truck with a bullhorn.

"Attention – This is the ranger - This is an emergency - The campground is now closed. Pack up your things and leave immediately."

"Didn't you hear what the ranger said, we need to get the hell out of here."

"Oh, sit down and enjoy your breakfast Carl ... and think."

"Think what, think about how I am going to be eaten by some rogue bear with rabies?"

"No, that bear was the one that was at our campsite last night. Remember how you left the dishes out with all that soap all over them?"

"Yeah."

"Yeah, well the bear licked all those dishes. The amount of soap you put on those things, I'd be foaming at the mouth too." I stopped cleaning up. "And no wonder that bear was panicked. Shit, the way that fucked-up kid was shrieking, he probably panicked every animal that could hear him."

I sat back down. "I bet you're right."

"Of course I'm right. Now enjoy your eggs."

Leonard and I sat calmly and enjoyed our breakfast. Around us there was chaos. Panic spread through the campground like a pox. Campers threw half-packed tents and sleeping bags into their cars. Breakfasts were left unfinished, steaming on paper plates at picnic tables. Grownups shouted out orders at their children, who were crying. One elderly couple halfway across the campground high-centered their Buick on a small stump backing out of their campsite. The old man, who was driving, filled the campground with acrid smoke from burning the car's tires trying to get off of it. Horns honked as people tried to get him to move the hell out of the way. The car was freed only after a young guy in a beat-up Jeep with a railroad tie for a bumper pushed the old man off, causing the Buick considerable body damage to the fender.

The whole scene was like watching an episode of Bugs Bunny and The Tasmanian Devil – the part at the beginning where all the animals of the forest flee in terror from the oncoming pestilence. Panic is entertaining.

We were working on our third cup of coffee by the time the campground cleared. Leonard took in a deep breath of the mountain air.

"I find it rather peaceful here."

"Yes it is," I agreed sarcastically. "We should get our stuff together and go nose around the park."

"Good plan."

We finished our coffee and went to work cleaning up the camp. The rain and soap method that Leonard had suggested, combined with a fastidious bear tongue licking, had left the dishes remarkably clean. I merely rinsed them and stuck them back in the supply box. Nothing else was really out except for the tent. Our decision to stay in the van had been a good one, on a number of levels. When we went to pack the tent, we found that it was under about three inches of water, both inside and out. Leonard was right - waterproof was a relative term. Had we in fact stayed in the tent the night before we would have been soaked. We poured the water out of the inside as best we could and loosely rolled it so that it would still dry. My guess was that that would be a couple of days.

Old Faithful

Since Leonard had driven all day the day before, I decided to take the wheel. While we let the van warm up, we looked over the pamphlet on the "Geothermal Phenomena of Yellowstone National Park." We decided that we would start with the Lower Geyser Basin about ten miles away. We would work our way up the valley stopping along the way at the Paint Pots, Black Sand Basin, the Morning Glory Pools, the infamous Bubbling Mud, and finish with Old Faithful. It would be a thirty-mile excursion of stinky water and tourists.

We also figured that since we had been driving like hell the past few days, and since we no longer had any schedule whatsoever, that we would stay at the park one more night - at a place called Lake Village. That would give us a break from driving and keep us inside the park, but only about twenty miles from the east entrance. The following day we planned to do the big drive. Our destination: Devil's Tower. That would require us to cross nearly the entire state of Wyoming - I figured roughly three hundred and twenty-five miles. I wanted to shorten that drive as much as possible, even if it was only by a couple of miles. I also hoped there was a phone there. I wanted to call Althea - badly. I was missing her like crazy and I know that she was expecting a call from me. She probably wondered where the hell I was.

We drove the ten miles to the Lower Geyser Basin without incident. We didn't see a single car along the way. Leonard had a theory that people had cleared out of the entire area because of the threatening news of the rabid bear. The way that folks had acted back at the campground, his theory seemed plausible.

The parking lot at our first stop was completely empty. It was mildly weird to have the place to ourselves, but it did mean that we didn't have to hide the fact that we were sitting in the van smoking pot. While we passed the pipe back and forth, we noticed that there were a number of large posters tacked up around the area. They were bright hazard red and had a big portrait of a snarling grizzly on them: "Caution - Dangerous Bear Alert."

"Looks like Ranger Hunk-Meat was here," said Leonard. "I guess that explains why the parking lot is empty." We were on our second full bowl when Leonard suggested that we take some toothpaste and froth up the mouth of the bear on one of the posters to make it seem more dramatic. I thought that it was a great idea, so I went back and rummaged through our supplies and got a tube of Crest Winterfresh Gel. After foaming up three of the posters Leonard and I were rolling in the middle of the parking lot laughing to the point of apoplexy. It was an effective addition.

We finally managed to get enough of a grip on ourselves to head out on the self-guided tour of the basin. After smoking two gigantic bowls of weed, we were both, as planned, completely stoned out of our marbles. Our first stop was a spectacle called the Imperial Geyser. In the center of a football field-sized sulfur-scarred deep blue steaming pool of water, a geyser pumped erratic spurts of boiling water fifty feet into the air. We stood by the railing staring at it in spaced-out awe. Bolted to the railing was a plaque explaining the history of the geyser. I read it.

There was a blurb about it being a relatively new geyser, nineteen twenty-seven or something like that, and that it had become famous because newspapermen visiting the area at the time wrote about it. It also said, "the estimated discharge is 500 gallons per minute." I shared that particular fact with Leonard. He responded by saying that it made him feel inadequate and that we should move on to the next thing. We both started laughing like mad again, but realizing the danger in the surrounding boiling water, kept ourselves under control.

The next sight was called Narcissus Geyser. In the center of a considerably smaller pool, probably only seventy-five feet in diameter, there was a proportionally smaller geyser. The pool was filled with milky sediment that had solidified in bulbous white blobs on the surrounding edge. The geyser sputtered only about fifteen feet in the air and made a kind of gurgling noise. I asked Leonard if this one made him feel inadequate as well.

He said, "No, not enough volume."

Like the last geyser, there was a plaque bolted to the railing that described it. I read through it. It was some tedious mythological story that had nothing to do with geysers.

"What's it say there, Carl?"

"It says that the pool was named after some young woman by the name of Narcissus Smith. It seems that she was a member of a Mormon party that was headed out West towards Provo around 1890. It says here that she was driven totally mad by the fanatical proselytizing of the leader of the party. When they arrived here at Yellowstone, instead of continuing on with them, she chose to end her life by throwing herself into the boiling pool." When I finished "reading," I looked up at Leonard who said, "Shit – that's a fucked-up story." It was not until I made eye contact with him that he realized that I had made it up.

We continued on. Along the path we saw a few signs pointing off toward other features some distance away. We were so stoned that neither one of us felt like hiking. We ignored them and decided to stay on the main path.

The last sight on the loop trail was a boiling cauldron called Ojo Caliente. Leonard, who spoke a little Spanish, translated the name into English for me.

"It means 'Hot Eye.'" Whatever you wanted to call it, it was a fifteen by forty-foot clear blue pool of scorching water that would rhythmically burp huge bubbles of noxious gas every few seconds. The intense sulfur smell was dizzying. In spite of it I found that in its own way the pool was actually quite pretty – that is, until Leonard spotted a large dead rat that had gotten too close to it.

The rat, or what remained of it, was just off the trail at the edge of the pool. His bones and heat-seared skin were petrified in a running position – not surprisingly heading away from the superheated pool. Apparently he had succumbed to the heat, or the gases, or a combination of both. Leonard lay down on the boardwalk and reached out for it.

"What the fuck are you doing, Leonard? Leave that disgusting thing alone." He stretched out his arm and grabbed the rat between his thumb and forefinger.

"No, man, we need a mascot."

"What?"

"You'll see ... I promise that you'll like it." He stood up and showed me the rat. "See, perfectly clean, nothing left here but skin and bones ... sterilized too."

I shook my head, "That's vile."

"Yes it is, Carl. You know, I think that we should rename this pool."

"To what?"

"I think that we should call it 'Rato Ojo Caliente.'" He made himself laugh.

"Come on man, let's get back to the van, and keep that thing away from me."

It was only about a hundred yards back to the parking lot. When we got there Leonard put the rat on the sidewalk, went into the supplies in the back of the van, and produced a spool of bailing wire that we had packed for unforeseen emergency repairs.

"What are you doing?"

"You'll see." He picked the rat back up and went over to the antenna of the van and proceeded to wire the rat to the top of it. When he was done, the running petrified rat stuck off like a weathervane.

"There, our new mascot – Mr. Rat."

"Oh, Jesus, Leonard."

"Oh, come on, Carl, I think that it's a rather nice addition, don't you?"

I stood there looking at the nose of the van with crushed grasshoppers all over it, and now a petrified rat waving from the antenna. The new addition certainly fit in with the motif. "I don't know if 'nice' is really the word that I would use ... but for some reason I like it."

We drove up the valley toward our next destination, Midway Basin, home of - according to the guide - a number of "mammoth-sized hot springs," and my personal favorite, the bubbling mud. The pamphlet also said that when the famous poet Rudyard Kipling visited the place in 1889 he called it "Hell's Half Acre." Good advertising. In my opinion it was all the more reason to visit it.

It was less than ten miles to the next basin, and again we saw no cars along the way. The rat looked good. When I got the van above fifty miles per hour, the slipstream actually seemed to breathe some life into him. He bobbed up and down in the wind in a rolling motion as if he were lazily running along with the van. I pointed this out to Leonard. He raised his palms up and spoke to the rat with a Slavic Dr. Frankenstein voice, "Live! Live!"

When we got there, as with the first basin, there was no one there. And, as with the first basin, there were bear warning posters stuck up everywhere. Apparently the ranger had cleared out this part of the park as well.

"My God, Carl, that ranger created a general public hysteria. I wonder if there's a tourist left in Yellowstone."

"So what? Maybe he did scare everyone away and we have our own private national park."

"Yeah, well, it's starting to give me the creeps."

"Yeah, well I'm starting to get the munchies ... I'm going to go aft and scrounge something up." I rummaged through our supplies in the back of the van while Leonard got out and went over to study the reader board near the picnic area.

After five minutes of digging around I found exactly nothing that I wanted to eat. I called out to Leonard, "Shit, don't we have any munchie food in this vehicle?"

Leonard called back in a Yogi Bear voice, "Hey, Boo Boo, don't you worry, I think that I found us some pic-i-nic baskets."

I pulled my head out of the back of the van to see what he was talking about. While I had been digging around in the van, Leonard had wandered though the picnic area. Sitting on the picnic table in front of him were two coolers, and a picnic basket. Apparently people had left the area in such a hurry that some had left a few items behind.

I played along with him, "Gee Yogi, I don't think that's a good idea. Don't you think that Ranger Smith will get mad if he catches us?"

Leonard kept up with the cartoon voice as he pulled items out, "Don't you worry, Boo Boo – I'm smarter than the average bear. Why, look what we have here, potato salad, macaroni salad, ice cream bars, potato chips, peanut butter and jelly sandwiches ..."

He kept pulling stuff and naming it until there was a good half table full of food in front of him. It was a Jellystone feast. For the next half an hour we proceeded to gorge ourselves on our windfall of abandoned food. When we were done, we were totally stuffed. And in spite of the vast amount of food that we had eaten, we still had a fair amount left. We wouldn't have to do any shopping for at least a couple of days.

We cleaned up our picnic booty, packed it in the van, and headed out. We were both so full that neither one of us particularly felt like going on a major hike. So we didn't, and frankly I don't think that we missed much.

The first geothermal wonder, Grand Prismatic Springs, which was supposed to be the highlight of the area, wasn't far. Unfortunately, when we got there neither one of us was particularly impressed.

"Ooh ... a big pool of stinky hot water," said Leonard sarcastically.

I tried to be slightly more excited about it. "Yeah, but still, I think that it's kind of pretty."

Leonard looked at me sideways, "I think that maybe for me to fully appreciate it I should have smoked some more weed before I saw it."

We moved on. The next, and what turned out to be our last, stop was what I had been so looking forward to - the bubbling mud pots. For a couple hundred yards, the boardwalk wound its way through about twenty or so pools of black-brown mud. They slowly bubbled and burped, while making somewhat vile gastronomic noises. It was even less exciting than the last stop. I guess that sometimes those things that you think are so cool as a kid are really not all that great when you grow up ... too bad. I tried to hide my disappointment, and pulled out my camera to snap a few shots.

I looked through the viewfinder and focused the lens. Just as I clicked the shutter, I saw a flash of movement in the viewfinder - I couldn't tell what it was. I pulled the camera away and looked at the mud pots. There was no other movement except for the slowly bubbling mud. Again, I put the camera to my eye and clicked. The same thing happened. This time I got a quick look at what it was – Leonard. At the last second of my shots he would stick his head in front of the camera and make faces.

I turned to him, "What the fuck is wrong with you? I'm trying to take a few pictures for posterity's sake here."

"Oh shit, this stuff is so lame, I think you'll like these pictures better." I took a final shot without his interference. "You know, Carl, I don't think that I really agree with Mr. Kipling's assessment of the area ... I think that I would maybe call this 'Heck's Half Acre.' Come on, let's get out of here."

"Yeah, I suppose you're right." I packed up the camera and we headed back for the van.

Maybe it was our overindulgence in food, the lameness of our last stop, or our waning high, but we both fell into somewhat of a funk. We drove the next few miles to Old Faithful in relative silence. Even watching Mr. Rat run next to the van didn't raise our spirits much.

When we got to the Old Faithful parking lot, I stopped the van at the entrance. It was a moderate zoo. There were two groups of tourists; those who had taken the ranger's bear warning seriously, and a handful of others who had ignored it. The latter group milled around and acted like regular tourists, snapping pictures, wandering into the gift shop, and eating their lunches from the tailgates of their cars. The ones who suffered from bear-o-phobia, though, rushed around re-packing their belongings and waiting in a sizeable line at the station for gas. They looked like refugees fleeing from an oncoming army. To add to the atmosphere, Ranger Testosterone had set up a rather sad-looking rabid bear central command center off of his tailgate at the far end of the parking lot. From it he barked out orders to a small platoon of volunteer forest workers who rushed around trying to carry them out. They didn't look like they were taking any of it seriously.

"My God, what is going on here?" said Leonard.

I offered an answer, "Panic?"

"Well, duh, Carl, it was more of a rhetorical question."

"Well, duh, Leonard." He ignored me.

"Park the van, man, and let's watch the festivities." I drove around and managed to find a spot at the far end of the lot near the command center. Along the way, I thought that I recognized one of the vehicles a few parking places down from us.

I pointed it out to Leonard, "Hey, isn't that the Germans' van?"

"Oh man, are those two going to follow us all of the way across the United fucking States?"

"I guess that means yes it is their van. And to answer your question, I believe they are."

I turned off the van and we got out. Being close to the command center, I immediately felt like we were being assaulted by a cacophony of complete pandemonium. Back at the gas station, people tried to get their belongings in order as they waited in line, inevitable arguments erupted, which in turn got a few of the children crying. Over all of it the ranger continued to bark orders.

I could feel myself cringe a little against the onslaught. Leonard, on the other hand, seemed completely at peace. He almost seemed satisfied with all of it. He stood in the parking lot looking around with a calm smile on his face, taking it all in.

"Man, this is great, just great. A person doesn't get to see this too often – a small preview of the complete fall of civilization right before their eyes."

"What are you talking about, Leonard?"

"Man, just look at them. They're just a step away, my friend, just a step away ..." He held his thumb and forefinger about a quarter inch apart to emphasize it.

As I looked around, I began to get what Leonard was talking about. Folks who had foolishly listened to the ranger had just simply fallen apart – and really, it took virtually nothing for it to happen, just a little "New Dawn – Now with Lemon." It was almost as if they had all been waiting for an excuse.

I said that to Leonard: "It's almost like they were waiting for an excuse."

"Yeah, well, maybe they were, Carl."

We drank in the spectacle for a few more minutes. It was, without a doubt, pretty darned entertaining to witness part of the American psyche crumble. It definitely pulled us out of our funk.

Finally I had had enough of it, though, and I turned to Leonard, "I'm ready for a little different scenery. I'm starting to get a little over-stimulated just watching all of this. Why don't we mellow out and go check out this Old Faithful thing?"

"Yeah, I have to agree with you, I'm starting to get a contact freak myself from watching these folks."

We wove our way out of the parking lot and toward the geyser. Somehow, not being part of it, people seemed to act as if we weren't there at all. We passed the visitor center and followed the signs for the path to Old Faithful. Once we were on the path, the humanity cleared. I took a deep breath and exhaled.

"Man, this feels better. Being around all of that was starting to make me a little uptight."

Leonard rolled his neck to stretch out his own tension. "Yeah, hysteria, no matter how interesting, is pretty exhausting." It was only a couple of hundred yards to the geyser. There were only about a dozen other people there, including Dieter and Marta.

They immediately spotted us. From the opposite side of the temporarily dormant geyser, both of them smiled and waved enthusiastically, "Ach, guten tag, mein friends, it is us, Dieter and Marta." They immediately headed on over to us.

Leonard leaned toward me, "Like we wouldn't have recognized them."

"It looks like they survived their encounter with Henry," I said.

"Yeah, but I wonder if Henry survived his encounter with them."

Dieter thrust out his hand as he approached, "Ach, it is good to see you mein friends." He took my hand in both of his and shook it vigorously. Then he turned to Leonard and did the same to him. Marta stood by, smiled wide-eyed, glowing at our reunion.

"We thought that we not see you again," she said sincerely and emphatically. "It made us sad." I thought to myself that it probably did make them sad. In a funny sort of way I was glad to see them too.

"Ya, is it not ironic that we see each other yet again?" I could tell that Dieter was pretty proud of himself that he now knew how to use the word so well.

"I think that it's a little more than ironic ... I think that it's actually a little weird," said Leonard. "It's like you two are following us across the country."

Dieter grinned, "Ach, and we could say the same for you."

"You know, he's right, Leonard. Are they following us or are we following them?"

Leonard rolled his eyes, "Why, thank you so much, Carl, for your observation."

"Just pointing it out there, Leonard." Leonard smiled thinly and turned back to the pair.

"So, what brings you two to Jellystone?"

They both looked puzzled. "Jellystone?" Dieter repeated.

"It's from a cartoon called ... oh never mind. What brings you to Yellowstone?"

"Ach yes ... Yellowstone." At the mention of the word, a look of peaceful knowing washed over both of their faces. I had seen that look before. They turned to each other beaming and nodded as if they shared a profound secret.

"Well?" Leonard was more impatient than amused with the pair.

Dieter looked at us and said simply, "Why, we are here to see Old Faithful," as if the answer were quite obvious. "The schedule over there says that it will erupt in another fifteen minutes," he continued excitedly. Marta nodded with him.

"Well, I bet it's quite a sight," I added.

"Ya, it is most beautiful, we have seen it ..." Marta interrupted exuberantly, "Seven time ... this will be eight!"

Leonard was staring at them with an almost perturbed look on his face and asked, "How long have you two been here?"

"Oh, we have been here since last night."

I tried to offer them some helpful tourist advice, "You know, Dieter, although Old Faithful is without a doubt pretty neat, there are actually some other pretty cool things to see around the rest of the park."

"Ya, we know." Dieter produced a stack of pamphlets from his rucksack. They were similar to the ones that we had been given by the ranger. "But we like the Old Faithful, it is magnificent."

Leonard shook his head and said under his breath, "What a couple of nuts." Thankfully, I don't think that they heard him.

I changed the subject. "So, Dieter, we've been wondering, how did everything work out back there with Henry?" At the mention of Henry, Dieter and Marta's expressions changed dramatically. Instantly an air of seriousness washed over Dieter. Marta's eyes narrowed intensely and she visibly set her jaw. Anger welled just a bit in her eyes.

Dieter apparently could feel her getting upset, and without even looking at her tried to calm her. He instinctively put his arm around her shoulder and said reassuringly, "Don't worry, he is with God now." Leonard caught the implication in these last couple of words.

"Oh shit, is he dead?"

Marta spoke tightly. "Nein, I think not, but he is very sick."

"Well I think that goes without saying. Of course he's sick, he's been sick."

"We kept trying to reason with him but he would not listen, the more that we tried, the madder that he got. Unt his face got redder unt redder the madder he got. A few minutes after you left us, his eyes, they rolled in his head, and his mouth, it make foam. Then he fall to the ground, shaking."

"It sounds like he had a stroke," I offered.

"Ya, maybe the stroke ... or maybe the poison within him. We carried him back to our van, and took him back to the ranger station. His wife, she was there. We help her put him in the house on the sofa. We tried to pray over him for God's help, but the more we prayed the more he shook. He is a very sick man indeed. We only hope that God will help him."

"How about his wife, was she upset?"

"Nein, this is most odd. She almost seems … happy. She say that this happen to him sometimes, and that he get better in a few days."

Leonard chimed in, "Hell, it's probably the only time that she ever gets any peace."

"What?"

"Oh, nothing, I'm just thinking that I'm sure that he'll be fine."

Just then the geyser let off an audible hiss and a small jet of water vapor shot a few feet in the air.

"Wow, that really was magnificent, it's too bad that we missed it," Leonard commented.

"Ach, yes, it is almost time." Again the German's didn't hear the sarcasm in Leonard's voice – I thought that maybe they didn't understand the concept. Dieter continued excitedly, "It does this a few minutes before the big eruption ... come with me," Dieter motioned for us to follow him to a better vantage point.

We followed them around the path to a spot that was downwind of the geyser's blowhole. "Here, this is good. From here we will be bathed in the spray of the geyser." I was uncertain if that was in fact a good thing, "Are you sure this is where we want to be? Isn't geyser water a little hot?"

Marta nodded and said confidently, "Yes, it is good."

Sharing the same spot was a conservative-looking couple in their mid-thirties. They had two children with them, a boy of about six and a girl who was a little younger. They looked like miniature copies of their parents, down to their clothing. The family seemed nearly as excited as the Germans.

The father readily offered us his hydrothermal opinion, "You're just in time. According to my watch it's gonna blow soon."

As if to punctuate his prophetic statement the geyser began to hiss again. This time the hissing was much louder.

"It comes!" Dieter called out. Seconds later a huge fountain of water burst from the ground and shot at least a hundred and fifty feet in the air. Steam plumed from the boiling tower. As the geyser continued to erupt, the plume drifted towards us. Soon we were all enveloped in a cloud of steam and warm mist.

I had to admit it really was a remarkable thing, and in spite of his initial skepticism Leonard thought so too.

"Man, this is something else."

"Yeah ..."

Dieter and Marta's reaction to the phenomenon was somewhat different. They stood next to us, arms out, palms up, heads back, and smiling.

Leonard leaned over to me. "What the fuck are they doing?"

"I think that they like it."

"Yeah, maybe too much."

After about three or four minutes the tower of water subsided and the steam and mist began to clear. The eruption was over. True to Dieter's prediction, we all got a little damp from the geyser's discharge.

Dieter looked to us and said, "Well, was that not beautiful?"

This time Leonard gave him some credit. "Yes, I have to hand it to you, Dieter, that was pretty darned cool."

"Ya, and the water, it is good, no?"

"Yes, it is good, yes," Leonard agreed, then ran his hand over his hair, wiping some of the excess water off. The family next to us seemed delighted with the spectacle.

The dad turned to his two children and said, "How about that, kids? That was really something now, wasn't it?"

The little boy looked up at him and said with deep awe, "Daddy, did Jesus make it do that?" The boy's words just hung there and everyone paused.

The father was about to answer him when Dieter knelt down on one knee next to the little boy.

He looked the boy right in the eyes and earnestly said, "Ya, it is the work of God. It is the holy water. We have witnessed the miracle." The little boy just stood there and blinked at him.

Dieter's words left everyone speechless for a moment - everyone except Leonard, who whispered to me, "Hell, it's not holy water, it's mild sulfuric acid." I masked my chuckle with a cough. I figured that it wasn't a totally appropriate time to burst out laughing. Besides, I didn't want to get drawn into this.

Finally the father spoke. Initially, he tried to politely avoid confrontation and simply put a little levity on Dieter's words. He said with a slight drawl, "Now, I don't know if I would call that a miracle, son. I sure would call it pretty, though."

"Ya, it was ..." Dieter politely challenged him.

The father now addressed Dieter directly. "Now see here, I don't want you to put any funny ideas ..."

Before he could go on, the man was interrupted by his wife. She was trying to keep the exchange civil. She said courteously, but firmly, to Dieter, "What he is trying to say is that we are a good Christian family. We go to church every Sunday, of course we believe in Jesus Christ, and of course we believe in miracles."

I whispered to Leonard, "Here we go." He nodded.

She went on, "Some things are miracles and some things are not miracles."

Leonard couldn't resist himself, "I have to agree with her there, Dieter, it may not have been a miracle, it may have just been hot water."

I tried to warn him off, "Stay out of it, Leonard."

Dieter and Marta looked disappointed. I think from their perspective they were only trying to point out what was an obvious explanation for the geyser.

Marta spoke gently, "Do you not believe that God created the earth?"

The man answered quickly, "Why of course we do."

"Unt that this is part of God's creation?"

"Well ... y-yes," The man stuttered, feeling a trap coming.

"Then why do you not believe in this miracle?" She stared at him as if her logic were indisputable. Unwilling or maybe unable to argue further he paused, then he took his son and daughter's hands in his and turned away from her.

"Oh for heaven's sa ..." He realized what he was going to say and stopped himself mid-sentence. He looked at his wife and said, "Come on honey, enough is enough ... we're on vacation." As the family hurried away down the path the boy continued to look over his shoulder at Dieter and Marta. He smiled back at them.

Dieter and Marta stood there silently, and watched them walk away until they were out of sight. When they were gone, Dieter stared out to the sky and said with a tone in his voice that sounded like a mixture of both frustration and failure, "Why do they not believe?" I think he was talking more to himself than anyone else.

Although I didn't necessarily agree with them I did feel a little sad for the pair. The glory of the world was before them and they so innocently wanted people to see what they saw as the sacredness in it. Neither Leonard nor I could answer his question.

Leonard broke the somberness of the moment with more practical matters.

"We should get going here, Carl. We need to go find a place to camp tonight."

"Yeah, you're right, we should get going here."

Dieter and Marta did not appear to have heard us. They were lost in their own thoughts ... or prayers.

I spoke directly to them, "Dieter, Marta." I startled them.

"Ya?"

"Sorry, I didn't mean to interrupt you. Leonard and I have to be going. It was good to see both of you again." Leonard nodded in agreement. In spite of the fact that they generally annoyed him, I could tell from the sincerity of his expression, that he felt kind of bad for them now as well. I put out my hand to Dieter, "Take care of yourselves. Maybe we'll see you again."

"Ya, we hope ..." Then still shaking my hand, he looked at me solemnly and said, "Bless both of you on your own pilgrimage."

Marta then in her European way, warmly kissed both of us on each cheek. "Goodbye, our friends."

When we were away from them Leonard said, "Carl?"

"Yeah, Leonard?"

"What do think was the deal with that comment that Dieter made about us on a pilgrimage?"

"Yeah, I caught that too ... I don't know. He apparently thinks that everyone who travels around is looking for something."

Leonard paused, then said almost under his breath, "Yeah ... I suppose."

When we returned to the van, we found that the parking lot had emptied a fair amount. The offensive din from all of the frantic commotion was gone as well. A good many of the tourists had apparently cleared out. Even the activity at the rabid bear command center had dwindled. The ranger was now there all by himself idly looking at a map. He looked disappointed.

"Well, it looks like everyone got the hell out of Dodge," I said to Leonard.

"You mean out of Yellowstone, Carl ... Yes it does look like it." As we approached the van, the ranger looked up from what he was doing.

"Good afternoon, men."

"Hi. Boy, it sure looks like a lot of folks cleared out of here."

"Yes, following my recommendation, many of the tourists have moved on," he replied officially.

Leonard, who knew exactly what the score was with the bear, asked innocently, "Did you have any luck tracking him down?"

The Ranger's expression turned to ice. He replied through tightly clenched jaws simply, "No." I guess he wasn't used to losing.

Leonard added sincerely, "Well, good luck ... he's out there somewhere. I'm sure if anyone can find him, you can, sir." The ranger took the comment as nothing more than a high compliment.

"You can count on that, men. You enjoy your stay, and remember, contact me if you see anything that might lead us to him." We both nodded an okay, got in the van, and waved as we drove back out to the road.

We drove without incident the forty or so miles to Lake Village, our campsite for the evening. The camp area was quiet, but not deserted. Apparently not everyone had left the park. We found a suitable spot down near the water. It was private, and from our picnic area we had a sweeping view of Yellowstone Lake. It was a pretty spot. It was five-thirty, and in spite of our huge lunch earlier we were both hungry. We got our picnic loot out and proceeded to gorge ourselves all over again.

After dinner, we smoked a bit of weed, talked, and let our food settle. As the evening wore on, a chill came to the air and we decided that a campfire was in order. We gathered a bunch of wood from the surrounding forest. All of it was totally soaked from the deluge the night before. Leonard and I fucked around for ten minutes trying to get a fire started. We burned every scrap of paper that we could find, and still had no luck.

I was on my hands and knees blowing on a smoldering twig when Leonard said from behind me, "Get the fuck out of the way, Carl. I'll get that thing going."

I got up and turned around. Leonard was at the picnic table pouring some white gas that we normally used for the stove and lantern into a cooking pot.

"That ought to do it," he said. I looked into the pot. He had poured in probably three cups of the explosive fluid.

"Jesus, Leonard, that stuff's pretty flammable. I don't know if I'd use that much."

"Oh, hell, Carl, you want a fire, right?"

Before I could argue with him about it, he grabbed the pot and from about ten feet away flung the gas onto the smoldering fire. We were too close. The moment that the gas touched the small flame there was a tremendous flash accompanied by a whooshing sound. Both Leonard and I were momentarily enveloped in flames. Not only had the fluid ignited, but so had the gaseous vapor that permeated the air of our campsite. Neither one of us was hurt, but it left us dazed.

When I came to my senses a few moments later, I quickly checked myself for flash burns. I had incurred no injury. I turned to Leonard.

"What the hell is wrong with you? You could have burned both of us alive!"

He said proudly and with a smile, "Yeah, but I didn't." He warmed his hands over the now-raging campfire, and said over and over again, "Burn, baby, burn! Burn, baby, burn! ..."

I grabbed a beer out of the cooler to calm my nerves.

"Could you grab me one too, Carl?" I lobbed one to Leonard. We sat down with our beers and made ourselves comfortable by the fire.

Just as we sat down, a young clean -cut fellow appeared from a trail through the bushes. He announced himself with a bluegrass drawl.

"Howdy."

"Hey, how ya doin'?"

"Hi my name's Gene - Gene Garland."

"I'm Carl, and this is Leonard." Leonard nodded and waved hi. We shook hands. "Care for a beer?"

"Sure, thanks." I reached into the cooler and handed him one.

"Me an' my wife an' my baby's out from Knoxville on vacation." He took a sip of beer and stepped closer to the fire.

"We're out from Mount Vernon. It's near Seattle," I said.

He nodded. "Yep, this here is the first time I seen my wife in six months. Hell, first time I seen my baby at all. See, I'm in the navy. My wife had the baby three months ago and they just got 'round to givin' me two weeks leave. Thought we'd come up out here an' spend some real time together." He took another long draw off of his beer. Then he said, "Say, I was wondering if I could ask you boys a question."

"Sure ... shoot."

"How'd you get this here fire goin'? I've been over there for an hour tryin' to get one goin'." He seemed embarrassed to ask, like being unable to make flame reflected poorly on his manhood.

Leonard smiled and reached for the can of white gas on the table and handed it to Gene, "Here ... this'll help." Gene smiled. Not only was he going to have fire, but his manhood was intact as well. He took the can from Leonard, and finished his beer in one long pull. He then stepped back from the campfire and filled the empty beer can with gas.

"I best be gettin' back to the family. I don't know how to thank you fellas."

"No thanks needed. I'm glad that we could help."

We shook hands and he disappeared back down the trail he had come in on. About three minutes later we heard a familiar whoosh from the direction of their campsite. We watched though the trees as flames shot up about fifteen feet in the air. Gene hollered, "Woooo hoooo!"

Leonard and I passed the rest of the evening drinking beer and talking by the fire. Inevitably our conversation came around to our girlfriends. This time I didn't beat up Leonard for his fugitive relationship with Gwendolyn. Hell, maybe if he thought about her enough they would get together again sometime. Weirder things had happened. I missed Althea like crazy. I also knew that she was going to be pissed at me for not having called her for a few days. I'd find a phone tomorrow.

Around ten o'clock we ran out of wood and the flames began to die down. The air got colder. It was time to get some sleep. We had not set up the tent, since it was no doubt still wet from the night before. We'd spend the night in the van again.

We crawled into our sleeping bags and hunkered down against the chill. My teeth were almost chattering.

"Man, Leonard, is it just me or is it colder than hell?" I could feel Leonard shaking next to me – it was a stupid question.

"Oh, no, C-C-Carl, it's not just you, it's colder than a witch's tit in here."

"Than a what? Where the hell did you get that?" Leonard didn't answer, he just shivered next to me.

In spite of the cold, I eventually fell asleep. I was wakened up sometime in the middle of the night, though, when Leonard clocked me in the forehead with his elbow when he rolled over. He didn't wake up. Awake, I lay there in my sleeping bag on the floor of the van. I noticed that it was quiet. Very, very quiet. Within minutes, I fell back asleep.

The Ninth Circle

"Hey, wake up, Carl! Wake up, man!" I was sound asleep when Leonard grabbed me by the shoulder and started shaking me.

"God, Leonard, knock it off, I'm asleep over here."

"Not any more you're not. Wake your ass up, man ... it snowed!"

I slowly opened my eyes. I figured that Leonard was bullshitting me as usual. When I opened my eyes the inside of the van was brightly lit. The sun was up. I looked at my watch – it was six-thirty. "Hey, maybe you can't sleep, Leonard, but man, it's no excuse to wake me up at six-thirty in the fucking morning."

Leonard was sitting up in his sleeping bag staring out the window.

"Look at it out there! Shit, it's really coming down." I still didn't believe him.

I raised myself up on my elbows half out of my bag – it was still cold. I looked over at the side windows of the van. Along the base of them was a six-inch rim of snow. "Jesus, you weren't bullshitting me ... it really did snow!"

"Yes Carl, it did really snow, and it is *still* snowing. Hard."

I got myself fully out of my bag and swung open the side doors of the van to investigate further. I was immediately hit by a blast of frigid air. There was at least a foot of snow on the ground and flakes the size of small kittens were still drifting down from the sky.

"Oh my God – look at this, Leonard!"

"Yeah, I'm looking, close that door, it's freezing." I did.

"How in the fuck are we going to get out of here?"

Leonard turned away from the window and said to me, "The same way that we got in here - drive."

"But shit, we don't even have chains. How are we supposed to drive in this without chains?"

"Carl, relax ... remember, it's not a car, it's a *Volkswagen*."

"Yeah, whatever, Leonard ... I'm going to go out there and see if there's a ranger around who can help us out." I put on my boots and jacket, opened up the doors and got out of the van. Leonard put on his own boots and joined me.

Outside of the van it was snowing hard. We walked out to the road and looked around the campground to see if there was anyone else around. There was no one. The campground was totally empty. The only indication that anyone had been there at all was a few sets of faint tire tracks, which were now quickly filling with snow.

"Oh, great, there's no one else here."

"Like I said, Carl, we're on our own, we gotta drive outa here." He was right. We had no other choice except for freezing to death and being found in the spring thaw. I didn't care for that option.

"Yeah, I suppose you're right. You want to drive or do you want me to?"

"Oh, I think you'd better drive, Carl. I've never driven in the snow before."

"Well fuck, neither have I."

"Excellent, then this will be a good learning experience."

In the cold, the van turned over painfully slowly. For a minute I wasn't even sure that it was going to start. Finally, I did get it going. I lit a cigarette and let the motor warm up. Leonard went aft and got out a tee shirt from his bag and wiped the windows. Volkswagens aren't known for an effective defrosting system.

I finished my cigarette, tentatively put in the clutch, and stuck the van in gear. I looked at the row of icons on the dashboard.

"Man, I hope these things work."

"Yeah, I hope so too," said Leonard, who reached out and rubbed Buddha's belly.

I let out the clutch and lightly gave the van some gas. I felt the rear end fishtail a little but the tires took and we were off. I was a little shaky at first, but the van handled well. "Hey, this ain't too bad... Leonard, wipe the window for me, will ya, I can't see."

"See, Carl, what did I tell ya, it's a Volkswagen."

When we got out to the main road, I finally had the courage to put the van into second and take it up to twenty-five.

"Hey, you're cooking with gas now, Carl," Leonard said with enthusiastic sarcasm.

"Oh, shut up, or I'll make you drive. Why don't you make yourself useful and tell me how far til we get to the ranger station." Leonard got the map out from under the seat and unfolded it. I lit another cigarette. I checked the pack. I only had four left.

"Hmmm, not too bad, looks like we only have about thirty miles to go." He grinned. "At this blistering rate, we should be out of here in about an hour or so."

We drove on through the snow for some time without any problems other than a few slips and slides. The further that we went, the more confident that I became of my ability to handle the van. About the same time that I began to relax some and was able to look at our surroundings, the snow began to let up and the sun came out. The entire landscape was covered in virgin snow. The sun sparkled off of it in the cold air. It was beautiful.

"You know, Leonard, it's really, really pretty out here."

Leonard agreed, "Yeah, Carl, it really is."

The sun stayed out and we kept moving on. The road, though, started to change. It began to wind a bit, and go up and down little grades as we wound our way through the trees. I felt the van slide more severely, and I began to tense up. Leonard felt it too.

"How ya doin' there, partner ... How about a cigarette?"

"Yeah, a cigarette would be good," I said tightly, not taking my eyes off of the road. I began to take my pack out of my pocket to hand to Leonard. "How much farther do you think?"

Leonard looked at the map. "You should be getting there, Carl, maybe five miles or ..."

I abruptly cut him off, "Oh, shit!"

As we came around the corner the road suddenly dropped steeply. At the bottom there was a tight curve. At the outside of that curve there was a drop-off that, from where we were, looked like it was at least a couple of hundred feet straight down. On top of it, it didn't look like there was a guardrail.

I tried desperately to put on the brakes, but the moment that I did, the van went into a full slide. We were only going about twenty-five miles an hour or so, but it was way too fast for the snow-covered grade. Leonard thought so too. I glanced over at him. He had one hand gripping the dashboard and the other on the door handle, as if ready to bail out.

"Oh Jesus, Carl, are we going to make that?" I couldn't answer him – I was scared shitless.

The curve came up fast. I turned the van's wheels. Nothing happened. I kept turning them. Still nothing. Out of panic, I hit the brakes, locking up all four wheels. We slid straight for the edge. "Oh, shit!" I braced for eternity.

Suddenly, about five feet from the edge of the abyss, I felt the front wheels take hold, and the front end of the van swerved back towards the road. I could fell the back end still sliding, so I let off the brakes and hit the gas hard. The motor roared, and I could feel the tires spin as they searched for traction. The back end continued to swing towards the edge. Then there was a loud "BANG" and the entire van shuttered and snapped around. The tires suddenly found something to grip, and we shot across the road. I wrestled with the wheel as the van fishtailed back and fourth. Gradually I regained control, pulled over to the shoulder of the road, and stopped. We had survived.

I turned off the motor. Just after I did I heard the passenger door close. I turned to Leonard.

"You asshole, you were going to bail out, weren't you?"

He looked at me with an only moderately embarrassed look on his face and said, "Don't worry, Carl, I would have gone to get help." I shook my head.

I got out of the van, and got out a cigarette. I tried to light it, but I was shaking like crazy. Finally I managed to get it lit and took a big drag. I turned and looked back at our tracks to see how close we had been to oblivion - very close. Leonard joined me.

"Look at that."

"Yeah ... I see it." I took another big drag and then handed the cigarette to Leonard. When he took it, I could feel that he was shaking too.

At the edge, right where the tires had taken hold, there was a large rock which was now exposed from under the snow. Leonard and I walked over. As we got closer, I could see that it was one of a half a dozen small boulders that served as a more decorative than functional guardrail. Then I noticed it - there was a broad dash of red paint on the rock.

"Leonard, take a look at this."

Leonard knelt down next to me. He reached out and touched the paint on the rock and said, "Is that us?"

I didn't answer him. We both turned around and looked at the van. On the left rear corner there was a small fresh dent. It all came together.

"Shit, Carl, if we hadn't hit that rock we would have gone right over this, back end first." I nodded as I looked down the sheer drop. There was a stream at the bottom.

"Close, huh?" I said.

Leonard whistled. "Yeah, close is right ..."

We got up and walked back to the van. "You know, Carl, I guess that all of those icons you put on the dashboard are working pretty hard for us." He actually sounded serious.

"Yeah, Leonard ... I guess you could say that we were stopped by the hand of God."

Leonard smiled and said, "Or by the hands of Vishnu ... or Buddha."

I shook another cigarette out of the pack. This one wasn't as hard to light.

"You want to drive, Leonard?"

"No, I do not, Carl. My robust, yet sensitive constitution doesn't permit me to get the bejeesus scared out of me twice in one day. You definitely have the hang of this snow-driving thing. On the other hand, if I take the wheel, I'll have to start at square one, and I predict that that will scare me."

"A simple 'No, you're doing fine' would have been sufficient."

"Maybe, Carl, but explanations make me feel closer to you." I rolled my eyes. We climbed into the cab and I fired up the van.

After our harrowing experience, I was a little hesitant to get back behind the wheel. Gradually, though, my confidence came back to me, but it was only a first gear confidence. The road helped - although it was still pretty curvy, it leveled out. I figured that we were past the worst of it. Leonard went back to the map.

"Like I was saying before we nearly drove off a cliff, I think that we're pretty close to getting out of here. It looks like we probably only have a few miles left to go."

"Yeah, well, at fifteen miles an hour that could take a while."

"Think positive, Carl ... at least we'll get there."

We kept plodding on. Leonard went aft and got us a stack of the chocolate chip cookies that Althea had given us for the trip.

"Breakfast?"

"Yeah, thanks, I could use a little sugar ... I could use some coffee too."

"Sorry partner, I'm not going to fire up the stove while we're driving."

"I wasn't asking you to actually do it, Leonard. It was a *wish,*" I said impatiently.

"Mmmm ... getting a little tight, are we?" I was going to answer him with an equally smart-ass reply when we rounded another curve in the road.

About five hundred feet ahead of us were four vehicles, one of which was an RV. They were parked by the side of the road at the base of a large hill. Apparently none of them could make it up it. I slowed the van to a crawl. As we approached I recognized the other three vehicles. One belonged to the Tennessee navy guy and his family; another, a Buick with fender damage, to the old man and woman who had hung up their car on the stump at our previous campground; and lastly, Dieter and Marta's van.

I pulled up next to the RV. It was an Oasis brand. Given the circumstances, it seemed appropriate. It had Vermont plates.

Leonard leaned out the window, "Knock, knock. Anyone home?" The side window of the RV slid open and a friendly, earthy looking middle-aged woman poked her head out.

"Hello there, young men, looks like you got stuck in the snow too." She had a Vermont lisp to her voice. "Why don't you pull over, come on in and warm up? Papa's just putting another stack of pancakes on the griddle ... got hot coffee here too."

I leaned over Leonard, "No, we got to get going here, but thanks though. We just stopped to make sure that everyone was okay."

"Oh, why, we are just fine. Got all the comforts of home in here."

Leonard got up, went past me, and started rummaging around in our supplies in the back.

I continued, "Has the ranger been by here?"

"No, we haven't seen him yet. I suppose he'll be by soon though," she said cheerfully like none of this was out of the ordinary.

Leonard came back up front with two Styrofoam cups. He handed them out the window to the woman. "We would be obliged if you could fill us up with some coffee."

"Oh, why sure." She took them and disappeared back into the RV. A few moments later she popped back out and handed the cups back to Leonard. The coffee steamed in the cold air.

"Thank you, ma'am." I reached down to the ignition to start the van. "We're going to make a run for the hill there. If we make it, as soon as we get to the ranger station we'll let him know that you folks are back here."

"Thank you so kindly. We certainly ... what?" She was listening to someone back in the RV. "Oh ... just a moment, boys."

She disappeared back into the RV. She came back with two paper plates, each with a stack of pancakes on them dripping with maple syrup.

"Have some breakfast."

"Thank you again, ma'am." Leonard took the plates from her.

"Wish us luck."

The woman smiled and waved. Leonard closed the window and I started the van. I pulled the van away slowly, letting the tires find their grip in the snow. We had only driven about twenty feet when Leonard spotted Dieter and Marta.

"Hey, Carl, you have to see this." He pointed towards them. They were lying side by side off in a snowdrift, like a pair of big children. They had big grins on their faces. They were making snow angels. Leonard and I waved to them and they waved back to us enthusiastically. They said something to us, but neither one of us could make it out over the sound of the motor.

"Boy, they may be nuts, but you sure have to give 'em points for tenacity."

"Yeah, that you do."

We only had about three hundred feet before we reached the hill. Once we passed Dieter and Marta, I gave the van some gas. I figured that we would need some momentum to get up the hill. When we reached the base of it we were doing a little over thirty in second gear. The motor roared. Leonard was encouraging.

"You go there, Carl ... hey, want a bite of pancake?"

"Yes I do." Leonard cut off a hunk from the stack and shoved the fork my direction. Without taking my hands off the wheel or my eyes off the road I took the bite, "Mmm, fees ar goo."

We got up the first half of the hill without sliding at all. Then, as we lost our momentum, the tires began to break loose. I gave the van more gas.

"Come on van, you can do it." The van continued to climb, but we were losing speed.

"I don't know if we're going to make it here, Leonard."

Leonard looked over at the speedometer and said, "Hell, I don't see why not, Carl, the speedometer says you're doing forty." I looked out the window. We were moving at a jogging pace. Without shifting, I gave the van still more gas – the motor screamed. I was somewhere near redline. We were only a couple hundred feet from the top of the hill now. The back end started to fishtail. I wrestled the wheel to keep us straight. Leonard started rocking back and forth in his seat as if to help shove us over the top. I started doing it too in rhythm with him – I think it might have actually helped. We finally cleared the top of the grade at a walking pace. We had made it.

Leonard turned around in his seat. "Look in your rearview mirror, Carl." Standing behind us at the base of the hill was the stranded party, clapping and cheering. I stuck my hand out the window, waved, and gave them a thumbs-up.

Once over the top of the hill, we could see that a ranger station, gas station and restaurant were only about a quarter mile away. It was, as Dieter would say, pretty ironic. There they were, folks trapped in a blizzard in the wilderness, trying to make the best of it, and just over the hill, civilization.

We pulled into the ranger station. The parking lot had been plowed. The ranger on duty must have seen us coming - he was at our van the moment that we pulled in. He was a guy in his fifties. He had big moustache that covered most of his mouth and he wore a cowboy hat. He was substantially less amped-up than Ranger Over-reaction.

He came over to Leonard's side and said with a folksy Montana accent, "Looks like you fellas got caught in the park in the big snow."

Leonard answered him, "Yes sir ... there is much snow."

"Yeah, it caught quite a few people by surprise. Around these parts it can snow just about any time of year."

He pushed the brim of his cowboy hat back. "Say, where did you fellas camp last night?"

"Back up at Lake Village."

"Did ya see anyone else on your way out? We're going to send some men in with snowmobiles, but it sure would help us out some if we had an idea where folks were ... it's a big park."

"As a matter of fact, that's why we stopped. There's a group of people stuck at the bottom of the hill just about a half a mile or so inside the park."

"Don't they know how close they are to the station?"

I broke in, "No, I don't think that they have a clue. They're pretty comfortable though. They're all holed up in an RV eating pancakes."

The ranger laughed a little through his moustache and shook his head. Then he leaned on the van door, looked at both of us intently and said with a prophetic seriousness, "Yeah, I guess most folks just don't see that their salvation is maybe only a few steps away."

I felt that same odd tingle at the back of my neck that I had with the old man back at Atomic City. I paused, nodded with understanding, then said, "Yeah ... I suppose that's true..." Like the old man, the ranger stared into my eyes, nodded and winked as if assured that I had fully understood his message. "Well, we best get going. We're going to head on over to the restaurant and get some food. We just wanted to stop and let you know about those people back there."

"Well, I sure appreciate it, and I'm sure they do too." I put the van in gear. "Hey, before you guys go, I just got to ask you ..."

"Yeah, what's that?" said Leonard.

"What is the deal with that?" The ranger pointed to the rat on the antenna, which now had a three-inch long windswept icicle hanging from his nose.

"Oh, him ... that's Mr. Rat. He's our mascot," Leonard said with complete seriousness.

The ranger just shook his head, laughed a little again and said, "You boys go on and have a good life." I guess he understood the joke. We waved him goodbye as we backed out.

It was just after ten o'clock when we finished our breakfast at the restaurant and got on the road. It had warmed up outside to a balmy fifty degrees. The snow was melting and the roads outside of the park had been plowed. Today was to be our long day of driving. I had hoped that we would have been on the road sooner. Snow ... nothing to be done about that. I guess that you just deal with the unexpected. Still, in spite of our moderately late start, I figured that we would be able to cover the three hundred and twenty-five miles to Devil's Tower by six o'clock.

Leonard had taken over at the wheel, and true to form he left a bit of rubber on the road when he went from first to second. "Shit, Leonard, would you quit doing that? I don't want to have to buy another tire."

"Hey, I'm just marking my territory, Carl," Leonard said in his defense.

"Well, mark it with your own tire."

"But think of the drama factor, Carl ... isn't that worth just a little bit of rubber? I mean, take McGarrett on Hawaii Five-O. Half of what makes him so cool is that he burns rubber everywhere he goes. And it's not like his buddy Danno is sitting in the seat next to him going in some pukey little voice, 'Steve, watch it, you're going to make the tires wear out.'"

"Well, this isn't TV, Leonard, and you aren't McGarrett."

"True, but I am nearly as cool." Leonard grinned. "I'll tell you what, Danno ... if we need a new tire I'll buy it, okay?"

"Yeah, you do that."

Pilgrimage

Almost as soon as we left the park, we began to drop out of the mountains. Before us we could see the rolling hills that marked the beginnings of the vast plains of the Midwest. We followed Highway 20 east toward Cody. With the grade in our favor, Leonard was doing nearly eighty. We were making good time.

It took us less than an hour to reach Cody. The moment that we drove into the city limits it was pretty clear that the town was hanging on tightly to its Wild West past. Judging from the looks of the town, it was probably because there was nothing else to hang on to.

We passed a rustic-looking sign made out of logs. It was complete with a six foot carved bust of Buffalo Bill: "Welcome to Cody - Home of Buffalo Bill - Enjoy your stay."

When we passed the sign, Leonard said, "Yeah, enjoy your stay as long as you're not a buffalo." I guess it was funny, in a sad sort of way. I didn't laugh; neither did Leonard. The highway took us right through the middle of the town. The Wild West theme continued. All the storefronts looked like they were straight from the late 1800's. Even the sidewalks were raised and planked. It felt like that we had entered a set for the television show "Gunsmoke." Having been weaned from a young age on such Hollywood entertainment, I thought that it was actually kind of cool.

I shared my thoughts with Leonard, "Hey, I'm kind of digging on this whole Wild West thing."

"Yeah, well I'm not ... this whole town gives me the creeps." After thinking about it for a minute, I understood what he meant. I guess television and reality are two different things. I didn't say anything else.

We kept on driving on Highway 20. We passed by the towns of Burlington and Emblem. When we got to Greybull we followed the highway south towards Worland and Thermopolis. I speculated on the latter's name.

"Hey, Leonard?"

"Yeah?"

"Why do you think that they call it Thermopolis?"

"Fuck, I don't know why they call it Thermopolis, maybe they make thermometers there."

"Or maybe they make thermoses there," I said.

Then Leonard turned to me wild-eyed and said slowly and deep-voiced, "Or maybe it's very, very, very hot there ... maybe it's really Hell, except they don't want to scare people away, so they don't call it that."

I played along. "Stop, Leonard, you're scaring me."

"Yeah, that's what it is ... it's Hell, and I'm driving us there." He threw his head back and laughed maniacally.

"Uh, excuse me, sir," I said like a scared kid, "I'd like you to please stop the van and let me out ... I think that you're completely insane."

"Oh no, no one gets out, my friend ... not on the ..." he paused, then he started singing at the top of his lungs, "Highway to Hell, yeah, yeah, yeah, yeah ... we're on a Highway to Hell ..."

I joined him, "a Highway to Hell, yeah, yeah, yeah, yeah ..."

About ten miles outside of Worland, Leonard said, "Ya know, this gas gauge has said three-quarters of a tank for the last hundred miles."

"Well, maybe it's because we've been going downhill since we left Jellystone ... so we're getting really good gas mileage. Live with it."

Leonard was doubtful. "Ah ... I don't think so, Carl," He leaned over and tapped on the gauge like he was a World War II fighter pilot.

"Man, you saw that in a movie." Just as I said that, the gauge's needle instantly dropped to empty.

"Oh, yeah, well maybe I did see it in a movie, but it sure the hell works. We'd better find a place to fuel up soon or we're going to be stuck in outer fucking nowhere."

I don't know if it was because I was now listening for it, but the motor began to sound like it was running a little lean. I decided not to say anything to Leonard about my observation and kept my eyes peeled for a filling station.

Not too many miles later I spotted a sign that said "Worland - 1 mile." As if to punctuate the urgency of our fuel situation, the van's motor missed.

"Was that you, Leonard?"

"No, that wasn't me, Carl ... that was the van." Then he changed his voice to a high cartoonish tone, like the van was talking. "I am so ... cough, cough ... thirsty … please ... I need a drink." The van's motor missed again, this time a little harder.

I ignored Leonard's talking van imitation and asked seriously, "You think that you can nurse it another mile 'til we get to Worland?"

"Hmmm, let me see," he put a thumb and forefinger to the side of his temple and rolled his eyes back in his head like he was a carnival clairvoyant. "I see a gas tank ... it is empty, wait, no ... there is, yes! There is a little gas in it, not much, though."

"You asshole."

"Wait, there is more ... I see a round orb, it is red. Clearer, clearer ... yes, inside the orb there is a word, T – E – X... A – C - O. There is gasoline at this place." He pretended to snap out of his trance, and he grinned at me.

"Okay, enough, Mr. Fucking Kreskin, here's the exit." As Leonard downshifted on the off ramp, the van missed again, this time almost dying completely, "Shit ..." We rounded a slight rise at the end of the off ramp. A large red sign loomed in the sky – a Texaco station.

Leonard saw it about the same time I did, "Ah, you doubted my powers!"

"Oh, shut up and drive."

Leonard hung a right and headed down the hill in the direction of the station. Fortunately it looked like it was only a couple of blocks away. The second that we began to head down the hill whatever gas was remaining in the tank must have been sloshed away from fuel line. The motor missed and died, this time completely.

"Oh, great ..." Leonard tried to restart it a couple of times with no success, "Come on baby ..." Finally he gave up.

The hill was fairly steep. Leonard tried a different tactic, coasting in. He gained as much speed as possible, not touching the brakes once. By the time we got to the bottom we were doing thirty-five.

"Ah, Leonard, I think that you want to make a left here at the next turn," I said with a nervous tone in my voice, as if to suggest that braking might not be such a bad idea.

"Yeah, I see it." He either didn't pick up on my suggestion or just chose to ignore it.

We hit the turn at a full thirty-five. The van fishtailed wildly and the tires squealed. I felt the van list hard to the right, come back, and then bounce a little. He'd had it up on two wheels.

"Fuck, Leonard!"

"Well, shit, Carl, I didn't feel like pushing us into the station."

"Well, I didn't feel like sliding in on our ass either."

"And, we're not ... we're totally under control and the station is just up ahead." I looked ahead; he was right, the station was only a block away.

"See, Carl," Leonard was now talking with an Italian accent, "A car is like a woman." He caressed the steering wheel, "You must drive her to her limit ... but at the same time you must be gentle. She must always know that although you take the risks, you are in control."

"God, Leonard, you're an idiot." He looked at me and raised his eyebrows. We both started laughing.

We rolled silently into the Texaco station. I got out and went back to fill the tank. There was a fair amount of resistance when I turned the gas cap. When I opened it, it made a loud sucking sound, like opening a vacuum-packed jar of pickles. We had been driving on fumes. I stood there and watched the gas pump numbers spin. When the counter went past ten gallons I called up to Leonard, "Hey, how many gallons do you think this tank holds?"

He called back, "Oh, probably ten gallons or so."

"Yeah, well, I've put in ten already, wait ..." the automatic filler clicked off, "... eleven point two gallons."

"Well then, it must be an eleven gallon tank, with point two in the fuel line."

"Thanks, Leonard."

"You're welcome, Carl."

Leonard handed me a twenty out the driver's window, "Here, I'll fill it this time."

As I walked between the pumps to go pay the cashier, I was nearly run over by a woman driving a blue '72 Dart who was pulling into the station. I didn't really get a look at her but I heard her lean out the window and say pleasantly, "Sorry." Without looking I kept walking and said, "It's okay."

I walked in. Behind the counter, the clerk, who was eating a jalapeno and cheese-injected corn dog, stared at a baseball game on a portable black and white TV that had a screen about half the size of a cereal box. Without looking up, he said, "Hi." He was maybe in his mid-twenties, but his exact age was hidden beneath his extreme corpulence. He was wearing a baseball hat and, although he was doing exactly nothing and it really wasn't that warm outside, he was sweating like mad.

"Hi," I said back.

"Is the gas going to be it for you?" he said politely without looking up.

"No, I'll be back in a second, I'm going to get a couple of sodas too."

He didn't say anything and kept watching the game. I went to the back of the store and grabbed a couple of Green Rivers out of the cooler. I only moderately liked their flavor but their unnatural green color combined with their high sugar content made me buy them whenever I found a store that carried them. On the way back up to the counter I picked up a bag of roasted peanuts as well.

By the time I got back up front there was a woman at the register buying a pack of Marlboros. I assumed, since no one else had pulled in, that she was the owner of the blue '72 Dart. She was a fine-looking woman. She wore tan Wranglers and a black leotard top. A black bra strap poked out from under the top and hung over her right shoulder. She had counterfeit blond curly hair that fell just past her shoulders. Silver earrings in the shape of small feathers hung from her ears. On her feet she was wearing beat-up black cowboy boots. Her look was a mixture of cowgirl and biker. She was one of those kinds of women who have an edge like a razor – you don't know you're cut 'til you're bleeding all over the place. For some irrational reason I had always been drawn to women like that. I realized I was staring.

"... And five makes ten. Thank you and have a nice day."

She took her change and her cigarettes from the counter and turned to leave. When she turned, she looked right at me, smiled, and said with a sweet predatory tone to her voice, "Sorry that I almost ran you over out there."

As our eyes met I felt myself melt a little inside. For a second I was unable to speak. Finally I stammered, "That ... that's okay ..." She walked slowly out of the store and, smiling, shot me one more glance over her shoulder. A little stunned, I continued to stare at her as she walked back to her car.

The fat guy behind the counter watched her too and observantly said, between bites of his corndog, "That woman is in really good shape."

I agreed and added, "In more ways than one."

Then he asked, like it was some big deep question, "Why is a fine-looking woman like that driving an old Dart?"

I paused and said, "Because it will run forever."

The fat guy stopped chewing and just blinked at me. He had no clue what I was talking about. Frankly, I wasn't sure if I did either, but somehow what I had said made sense to me.

"So what do I owe you?"

"Oh ... yeah, ah, let's see, that's nine seventy two on pump three, and with the pop and peanuts ..."

"Give me a pack of Camel filters too."

"Okay, that'll be twelve eighty nine." I paid him and left.

When I got outside of the store, the blue Dart woman was sitting in her car on the other side of the parking lot. She was smoking a cigarette and looking right at me. She was smiling. I stared and smiled back. Without either one of us moving we watched each other for probably thirty seconds. Finally, and I don't know why, I decided to walk over to her. It was almost like it was a reflex. Inside I felt like a moth flying towards a flame. On the surface I was instinctually drawn, but way, way deep down inside I knew it was wrong. Still I couldn't, or didn't stop myself. As I approached the car window she put her hand out.

As I took it, she said pleasantly, "Hi, my name's Melody." I just stood there saying nothing. Her hand was soft yet strong and as I held it in mine I felt an erotic tingling magnetism. Finally she said prompting me, almost laughing a little, "And yours is..." Her voice snapped me out of my moth-like trance and I realized that I had just been standing there looking at her, and holding her hand.

"I'm Carl." A little embarrassed, I took my hand back. As I did, I felt her hold on just a bit, as if to say, "It's okay, I want you to do that."

"So what brings you all the way out here to Wyoming?" She was now leaning innocently and coyly on the door frame with her head resting on top of her hands.

"Oh, me and my friend are just taking a little road trip. No real plans, ya know, just road trippin'." I was stumbling all over myself.

For a few moments she didn't say anything. She just looked at me, smiling. Then, without breaking her look, she licked her bottom lip with just the very tip of her tongue and said, "Well, if you have nowhere where you need to be, maybe you could stop by for dinner tonight. I live just up at the end of the road about ten miles." She motioned with a tilt of her head, smiled, and with the look that was in her eyes, I knew what "dinner" really meant.

I felt a little surge of lust-fueled adrenaline in my chest. We continued to stare at each other, and as we did I felt myself slipping towards one of two answers - yes. I sensed that she knew that.

After what was probably a minute or so I opened my mouth and said quietly and almost apologetically, "I'm sorry... I, I can't. We need to get back on the road." My words sounded distant, as if they weren't mine.

She smiled like she didn't really believe me, "I understand." She put out her hand again, "It was nice meeting you. If you change your mind, I'm just up the road."

As I took my hand away from our parting I felt her fingertip wisp across my palm. Then she started up her car, and as she drove away she stuck her arm out the window, waving like she would see me later.

I just stood there for a moment, then turned and walked all the way back across the parking lot to the van.

Leonard had watched the whole scene. "Jesus Christ, Carl, what the hell was that all about?"

"I have no idea."

"Man, even from here that woman looked like she wanted to eat you for breakfast, lunch, dinner, and maybe a snack too."

"Yeah, she did, didn't she," I said smiling. "I suppose I wouldn't mind being a meal. As a matter of fact, she wanted me to come over for dinner."

Leonard didn't immediately say anything. He just leaned on the steering wheel and looked at me.

"What?" I tried to sound innocent even though I didn't feel like I was.

"I'll tell you something else, too, Carl." Leonard now sounded more serious.

"What's that?"

"If Althea had seen that little exchange there, she would have clawed that woman's eyes out and then kicked your ass back to Mount Vernon."

I didn't have to think about it - he was right. Althea had a bad, though not often seen, temper. I tried weakly to defend myself with a classic line, "Hey, I may be in a relationship, Leonard, but I'm not dead."

"Yeah ... well maybe not, but you very well could be, and maybe I wouldn't blame her. I would call it justifiable homicide." Then he added, looking at me hard, "You know, Carl, you ought to hang on tightly to the good things you have. You'd miss them if they were gone."

I didn't try saying anything more. There wasn't anything more to say. Leonard made me think. During the whole exchange with Melody the thought of Althea hadn't consciously entered my head. Hell, I didn't simply tell Melody I had a girlfriend. I told her we had to get back on the road. I felt like a jerk.

We headed out from Worland on Highway 16 toward Buffalo. It was one-thirty. Leonard started whistling. It was okay at first, but he kept it up, the same song over and over. It became annoying, in part because it was vaguely familiar, but I couldn't put a name to the tune.

"Hey, Leonard, do you mind?"

"Mind what?"

"Mind whistling something else ... or better yet, not whistling at all, it's driving me crazy."

"Oh, no problem," he said suspiciously cheerfully. There was silence, for a moment. Then he started humming, the same fucking song.

"Knock it off, Leonard, I mean it. Man, half of what's driving me crazy is that stupid song."

"Oh, sorry," he said, again suspiciously cheerfully. I knew something else was coming. Sure enough, there was silence, for a moment. Then he started bobbing his head to the rhythm and sang... "Devil with the blue Dart, blue Dart, blue Dart, devil with the blue Dart car."

"Oh God, Leonard, leave it alone." I knew that he was teasing me, but at the same time he was a little serious too. He was driving his point home.

"Leave it alone nothin', Carl, that was just like in the movies back there. And you know what the best part is?"

"What's that?"

"I can blackmail you with it later."

I knew he wouldn't, but I played along anyway. "Fuck you, I'll deny everything, you dirty little extortionist."

"Sure you will, Carl, sure you will. Oh, and I prefer 'blackmail.' Extortion is such a dirty word."

We were interrupted when raindrops - big raindrops - began hitting the windows.

"Here we go, thunderstorm." Leonard switched the wipers on. Lightning flashed.

"Yeah, well, at least it ain't snow."

"True ... and at least it ain't grasshoppers."

The sky darkened to a deep purple-black and a strong wind started to pick up. We kept driving. Leonard slowed the van both in order to see and in order to keep it on the road against the wind. The rat whipped back and forth wildly on the antenna.

"Mr. Rat says that the wind is out of the south," I observed. Lightning flashed again.

"I don't give a shit what direction it's coming from ... God, this is like driving a piece of fucking plywood down the highway."

"Hey, there's no hurry, Leonard, just get us there alive."

"I case you couldn't tell I'm not, and I'm trying to." Leonard said tightly. I felt the van hydroplane slightly, then snap back.

The rain was coming even harder now, and there was about an inch of standing water across the highway. The sky was like night. Leonard reached down and switched the wipers to frantic mode and slowed the van to a crawl. It didn't help.

The road conditions were deteriorating rapidly and I was starting to feel nervous. I had never seen weather quite like this before. "Maybe we should just pull off, smoke some weed, and watch the storm," I suggested.

"Maybe that's a good idea, before something tragic happens." Leonard wrestled the van against another strong gust. "There's an overpass up there. I'm gonna pull off underneath it."

"Good plan."

"Yes it is."

Leonard pulled the van over onto a flat grassy spot as far off of the shoulder of the road as he could. The rain seemed even more intense under the protection of the overpass. There were two close flashes of lightning. Thunder roared. The van shook. We both jumped.

"Woah, that shit was close," I said.

"Yeah, very ..."

I reached into the glove box and got out the pipe and the Wiccan weed. I quickly filled the pipe and lit it. *Flash – Wham.* Another close strike. I held the smoke and handed the pipe to Leonard.

"Man, good thing we got off the road when we did."

Leonard nodded in agreement as he took a deep draw on the weed. In spite of the rain, it was hot and I opened the side window. The warm air rushed in. It smelled heavily like electricity.

"Hey, Leonard?"

"Yeah?" He was still holding his breath.

"Does this feel a little apocalyptic to you?"

He let the smoke out, then said, "What *exactly* do you mean, Carl?"

"Well ... like I sort of get the feeling that something's going to happen."

Leonard looked at me blankly for a moment then said, "Hey Carl, news flash – something *is* happening. We're in a whoop-ass thunderstorm in Wyoming." He handed the pipe back to me and added, "If you're going to say high stuff then you ought to be high."

I took the pipe from him and took another drag. Leonard was probably right. Having never been in a thunderstorm of this intensity, I was probably just being paranoid.

We finished the weed and sat in the van under the protection of the overpass. The storm lasted a good long time. Both of us sat there in complete awe as we watched the rain pound down and the sky flash and rumble around us. It was a dramatic and very cool thing to experience, but still I couldn't shake my ominous feelings.

Finally the storm passed about forty-five minutes later. When it did, we decided that it was time to move on. Leonard started the van and pulled back onto the highway. The sun was out, but there was still about a half inch of standing water on the road and Leonard wasn't able to do any better than fifty-five.

"It looks like there goes our getting to Devil's Tower by six."

"No, it doesn't really look like we're going to do it, does it." I said. I pulled out the map. "Hmm."

"Hmm, what?"

"Hmm ... we have about two hundred and twenty miles to go."

"What!?"

"Like I said, we have about two hundred and twenty miles to go. So ..." I looked down at the speedometer, "... if you keep up this speed, and don't have to stop for a thing, then it should take us about four hours or so. We'll get there around seven."

"You know, Carl, you're really a shitty navigator," Leonard teased.

"How do you figure?"

"You *always* miscalculate how long it will take us to get anywhere."

"Hey buddy, I don't write the miles, I just read them."

"Yeah, well, your math sucks."

"Yeah, well, I'll show you," I said with a tone in my voice like an affected prep school kid, and went back to studying the map to see if I could knock a few miles off of the drive.

In my half-high state, my mind wandered from the task at hand. Instead of looking for a better route, I got caught up in the interesting names that had been given to the small towns.

"Hey, Leonard."

"Yeah?"

"There's a town here called Yonder. Isn't that a weird name for a town?"

"Yes, Carl ... it is, very interesting." He didn't sound interested.

"Here's another called Hadtsell." He didn't say anything.

"Oh, and here's a really weird one," I didn't even think before I said it. "It's called Closed in Winter."

Leonard looked over at me, "Oh, really, Carl? Is it near I-can't-read-a-map?" He said it like it was one word.

I tried to brush off my mistake as intentional. "Hey, I was just kidding," but it was too late. He knew it was a high mistake. He was laughing like crazy.

"Shit!" Leonard said, and I felt the van slide slightly. I looked up from the map.

"Shit, what?"

"There's something on the road, and it's slicker than hell." Leonard throttled down the van. It backfired - we slid a little bit again.

"Hey, slow it down, Leonard."

"That's what I'm doing! What the hell is all of this stuff on the road? – Fuck, it's moving!"

Both of us were leaning forward looking out of the front window trying to determine what the hell on the roadway was causing our sudden loss in traction. Suddenly, a frog hit the front window and we reflexively jumped back in our seats. "What the ..."

Then came another, and another – little bright green frogs with red eyes. They bounced off of the window and off the front of the van as they hopped on the highway. Leonard began to freak out. He was rocking back and forth in the driver's seat saying, "Oh, no, no, no, no ... this is so wrong ..."

As far as I could see, the road ahead was absolutely covered with thousands and thousands of frogs. It was bizarre all right, but I wasn't as freaked out about it as Leonard was. He had always thought that cold-blooded creatures were a little creepy. I had to agree with him about one thing though.

"You're right, Leonard, driving over hundreds of these guys is so wrong."

As if to punctuate the wrongness of it, a frog leaped up from the road and landed right in the middle of the driver's side of the windshield. He hung there, stuck to the glass with the little suction cups on the ends of each of his toes. He stared in at us with little beady red amphibian eyes. Leonard recoiled back in his seat – his own eyes wide with horror.

I couldn't help myself. I said in a squeaky little voice, "Why, oh why do you squish my brothers?" I thought I was funny as hell and I started to laugh.

Leonard whipped around and glared at me, "Shut the fuck up, Carl, I'm serious, that's the last thing I need right now!" Then he turned his attention back to the frog, reached down and switched on the windshield wipers and said, "Quit looking at me, you little fucker!" The little frog jumped off unscathed. He must have seen the wiper arm coming.

I could see that Leonard was sincerely upset. I tried to be helpful and offer a solution. "Maybe we should wait this whole frog migration thing out by the side of the road."

Leonard would have none of it. "Wait? Wait for what? Wait for them to cover the van by the thousands and then contract their sticky little feet all at once so that they can break the windows and get to us?" The van slipped a little again.

"Shit, Leonard, calm down. They're frogs, not rattlesnakes."

"Shit calm down nothin,' I know about these things, they aren't as harmless as they look. I saw frogs just like this on a nature show once. They're poison fucking dart fucking frogs. They secrete curare from their skin. Just touch one of them and you're in for an excruciatingly painful writhing death. They showed a monkey on the show that had been playing with one of them. He started twitching and shit, then he started screaming in pain. Before he died he chewed off his own fingers."

While I considered a response to Leonard's venomous story, two more frogs hit the window and bounced off. Another one landed on Mr. Rat and hung on for a good while.

Finally I said calmly, "Um, I think that those kinds of frogs only live in the Amazon."

Leonard immediately shot back, "Oh really, Mr. Goddamn Frog Expert? Well I've got news for you, killer bees are from the Amazon too, and they sting the shit out of people around here all the time." I thought about it for a minute then concluded that he might be right.

I raised an eyebrow and said, "You have a good point there, Leonard - keep driving."

"Goddamn right I have a good point," and with that he gave the van a little more gas. When he did, it slid again a little.

We drove for at least another five miles through frogs before we were finally clear of them. When it was over we were both considerably traumatized by the experience. Leonard remained reasonably stoic, although I did hear him whimper quietly a couple of times when we hit some fairly large concentrations of the critters. Myself, toward the end I was beginning to feel each bump as the van ran over them. It was making me feel moderately sick both emotionally and physically.

"I've seen some weird stuff, but nothing quite that weird," I said.

Leonard, who was more shaken than I was, replied, "Oh my fucking God, I'm going to need years of therapy to get over that." I didn't think that he was kidding about it.

I replied, "Well, I guess then I won't ask you to wash the van later."

Leonard gave me a look that said, "I am ignoring your comment, asshole." Then he said, "Why am I always at the wheel when this shit happens?"

"I don't know, Leonard ... luck?"

"You know what else, Carl?"

"What?"

He looked right at me and said seriously, "Man, this shit is getting biblical." I didn't say anything, but the same thought had occurred to me.

The frog incident had slowed us up considerably. We were still over an hour away from Buffalo when we drove through Powder River Pass. It was a long slow haul up the 9,677 feet to the top. The van labored under the steep grade even though we were in third gear. Once over the top, Leonard rocketed down the backside trying to make up for lost time. But after a couple of tire-shrieking, pants-soiling, fingernails-on-the-dashboard-clinging turns on sudden tight corners with sheer drops, I convinced him to slow down.

"If you don't cool it, Leonard, I promise I will projectile hurl all over the inside of this van." Leonard took the threat seriously and considered how it would play out.

"Oooh ... and if you hurl, it'll start a chain reaction, and I'll hurl too ... That will make the van smell like hurl and then every time that I get into the van I'll hurl again. You might even hurl again too. Hmmm ..." he put his forefinger to his lower lip as if to ponder what to do. Finally he said, "I guess I'll slow down."

We passed through Buffalo at a quarter after five. The drive eased up as we left the winding two-lane highway and turned onto Interstate 90 headed east toward Gillette. It had been a long day in the van and we both were exhausted. We drove on without conversation for a good half hour. Lulled by the drone of the van's motor, I half-napped as I watched the high plains whip by outside the window.

Leonard broke the silence.

"Carl?"

"Yeah?" I said groggily.

"I need to get the fuck out of this van before I go monkey dung."

I slowly roused myself and got out the map. "I hear ya... let me see if I can find somewhere to pull off and get some coffee ... by the way, how are we doing on gas?"

"Hmm, looks like we have about a third of a tank. We should probably top it up if we can find a station."

I studied the map in search of a town that might offer what we needed. Since I had been napping, I hadn't been paying much attention to any landmarks. As far as I could tell from the map, though, we were most likely in the middle of a whole lot of nothing.

"Hey, Leonard?"

"Yeah?"

"Have you seen anything recently that I can use as a landmark?"

"Yeah, we passed over Crazy Woman Creek about ten miles ago."

"Thanks ... have we passed the Powder River yet?"

"Nope."

"Good, that should be coming up here pretty soon. Right after that, there's a town about five miles off of the freeway called Bliss. It looks pretty small, but it's the only town 'til Gillette, and that's about an hour away from here."

We drove on for another ten miles or so before we came to the Powder River.

"Here we go, Bliss should be coming up here pretty soon."

Leonard surveyed the landscape. "Why in the hell would they call a town out here Bliss? Jesus, there isn't anything thing out here."

"Yeah, well it's near Crazy Woman Creek, isn't it? Maybe that has something to do with it."

A couple of miles later we came to a freeway sign that simply said "Bliss." Leonard took the exit and said, "Ah, I feel peaceful already." As soon as we were off of the freeway though the road turned to rough gravel. "Man, you would think that the road to Bliss would be smoother ... how far did you say 'til we get there?"

"Looks like from the map maybe five miles, tops. It's hard to tell, though."

Leonard drove slowly down the road, which was heavily washboarded. He erratically wove the van back and forth to try and avoid the deepest of the potholes. We had only gone a mile or so when Leonard said, "Just a guess, Carl, but I bet this place isn't a metropolis."

"Good guess." I pointed to a tilted blue sign by the side of the road, "Welcome to Bliss - Pop. 13."

From what I could see, the town of Bliss consisted of exactly eight buildings - a restaurant, a general store, five homes, and a small church that had a fresh coat of white paint. I expected Laura Ingalls to come bounding out of one of the houses. She didn't. I stated the obvious, "Not much here, but it sure looks pleasant."

"No, there isn't, and yes it does. I wonder what they're hiding," Leonard said cynically.

We stopped the van in front of the general store, got out, and stretched. The only sound was of the wind whooshing around the buildings, and an occasional squeak from the rusted steel sign that hung above the door of the general store.

In the yard of one of the houses, a woman in a faded yellow gingham dress patiently hung up clothes on the line to dry while a little girl at her feet played with the basket of clothespins. Neither one of them paid us any attention. Then just above the sound of the wind, I heard a piano start to play. It came from one of the houses. Whoever was playing wasn't a virtuoso, but the song they played was sweet. The town, no matter how small, was alive.

I walked over to the door of the store and tried it. It was locked.

"Well?" Leonard called from over by the van.

"They're closed." I peered in through the window to see if there was anyone there. The lights in the store were off. From the window I could see that the store was well stocked. There was something odd about it, though, but I couldn't place what.

Cans and jars were stacked neatly on shelves that ran from the worn wood floor to the high ceiling. Various other goods such as lanterns, gas cans, and sickles hung from the rafters. One shelf was stacked with neatly folded faded green wool blankets. Right next to the blanket were rows of hand tools. Towards the counter at the back of the store there was a barrel that was filled with axe handles. There were two other barrels at the other end of the counter but I couldn't tell what was in them.

I was about to walk away when it came to me. Everything in the store was old, very old. The labels on the cans and jars looked like they were from the twenties or thirties. The tools and other dry goods were of a style from a time long since passed. The posters on the walls advertised brand names I had never heard of. I felt like I was looking through a strange window that was a portal to another time.

I returned to the van and to Leonard. I decided that a lengthy explanation about the store wasn't necessary and simply said to him, "Nobody home, maybe we should try over at the restaurant." We walked across the dry dirt street to the restaurant. The door to the restaurant was propped wide open and the lights were on.

Inside, the restaurant was clean and neat, and there were a place settings and menus at every table. In the middle of the dining area stood a tall skinny man who slowly swept the floor. Aside from us, he was the only person there. He wore a tired-looking white collarless dress shirt, and his dark baggy trousers were held up with suspenders. His graying hair was uncombed and he had a couple of days' growth of beard. He looked like a tenant farmer straight out of the depression. He looked melancholy.

He didn't look up when we walked in. I cleared my throat, "Excuse me." He still didn't look up, although I was sure that he had to have heard me in the empty restaurant. I said it again this time a little bit louder, "Excuse me." He stopped his sweeping and slowly raised his head. He looked at us with a blank emotionless stare. "Excuse me, I was wondering if we could get a couple of cups of coffee to go." Still, he said nothing, and his lack of facial expression didn't reveal that he had heard a word I said. I repeated myself, this time I said it more slowly, "My friend and I were wondering if we could get a couple of cups of coffee to go." My words echoed off of the empty walls. The restaurant fell silent again.

I was just about to ask again, when he spoke. His voice was quiet and dry. It suited him. "Coffee? ... coffee? ... coffee... yes, yes, coffee." He perked up a little, as if the sounds of his own voice woke him out from a long deep dream. "Yes, coffee would be nice ... amen." His words trailed off and he smiled a little at the corners of his mouth. He turned and looked out the window.

Leonard spoke to him this time. He was direct, but polite, "Yes, coffee would be nice ... could we please get a couple of cups to go?"

Slowly the man turned back towards us. He paused for a moment then said, "Sorry ... we've been closed for a few years now." The smile faded from his mouth, he lowered his head, and he began sweeping again.

Without saying anything else to him, Leonard and I left the restaurant and walked back to the van.

"Man, Carl, what was the deal with that guy?"

"No clue ..."

"I mean if they've been closed for years now why in the fuck is he in there sweeping the floor?"

I shook my head. "I don't know, Leonard."

"And what's the deal with naming this town Bliss?" Then he added, "Man, I don't think so ..."

I couldn't answer him. I just shrugged my shoulders.

We got back in the van and drove out of town. Halfway to the freeway a bell rang from back in the direction of the town. I listened for a moment and then said, "You know, Leonard, people tell themselves and other folks all sorts of things. I suppose that's what having faith is all about ... you just have to believe."

Leonard nodded, then looked over at me, "Yeah, maybe someone told them that it was ... Bliss."

We got back on the interstate and continued to head east toward Gillette. It was now after seven and the sun was starting to get low in the sky. We had about an hour to Gillette and close to two to Devil's Tower. Leonard was hunched over the steering wheel, more leaning on it than gripping it.

"Tell me this, Carl ..."

"Tell you what?"

"I want you to be honest with me now, but please be gentle." He sounded like a suspicious lover.

"Yeah?"

"I can take it, so don't lie to me, I'll know if you are ... I need to know the truth."

"What? – Just fucking say what you're going to fucking say." I was growing inpatient with him.

I hated this game in real life, and I was getting moderately bugged by it now, even though I knew he was teasing. Leonard continued, "Now don't act like that. I think that if you're honest it will make us closer, even if I don't like the truth."

"Oh, for God's sake, would you just ask me?"

"No, forget it ... if you're going to act like that about it."

"Oh, Jesus, Leonard ..."

I stopped myself and changed my tone, "Okay, okay ... Please ask me what you were going to ask me."

"Thank you Carl, that was much nicer ... but I don't think that you're sincere." I felt my blood pressure rising. I kept a lid on it, though, and stayed syrupy.

"No, really I am ... I want to know. Your feelings are important to me," I was pleading now – I hated this part, even if we were kidding around.

"Really?"

"Yes Leonard, really."

"Well okay ... here it goes ... we aren't going to make it to Devil's Tower today, are we?" He smiled, he knew what was coming.

I looked straight at him and unleashed, "No you little weevil-faced turd, we are not going to fucking make it to Devil's fucking Tower today!"

"Oh Carl, thank you ... I knew you'd be gentle with me... you are so sensitive." We both laughed like crazy.

Purgatory

We rolled into Gillette at eight-fifteen. It wasn't much to look at. It was nothing more than a crappy little coal-mining town in the middle of the prairie. Everything looked dirty and harsh. True to the industry that kept the city alive, a fine layer of coal dust covered everything. There were a couple of older, more classic-looking stone buildings at the center of the town that looked like they had been built a hundred years ago. Aside from them, most of the rest of the architecture was post-modern strip mall. Surrounding the low hills around the city were the residential neighborhoods - if you can call rows and rows of singlewide mobile homes laid out on a grid of blacktop streets neighborhoods.

"What an utter shit hole," Leonard said in disgust.

"Yeah, I wouldn't really call this a vacation destination..."

My words were drowned out by a '72 Ford F250 that roared by - apparently mufflers were optional in this city. Across the rear window there was a confederate flag, and on the bumper a sticker that warned prophetically, "South's Gonna Rise Again." Inside was a pair of whooping cowboy coal miners who were drunker than monkeys. As they rounded the corner at the end of the street, an empty half rack of Coors was ejected from the passenger window. It broke apart when it hit the concrete and cans skittered loudly across the road.

After they had passed around the corner, Leonard said sarcastically, "Whoo-weee, them's some deep-thinkin' good 'ol boys. Too bad they're gone, I wanted to par-tay with 'em tonight."

"Yeah, I bet we could sit around, read some poetry and maybe have a good cry."

Leonard laughed, but only briefly, at my comment, and then said vehemently, "What a couple of fucking assholes. I fucking hate people like that. And you know what?"

"What?"

"I bet this fucking town is full of idiots like that." Then he added, "Shit, Carl, do we have to stay here tonight?"

"No, we don't, but it's headed towards eight-thirty and it's still over an hour to Devil's Tower. I don't know about you, but I'm tired as hell. I vote for staying here tonight. We can make it as painless as possible. We'll just get a hotel room and blast out of here first thing in the morning. I saw a Super 8 out towards the edge of town."

"All right, but you know what, Carl?" He didn't give me a chance to answer him. "As long as we are in this shit hole, I cannot be held responsible for my actions."

I nodded, "Seems fair enough to me."

"Fair doesn't have anything to do with it, Carl."

We backtracked through town and without incident found the Super 8. It was exactly like every other Super 8 in the universe except that underneath the sign it said, "The Wrangler." I guess it was their way of letting their guests know, in case they'd forgotten, that they were still in Wyoming. In keeping with the motel's theme, attached to the motel was a restaurant and bar, "The Corral" and "The Round-up Room."

They had built the motel next to the only major tourist attraction in town, the Campbell County Rockpile Museum. It was a gigantic two hundred and fifty foot tall by quarter-mile square mound of mine tailings. I found out later from a pamphlet that I got in the motel room that it was a tribute to Gillette's ("The Powerhouse of the Nation") coal mining industry. The museum was nothing more than a self-guided tour of everything that you ever wanted to know about coal mining, which for me wasn't much. Also included was a memorial wall that listed on little brass plaques everyone in

Gillette who had been killed in various mining accidents. It was a big wall.

Leonard parked the van in front of the motel lobby. We grabbed our stuff for the evening from in back and went to get a room. When Leonard passed the rat on the antenna, he rubbed it on the nose with his finger and said, "Goodnight Mr. Rat, protect the van."

"How can you touch that thing, Leonard?"

"Easy, man – it's just like rubbing the belly of a Buddha. Mr. Rat gives you luck." He smiled.

"Yeah, whatever ..."

"Oh, you just wait and see, my friend. I'll bet you a beer that the van is still right here where we left it tomorrow morning."

"Yeah, but that doesn't have anything to do with Mr. Rat."

"Don't be too sure, Carl. If I were going to steal a van, it sure wouldn't be one with a dead rat hanging from the antenna."

"Good point, Leonard ... no bet."

As soon as we walked into the motel lobby I felt relieved. Even if it was Gillette, it was civilization – sort of. I wanted a hot shower, a cold beer, and a real bed. I also wanted to call Althea.

Behind the front desk there was a rodent-like fellow with slicked back hair. In front of him on the counter there was a sign that identified him as Daryl. His beady eyes followed us we approached the front desk.

"Good evening, Daryl," Leonard said formally, "Are you by chance the concierge for this establishment?"

Daryl was obviously confused by the question and replied, "No, I'm a Baptist, why?"

Leonard rephrased the question for him, "Are you the desk guy?"

Given a question that he could understand, Daryl perked up slightly, "Yes I am, how can I help you?" He smiled. His crooked teeth looked like he had used roofing tar as a substitute for chewing gum for most of his life. I winced a little.

"We're after a room for the night."

"Well, I can sure help you out with that, we got plenty... how about a double for twenty-nine dollars? Got two beds and cable."

Leonard smiled back at him politely and said, "That sounds good, but we were after something, well ... a bit more special. Do you have a honeymoon suite?" Daryl looked at us slack-jawed like he didn't want to understand the question.

Leonard let him twist for a few moments then saved him. "Hey man, I'm just kidding, the twenty-nine dollar double sounds great." Daryl looked relieved, yet still a little homophobically suspicious. He wanted us to go away.

Quickly he said, "Yes, sir," and handed me some paperwork to fill out while he got the keys to the room. "You're in room 212. The restaurant serves dinner 'til eleven and the bar's open 'til two."

"Sounds good. Thanks for your help." I said as I took the keys from him.

I felt him watch us as we walked down the hall to our room. I turned to Leonard, "Jesus, was that comment about the honeymoon suite really necessary? We're in Gillette, Wyoming, for God's sake."

"Yes Carl, I believe it was. Remember what I told you?"

"What's that?"

"As long as we're in this shit hole, I'm not responsible for my actions." And with that he reached around behind me and patted my ass.

When we got to the room we flipped for who got first shot at the shower. Leonard won. While I waited for my turn, I laid on the bed surfing through the fifty-seven channels of idiocy on the TV. I finally settled on a black and white movie called "Forbidden Planet." I had seen it before. It was a science fiction adaptation of Shakespeare's play, "The Tempest." It was weird, but I thought it was good.

The movie went through three commercial interruptions and was headed for a fourth when Leonard finally decided to get out of the shower. He had been in there so long that when he came out I was surprised to see that he wasn't pruned beyond recognition.

"Gee, don't you want to take a little more time there, buddy? I feel like you sort of rushed your shower."

"Hey, I was just trying to wash the filth of Gillette off of me."

"Good luck."

"Yeah, well, it didn't work."

"Oh ... I'm sorry to hear that."

"Screw you, Carl ... what the hell are you watching?"

"It's called 'Forbidden Planet.' It's good."

"Oh, I'm sure it is, Carl ..." Leonard said, then added, "The shower's all yours."

"Thanks, is there any hot water left?"

"No there isn't, I made sure that I used it all up."

"Good ... cuz you know, Leonard, rugged guys like me like my women hot and my showers cold." I started laughing. Leonard rolled his eyes.

The shower not only felt good, but I think that I probably needed it. It had been days since the last one and, although I couldn't smell myself, I was sure that I was getting a little ripe. When I got out, Leonard had taken the liberty of changing the channels. He was watching a rerun of "I Dream of Jeannie."

"Hey, why did you change the channel?"

"Because the movie that you were watching was stupid, Carl."

"Oh, and 'I Dream of Jeannie' isn't?"

"Oh, sure it is, but shit, who cares? You get to see Barbara Eden run around in that harem outfit."

"Come on, man, turn that off and let's go down to the restaurant and get some dinner. I'm starving." Leonard reluctantly switched off the TV and we left.

Inside, The Corral Restaurant was just what I thought it would be ... and more. The theme was - not surprisingly - Western. The booths had facades of fakey-looking fence rails, and the walls were covered with made-to-look-old pictures and posters depicting scenes out of the Old West. There were other knick-knacks screwed into the walls as well: a six gun, some spurs, an old saddle, a bridle and bit, some rusty barbed wire, and some other hardware that I couldn't identify. The place smelled like cooked meat, French fries, and cigarette smoke.

A tough-looking fire hydrant of a woman who looked like she could hold her own in a rodeo ring approached us, "Table for two?"

"Yeah, thanks."

"Come with me." She was medium-polite, but not particularly friendly. She sat us down at a table and handed us a couple of menus. "You want to hear the specials for this evening?"

"Yeah ..."

"We have an eighteen ounce porterhouse steak that comes with fries and a salad – that's thirteen ninety-five. We have prime rib that comes with baked potato and salad for twelve ninety-five. We have liver and onions, also with fries and a salad – that's ten ninety-five. We have ..." She rattled on through an extensive list of meat-centered dishes. When she was done, I figured that she had probably listed everything that was edible on a cow – and some parts that maybe weren't. "Name's Connie – I'll give you a few minutes ..."

"Thanks." She nodded, forced a slight smile and walked away.

"Leonard?"

"Yeah?"

"You know where we are?"

"Where, Carl?"

I leaned across the table and said in a lowered voice, "We are in vegetarian hell."

Leonard looked from side to side as if to make sure no one was listening. "Shhhhh ... yes, we are, Carl, now keep it down, we don't want to let anyone find out that we're cows in disguise working for the resistance."

I nodded, "Roger."

Leonard lowed, folded up the menu and slid it onto the table. I lit a cigarette, "So what are ya going to have?"

Leonard reached over to the pack on the table and took a cigarette out of for himself. As always, he broke off the filter, then said, "I think I'll have the bacon and cheese burger ... that way I won't blow my cover. You?"

"Good plan, I was going to have the double cheeseburger."

As soon as we both put down our menus, Connie returned and we ordered up. The food didn't take long and when it arrived it was huge. Both of us were starving, and we ate voraciously without much conversation.

Leonard finished his Coke, loudly sucking air through the straw. He reclined in the booth, and to emphasize the fact that he was done, let out a huge belch. It was loud enough that a couple three seats down looked over the wall of their booth at us in disgust. Leonard waved and called down to them apologetically, "Sorry, my fault ... I'm just making room for dessert."

The woman sniffed and gave him an even dirtier look.

"Hmm, I guess she didn't accept my apology."

"I guess not, too sensitive," I let out a belch of my own, yet not nearly as loud as Leonard's was.

Connie returned, cleared our plates, and asked unconvincingly, "How was everything?"

"Fine, good burgers."

"You boys interested in dessert?"

"No, ma'am, I'm full as a tick," Leonard answered.

She was not even remotely amused by the tick comment. She stared at him for a few seconds with a peeved expression on her face, then turned to me, "How about you?"

"No thanks, I'm fine too."

She quickly added up our bill and slapped it on the table. "You can pay here or up front." She was gone before I could thank her.

"She was about as friendly as a wet weasel in a gunny sack," I said.

"Yeah, clearly no appreciation for intellectual humor. Do we really have to tip her?"

"I think so, unless you want to get your arm chewed from the elbow down."

Leonard thought over the options aloud, "Hmm, mutilated arm ... tip ... mutilated arm ... tip..." Finally he pulled out his wallet, flipped over the tab, and said, "I think I'll go with the tip this time."

I began to reach for my wallet as well. "What do we owe 'em?"

"Forget it, this one's on me. Tell you what, buy me a beer." He put fifteen dollars on the table.

"Done – thanks, Leonard."

On the way out of the restaurant and over to the bar I said to Leonard, "I'll meet you in there. I'm going to give Althea a call."

He raised an eyebrow in understanding, "Good plan, my friend. It's been a few days and a couple of states since you've talked to her." I nodded and smiled uncomfortably. Although I had done exactly nothing wrong, and realistically hadn't really had the time to call, I had an uneasy guilt. I headed back to the motel room, while Leonard headed into the bar.

I could hear the phone ringing on the other end of the line, three, four, five ... With each successive ring, I felt farther away. On the seventh ring, I figured she wasn't home and I was just taking the receiver away from my ear to hang up when the line clicked and Althea answered.

"Hello?"

"Hey Althea ..." There was a long, uncomfortable pause. When she didn't answer me, I thought for a second that I had lost the connection. "Hey, are you there?"

There was more silence. I was just about to ask again when she said coldly, "Hi, Carl." She was pissed – big pissed. I instinctively decided to go down the "I'll pretend that nothing's wrong" route and see where it would take me.

"Hey Althea, how are ya doing?" Silence.

I said cheerfully, "I miss you like crazy." There was more silence. Evidently that route was not a through street.

"Where are you, Carl?" The tone in her voice told me that she was going to be extra double-pissed when I informed her that I was in eastern Wyoming – nearly three states away from when I last called her. I thought for a second about concocting some story about how we just escaped from the compound of a group of outlaw biker white supremacists after being abducted on a lonely back road in Idaho. I figured it was a weak fantastical story that she'd see right through, and I would only make things worse by lying. I told her the truth and braced myself.

"Um ... we're at a Super 8 out here in Gillette, Wyoming. It's kind of in the middle of Wyoming." I should have left the "middle" part out.

She exploded, "Kind of in the middle?! You bastard, how bad do you think my fucking geography is? You're nearly in fucking South Dakota!" I pulled the phone away from my ear a little. "Where have you been? What have you two been doing? Goddamn it, you said you were going to call ... why haven't you called me!" Her anger sounded like it was bouncing back and forth between a mixture of genuine hurt and indignant rage. Althea had a deep capacity for passionate jealousy and I was witnessing it.

I felt disoriented and stumbled for words, an explanation, "Well ... um, we went to Idaho to this Craters of the Moon place, and then we went to Yellowstone ... Yellowstone was really cool." I tried to sound casual. "We're heading to Devil's Tower tomorrow. Oh yeah, and it snowed in Yellowstone ..." My sketchy and disjointed story made me sound guilty even to me, but for what I don't know. Then, just for a millisecond I thought about Melody the blue Dart woman. Leonard was right. I felt like shit. I hoped that Althea wasn't telepathic. I tried a different tack.

"Look, Althea, I'm really sorry that I didn't call you. I've been thinking about you all the time, but I just haven't been anywhere near a phone." Again there was a pause.

"I thought that you were going to be at Devil's Tower a couple of days ago." She was accusatory, but she sounded like she was calming down ... some, but not much.

"We were, but we got side-tracked."

"By what?" She said tersely. Here was the drill – I hoped that I answered well. I tried to pawn some of the responsibility off.

"Well, we started to run behind schedule, so Leonard threw all the plans out the window. After that, we sort of started to wing it."

"And how did you end up in Yellowstone?"

"That was the 'wing it' part. It was Leonard's idea," I lied.

"Hmmm ..." She was considering the credibility of my explanation. After a couple of moments she said, "Well, I still think that you could have at least called me to let me know where the hell you were. I mean, don't they have telephones in Yellowstone?" She wasn't letting go of it and I was beginning to get a little frustrated myself.

"Shit! - I told you, Althea ... it snowed," I said shortly. The line went quiet again. I wasn't sure which way it was going to go. But now I was getting pissed too. "Well?" I said.

Finally she said in a calmer voice, "I'm just asking, Carl. I was really just worried about you, that's all. I thought that something might have happened to you or something."

While she was talking, I thought to myself, "I've heard all of this before. I wonder how much of it is concern and how much of it is suspicion." I decided not to share my thoughts with her and attempted to normalize the conversation, "Yeah ... I understand ... so how have you been?"

"Pretty good ... I miss you, Carl." She sounded a little apologetic.

"I miss you too, Althea," I tried to sound apologetic too.

"I've just been painting and working ... you know, the same stuff, nothing too special ..." She trailed off, paused, then said tenderly, "I love you Carl. I'm sorry."

"I know you do – I love you too, Althea."

We talked for another ten minutes, but the way that our conversation had started out left the rest of it feeling awkward. We tried to act like everything was normal. It didn't work. We both recognized it, yet neither one of us wanted to hang up. I missed her, and I knew that she missed me, but I didn't want this. Finally I decided that it wasn't going to get any better, and it was best to go.

"I've got to get back to Leonard. I left him in the restaurant," I lied again. I figured that telling her that all I wanted to do was go and have a stiff drink or three wasn't a good idea.

"I understand, Carl," she said, like she really meant it. "You promise me that you'll call again soon?"

"I promise, Althea ... really. I'll call you again in a day or two – Rama, Rama." I knew that that would make her feel a little bit better. I also knew that in a couple of days, no matter where we were, I would find a phone. I wanted to make this right.

"I love you, Carl."

"I love you too, Althea ... Goodbye."

Hanging up the phone, I felt empty and distant. It had not been what I had wanted or expected. I felt even stranger because the word "goodbye" had come out of my mouth. I tried intentionally to never use the word because I thought that it sounded so final and sad. I wondered why I had said it now.

On the way back to the bar, I thought about our conversation some more. I wondered if her outbursts of jealous anger were something that she would outgrow. In the beginning it had been flattering. But as time had gone on they had increased in frequency and I was starting to feel suffocated. I knew that it wasn't something that I was willing to live with forever. Still, I loved Althea like mad.

By the time I arrived at the bar Leonard was at full speed, and was finishing his second beer-and-shot-of-bourbon combination.

"Oh, hi Carl, how nice of you to join me. I was beginning to think that you had jumped in the van and had started driving back to Mount Vernon."

"Man, don't you start in on me now." In spite of his pre-inebriated state, Leonard could tell that my telephone conversation with Althea had not gone well.

He got serious, and said sincerely, "Sorry, buddy. Let's get a cure and talk about it." He motioned for the barmaid who wandered over from the far end of the bar in slow motion.

She was at least eighty years old if she was a day. Her immaculate jet-black hair seemed unlikely for a woman of her age - particularly a woman who had been half-mummified from years of working in an alcohol and cigarette-smoke-permeated environment.

When she finally arrived, she stood in front of us and said nothing, probably saving what precious little life energy she had left in her.

"Could I have another round please, and the same for my friend here." Wordlessly, she turned around and shuffled away, presumably to get our order. I hoped she lived long enough to get back. I wanted a beer badly.

"So, talk to me, Carl ... what happened between you and Althea?"

"Oh, shit, I don't know if it's even worth talking about..."

Leonard stared at me as if to say, "And?"

I thought about it for a moment. Leonard was a good friend and he wasn't going to just let this go.

Finally I said, "Oh, you know how Althea is. She was pissed as hell that I hadn't called."

"Yeah, so? What's new? She's always getting pissed at you over shit like that." The barmaid returned with two beers and two bourbons. With a shaking hand she set them down in front of us. "Thanks," Leonard said. She nodded once slowly.

I took a drink from the shot of bourbon. I could feel the hot, smoky-tasting liquor make its way into my belly. It felt good. I followed it with a pull from the cold beer.

I continued, "I'm sick of it ... I'm sick of her always getting so fucking pissed off with me for fucking nothing. Man, I'm just hanging out with friends and stuff. I don't have to tell her every single little thing that I do. My God, she's suffocating me." I took another long drink from the beer then continued, "All I wanted to do was give her a call and have a nice conversation with her. We haven't talked for days and ... Jesus Christ, she acts like I'm always out looking for other women or something. It's total bullshit."

"Did she say that to you ... that stuff about other women?"

I was getting worked up. "No, she never comes right out and says it, but fuck, I know what she's driving at."

Leonard said quietly, "You two gotta have a real talk, man."

"About what? About how I'm not fucking other women?"

The alcohol was already loosening me up and as it did I raised my voice. Leonard took a drink from his beer and stared at me. His eyes were intense and serious. He didn't say anything for a while. The silence between us became uncomfortably long.

Then he said calmly, "You know, Carl, maybe she sees something in you to question."

"What? Question what?" I was medium defensive at the suggestion of any kind of responsibility on my part.

"Answer me this, Carl – do you love her?"

"Well yeah, I love her. I'm crazy about her."

"Really?" he said with a skeptical tone to his voice.

"Yeah, really, shit, you know that."

Leonard let my words fall into silence again. They were mine and he wasn't going to touch them. Then he hit me head on, hard and honestly. He raised his own voice, "Then why the fuck haven't you called her for days? And what the fuck was the deal back there at the gas station with the woman with the blue Dart? What, you think that Althea doesn't sense that shit like that goes on when she's not around? Man, she doesn't have to see it to know it. If you were really committed to her, shit like that wouldn't happen. Take some fucking responsibility. Yeah sure, she might be little sensitive about stuff, hell, nobody's perfect, but you're sure as hell not helping things any ... you're making her crazy, Carl."

At emotional times like this I could always count on Leonard for a direct and sincere opinion – and one that didn't necessarily agree with everything that I said. This was one of those times. I thought about what he had said, and took another drink of my beer. I came to the conclusion that, Leonard, as he often was, was right.

During my toxic conversation with Althea, my thoughts had turned to the woman with the blue Dart, and I knew, even without Leonard pointing it out to me, that it was wrong. I was not without sin. I took another couple of sips from my beer then I told Leonard just that. "You're right ... I don't want to lose her." He smiled, nodded his head and motioned the barmaid for another round.

I was so distracted when I first came into the bar that I hadn't really looked around at the surroundings. I scanned the lounge while waiting for the second round of drinks to arrive. The Round-up Room was done in exactly the same Western theme as the attached Corral restaurant. There were the same fakey-looking fence rails separating the booths, and the walls were similarly covered with made-to-look-old pictures – except that most of them in the bar depicted gunfights and other homicide-related events. There were also at least eight or nine "Wanted – Dead or Alive" posters up. I briefly wondered if they were actually recent pictures of real criminals that the local county sheriff had put up in the hopes that someone might tip him a lead.

They had added a few other homey touches as well. All around the walls of the room there were various game animals that had been stuffed and mounted. I guess back in the restaurant they figured that it was a bad idea to have critters staring down at folks eating steaks – it might adversely affect their appetites. There was an elk, two deer (one of which had shamefully small antlers), a moose, an antelope, three ducks, a pheasant, an owl, a prairie dog, and a jackrabbit that had been converted into a jackalope. Given the vast amounts of meat that they served in the restaurant, I wondered why they didn't put a cow head up there. I guess that they figured that cow wasn't really considered "game," but then again, I never thought a prairie dog was either.

"Man, check out all of these animals, Leonard ... I wonder if there is anything left alive out in the wild."

"There won't be if the hunters in this state have anything to do with it. Maybe we should bring in Mr. Rat and see if they'll put him up there with the rest of the critters." After two beers and two shots of bourbon, I thought that that was tremendously funny and started laughing so hard that I got tears in my eyes. Leonard laughed as well, but not nearly so hard. I think that he was actually serious about the comment.

When we finally recovered, I noticed that the other half dozen folks in the bar were staring at us. Apparently drinking was serious business around these parts. Two big bronco-busting guys a few barstools down from us continued to stare at us long after the rest of the folks in the bar went back to their conversations. I guess they didn't like the looks of us much. I didn't really care.

We kept on drinking and laughing in spite of whatever cultural norms we were shattering at the bar. I felt better. When we were halfway through our fourth round of drinks, though, the conversation turned a different direction.

Leonard got serious. He turned to me and said loudly, "You know what, Carl?"

"What, Leonard?"

"Wyoming sucks." I nodded a little in agreement.

"Wow, man, you really hate this state, don't you?"

"Yes I do, Carl – with a fucking passion."

In my current state of inebriation, I had forgotten about the close proximity of the two bronco-busting guys. They stopped their conversation and turned our direction. When I saw that they had heard us I prayed to myself, "Jesus God Mother of Mercy, don't take me now."

I thought that maybe I should warn Leonard, but before I could stop him from elaborating any more, he continued, "I hate this fucking state. It's filled with a bunch of backward-ass slack-jawed fuck-heads. Christ, they named everything in the state after a bunch of assholes - like they're proud of it."

I could see the bronco-busting pair behind Leonard begin to tighten up. Leonard kept going. I couldn't stop him.

"Shit ... Sheridan, Cody, Casper, Laramie, come on ... and the biggest asshole of them all – Custer. What would people think if we named a city Hitler, or Mussoliniville? Oh, or how about this one – Genocide ... oh that has a nice ring to it, doesn't it? – Genocide, Wyoming."

Leonard had raised his voice loud enough that everyone in the bar could hear him clearly. Leonard was, of course, right, and I completely agreed with him. Unfortunately, his choice of where to air his opinion was probably not the best. The pair began to get up off of their barstools.

"Fuck ... you know what it says on their license plates?" He didn't wait for me to answer. "'Wyoming – The Equality State. Oh yeah, that's a nice little dream ... equality if you're a white, carnivorous, pencil-lipped, fucking idiot." Finally Leonard had to take a breath and I used the opportunity to get in a couple of words of warning. The bronco boys were now headed our way.

"Ah, Leonard, cowpokes at twelve o'clock."

"Good, then I can say it to them. They probably could use some education."

Leonard turned and stood up off of his barstool to meet them. I did the same. I was going to back him up the whole way. I figured that it was probably going to get physical but I also figured that we were both drunk enough that it wouldn't be too painful.

The pair were large – at least six foot two and somewhere around two twenty. They had ruddy permanently sunburned complexions and crew cuts that looked like they had been done with sheep shears. I decided not to vocalize my observations on their haircuts, this being cattle country and all.

The slightly bigger of the two opened his mouth first, "I hear you boys don't like Wyoming," he said it slowly like he was throwing down a gauntlet.

I thought, "Here it comes, the beginning of our personal apocalypse." I felt myself suddenly fill with adrenaline. It was like I had drunk seventeen cups of coffee all at once. I wondered if my internal shaking was actually visible, but I didn't want to look down at my hands to check. Leonard, on the other hand, appeared steady, and didn't immediately say anything. He just looked at them. It made the situation even more tense.

I was just about to start to try to talk our way out of it when Leonard politely corrected him and said, "Oh no, you misunderstood me, I didn't say that I didn't like Wyoming – what I said was I don't like the *people* in Wyoming." He smiled. They were stunned. It was like both of them had been hit with a ball-peen hammer right between the eyes. Neither one of them could believe that Leonard wasn't even remotely threatened by them. While they were still stunned Leonard continued.

This time he raised his voice, "I also said that you name shit in this state pretty fucked-up names ... like Gillette ..." *Bang!* He slammed his hand so hard on the bar top that it sounded like a rifle shot. The pair reflexively jumped. Then Leonard took a step forward and screamed, "Hey! – I don't think that you are fucking listening to me, goddamn it!" The pair looked confused - this was not the way that this was supposed to go.

Leonard kept going, but now he was totally calm and pleasant, like he had flicked a switch in his head. He was smiling again, "... As I was saying ... Gillette ... you know what Gillette means in French?" They stared at him and waited for the answer. Leonard switched again. *Bang!* He hit the bar top, and yelled, "I asked you a fucking question - answer me, goddamn it! This is going to be on the test ... do you know what Gillette means in French?!" He enunciated every word. The pair looked uneasy. Leonard waited. The bar was silent.

After a few moments, Leonard took another step forward. His eyes were intense and wild. The pair stepped back. Then Leonard changed again. He raised his eyebrows and said calmly, quietly, and with an intellectual tone, "The linguistic background of Gillette is very interesting. It comes from two words – 'gill,' meaning 'smooth' and 'ette,' meaning ass ..." He paused and smiled pleasantly, "... so Gillette means 'Smooth Ass' in French." He said the last part with a clenched jaw – like it pissed him off.

The pair was at a total loss of how to respond. They had expected to beat us to a pulp and were instead confronted with a raving maniac. I'm sure that only a few seconds passed, but they felt like minutes. I wasn't entirely sure which way things were going to go.

Finally the smaller of the pair said, "Come on, Bud, let's get the hell out of here ... this guy is crazy." The bigger guy nodded, and looked relieved.

Anyone who has ever been in a fight knows that the guy that you want to stay away from, no matter how tough you are, is the crazy guy. Crazy guys are unpredictable. Unpredictable is dangerous. Leonard was both.

The smaller guy pulled out his wallet and put a ten and a five on the bar and said, "This ought to cover it, Myrtle." She didn't say anything. She didn't look particularly rattled either. Then, the bronco boys made their way towards the door slowly. Neither one of them took their eyes off of us.

It wasn't until after they were gone, and that I picked up my bourbon to calm myself, that I realized that I was shaking like crazy. I spilled a fair amount of the liquid trying to get the glass to my mouth. Leonard on the other hand sat back down calmly, took a drink of his beer and said, "Well, that was an interesting little exchange now, wasn't it?"

"Ah ... yeah, Leonard, I suppose you could call it that ... um, maybe we should get going here."

Leonard turned, looked at me and said earnestly, "Why?" I looked around the bar. Everyone had gone back to the business of drinking like nothing out of the ordinary had happened. With the bronco boys now gone, I couldn't think of a good reason to leave. No one in their right mind was going to fuck with us now, and I sure wanted another drink.

I motioned the barmaid, and she brought us one more round. While we were drinking I said to Leonard, "Man, that was great ... I thought that those guys were going to kill us. How did you know that they were going to back down like that?"

"They were, and I didn't. When somebody pushes you, though, Carl, push them back – push them back hard." I nodded.

Then I said, "I do have a question for you, though."

"What's that, Carl?"

"Does Gillette really mean 'smooth ass' in French?" Leonard looked at me like he pretended that I was kidding with the question.

Then he leaned over to me and said in a lowered voice, "No, Carl, but I bet within a week everyone in this state will think that it does." We both laughed like crazy.

We finished our drinks, paid the tab and headed back to the motel room. By the time we got back to our room my adrenaline rush was completely gone and I was beginning to seriously feel the effects of the vast quantities of alcohol that I had consumed in the bar. The mysterious and complex task of walking became something that I actually had to think about. Apparently Leonard was having the same problem. When we got to our room he fumbled with the lock – initially trying to open the motel room door with his own house key.

Giggling stupidly, we finally managed to break the not-so-secret code of our room door. When we got in, I immediately headed for bed. Not only was I tremendously drunk, I was exhausted.

Leonard, while saying "shit," repeatedly, chased the TV remote around like it was a live squid after he knocked it to the floor. When he finally got a hold of the slippery little invertebrate he turned on the TV. "Lost in Space" was on.

"Perfect," said Leonard.

As I lay on the bed, the TV faded in and out of focus and I had a difficult time following the plot. "Danger, Will Robinson ... Danger ..." For some reason Robbie the Robot's mechanical words sounded appropriately prophetic and I started to laugh uncontrollably.

"What the fuck is so funny?" Leonard said, his articulation sloppy.

I got up from the bed and with arms flailing said in an automaton-like voice, "Danger, Dr. Smith ... Danger ..." I fell back to the bed laughing. Leonard started laughing too, but I think it was more at me than with me.

I woke up at around three AM to the TV blaring. I didn't remember falling asleep ... or more appropriately, passing out. Since the TV was still on, I figured that Leonard must have passed out too.

On the screen, there was a short fat white guy in a bad blue leisure suit slapping people on the forehead and yelling, "Heal!" When I finally focused my eyes, I recognized him as the preacher/faith healer, Earnest Angley. He was a personal favorite of both Althea and I – we found him extremely entertaining and occasionally late at night would tune in to his show.

At three AM, though, and on the beginning of a hangover, I found him annoying. I got up, and in the middle of another miracle, "Heal! – Evil spirits ..." switched the TV off and went back to bed. With the background noise of the TV gone I could hear that Leonard was snoring the big snore. I immediately fell back asleep.

I woke up to the phone ringing. I looked at my watch - it was exactly ten o'clock. I turned over, grunted, and stuck my head under my pillow and tried to tune out the annoying ringing, figuring that it would eventually go away. It didn't.

I pulled my head out from under the pillow and said groggily, "Hey Leonard, could you get the phone?"

Leonard mumbled something unintelligible then slowly hoisted himself up on his elbows, looked at me sleepily, said, "Yes..." then fell back down face up on the bed. The phone continued to ring.

"Oh, shit, forget it ... I'll fucking get it."

It was on probably the twentieth or so ring when I answered, "Yeah?"

I didn't even try to hide the fact that I was annoyed. It was Daryl from the front desk: "Checkout is at eleven." It was more of a statement than an informative request. He hung up before I had a chance to answer.

"Who the fuck was it?"

"It was the rodent at the front desk, Daryl ... he says that checkout is at eleven."

"What time is it now?" Leonard groaned.

"It's four minutes after ten." He mumbled something else and rolled over.

"I'm going to take a shower." Leonard mumbled something again that sounded like a "yeah."

I hopped in the shower. As I stood under the water, I was actually surprised at how well I felt ... not just well, but actually good, really good. It was curious, but from what I could tell, I didn't have any traces of a hangover whatsoever. And, from what I could tell, I wasn't still drunk either.

I finished up my shower, shaved, and put on fresh clothes. When I came out of the bathroom I found that Leonard had fallen back asleep.

"Hey Leonard." He moved a little, but didn't appear to fully wake up. I said it louder, "Hey, Sleeping Beauty, wake up! It's ten thirty and if you want to get a shower before we leave you better get up." The last part about the shower seemed to get him. He raised himself off of the bed.

"Oh man ..." At first he appeared to be a little worse for the wear than I was, which made no sense to me because the night before we had matched each other drink for drink.

He got up, stretched, and yawned.

"How ya feelin' there partner?"

He blinked the sleep out of his eyes and said with puzzlement in his voice, like he wasn't expecting it, "Fine ... I feel just fine."

"I'll tell you what, I'll go up to the desk and take care of the room while you take a shower."

"Yeah, good idea." He still sounded like he didn't believe that he wasn't horrendously hung over.

Daryl the rodent peered over the front desk as I approached.

"Hi," I said.

"Hello," Daryl answered flatly.

"Hey, thanks for the wake-up call ... whew, we really tied one on over in the Round-up Room last night. Who knows when we would have woken up."

Daryl broke eye contact with me, shuffled some papers on the desk, and said, "I heard."

I thought to myself, "I bet you did."

"So, my buddy is just finishing up a shower and we should be out of here in a few minutes. What do I owe you?"

We had eye contact again. Daryl got out the papers for the room, paused and then said seriously, "Did you break anything?"

I pretended to think about it for a minute and then said, "No, but we sure thought about it." Daryl heard my comment, but pretended to hear nothing more than "No."

"That'll be thirty three fifteen, that includes tax." I reached into my wallet and got out a pair of twenties and handed them to him.

"Here you go."

He handed my change back to me without saying a word.

"Well, thanks again for your hospitality," I smiled. He knew that I didn't mean a word of it. He nodded once, and didn't smile back.

I went back to the room to get Leonard, and we made our way out to the parking lot and to the van. As soon as we exited the motel, Leonard pointed out that Mr. Rat was still hanging faithfully from the antenna, and that the van was in fact untouched.

"What did I tell you, Carl?"

"Yeah, yeah, Leonard, so you were right ... is that what you want?"

"Yes it is, Carl, I need to hear things like that, it helps my fragile self-esteem." I unlocked the driver's door and got in.

"You know what, Leonard?"

"What's that, Carl?" I started the van and gunned it a couple of times. The roar echoed across the parking lot.

"I don't think that anyone in that motel, restaurant, or bar was particularly sad to see us go."

"Carl, this is just one of the many things I like about you ... sometimes you are so perceptive."

The Promised Land

We headed out on Interstate 90 toward Devil's Tower. By the map, it was less than sixty miles away. We would be there in less than an hour. At the town of Moorcroft we left the freeway and headed north on Highway 24. Twenty-five more miles to go. It was just before noon.

Leonard pulled out the pipe and filled it to the brim with Wiccan weed. "Isn't it a little early for that, Leonard?"

"No, it is not ... it's never too early for that. Besides, if you're trying to stick to etiquette it's past noon."

I looked again at my watch, "No it's not, it's five to twelve."

"Carl, we passed a time zone back in Idaho, it's one in the afternoon."

All of a sudden a light bulb came on. "Ohhhh ... that's why Daryl called us up and was all pissy and shit ... it wasn't ten, it was really eleven."

Leonard fired up the weed, took a drag, and said breathlessly as he exhaled, "Duh." He then steered the van from the passenger's seat while I took the pipe and Zippo and took a drag myself.

"Yeah, this is supposed to be a pretty cool place, Carl, really spiritual."

I nodded, my eyes tearing from trying not to cough. After a few seconds I couldn't hold the smoke any longer and let it out. I caught my breath. "Yeah, that's what I hear. We should be there pretty soon." Leonard took the pipe and lighter from me and I resumed driving. "You know, we should probably stop and get a few supplies."

Leonard, who was in the middle of another drag and couldn't talk, nodded.

"Why don't you get out the map and see if there's any place we can stop before we get there."

Leonard nodded again. He was still holding his breath. He grabbed the map off of the floor and let his breath out with a whoosh. "Hmm, it looks like there is one town on the way. It should be coming up here any time." He threw the map back on the floor and went back to the pipe and the Wiccan weed.

We drove on for another five minutes through the beautiful rolling hills and spotty pine forests leading up to Devil's Tower before we came up over a rise to the town of Carlile. From what I could tell, Carlile wasn't really a town at all. It was nothing more than a general store and a singlewide trailer – presumably the residence of whoever ran the store. When we pulled into the gravel parking lot, which was just off of the highway, I noticed a sign in the window of the store that said "US Post Office." I figured that was probably what gave the place its "town" status.

There was only one other car in the lot, a half-rusted dirty brown Ford van. It had a bumper sticker on the back that said, "Fat People are Harder to Kidnap." I pointed it out to Leonard.

"Hey, check out the bumper sticker ..." I was already laughing.

Leonard added, "Yeah, I bet the guy who drives that thing is really underfed." Just as Leonard said it, the door of the store opened up and a fantastically obese couple came out carrying two huge bags of groceries. The man must have weighed close to four hundred and fifty pounds, but he looked comfortable with it. He had a spotty, ratty-looking beard and was chewing on an unlit stub of a cigar. His wife, who was similarly huge, gnawed on a submarine sandwich that was loaded with the works.

By now we were out of our own van. The woman, who was mid-bite in her sandwich, walked past the front of our vehicle and within inches of Mr. Rat. She noticed him and with a tremendously screwed-up look on her face remarked, through a mouthful of food, "My God – that is disgusting!"

As she said it, I could see the half-eaten sandwich masticate around in her mouth. It was revolting. Leonard, who had composed himself after his witty comment, looked at her and said understandingly, "Yes it is, ma'am, it certainly is ... but we're too afraid to touch it to get it off of there."

She knew he was full of shit. She sniffed, took another bite of her sandwich, belched, and got in their van. While they drove out of the lot, Leonard turned to me and said, "Don't you think that it's just a little more than ironic that a repulsively obese human being like that calls a petrified rat disgusting?"

I was laughing like crazy, but I managed to get out a "Yes ..."

After purchasing supplies, we were back on the road. The woman behind the counter at the store said that we only had another few miles to go. I let Leonard drive. Back at the store I had splurged and bought a four-inch ceramic jackalope with a magnetic base. I wanted to find an appropriate place for it on the van's dashboard.

"What the fuck is the deal with those things?" Leonard said.

"Hell, I don't know ... I think that they're funny as shit, though."

"Yeah, well, I think that they're weird as hell. They're probably the creation of some psychotic taxidermist who got stuck inside all winter and then started gluing spare animal parts together."

"Yes ... and your point is?"

Leonard didn't answer me.

I moved the jackalope around and finally settled on a spot next to a similar-sized statue of Mary. She looked his direction with a serious expression on her face. I thought to myself, "All God's creatures." I smiled and sniffed a chuckle.

"What, Carl?"

"Oh ... nothing."

I was still admiring my jackalope when Leonard said, "Hey, there it is, Carl ... we're here."

I looked up, and ahead a couple of miles or so a massive pillar of rock rose out of the rolling hills. It must have been seven or eight hundred feet tall. Completely in awe, I could think of nothing more profound to say than, "Man ... that is totally cool."

Leonard was affected the same way by it and simply said, "No shit." Neither one of us said another word until we arrived at the park's entrance station.

Leonard pulled up next to the ranger's booth. A cheerful, attractive, and wholesome-looking woman in an obligatory Forest Service green uniform greeted us. "Good afternoon."

"Hi," we both said in unison. It sounded high to me. I wondered if she could tell.

"Are you here to camp, or just to visit for the day?"

Leonard handled it. He looked straight at her and said, "Ah, we're going to be spending the night." It was a harmless and accurate answer, but for some reason she blushed a little when he said it. She must have been thinking about something else.

She cleared her throat and said, "Yeah ... um, that will be six dollars and fifty cents." Leonard took out a ten and handed it to her. She made change and handed it back to him along with some literature and a map of the area. "Here you are. You shouldn't have any trouble finding a place to camp, the campground is nearly empty." She leaned out the window slightly and pointed, "Just follow this road for about a quarter of a mile. There will be a sign marking another road to the campground." She looked back at Leonard, gave him a huge smile and said, "Have a nice stay."

Leonard smiled back, "Thanks, we will."

The ranger was right, when we got to the campground it was nearly empty. I only saw two other campers. We drove around the circular drive a couple of times to scope for the best spot. We settled on one that was on the very south corner, about a hundred yards from the Belle Fourche River.

We pulled in, parked, and got out. It was a beautiful day, maybe seventy-five or eighty degrees with a slight wind. I could hear a few birds and the gently flowing river nearby. It was totally serene.

As we unpacked the van, I couldn't help but keep looking back at the monolith that spectacularly rose up out of the earth just a half mile away. There certainly was something spiritual about all of it.

While we set up the tent I said pensively to Leonard, "I wonder why they called it Devil's Tower ..." I stopped what I was doing and looked up at it, "Man, it's nothing but beautiful."

Leonard was looking at it too, "Yeah, I know what you're saying, Carl ... I can't answer that."

We finished with the tent and got the stove and lantern set up. I looked around, "Hey, no sign of Dieter and Marta."

"No, and I bet we aren't going to see them here either."

"Yeah, they're never going to come to this place just because of its name."

"Yeah, what a shame ... I think that they really would like it."

"Yeah, I think they would too. You know what else, Leonard? I know it sounds weird, but I sort of miss them."

Leonard paused. "Yeah, I know what you mean. They're a pretty goofy pair, but they sort of grow on you."

"Yeah ... they sure do."

After we got done setting up camp, I rummaged around in the cooler and found a Coke. "You want one?" I said to Leonard.

"Yeah, a Coke sounds good ... thanks." I handed him one and joined him at the table. Both of us sat there wordlessly for a while staring at our surroundings and taking it all in. I felt totally at peace.

"So, you still think that Wyoming sucks?"

"I never thought that Wyoming sucked, Carl ... I just thought that the people in Gillette sucked." I nodded.

"So, maybe we should take off and hike around here a bit ... we have a good chunk of the afternoon."

"In a few minutes, Carl. This is great just sitting here."

While we sat there I picked up the literature and the map of the area that the ranger had given us and started reading. Some of the history was actually pretty interesting.

"Hey, Leonard."

"Yeah?"

"It says here that some of the Native American tribes around here believe that the tower is sacred ground. One Native American name for it is 'Bear Lodge' ... maybe that explains some of this spiritual feeling that we're both picking up on ... what do ya think?"

"Well I'll tell you what I think ... I think that 'Bear Lodge' sounds a hell of a lot better than Devil's Tower. The rest of all that spiritual stuff ... hell, I don't know ... I'm not from around here."

The Oracle

For the next hour and a half, we lay out on the grass and napped off and on while taking in the sun and surroundings. As the afternoon wore on and the sun reached its peak, it got hotter. Lazily, Leonard said, "I'm frying out here, how about you?"

"Yeah, I am too." I was bathed in a pool of sweat, and I could feel a sunburn coming on. It felt good.

"What do you say about going and stretching our legs here ... I think that I'm ready for that hike."

I sat up, maybe too quickly – the heat made me light-headed. "I'm with you, Leonard, I think that we ought to get out of this sun." The light-headedness passed, and I went over to get another Coke from the cooler. "Want another one of these?"

Leonard, who was over in the van digging around for something, hollered back, "Yeah ..." When he came back I handed him the Coke.

"What the hell were you looking for?"

"These." Leonard held up the bag of mushrooms that the Wiccans had given us. "You know, you have to be in the right frame of mind for this sort of thing. This place has good energy. Good energy makes for a good trip."

Leonard was so right. I had only taken mushrooms a couple of times, but I knew that the experiences could be vastly different. So much of the journey depended on where you were at, who you were with, and what you were doing. With the good vibes that we both picked up on around here, and the good company, I predicted that the experience would be no less than great.

"I almost forgot that we had those on board. Good call, Leonard."

We dumped the mushroom out on a plate to count out how many we had – thirty. Figuring out dosage was a tricky thing with something organic like mushrooms. You had to know not only what kind they were, but how potent they were as well. We knew neither.

After a little discussion, we surmised that they were probably similar in strength to the weed that the Wiccans had given us – moderate. Still, we had no idea what kind they were. We eventually settled on eleven apiece. Ten somehow just seemed like too few, but eating all of them might send us into outer space. Now our only challenge was how to actually eat them. Their flavor didn't appeal to either one of us - they tasted like dirt. Leonard suggested that we make a tea out of them, but it was far too hot out for that. Since I didn't want to swallow them whole, I instead tried chewing them a couple of times and then washing them down with the Coke to try to mask the flavor. It didn't work. I still felt like I was eating dirt.

"My God, these things taste terrible."

Leonard swallowed hard on his eighth mushroom and took another drink of Coke. "Focus on the goal, Carl, focus ... just get 'em down." He popped another one in his mouth, chewed twice, swallowed hard, and smiled. Finally both of us had managed to eat our portion. By the end I had such a horrible taste in my mouth that I wanted to go brush my teeth. I figured I would look too anal if I did. Instead I grabbed another Coke out of the cooler to wash the taste out of my mouth. Leonard did the same.

"Well, my friend, I think that we are now ready for our journey." Leonard grabbed the map off of the table and began to study it. "So, where do you want to go?"

"I was looking at that Red Beds Trail. It's about three miles long and goes completely around the tower."

Leonard folded up the map. "Good plan ... let's go."

As we were leaving our camp I happened to look at the sky to the south. It looked like clouds were building. "Hey, Leonard."

"Yeah?"

"Look at the clouds out there ... maybe we should take a jacket with us."

Leonard looked up at the sky. "I don't think those are rain clouds, Carl ... I think that they're just cloud clouds. Besides, we shouldn't be gone all that long."

"Yeah, I suppose you're right," I shrugged.

We had only gone a hundred yards from our camp when Leonard stopped and looked up at the clouds again.

"What?"

"Uh, I just have a feeling ... maybe you're right, I suppose it can't hurt to take a jacket." He trotted back to the van.

"Hey, grab mine too, would ya? And get my camera, too." Leonard waved that he heard me.

Jackets in hand, we were back on the trail, which started out following the Belle Fourche River. The quiet river had, over time, patiently carved a meandering path through the landscape. Now deep red earth bluffs rose up roughly a hundred feet right next to it. Cottonwood trees lined its bank on the opposite side. After a half a mile or so the trail began to turn away from the river and head towards Devil's Tower. I checked my consciousness to see if I felt any of the effects of the mushrooms yet ... nothing.

I asked Leonard, "You feel anything?"

"Nope, not yet." We kept walking.

Only a couple of minutes later we broke out of the tall grass and came to a flat spot in the landscape. The grass looked like it had been mowed. We stopped.

"What the hell is going on here?" I asked Leonard. Then out of the corner of my eye I saw some movement and heard an "eeep!"

"Prairie dogs, Carl."

I vaguely remembered seeing them as a kid, but the memory was a hazy one. I scanned the landscape to see if I could catch a glimpse of one of the critters. It wasn't hard – the entire plain was alive with them. There must have been hundreds.

"Oh my God, these things are cute as all hell."

"Cute?" Leonard looked at me, raising one eyebrow.

"Well yeah, Leonard, what would you call them?" He didn't answer. I slowly walked a few steps into the town sending the closest prairie dogs scurrying for their holes. I couldn't help but smile. I sat down, hoping that my low profile would bring the closest ones back out so I might get a picture. Leonard sat down next to me.

As I took out my camera, about five feet away one particularly curious prairie dog surfaced from his hole and started to "eeep" repeatedly at us. He stood on his hind legs and with each "eeep" his whole body shook. It was tremendously funny and I started to laugh. I wanted to take his picture, but the more I looked at him the funnier it seemed. Leonard started laughing too, although I don't know if he was laughing at me or at the prairie dog. Other prairie dogs now started to pop up from their holes around us and "eeep." With each one that surfaced, I laughed harder. Eventually I was laughing so hard that I was crying. I fell on my back and looked up at the clear deep blue sky, laughing and listening to the "eeeps" all around me.

I don't know what happened first - either my laughter faded or the "eeeps" stopped. But suddenly all I could hear was the wind. I remarked, "My God, the sky is beautiful."

I wasn't sure if I had said it to myself or said it out loud, until Leonard answered, "Yes it is, Carl ... it is very beautiful."

I turned and looked at him next to me and said, "Did you say that or did I just think you said that?"

Then I heard his voice in my head, "You heard what I thought, Carl." Leonard's lips didn't move. He turned to me and smiled.

"Good mushrooms – nice Wiccans." This time his lips moved. I nodded.

I stood up. My body felt light and ethereal, but at the same time completely sensitized. I took a deep breath and closed my eyes. I could feel the wind touch every strand of my hair. It felt as if it was being stroked gently by a human hand.

It was a good feeling, and I could feel myself sway back and forth to its unseen rhythm.

"Shall we go?" Leonard's voice again. I opened my eyes. He was in front of me, smiling.

"Yeah, let's do that," I said.

I followed behind Leonard as we made our way up the trail and toward the tower. Neither of us talked. With each step closer I could feel an increase in energy. It was an electrical kind of feeling, but softer. I tried to roll with it and I thought to myself, "This is about as high as I am going to get."

As soon as I thought the words, a tremendous "Hmmm" erupted, like a thousand crickets buzzing in the heat. The sound enveloped me and seemed to follow the rhythm of the soft energy. Then all of a sudden my mind felt as if it was being shot out of a cannon. I heard a whoosh and for a second everything around me sped by. Then it was quiet again. I had come to another level.

"You okay there, Carl?" Leonard was standing in the trail about twenty feet in front of me. All around him hung a warm yellow glow. I smiled.

"Yeah, I'm fine, Leonard ... how are you?" I watched as my words traveled through the air and splashed into the peaceful radiance around him.

"You too, huh, Carl?" he said. I watched as his words floated back to me. When they arrived, I felt them splash into my own luminescence. It tickled.

I laughed and said, "Yeah ... me too." He turned and we continued up the trail.

We got closer and closer to the tower. The closer we got, the more I felt like I was floating rather than walking. I looked down at my feet to check and see if it was so. I was not surprised when I saw golden light emitting from the bottoms of my feet, which were now six inches off of the ground. I wanted to show Leonard what I had discovered and I called to him up the trail.

"Leonard – come here, look at this." Leonard turned around and half swam down the trail to me, light following behind him. He floated gracefully around me, and lit on a spot next to me.

He looked down at my feet, and simply said, "Yes." I understood.

We floated together the last few feet up to the base of the tower. We were close enough now that the auras that surrounded us touched and blended. It seemed to at least double their intensity and I felt warm and close to Leonard as if we were touching each other's souls.

At the base of the tower we found a large flat rock. We sat down, leaned back and stared up at the monolith before us. As I looked at it, I noticed that it wasn't a single rock but rather thousands of individual pillars bound as one, all thrusting upwards together. I thought to myself, "This means something." Then it happened again. As soon as the thought entered my mind, a tremendous "hmmm" filled the air. This time it was louder than before. I could feel the soft energy become more intense and I felt as if my light was merging to become part of it. The tower began to glow the same golden glow that surrounded us.

I said, "Is this me?"

And I heard Leonard's voice inside my head answer comfortingly, "No, we feel it too."

I turned and looked at him, and said "We?"

He smiled, nodded and said, "Watch." He motioned his head towards the tower. When I turned to look, the "hmmm" was replaced again by the whoosh. The world raced by at an insane speed and within an instant I was looking down a long bright tunnel. I struggled to focus my eyes to see what was at the end of it ... slowly, slowly ... slowly it came clear. It was the tower. As soon as I recognized it, the tunnel shattered like glass and sparkling pieces trailed off and evaporated into the air.

My vision snapped clear and I was staring upwards into the blue sky again. The tower glowed, increasingly brighter now, and the brighter it glowed, the taller it became. Each fingered pillar reached for the sky. I followed it up and up and felt inside a profound understanding the higher I went. Slowly, a slender shaft of light rose up from the top of the tower and went up into the heavens as far as I could see. It was brilliantly infinite. Smiling, I stared at it and said, "I know." Then I started to cry.

I closed my eyes, and as soon as I did the hum stopped. I found the silence louder. I opened my eyes again and looked at the tower. The glow was gone, as was the shaft of light. It was rock once more. The world was again as it was.

I turned to see if Leonard was still with me. He was right beside me. He blinked as if waking up from a dream. His cheeks were streaked and his eyes were bloodshot. He looked like he had been crying hard for a long time, yet he did not look sad.

"Leonard?" He turned to me, and although he looked peaceful, I could tell he was struggling with the transformation.

His eyes fixed on mine and he said, "You too, Carl?"

"Yeah, Leonard ... me too."

Neither Leonard nor I said anything else for a long, long time. We just sat there together on the rock. I wanted to ask him what had just happened, but I didn't know how to put words to the experience. My entire body was tingling. The tips of my fingers prickled as if I had touched a very high voltage wire. I felt weak, but at the same time charged and extremely lucid. I sensed that Leonard felt exactly the same way. Although the world was less dramatic, I knew that the mushrooms were still with us.

Time seemed have slowed now and I was amazingly attuned to my surroundings. I felt free to plainly see what was around me. It was obvious ... uncomplicated. The forest, rocks, earth, and sky were magnificent and I could sense life in all of them. I took a deep breath and felt that life run through me. It was quiet now except for the wind, which whispered through the pine trees. The more that I listened to the sound, the more I thought I could hear a chorus of voices speaking, but I couldn't make out the words.

I don't know how long we sat there, but after a time the sky began to darken. At first just a few clouds danced by the sun and were gone. Gradually, though, the clouds increased, thickened, and stayed. Finally the azure sky was replaced by a purple-black curtain that hung ominously. The air stilled and the birds became silent.

Leonard broke our own quiet and said, "Thunder storm."

"What?" I had not spoken for a long time and the act of making a word seemed like a foreign thing to me. It echoed in my head.

Leonard shifted his eyes upward, got up and repeated it, "Thunder storm, Carl. We should find a place to wait it out." I stood up with him.

I felt more comfortable with language now and strung together a sentence, "I'll follow you, Leonard." My words still echoed in my head.

We followed the trail, which hugged the tower, for another three hundred yards or so before we came to a fork. One leg continued on around the base of tower and the other went off into the forest. A few drops of warm rain landed on my cheek.

"You feel that, Leonard?"

"Yeah, here it comes. This way, into the woods away from the tower – it's a lightning rod."

The storm was imminent and we hurried down the trail in search of anything that might offer us shelter. The sky had darkened to such a degree that it was becoming hard to see in the woods. I'm sure that the mushrooms weren't helping my spatial abilities any either. Both of us tripped several times over rocks and roots in the trail.

Then, without warning, there was an enormous flash, which was followed almost instantaneously by a tremendous "BOOM." I instinctively jumped. For a second the woods lit up and I could see Leonard's figure in front of me frozen mid-step as if caught by a camera flash. His image lingered and shimmered like an apparition long after the light disappeared. I wondered if I looked the same to him.

"Shit, that was close!" I said. My voice sounded distant, like I was talking into a large tin drum. I barely got the words out when there was another flash. This time though the "BOOM" was simultaneous. The sound enveloped me and reverberated against my body. It was accompanied by an almost metallic tearing sound, and the air was permeated with the smell of ozone. Leonard, whose spirit-like image had disappeared in the last flash, was now next to me.

He corrected me by saying, "No, Carl, *that* was close."

Rain began to flood down on us - the clouds had been ripped open by the strike. Water washed over me as if I were standing under a falls. It was warm and good - it felt safe. It was totally dark, yet I could clearly see glistening silver rivulets of water, like strands of mercury, running down all over my naked body. I thought to myself, "When did I shed my clothes?" Before I could answer myself there was another flash and a close "BOOM." In the brief light, I could see that I was again clothed ... maybe I never wasn't. I closed my eyes and took a deep breath – ozone.

Leonard said to me, "Carl, we should get out of this." I felt no danger at all, but somewhere deep in the back of my mind, intellectually I knew that being out in the open in a thunderstorm was not safe. I nodded. I wasn't sure if he could even see me. I felt intangible.

We bumped and tripped on down the trail, finding our way between the intermittent flashes of lightning. Finally we came to a large boulder that was half buried in the hillside. The ground was eroded out from underneath it on the downhill side and a lip jutted out over it, offering a dry cave-like shelter.

"Here," Leonard said. I followed him into the place under the boulder. There wasn't a lot of room in the shelter; just enough for Leonard and me, but it was dry and safe from lightning strikes.

I said to Leonard, "This is a good place." Lightning flashed again, as if to emphasize my point.

"Yes, it is, Carl."

I'm not sure how long Leonard and I lay on our bellies looking out at the fantastic thunderstorm as it raged, but we were there for a while. I, as did Leonard, I'm sure, bounced back and forth in and out between hallucination and reality. Increasingly the line between the two blurred and it became impossible to tell which was which. I ceased to care and just went with it. It was irrelevant.

Twice we heard trees nearby get hit by lightning and explode in a scream that sounded more like a voice in agony than shattering wood. At one point, when a strike lit up the inside of our cave, I thought I saw Leonard's facial features change. I guess that I must have been thinking about other critters that lived in caves too, because for a brief moment, although he was still human, he was feline as well – part puma and part man. It was so Wizard of Oz-like that I started laughing hysterically. I wondered what character I was.

"What the hell is so funny, Carl?" There was another flash and I could see that he was just plain old Leonard again.

I composed myself and instead of telling him what I had seen, I said, "Nothing, man, I'm just tripping."

Leonard paused, then said to me, "Well, trip with me, Dorothy – we're not in Kansas anymore." As soon as the words left his mouth we both started laughing uncontrollably.

Eventually the storm moved on. The rain stopped, the lightning faded, and the thunder became just a faint rumble in the distance. The clouds dissipated revealing a freshly washed blue sky. Sunlight flooded the forest and the aroma of sweet pine permeated the air.

Leonard and I crawled out from our shelter under the rock. We both stretched. We were stiff from lying in the confined space. My mind felt clear, and not as unpredictable. I was fairly sure that most of the effects of the mushrooms were gone.

"Man, Leonard, that was one hell of a thunderstorm. How long do you think that went on for?"

"No clue, Carl. I'll tell you what though ... that was one hell of a trip. I don't think that I'll be forgetting any of that anytime soon."

"No shit ... I guess I now know why they call them magic mushrooms."

"Yeah, magic is right – nice Wiccans."

The Shepherds

Leonard and I got back on what we thought was the trail and headed back in what we thought was the direction of the campsite. We ended up wandering around for about twenty minutes before we realized that what we were following was a deer track.

Realizing our mistake, Leonard stopped and said, "Oh, fucking great, Mr. Lewis – we're lost."

I couldn't resist it and said, "Mr. Clark, might I remind you ... not all who wander are lost." I barely said it with a straight face.

Leonard gave me a look like he wanted to pummel me and said, "Mr. Lewis?"

"Yes Mr. Clark?"

"Fuck off."

I started laughing like crazy, and Leonard did too. I thought to myself, "I bet at least once on their cross-continental journey somebody in the Corps of Discovery said just those very words."

Leonard suggested that we try to find a clearing to see if we could spot the tower. If we could at least find that, then we could find our way back. I agreed and we walked though the woods for a few more minutes before we did in fact find a large grassy clearing. Both of us looked back and forth and tried to crane our necks above the trees to see if we could spot the monolith. We had two false sightings, once when I saw what proved on closer examination to be a hill about a half a mile away, and another when Leonard spotted a boulder in the woods.

After the second false alarm, Leonard said, "Shit, I still can't see a fucking thing. One of us is going to have to climb a tree and get some height."

"Well Leonard, that is just a wonderful suggestion ... you go right ahead." I half-bowed and motioned with my arm graciously towards the nearest pine tree.

"No, no, no, Carl, I think we should be fair about this. I don't particularly want to get covered in sap climbing a fucking pine tree."

"Yeah, well, I'm scared shitless of heights and I would rather not soil my pants climbing one either."

"Well then ...?"

"Let's do this, Leonard ... we'll draw straws on it." I picked up a stick, turned around, broke off two short pieces, and stuck them in my fist. I turned back around: "Here ... short straw goes up."

Leonard reached out and pulled a stick from my hand. "Woah, looks like you got the short one there, partner."

He gave me a nasty look. He knew, but he decided to do me a favor and said, "You owe me one, asshole. Hold my jacket."

Leonard was sizing up a tree, trying to figure out his strategy before he was in it, when I heard a noise off in the woods. "Hey, hang on for a second, Leonard, did you hear that?"

"Hear what?"

"Hang on ..." We both listened intently for a moment but heard nothing.

"Flashback, Carl. It's probably just a chipmunk. Now let's get this over with, give me a leg up to the first branch here." I bent down and locked my fingers together to give Leonard a little extra height. Then I heard it again – a rustling and a stick crack.

"Okay, man, you had to have heard that."

"Yeah, I did ..."

Leonard took his foot down from my cupped hands and I stood up. We both looked to the direction of the sound. We heard it together. It was getting closer.

Off in the woods maybe a couple of hundred yards or so, we could hear more rustling of underbrush and more sticks snapping. Whatever it was, it was big.

I whispered to Leonard, "What the fuck do you think it is, bear? Cougar maybe?"

"Shut up, man, I'm listening," Leonard whispered back. I slowly inched myself closer to the tree next to us. Fear of heights or not I figured that my only avenue for escape might be climbing a tree. If attacked by a wild carnivore I would probably crap my pants anyway.

We strained to see what was making the sound, but in the dense forest we could see nothing. Then, just when the noise sounded like it was on top of us, two men emerged from the woods on the opposite side of the clearing. I think they were just about as surprised to see us as we were to see them.

As soon as they spotted us, they stopped and stood still. They were extraordinarily short – maybe five-two or five-three. They both had onyx black hair and were very dark-skinned. They appeared to be maybe Hispanic. They wore dark brown wool ponchos that had complex brightly colored geometric patterns woven into them. Over their shoulders they carried rugged looking leather bags. One of the men had a long stick that was crooked at the top.

I whispered to Leonard, "Who the fuck are those guys?" While I was saying it, the man without the staff leaned over to his partner and said something to him. It was probably the same thing I said to Leonard.

We stood there for what seemed like a couple of minutes or so just staring at each other. Leonard, who hadn't answered my question, finally said, "Maybe we're still in Oz ... they're short enough to be Munchkins."

"Yeah, maybe ... but Munchkins don't wear ponchos, and besides, they're not Technicolor enough."

"True ..."

I started to laugh quietly. Leonard leaned over and said, "Don't laugh, it's not polite." It made it worse. The two men saw that we were laughing and apparently thought we were safe enough to approach. Broad smiles appeared on their faces as they started to walk across the clearing towards us.

"Come on, Carl," Leonard nudged my arm. We headed over to meet them.

In the center of the clearing we stood facing each other. Our difference in size was considerable. We towered over them - it was almost comical. I wondered if they were intimidated by us – if they were, they didn't show it.

"Howdy, partner," Leonard said, and put out his hand. I did the same. The two men looked confused, like they didn't know what to do. They looked at our outstretched hands, then they briefly looked at each other as if the other one might know the answer.

I said to Leonard in a lowered voice, "Maybe they don't speak English."

"Maybe …" Leonard let his hand fall. I had already lowered mine.

"I sort of thought that the handshake thing was a universal deal," Leonard said with a genuinely perplexed tone to his voice.

"Well, Leonard, apparently it's not where they come from, now, is it." I gave him a smart-ass smirk to go with my smart-ass answer.

Leonard was just about ready to give me shit back when the fellow who was holding the staff said clearly, "Oh … I speaks English." He grinned. Half of his teeth were capped in gold, the rest were brilliant white. His partner smiled too. His teeth were similar. He didn't say anything.

He continued, "I am sorry, but we not know what is 'howdy partner' you say."

Leonard broke in, "Hey, don't worry about it, just another way of saying hi ..." They both nodded and continued to smile politely, but Leonard's lack of a full cultural explanation didn't seem to help them much.

The man with the staff changed the subject, "We are, how to say … um … sur, sur ..."

I helped him out, "Surprised?"

"Yes, this is it … we are surprised to see you here. We have been in the woods much time. We no see anyone."

I nodded and said, "Yeah well, we were a little surprised to see you out here in the middle of nowhere too." I paused, then said casually, "So, are you guys from around here?" I knew they weren't.

They looked at each other and said something in what sounded sort of like Spanish, "Los extranjeros son locos." They laughed a little, then turned back to me and gave me a look like the question that I had asked was a stupid one, but they were too polite to say it.

The man with the staff spoke, "Yes, of course, we live here. Where do you come from?"

"Oh, we came from Mount Vernon." They both looked at me blinking. From their reaction, I may as well have said, "Oh, we come from a dark and mysterious planet on the far side of the sun."

Then the man said carefully, "Where is this place, Mount Ver-non?" His first try at pronouncing it was difficult for him.

"Well, um, it's back in Washington State."

They looked at each other, and said in their Spanish-something else dialect, "Washington ... Casa de la Presidente Reagan – en los Estados Unidos?!" I could understand enough of what they were saying, and I thought to myself, "Oh, great, shit ... now they think we're spies for the CIA."

He turned back to me, suspicious now, "Where is this Washington State that you talk of?" The whole conversation was beginning to get very, very weird, and I was clearly not making things better.

Leonard, who was getting impatient with all of it, and saw where it was going, broke in and said earnestly, "No, man, we're not from Washington D.C. – no government," He pointed to himself and shook his head no, " ... different place, we're from Washington *State*."

The pair still looked a little confused, but they also looked visibly relieved at Leonard's statement that we were not in fact agents on some Secret Squirrel mission for the American government. The translator for the pair was now friendly again, "My friends ... then you have come a very long way." He sounded like he was totally impressed.

Leonard quipped offhandedly, "Yeah, I suppose we have ... it's probably ... what do you think, Carl, eleven, twelve hundred miles or so?"

"Yeah, Leonard, it's something like that, but I don't really think that's what they think."

"What do you mean?"

I didn't answer him and instead said directly to the two men, "What is the name of the country that you come from?"

They both said in unison – "Peru."

Leonard, who still wasn't following all of this, said, "And so what brings you up here to Wyoming?"

Before either one of them could answer me, a crowd of noise and movement erupted from the forest behind the two men. Suddenly, out of the underbrush, a sheep appeared, then another, and another ... they kept coming and coming until the entire field was filled with sheep. Bleating, they bumped and nudged up against us until we were awash in an ocean of sheep.

I looked around the field, "Shit, Leonard, there must be over three hundred sheep here."

The man with the staff said, "Oh yes, and there are many more in the woods. We are shepherds and our flock is large." He was proud of it. Then he added, "Our sheep, they are over a thousand."

"What?" Leonard said with amazement.

"Yes ... and we have walked many miles to look for good grasses for them." He smiled.

"And so, exactly how far do you think that you have walked?" I asked cautiously.

"Oh, that I do not know. We have been in the mountains for months." A sheep bumped up against my leg, bleated, and looked up at me.

I gathered myself for the big, big weirdness question. I took a little breath then said, "So ... do you two by any chance *live* in Peru?" Neither one of them had to say anything. I was pretty sure that I knew what their answer was going to be. Leonard looked at me – he was beginning to get it.

"Oh no, man ... no, you don't think that ..." He shook his head in disbelief.

The pair rattled off a few words between themselves then turned to us and said in English simply, "Live in Peru? Yes, senors."

In spite of being somewhat ready for it, their answer briefly left Leonard and I at a loss for words. Finally Leonard said to me, "Do you really think that these guys don't know that they are currently in Wyoming?" A couple more sheep bumped against us and bleated.

"Ah, no, Leonard ... I really don't think that they do ..."

"Well," Leonard continued, "I think that someone needs to take some responsibility here and inform these two that they're just a little off course."

"Yeah, well you go right ahead there, Leonard, and do that."

"I will."

He turned to them and said gently, "Excuse me ... I know that this might sound just a little fantastic, but are you aware that you are in Wyoming?"

They blinked, and one of them said to the other, "Donde esta Wyoming?"

Leonard, whose command of Spanish was far better than mine, replied calmly, "It's in the United States."

Their eyes got wide and they said together excitedly, "los Estados Unidos aqui – Dios mio! No es verdad!"

"Yeah ..." Leonard said, raising his eyebrows and nodding.

The pair talked excitedly between themselves, apparently trying to comprehend exactly how they had gone from the mountains of Peru to the Wild West of the United States. Finally the one with the staff said to us in English, "It is amazing what you tell us, but we believe it to be true. Many things have been strange for many days now - we have not seen country like this before ... and the winter season, she never come ..." His voice trailed off. His friend hung his head solemnly. Then he said almost ashamedly, "We do not know how we could have become so lost ... we do as we always do ... we follow the stars."

While he was talking, Leonard dug around in his jacket pocket and found his old compass. When the man finished speaking, Leonard put out his hand, handed him the compass, and said earnestly, "Here man, this should help get you two home again ... just follow the needle south. Sud."

The man took the compass, smiled in appreciation and said, "Gracias, we thank you." His partner smiled too.

"Hey, it's no problem," Leonard said, and then added, "We should get going here too ... we need to get back to our own camp."

"Yes, we know. May your journey be safe ..."

The Peruvians said something to the sheep in Spanish and they parted, leaving us a path out of the clearing. When we neared the edge of the woods, we turned around and waved goodbye to them. The Peruvians waved back enthusiastically and the sheep began to bah nearly in unison as if to say goodbye as well. One sheep next to me intentionally nudged my leg. I looked down at him, and his deep yellow eyes met mine. They looked knowing. He opened his lips and said to me, "Baaaaah con Dios."

I figured it was just another flashback.

Once back in the woods, we almost immediately found a clearly marked trail. "Hey, here we go, Leonard ... I think we found the path."

"Yeah, I think you're right, Carl."

We picked it up and started what I hoped was our hike back to our camp. "So, do you really think those guys really walked all the way from Peru?"

"Hell, I guess so, Carl ... I guess we now know why they call it 'Peruvian Marching Powder.' It is pretty weird though, I'll give you that."

"Yeah," I agreed with him, "I would say that pretty weird is kind of an understatement."

"You know, you just hope that the locals don't find out that they've got a thousand head of sheep wandering around in their cattle country." I think Leonard was trying to be funny, but it did seem like a very real danger. Then I thought about what the sheep had said to me back at the clearing. I smiled to myself and said, "Ah, I wouldn't worry about it too much, Leonard."

We followed the trail through the woods for about ten minutes or so until we reached a junction and a sign that said, "South Side Trail/Belle Fourche Campground 0.6 m." Less than a hundred feet later we broke out of the woods and onto the open prairie. From the rise we could see the campground and the van in the distance. Now, out of the woods, I could feel the warm sun against my skin. It was a beautiful day, but I still felt a little disoriented from our experience at the Tower.

I looked at my watch, "That's weird."

"What, Carl?"

"I just looked at my watch and it says that it's eleven thirty."

"What?"

I looked at it again and saw by the second hand that it was in fact running. "Yeah, it says eleven thirty ... I wonder if I bumped it or something while we were tripping out there."

"Yeah, probably. We'll get the time from somebody when we get back to the camp."

We had only been back at our camp for a few minutes, and I was just putting on some coffee, when the ranger pulled up in her official celeste green Forest Service pickup. She was apparently making her campground rounds. We both waved and she got out of her truck and started walking our direction. We met her halfway.

"Good morning," she said cheerfully, again primarily addressing Leonard.

"Hi, how you doin'?" Leonard said.

"I'm doing fine, but I guess I really should be asking you that," she said with a note of genuine concern in her voice. "How did you do with that thunderstorm last night? Did either of you get any sleep?"

Leonard and I looked at each other. The confused look on Leonard's face mirrored what I was thinking inside. Leonard beat me to it and said, "Last night?"

Now the ranger looked confused. She was probably thinking, "Where the fuck were you two? Didn't you hear the end of the world?" She was polite, though, and kept smiling and said, "Ah ... yes ... the big thunderstorm last night, is everything okay at your camp?"

I looked at my watch again to verify the time, and Leonard said rather unconvincingly, "Uh ... yeah, it was a little rough but we're fine. We'll probably just take a nap this afternoon."

"Are you going to stay this evening?" Leonard looked at me. I shrugged.

He turned back to her and said, "Yeah, I guess we probably will stay another night."

"Good, I'm telling people that considering the bad weather last night they are welcome to stay this evening for free."

"Well, thank you very much, that's very kind of you," Leonard was pouring on the charm.

"You're welcome. I'll stop by again later and check in and see if you need any firewood or anything else." She started to blush as soon as she said "anything else." Leonard had evidently restored our credibility with the ranger. I decided it was best not to tell her about the Peruvians.

By the time the ranger left, the coffee was done brewing. I poured Leonard and I each a cup and then proceeded to fix us up a huge dinner/breakfast/lunch of bacon, eggs and hash browns. We were both, understandably, starving. Neither one of us said much while we ate. Having apparently been up all night, we were exhausted as well.

After we finished, Leonard went back to the van, got a blanket, spread it out on a grassy spot under the shade of a nearby cottonwood, and lay down. I shoved the dishes into a pile on one end of the table and joined him. A nap was definitely in order.

Under the tree, we lay there on our backs next to each other watching the leaves dance and rustle in the wind. It felt good. Off in the tall grass I could hear a pair of meadowlarks call back and forth. It was a sweet sound. I closed my eyes and drifted. Just before I fell asleep, Leonard said to me, "That was something out there last night, wasn't it."

A meadowlark called again. I waited until it was done. "Yeah, it sure was ..." I wanted to say more, something deep, but I couldn't think of what to say.

In the end, that was all either one of us could say about it – those two brief sentences. Even later, we didn't really talk much about what we had actually experienced, but we both knew that we had shared the same trip – we knew that it had happened. It made us closer in a way that words would not do justice to, and without saying so, I think we both decided not to ruin it with explanations.

Faith, Virtue, and Love

When I woke up, the sun had dropped low in the sky. I raised myself up to a sitting position and looked at my watch – it was after six o'clock. Leonard was up, and was sitting at the picnic table drinking a beer and playing solitaire. He flipped another card off the deck, looked over at me and said, "Mornin' sunshine."

"Hey, Leonard. How long have you been up?"

"Oh, just a little while. Man, did that feel good or what to get a little shut-eye."

"Yeah, no shit. I'm still tired though." I got up and rubbed my eyes, trying to fully wake up. "Man, my brain still doesn't feel right."

"I hear you, Carl. Mushrooms always do that to me too. You want a beer? It might level you out. It's working for me." He raised the can in front of him, took another sip, and grinned.

"Yeah, a beer sounds good."

I sat down at the table while he rooted around in the cooler and got a beer. "Here ya go ..."

"Thanks, Leonard."

In spite of the nearly eighty-degree heat the beer was still cold. I opened it and took a drink. It tasted better than I thought it would. Leonard set down the cards, "Fuck, I have no idea why I ever play this, I never win."

"Remember, Leonard, its not whether you win or lose ... it's how you play the game."

"That is such a wonderful little platitude, Carl - how profound," Leonard said sarcastically.

I took another sip of beer, "Why, thank you, Leonard."

"You're so welcome, Carl ... So what do you want to do about dinner here?" He rubbed his belly, then stretched.

"I don't know, what do we have?"

Leonard was already at the box of food investigating. "Well ... we have a can of refried beans, and I saw some tortillas and cheese in the cooler ... how about burritos?"

"Burritos sound good, but you'll have to promise me that you won't smoke in the tent tonight. I'd rather not die in a methane gas explosion."

Leonard looked at me like I was an idiot. "Sure, Carl, I promise."

I kept going with it. "Well ... it could happen. I remember I saw this movie once about these coal miners in Kentucky ... See, they were working way down in this shaft, and then there was this mine gas explosion, and ..."

"Oh, shut up Carl, that was a coal mine, not your colon." We both started laughing.

We had just finished dinner and were working on fresh beers when the ranger returned. She smiled and waved through the windshield as she pulled in next to our van. We waved back.

"You know, Leonard, that ranger sure is attentive."

"Yeah, she's pretty nice."

"And easy on the eyes, too ... I think she's got it bad for you, buddy."

"God, Carl, would you quit trying to live out your sick fantasies through me?"

"Why? It's fun ... shhh, here she comes."

As she neared the table we both acted like we were having a civil conversation.

"Hi, how are you guys doing?"

"Hi, we're doing just fine. Had a little nap, had a little food, now we're having a little beer ... have a seat, want one?" Leonard asked.

The ranger sat down, "Thanks, that would be nice. I just finished my shift." She had tipped her hand – I kicked Leonard under the table. I knew that he felt it, but he didn't show it in the slightest. Leonard handed her a beer.

"Well, it was darn nice of you to come by after work and check on us."

"Ummm ... yeah." She was slightly embarrassed. She quickly took a sip of her beer to hide it.

"So, we haven't properly introduced ourselves. My name is Leonard, and this is my friend Carl. We're from Mount Vernon, back up in Washington State."

"It's nice to meet you. My name is Mary. I'm from Havre, Montana. I'm an elementary teacher during the school year and I do this in the summers."

"What a great gig," I said.

"It is ... I love my students, and I love teaching, but I love the outdoors too. This place is special to me. My parents used to take us down here every summer when I was a kid. They said that this was a mystical place; I always thought so too. At least once each vacation my dad would take us for a hike around the tower. He said that it was sacred up there. I remember that during those hikes none of us ever said anything. It wasn't like it was a rule or anything ... we just knew he was right. You know, you just don't talk in churches and places like that.

The rest of the time my brother and I would run around looking for arrowheads and fossils in the creek bed. In the evening, we would all get together around the campfire and tell stories and roast marshmallows."

She paused, and I could tell that she was awash in her memories. Then she said, "I loved my parents very much ..." She sighed quietly, "I guess I still get to spend time with them, though ... you know, being here every summer."

She couldn't have been older than twenty-five or twenty-six. I figured that her parents probably didn't die of old age. I felt sad for her. It sounded like she'd had a good family, a close family, the kind of family that a lot of people dream about. I remembered that I had done some of the very same things with my own parents before their relationship exploded into a devastatingly messy divorce. It was reassuring to hear that it didn't have to be that way. I suppose in a tragic sort of way she was lucky, too.

We sat at the table silently. I finished my beer in a final large gulp and reached into the cooler for another. "Anybody need another beer?"

"Yeah, I'll have another," Leonard said. I was pretty sure that he wasn't done with his last one - I think he was just trying to make conversation.

Mary sensed our uneasiness, "Hey, you guys – sorry about that, I didn't mean to be a bummer or anything."

Leonard reassured her, "Hey, it's no problem. It sounds like you had a pretty cool family."

"Thank you ... I did." She said it with the beginning of tears in her eyes. She continued, changing the subject, "So you came all the way from Mount Vernon?"

"Yeah ..."

"And what made you decide to come here?"

"Well, we didn't really decide to, it just happened that way. We had a big elaborate plan when we started, but Leonard threw it out the window back in Oregon." I looked over at him.

"Yes I did, Carl, and you know what?"

"What?"

"I'd do it again, just like that." He gave me a forced petulant smile back.

"Well, no matter how you decided to come here, I'm glad that you did. This is a magical place and, and ... I got to meet you." She said the last part looking directly at Leonard. She was flirting hard.

The three of us sat at there at the table and talked on into the evening. The more I listened to what Mary had to say, the more I liked her. She was a deep and interesting person, but she also had a well-grounded wholesomeness about her. Her demeanor was unpretentious and straightforward. I'm sure she got some of that from being raised in a small town in Montana. I could tell that Leonard was taken with her as well. But despite her flirting, he innocently kept his distance.

At one point in the evening the sun dipped to the horizon, and we were treated to a brilliant sunset. The whole sky lit up a vivid magenta. It reflected on everything, including the tower-it glowed. It reminded me of our experience the night before and as I watched it I half expected it to start to metamorphose. It didn't. I didn't share my thoughts, but I know that Leonard was probably thinking about it too. I glanced over at Mary, and as she looked at the tower, I recognized a familiar look in her eyes. I wondered if it was possible that Mary had experienced something similar, and that it was part of the "magic" that she talked about.

After the sun went down, I stayed up and had a couple more beers. But by the time that nine o'clock rolled around, the need for sleep caught up with me.

I interrupted the conversation, "Hey you guys, I'm pretty beat here. I think that I'm going to go crash for the evening."

"Sounds good, Carl. I think I'm going to stay up for a while longer and talk. I promise we'll be quiet though."

"Hey, don't worry about it, I'm so tired I doubt if your talking could keep me up." I got up and turned to Mary, "Good night. It was really nice meeting you. I'll probably see you tomorrow morning on our way out of here."

Mary did not look disappointed that I was going to bed, leaving her and Leonard alone. She smiled and politely said, "Good night - it was nice meeting you too."

I crawled into the tent and then into my sleeping bag. It felt good to lie down – very, very good. As I lay there in the darkness, I was lulled by the night song of the crickets and the conversation between Leonard and Mary. On the side of the tent wall I could vaguely see their shadows projected by the lantern. Just before I fell asleep I heard Leonard say, "I'm sorry, but I have a girlfriend."

When I woke up it was utterly still. I could tell that it was early - the light was still soft. I didn't bother looking at the time. I didn't really care, and it didn't really matter. At some point the night before, Leonard had climbed into the tent with me. I never heard him. He was so sound asleep he barely made a sound, just a quiet sigh with each slow breath. I unzipped the tent and got out. I had no idea how late he had been up. I figured I'd just let him sleep.

The early morning air was fresh and clean and I felt great. Whatever sleep I had lost a couple of nights before I had regained last night. I went and put on some coffee, trying to be as quiet as possible so as not to wake Leonard. As it was brewing, I sat and took in the landscape. It was beautiful here - probably one of the most beautiful places that I had ever been in my life. With all that had happened I felt a kinship with the place. It also felt like we had been here a hell of a lot longer than just two days. I was sad that we were going to be leaving, but I also knew that we had to get moving on.

The coffee finished brewing and I poured myself a cup. Leonard was still sound asleep and he probably would be for a while. I thought that now would probably be a good time for me to give Althea a call. I had seen a telephone back at the entrance to the campground. I refreshed my mug and walked up there.

I set my mug down on top of the pay phone, shook a cigarette out of my pack and lit it. I hadn't been smoking much and the first drag made me a little lightheaded. I looked at my watch, which was still on Mount Vernon time. It was seven fifteen. Now it mattered. I knew that Althea would still be asleep, but I figured that that she wouldn't be too pissed if I woke her up. After all, I had promised that I would call her as soon as I could.

I picked up the phone, dropped two and a half-dollars worth of change into the slot, and dialed. I listened to the phone ring at the other end of the line ... two, three, four ... With each ring that passed I felt a growing anxiousness rise inside me ... what if she was pissed again? Then another thought occurred to me - what if she wasn't home? I tried to shove the distorted possibility out of my mind.

After the eighth ring, she answered groggily, "Hello?"

"Hey Althea, sorry if I woke you up."

At the sound of my voice, she immediately perked up. She was not pissed. "Hi Carl ... Oh sweetheart, I am so glad that you called. It's so good to hear your voice."

"Yeah, Althea, it's good to hear yours too." I could hear sheets rustle on the other end of the line and I thought how good it would be to be in bed with her right now. It immediately made me homesick.

"So where are you?"

"We're out at Devil's Tower."

"Oh, so you finally made it there. What's it like?" she said enthusiastically.

I turned around and looked at the tower. "Yeah, we finally made it ... it's cool, really cool, Althea. I know that you'd like it a lot. We'll have to come out here together sometime."

I decided not to elaborate on Leonard's and my experience. That was something that happened between the two of us and it needed to stay that way.

"I'd like that, Carl ... oh, I miss you so much."

"I know, Althea, I miss you too."

"How much longer are you going to be away?"

"Oh, probably not too much longer ... just a few more days. I'll talk with Leonard today and we'll figure out when we're going to start heading back. I'll let you know."

"Well, come home as soon as you can – okay?" I really didn't feel like she was pushing, but she quickly added, "No pressure or anything, Carl ... really, it ... it just feels like you've been gone forever." She was right. We had only been gone for ten days, but it felt more like a month.

Althea and I talked for another twenty minutes or so about everything that we had been missing in each other's lives, until I ran out of change. Our conversation was far better than our last one, and by the time we had to go I missed her terribly. Finally, we shot a barrage of "I love you's" at each other as the phone timed out. Althea was in the middle of sending me a loud smoochy kiss when the line clicked and I heard the dial tone. I reluctantly hung up the phone, sat down on the dew-damp grass, and thought about home.

When I got back to camp Leonard was up. "Hey, buddy, where have you been? Did you call Althea?"

"Yeah ..." I said, a little quietly.

"What's wrong, man, another bad conversation?"

"No, a good one. I guess talking to her made me kind of homesick."

"Yeah, I hear you, we've been gone for a while. Hey, how about another cup of coffee? I made a fresh pot."

I handed him my mug. "Thanks." He handed it back to me and I took a sip of fresh coffee.

"What are you thinking there, Carl?"

"Well, we've been gone here for ten days ... we should maybe think about when we're going to start heading back."

Just for a moment, Leonard looked a little impatient, but he took a sip of his own coffee. It went away. "Hey, don't worry about that homesick thing, Carl, it'll pass. I mean, look at it this way, it's good that you are. We'll be turning around here in a couple of days, okay? In the meantime let's just enjoy it."

"Yeah, you're right, Leonard ... you're always fucking right."

"I know I am," he smiled and took another sip of coffee.

We had a quick breakfast and packed up our camp.

"You want me to drive, Leonard?" I already had my keys out.

"No, man, I'll take the first shift. It'll help me wake up."

"You sure?"

"Yeah, I'm sure. I'll let you take over in an hour or so ... promise."

"Okay ..."

As Leonard passed around the front of the van he said cheerfully, "Good morning, Mr. Rat," and petted it on the nose with his index finger.

"Shit, Leonard, how can you touch that thing?" He didn't say anything. He just smiled, went back, and petted it again.

We got in, Leonard turned the ignition, and the van fired up with a roar. "Hey, how about one of those cigarette things, Carl, while I let this canister warm up?" I shook one out of the pack and handed him the lighter. He broke the filter off and threw it in the ashtray.

"Why don't you just buy your own pack of straights and quit busting the filters off of mine?"

"Because, Carl, I hate buying cigarettes. If you were a real friend you'd buy straights to make me happy." And with that, he put the van in gear and punched it. The rear tires chirped and we leapt out of the campsite. I shook my head, but said nothing to him. I wasn't going to feed it.

"Well?"

"Well what, Leonard?"

"Aren't you going to say it?"

"Say what?" I played innocent.

"Come on, Carl, give me shit for burning out ... please."

"No way."

"Come on man, you hate it when I do that."

"Yes I do."

"Then why aren't you giving me shit?"

"Because, Leonard, if I let you know that I'm pissed off then you'll keep doing it."

"Ha – then you are pissed off!"

"I didn't say that." He punched the accelerator hard again, fishtailing the back end of the van.

"Are you sure you're not pissed off?"

"Nope ..." He stopped the van and turned and looked at me. He had an impish look on his face.

"What are you stopping for?"

"Are you sure, Carl?"

"Yeah, I'm sure ..."

"Okay ..." Leonard floored the accelerator. The tires squealed and loose gravel ricocheted out of the fender wells, pinging against the sheet tin loudly. I could feel the front end of the van literally begin to lift off under the sudden surge of horsepower.

"You asshole – what the fuck are you doing?!"

"Are you pissed now?"

"You're goddamn right I'm pissed, you maniacal turd!"

He immediately relaxed the throttle. "Ah, ha, ha, ha, ha... then I have won!" He raised a fist in the air like he was part of some revolution.

"Well, don't fucking gloat over it, butthole, just drive."

"Okay, Carl ... whatever you say." We looked at each other and burst out laughing.

When we arrived at the park exit, Mary was in the ranger's booth. Leonard pulled up the van, shut it off, and leaned out the window. Now I knew why he had wanted to drive. Maybe he had a girlfriend, but he wasn't beyond flirting, especially now that he had made that fact totally clear.

"Hey, Mary, just thought that we'd stop by and say goodbye. We're heading out."

Mary leaned out of the window. "I'm sorry to see you go, but I'm glad that you came." She blushed slightly.

I leaned over Leonard, "It was good to meet you. Maybe we'll be out again next year ... this is a completely cool place."

"I hope so." She wasn't looking at me. "I'll still be here – you know, every year."

"Yeah ..." Leonard broke in, "Well, we need to get going here, we've got a drive ahead of us." He tried to sound casual about it, but there was a slight catch in his voice.

Mary leaned out the window and ever so gently kissed him on the cheek, "You take care, okay?" She said it so quietly I could barely hear her. "Please come back and see me sometime." She looked like she was going to cry.

"Hey ..." Leonard looked directly into her eyes, "We'll see each other again ... really."

"Yeah, sure ..."

Leonard started the van. "Take care, Mary ... goodbye."

As we drove away, Leonard kept glancing in the rearview mirror, until finally we came up over a rise and around a corner, leaving Devil's Tower, and more importantly the ranger's station, out of sight. I think that he was wrestling with himself, wondering if he had done the right thing with Mary. After all, although he called Gwendolyn his girlfriend, from my perspective, I still had my doubts that he would ever see her again. At least, that was my reality.

Neither one of us said a word for at least ten minutes. I could tell that he was bumming and I thought it best to let him be alone with his thoughts for a little while. I picked up the atlas and I busied myself looking for possible destinations. I had no idea where we were going.

Finally Leonard broke the silence and said, "So, what do you see there, Carl?"

I put the map down. "Oh, I don't know, we have a few options ..."

"Like what?" It was just talk. He didn't sound like he was particularly interested.

"Like, you want to talk about it?"

"About what?"

"The Mary thing."

Leonard paused for a few moments, then looked at me and said, "I don't know if there's a whole lot to talk about, Carl."

"Yeah, well, I think there probably is. You know, I was pretty sure that you and Mary were going to hook up last night."

Leonard looked at me with a little bit of a baffled expression on his face and said, "What makes you say that?"

"Well ... she's pretty, and you both obviously have a connection."

Leonard thought about it for a second and then said frankly, "I have a girlfriend, Carl."

"Yeah, I know, Gwendolyn ... but you thought about it, didn't you?"

"Yeah, I thought about it, Carl. And you know, it makes me feel guilty that I did."

"Why? You're not even sure that you'll see Gwendolyn again."

"I guess ..." he faltered. "I guess for a while I started to question it too. But you know what?" He looked off across the rolling pine-covered hills, and said, "I'll see her again, I have faith in that."

I believed him.

South Dakota

There was no more to be said about it, so I picked up the map again, and got back to the business of trying to figure out what we were doing.

"Where the hell exactly are we going, Leonard?"

"Fuck, no clue ... You said we had options."

"Yeah, I suppose it depends how much farther you want to drive. It looks like the Black Hills aren't too far from here ... maybe three hours, tops. Beyond that," I glanced back down at the map of South Dakota, "there is pretty much nothing for a few hundred miles."

"Well, I guess that settles it, we're going to the Black Hills. So what road do I pick up?"

"I don't know, what are we on now?"

"We're on 14 heading south. Interstate 90 should be coming up here anytime."

"Hmmm, it looks like we take 90 east for just a couple of miles, then head south on ... oh what the hell is that ..."

"Carl, you are not instilling me with confidence here."

"Yeah, yeah ... Here it is, Route 585 going south."

"Are you sure?"

"Sure I'm sure, it runs into U.S. 85, which takes us right there."

"Okay, against my better judgment, I'm going to trust you."

"Gosh, Leonard, thanks so much for the second chance... after all, I've screwed you so many times in the past."

"Oh, no man, I'm not saying that you have intentionally screwed me ... what I am saying is that your ability to read a map is, well, somewhat impaired." He tried to sound clinical. "You're what I would call navigationally challenged. I also think that you can't help it ... it's a genetic thing."

"Well, thank you so much for your deep insight, doctor. The real question is ... can you help me?"

Leonard continued with the physician routine. He looked over at me and with a serious look on his face shook his head no, as if what I had was a terribly rare, virulent, and fatal illness. "I'm sorry, Carl ..."

A few minutes later we picked up 90, then shortly came to the junction with 585 and headed south. We drove for a half an hour through rolling grassland. To the west the prairie seemed endless. To the east, not far away, we could see the forests of the Black Hills.

We passed through the town of Horton and not long later, at the town of Four Corners, we picked up Route 85. "See, what did I tell you, Leonard ... I'm doing pretty good here. Maybe I'm not as sick as you think I am."

Leonard raised one eyebrow, "Sure, Carl, sure. Whatever you need to tell yourself to feel better."

Twenty minutes later we came to Newcastle and the junction with Route 16, which would take us east into the Black Hills. Here the country changed considerably - we were out of the grasslands and into spotty forest. Leonard deemed that it was time to fuel up the van and get a few supplies, so we pulled off at the first exit in search of a gas station.

"Let me know if you see a station, okay Carl?"

"Will do, Leonard ..."

As we drove through the town I found that it was actually a fairly decent place. The downtown buildings were small, and every one of them without exception was made of brick. Large hardwood trees canopied over the streets and sidewalks. Everything was neat and clean - clearly the citizens had a fair amount of civic pride.

"You know, Leonard, this ain't such a bad little town ... especially for being in Wyoming."

"Yeah, I suppose so, but the key word here is Wyoming."

"Well, maybe we're close enough to South Dakota that some of that state rubbed off on 'em."

"Maybe. I think it's all a facade though."

I interrupted our conversation, "Hey, over there, Leonard!"

"What?" Leonard slowed the van, "do you see a gas station?"

"Oh, nope, my mistake, it's a Laundromat." Leonard gave me a look. We continued down the street. A half a block later I said it again, "Hey, wait ... over there."

"What?"

"Oh, oops, sorry. Convenience store." I tried to sound genuinely apologetic. Leonard glared at me, but still didn't say anything. When the buildings on the main street started to thin out Leonard turned and went back around the block. As soon as we got around the corner, I again said with sincerity, "Hey, here we go, yeah... Oh, damn, my mistake again, sorry ... just a house."

Leonard calmly pulled the van over to the curb, rested his arms on the steering wheel and looked at me. "What the fuck is exactly wrong with you, Carl?"

"What?" I tried to sound innocent.

"Don't give me that 'what?' shit, you know what." He stared at me, demanding an answer.

"Am I pissing you off?"

He blinked hard once, took a deep breath and said slowly, as if it took all his patience, "Yes, Carl, you are pissing me off."

"Oh, sorry ... my fault." I smiled at him.

"God damn it, Carl, would you knock it off with the fucking 'sorry my fault' routine."

I couldn't resist it, "Oh, sure, sorry ..."

"Fuck - don't even say it!"

"Hey, I'm just getting you back for about seven thousand miles worth of rubber."

"Okay, so we're even ..." He smiled slightly, and added almost under his breath, "for now ..."

We ended up driving around for another five minutes until we decided that perhaps we needed some guidance in finding the elusive filling station. Leonard spotted a kid riding his bike, slowed, and asked, "Hey kid, where's a gas station around here?"

The kid looked at Leonard like it was a trick question. He pointed across the street, and said with a squeaky voice, "Um, it's right over there, mister." He rode off quickly on his beat-up Schwinn as if he were afraid we were going to ask him anything else.

Once we had fueled up, and with two full grocery bags full of fresh supplies, we were ready to be on the road again. I took over at the driver's seat to give Leonard a break.

"So, you think that you can find your way back to the highway, Carl?"

"Yeah, probably."

"Probably is not what I want to hear, buddy."

"Well, maybe you can fucking spot for a fucking sign, Mr. Critical Guy, and help me out ... how about that?"

"I was just going to suggest that, Carl ... you know the first sign of healing is knowing that you need help."

"Oh, fuck off, Leonard." I pulled out of the gas station.

We drove in what seemed like circles for nearly ten minutes in search of the highway. Leonard ranted, "What the hell is wrong with this town, don't they believe in signs? First we can't find a friggin' gas station, now we can't find a friggin' sign to get us back to the highway."

I responded with a Rod Serling imitation, "Picture if you will ... two men on a lonely long road trip, trapped in a town called ... Nowhere. Stop at the light, next exit ... The Twilight Zone."

Leonard stared at me and said, "My God you are strange, Carl."

"Thank you, Leonard."

"You're welcome, Carl."

At last we spotted the highway, and after a few more minutes of driving around actually managed to figure out how to get on it.

"Jesus Christ – finally."

"Hey, but we're there, Leonard. Just another half an hour or so and we should be in the Black Hills National Forest."

Leonard rolled his eyes as he got up and headed aft, "Sure, Carl." He called from in back, "You want one of these?"

I looked in the rearview mirror and saw he was holding a soda. "Yeah, I suppose so ..." He came back up front and handed it to me. The highway was straight and easy, and the day was beautiful. We drank our sodas and enjoyed the scenery as we drove on.

After a few minutes Leonard said, "Aren't we supposed to be headed east?"

"Yeah, why?"

He nodded out the window, "Well, because it looks more like we're headed south."

I looked up at the sun, studied it for a moment and said, "So you are right Leonard, we are definitely heading south. We must have picked up 85 instead of 16 back there."

Leonard calmly grabbed the map up off of the floor. He looked at it for a moment, "Yeah, that's what we did alright," then threw it back down.

"So, what do you want me to do here, keep going or turn around?"

"Ah, keep going, there's a junction with Route 18 coming up here soon ... that'll get us there too."

Given his general impatience with these sorts of logistical errors, Leonard seemed surprisingly nonchalant about it. "Aren't you pissed?"

"No Carl, I am not. I need to be gentle with you during your sensitive recovery period. Getting pissed at you could trigger a catastrophic relapse and we could end up in Nebraska."

"You are such an asshole, Leonard."

He smiled at me and said, "Yes, Carl, sometimes I am."

Twenty minutes later, our southbound theory became reality when we saw a blue sign that said, "U.S. 18 – East – One Mile." We took the cutoff at Mule Creek and headed east toward the town of Edgemont, South Dakota. Leonard did a little cheer when he spotted another sign that said, "Thank you for Visiting Wyoming – Come Back Soon."

"Come back soon my ass, I'd rather have an enema." I was surprised when he turned around and waved goodbye. I thought he was going to give the state the finger. He then settled back into his seat and took a deep breath as if he had been holding it for the entire state. "Man, I feel better already."

"Oh, come on, Leonard, Wyoming wasn't all that bad."

He stared at me like I was speaking Swahili.

"No, seriously. Hell, they've got Yellowstone and Devil's Tower ... and hey, we met Mary there ..."

He pondered my point for a minute then said, "Well, you're right, sort of ... BUT those places don't count ... they're national parks, so they're not really part of Wyoming." He smiled smugly then added, "And Mary, she's from Montana." There was no point in arguing with him.

A short time later we saw a brown sign that said, "You Are Now Entering the Black Hills National Forest."

"Hey, Leonard, we made it."

"Yes, we did, Carl, and this is good." He patted my shoulder. "So, all we need to do now is find a place to camp."

"Yep, that's about it."

"Any ideas?"

"Nope, I didn't get that far."

Leonard was just about ready to pick up the map and do some research when yet another sign appeared by the side of the road: "Hot Springs 3 miles – Wind Cave National Park 12 miles." Almost immediately another followed that simply asked, "Have you Dug Wall Drug?"

"Damn, what is the deal with all of the signs, what did they do, steal them all from Wyoming?"

"Hell, I don't know. Possibly. Maybe they hate Wyoming as much as you do."

"Carl, no one hates Wyoming as much as I do."

"I'm pretty clear on that point, Leonard." I didn't want to get into it any further, and returned to the subject at hand. "Well, my vote is for the Wind Cave place. It sounds cool."

"Sounds cool to me too ... let's do it."

We passed though the more-tourist-trap-than-town of Hot Springs and headed up toward the park. In the nine miles between the town and the park we saw four more signs advertising Wall Drug. After the third sign, I pretended to be in a trance-like state and repeated in a monotone voice over and over, "Must go to Wall Drug, must go to Wall Drug ..."

I was on my fifth round of it when Leonard said matter of factly, "You know, Carl, the traditional way to snap someone out of a hypnotic state is to slap the shit out of them." I looked over at him. He raised his eyebrows.

"No need for that, Leonard, suddenly I seem to be over it."

"I thought so."

It was only twelve-thirty when we arrived at the entrance to the park. In spite of the few glitches on this last leg of our trip, we had actually made pretty good time. The ranger, a middle-aged, seasoned looking guy, was polite but not overly helpful. After we paid our campground fee, he handed us the obligatory literature and maps for the park. Barely making eye contact with us, he half-pointed up the road and said in a monotone like he had said it a million times, "Follow the road, you'll come to the campground in a couple of miles. It's well marked." Then almost as an afterthought, he said a little insincerely, "Enjoy your stay." Neither Leonard nor I took it personally. It was the end of the season and he had probably seen enough tourists to last a lifetime. We were just one more pair.

On the way to the campground we saw our first buffalo. Leonard spotted them first, and I pulled the van over at a turnout at the side of the road so we could get a better look. A pair of them was grazing in an open field maybe four hundred yards away. Even from that distance they looked big. We sat for a few minutes quietly watching them. They were beautiful, and in spite of their size, graceful-looking animals. After a bit Leonard said, "We should get going here, Carl, we need to get set up. Just a guess, but I bet those aren't the only ones we'll see here."

"You're probably right." I started the van and got back on the road toward the campground.

We arrived at the Elk Mountain Campground minutes later. We circled around to find our spot – number thirty-three. Although there were seventy-five sites, we could see only two others occupied. We had the place nearly to ourselves. We found our spot and pulled in. In spite of the ranger's apparent indifference, he had given us what appeared to be one of the best sites in the entire campground. The tent clearing was a nice grassy place nestled down in a grove of filbert trees at the bottom of a small slope. Next to it was a gentle, clear running brook. From the road it was not visible at all. "Man, Leonard, this is a sweet spot."

"Yeah, no shit – nice ranger."

We got set up without difficulty and when we were done sat down at the picnic table with a couple of sodas. "So, what do you want to do with the afternoon, Leonard?"

"I don't know. This is a pretty nice little place we have here. I could just lay around here, get stoned and veg."

"Yeah, I suppose that's one option."

"You don't sound too thrilled with that idea ... what did you have in mind?"

"Well, I was sort of thinking that we could do a little exploring ... maybe even check out the cave."

"Cave?" Leonard said tenuously and took a sip of soda.

"Yeah, cave." I rifled through our stack of park literature on the table and found the pamphlet and map that the ranger had given us. "It says here that Wind Cave is one of the largest cave systems in the world. Here, listen to this." I read:

"'The cave system started forming over three hundred and twenty million years ago when water began to dissolve limestone sedimentary layers buried within harder rock. Inside the cave there are many extraordinary calcite formations, some of which are found nowhere else in the world. These include boxwork, flowstone, helictites, and frostwork. The cave was first discovered in 1881 by Jessie and Tom Bingham, who, when herding cattle in the area, heard a whistling noise. When they went to investigate, they discovered a hole in the ground, out of which wind was blowing. The wind, for which the cave is named, is generated by the difference in air pressure between the outside air and the air in the cave itself. Although the cave has been extensively explored, it is estimated that only about 5 percent of it has actually been discovered. Ranger-led tours of the cave are offered year-round. Tour schedules are available at the visitor's center.'"

"Well, what do you think?" I looked up at Leonard, "I think it sounds pretty groovy."

Leonard looked slightly nervous, didn't say anything and took another drink of his soda.

"What?"

"Gimme a cigarette would ya, Carl?"

"Sure ..." I reached into my pocket and handed him the pack. Leonard busted the filter off of one, lit it, and took a deep drag. "What's wrong, man?"

"Oh, forget it, you're going to think I'm a weenie."

"No man, seriously, what's wrong?"

Leonard took another deep drag. "Well ..." He checked himself for a moment then continued, "... Okay, here it is, Carl, I really don't like being in closed places."

"Yeah, so? - I had no idea." I tried to sound casual about it. "Hey, we'll just do something else."

Leonard looked serious.

"What?"

"I don't want to do something else, Carl."

"Well, why the hell not? Shit, if you're claustrophobic why the hell would you want to go down in a fucking cave? There's tons of other stuff to do around here." Leonard continued to look at me intensely. I tried to reassure him, "Hey, man, it's no big deal ... really."

"Yes it is, Carl ... it is a *very* big deal. Call it personal pride, but I refuse to let irrational fear stop me from doing anything ... it's just not who I am. Come on, let's get going." He got up and started to head for the van.

"Hey Leonard, hang on a minute ... I'm serious, we don't need to go."

He stopped, turned around, and said determinedly, "Yes we do, Carl - come on."

As soon as we got in the van, Leonard pulled out the pipe and some Wiccan weed. "Hey, are you sure you want to do that before we go down in a cave?"

"Why not?"

"Well, you know ... that whole pot -paranoia thing."

Leonard finished filling the pipe, then put a match to it and took a healthy drag. He held the smoke for a minute, then exhaled and said, "Pot doesn't make me paranoid ... it helps me focus." I shrugged my shoulders, took the pipe from him, and took a drag myself.

Once we finished the weed, we got underway. I had a pleasant but not overwhelming buzz on. Leonard briefly looked over the pamphlet on the cave, then put it aside and looked at the rest of what the ranger had given us. All of a sudden he started laughing.

"What?"

"Oh man, you need to see this." He held a booklet up. It was titled simply, "Buffalo and You." He turned the page. There was a picture of a smashed-up late model pickup truck. Underneath it, it said in red bold letters, "Warning - Bison can be unpredictable and dangerous!"

"My God, I think that's a bit of an understatement."

"Yeah, it says here that some guy who was apparently unfamiliar with 'buffalo temperament' honked at one to get him to move out of the road. It was during the rutting season and the eighteen-hundred-pound bull attacked his truck and turned it into scrap metal."

"Jesus, are you serious?"

"Yeah, I'm serious." Leonard looked up, shook his head in disbelief and said, "My God, people are stupid!" He continued, "You know what they should have titled this flyer?"

"What's that, Leonard?"

"Natural Selection and You." We both busted up laughing.

We were still laughing when moments later we rounded a blind corner. About a hundred feet ahead of us, in the middle of the road, there was a herd of about thirty buffalo. I slammed on the brakes, sending the van into a screeching four-wheel lock-up. We slid to a stop about twenty feet from them. A huge bull raised his head and looked directly at us with an expression that said, "What the fuck do you think you're doing?"

He took a couple of steps toward us, and for a moment I thought he was going to come over to the van to investigate further. Instead, he stopped and stared at us, then went right back to what he was doing, grazing by the side of the road. I said quietly, "Oh shit, that was close."

"Yes it was, Carl," Leonard answered.

"I think I'll just wait here patiently until they decide to move on."

"I think that is an excellent idea, Carl." I switched the van off and we made ourselves comfortable. We were on buffalo standard time.

Gradually the herd began to move. The direction that they chose was toward us. They lazily walked around us, and at one point we were completely surrounded by buffalo. We both stayed quiet and tried not to move. Somehow the situation seemed more serious than the sheep that we had encountered back at Devil's Tower. As they passed I spotted a calf with its mother. It couldn't have been more than a few days old. I whispered to Leonard, "Check it out ... a calf. Is that cute or what?"

Leonard whispered back, "I'll give you a dollar if you go out and pet him." I tried hard not to laugh. Trying only made it worse, but I managed to hold it in.

Finally the herd was behind us by about fifty feet. We deemed that they were far enough away that even if one of them did decide to charge us, we could probably outrun them. Looking in the rearview mirror, I fired up the van. The big bull that had threateningly glared at us earlier immediately took notice of the roar of the van's motor and began walking toward us. As he did, the herd cleared a path for him.

"Hey Carl, just a suggestion, but I would think about putting a little pedal to metal right now."

"I so hear you, Leonard ..."

I rammed the van into gear and punched it. As I did, I again glanced in the mirror. As soon as the van started moving, so did the bull. He was at a trot now. I started to put some real estate between the bull and us. After only a couple of hundred feet or so, though, I felt the van begin to slide, and we immediately lost our momentum. "What the fuck!?" I turned around. I had been looking more in the rearview mirror than at the road ahead.

In front of us, the road was completely covered for at least a hundred yards with about eight inches of buffalo manure. The van's tires spun and slid, occasionally grabbing traction on the pavement underneath.

"Oh shit!"

Leonard looked at me and said, "Literally ..."

"Fuck off, Leonard, this is serious!"

"I am, Carl - punch it!" The van lurched ahead, but we were losing speed. I looked in the mirror - the bull was gaining on us. "Come on, come on ..." I coaxed the van. We had about a hundred and fifty feet to go. I looked back in the mirror and could see the bull seriously start to close in on us. I thought to myself, "Objects in the mirror may be closer than they appear." I shared that thought with Leonard. "Where's he at?"

"Close, Carl, very close ..." We had maybe fifty feet to go until clear pavement. The van's motor screamed under the high revs.

"How close, Leonard?"

He turned around and quickly grabbed the dashboard handle with both hands, "Too close - prepare for contact!"
WHUMP!
All of a sudden the van jumped violently forward. I put my foot hard into the accelerator, the motor sang. I braced myself for another blow. Instead, unexpectedly, the tires found full traction. The van shuddered and squealed ahead with newfound thrust.

Apparently the blow from the buffalo had been enough to push us clear of the manure and we were on solid ground again. I again looked in the mirror and saw the bull standing in the middle of the road, his face covered in dung flung up from the wheels of the van. He looked pissed.

Leonard turned around and looked back, "I'll tell you what, Carl, you'd better pray that he can't read license plates."

"Yeah, no ..."

Leonard cut me off, "Don't even say it."

We arrived, without further incident, at the visitor's center a few minutes later. Unlike the campground, the parking lot here was about half full. There was an open parking spot almost directly in front of the center, and I pulled in. As soon as we got out of the van we were both immediately assaulted with the overwhelming stench of buffalo manure. A thick layer of fresh dung packed the wheel wells and sprayed up along the sides of the van. Leonard winced at the odor and took a couple of steps back, "Jesus Christ, Carl, it smells like a fucking outhouse on wheels." He started laughing - he thought he was pretty clever.

"Yeah, well, since you were riding in it, I guess that makes you a turd."

He stopped laughing. "That's Mr. Turd to you, buddy."

"So, are you sure that you still want to do this?"

"Hey I told you already, yeah," he said emphatically, "Now come on, let's go ... I'm going to hurl if I stand here any longer."

"Okay, but hang on for a second, I want to see if we picked up any body damage."

I circled around to the back of the van. Leonard followed with his hand over his mouth and nose.

"Aw, hell ..." Dead center of the engine lid there was a two-and-a-half foot wide dent. On either side of it, two ragged three-inch holes were punched in the sheet metal.

Leonard reassuringly put his hand on my shoulder, "Hey Carl, don't worry about it, it adds character ... battle scars, man." Then he put a finger in one of the holes and added optimistically, "And ventilation, too."

I was still displeased about it, but it was done. "Yeah, whatever ... come on, let's go." We headed on into the center.

The Netherworld

Walking into the building was like walking into a cave. The ceilings were high, but the low lighting and the lack of windows made it feel distinctly cavernous. All around the walls there were lighted display cases of various geologic specimens – specimens that I assumed came from the cave below. I looked at Leonard to see what his reaction was. He looked slightly nervous. "How you doin' there, Leonard?"

"I'm doin' fine. How are you?" He refused to acknowledge that he was nervous.

We went over to the information counter where we were greeted by two rangers, a man and a woman, both in their mid-forties. They seemed like they were a couple. They were far more enthusiastic than the fellow that we had met at the park entrance had been.

"Hi, how are you today? Can we help you?"

"We're doing fine ... we were wondering about when the next tour is." Leonard had wandered over to a large map of the area near the counter so I handled the logistics.

"Well ..." She turned around and glanced at the clock behind her, "We have another tour leaving in about ten minutes." She smiled pleasantly.

"That sounds great, so what do we do?"

"Will it be just the two of you?"

"Ah, yeah ..."

"Well then, that will be three dollars each." I reached into my wallet and got out a ten and handed it to her.

"Thank you." She reached under the counter. "Here is some information that we have about the cave. I'll be back with your change in a moment."

"Thanks."

"Hey, Leonard." He didn't answer - he was intently studying the map. I tried again a little louder, "Hey, Leonard, I got us signed up for a tour ... it starts in about ten minutes." He still didn't answer.

I was just about to walk over to him when suddenly he said, "Fucking Custer State Park – they named a park after that asshole?!" He nearly yelled it. The room fell silent, and everyone turned their attention to him. "Oh my God, one of the most egotistical, genocidal sons of bitches in American history, and they have the fucking audacity to name a fucking park after him?! What the fuck is that all about?!"

I left the counter and went on over to him. When I got closer I could see that he was actually breathing hard. He was raging.

"Hey Leonard, maybe we should get out ..."

He ignored me and cut me off mid-sentence. "Look at this, Carl!" He pointed to the map. Just north of Wind Cave there it was... Custer State Park.

"Jesus, Leonard ..."

"Jesus is right. What the hell were they exactly thinking?!"

"I can't answer ..."

He cut me off again, but this time he had heard me. He lowered his voice a little. "Yeah, it's insane – it's fucking insane, man..." He turned to me and our eyes met. He had tears in them, he was so angry. For a few moments he just stood there looking into my eyes. He breathed heavily. A couple of times he started to say something, but then stopped to catch his breath. Finally he said just one word ... "Shit."

"Come on, man, let's go have a cigarette." For a second, Leonard didn't acknowledge that he had heard me, then he nodded. We headed for the door. On our way out it was stone silent. No one said a word. Either they were afraid of Leonard's anger, or they agreed with it – both were appropriate.

As soon as we were outside, Leonard said, "Over there." He motioned toward an open piece of lawn that was under the shade of a small grove of trees across from the visitor's center. I followed him. He laid down flat on his back in the grass and closed his eyes. I knelt down next to him. He squeezed his eyes shut so hard that a few of the tears of anger were forced out of them and ran down his cheeks.

I gave him a few minutes to still himself then finally said, "Hey, how 'bout that cigarette?" I knew he didn't want one but I said it anyway.

"No, Carl - thanks." His voice was hoarse and dry as if he had been yelling for a long time. He didn't open his eyes.

I knelt next to him quietly for a few more minutes. He kept his eyes tightly shut and he didn't move. When his breathing became less labored I said, "I'm going to go in and get our dough back ... I'll be back in a minute."

Leonard took a deep breath and said, "I thought that you wanted to go down into the cave." He opened his eyes and looked up at me.

"Yeah, well, I did, but ..."

"So why don't you find out if they have another tour later?" He was sincere about it. I knew if I said no he would think that I was being patronizing. "I'll go check. I'll be back in a minute." Leonard nodded.

On the way back into the visitor's center I thought briefly that I might just come back and tell him that they didn't have another tour. We'd just forget the whole thing. I figured, though, that he would see right through it, and besides, I thought it would be pretty fucked up to lie to him. You don't lie to friends, not ever.

When I approached the counter the ranger didn't give me even an ounce of shit. She smiled slightly and simply said, "You missed the last tour. If you would like to go on the next tour, it starts in about a half an hour. If not, I would be happy to refund your money."

"Thanks, I appreciate that. I think that my friend and I are going to take the next tour." She brightened up and actually seemed happy that we were going to go.

"Good ... then just meet me here by three-thirty."

"Sounds great, we'll be back in a bit."

I went back and joined Leonard.

"Well?"

"She says that there's another tour leaving in about a half an hour."

"Cool." He sat up. "You know what, Carl?"

"What's that, Leonard?"

He paused for a second, as if he questioned whether he should say what he was going to say. "When you went back in there it crossed my mind that you might just come back and tell me that that was the last tour, so we could just forget the whole thing."

"Yeah?"

"Yeah ... But then I said to myself, hey, friends don't lie to each other."

I swallowed a lump in my throat and said, "No, they don't, Leonard ... they don't."

Leonard and I hung out together on the grass and smoked a couple of cigarettes until it was time to go. Leonard's raw anger seemed to abate some, but the indignation was still there. I didn't have a buzz on any longer, and I suspected that if I didn't, Leonard sure didn't either.

"Hey, Leonard, do you want to smoke a little more weed before we head on in?"

"Nah, I'm good."

"You sure? I thought you said that weed helps you focus."

"It does, Carl, but you know, I'm feeling pretty focused right now without it."

We were just a couple of minutes late for the tour when we got into the visitor's center. The room was empty and there was only one ranger behind the counter. He said, "You just missed them."

"Oh shit ... I mean, excuse me, damn."

"Look, I tell you what, I'm not supposed to let anyone down there without a guide, but if you hurry you'll catch up with them. Just be careful. If you don't see anyone by the time you get to the bottom of the stairs then come on back up. Hell, there's about a million miles of cave down there ... don't want you getting lost." He motioned across the room with his hand. "Just go through that door over there."

"Thanks, man." We made for the door. I put my hand on the doorknob and said, "You still okay with this, Leonard?"

"Quit asking, Carl."

I opened it and we went in. Inside, the air was much cooler, maybe fifty or fifty-five degrees, and although there was electric lighting it was still dim inside. It took a few moments for our eyes to adjust.

"Man, it's cold as hell in here."

"Well, what did you expect, Carl? It's a frickin' cave."

"Hey, it was just an observation."

We walked the few steps from the alcove to the top of the stairs and looked down the passageway that led to the cave below.

"Whew, I'll tell you what, them are some steep stairs." Leonard didn't say anything: he just stood there staring down into the abyss. I figured that standing there and looking was worse than just doing.

"Come on, Leonard, just follow me." We began our descent.

The stairs were extremely steep, and although I didn't suffer from claustrophobia as Leonard did, I did suffer from a healthy respect for heights. I hung onto the railings tightly. My knuckles were white. Leonard, in his own hypersensitized state, noticed my uneasiness.

"Hey, is this bugging you, Carl?"

"Yeah, a little ... Not the cave part, though, it's these fucking stairs. Do you think they could have made these any steeper?"

"Yes, Carl, as a matter of fact I think they probably could have."

"I know that they *could have*. It was more of a rhetorical question."

"Duh, Carl. I just like giving you shit. It makes me feel better."

"Well, I'm so glad that I can be helpful to you."

"I am too."

It took us nearly five minutes to make the descent into the cave. The further we went, the more clearly we could hear voices. We were going to catch up. Finally, we could see the bottom. I could just make out the last person in the group clearing the last stair.

We stepped into the large cavern and joined the group of about thirty other people. The ranger, who we had met in the lobby above, was leading the group. She was standing on a rock which served as a pedestal at the far end of the room.

"... Under no circumstances is anyone to leave the group. There are hundreds of miles of passageways in the Wind Cave system, many of which are unexplored. Some of these passageways have false floors and can be quite dangerous. Should you for some reason become separated, stay where you are. It gives us the best chance to find you. Even people who are very experienced can become confused. A couple of years ago one of our rangers came down to explore some new areas of the cave. She became disoriented and eventually got lost. It took us over three days to find her ... the batteries in her flashlight only lasted for one."

I looked over at Leonard to see how he was taking the ranger's speech. He looked a little edgy. He leaned over to me, "This is not really making me feel extra comfortable, Carl."

"Yeah, I know, me neither ... let's just stick with the group."

"Oh, no, Carl, I was thinking screw the ranger, let's just wander off on our own tour."

I smiled at him and said, "Oh shut up, Leonard, you know what I mean."

The ranger continued to talk about some of the history about the cave. As she talked I looked around. The cave was magnificent. All around us the walls and ceiling were covered in strange white honeycombed structures. It was like being inside of a gigantic hive.

"Man, this is insanely cool."

Leonard was looking around too. "Yeah, it's a complete trip." He sounded slightly more comfortable.

At last the ranger came to the end of her speech. "The complete tour is going to last a little over an hour. Is there anyone with us who is feeling at all uncomfortable with being down here? Many people are claustrophobic ... don't be embarrassed to say something. We want you to enjoy the tour." She paused for a minute to see if anyone would answer. I glanced at Leonard. He raised one eyebrow – he was not going to give in. "All right, then, follow me. Our first stop is a room called 'The Methodist Church.'"

She headed down the wide passageway and the group followed her. We were last in the line. Leonard leaned over to me and said, "Gee, with a name like that, I'm surprised that Dieter and Marta aren't here."

"Um, I think they're Lutherans, Leonard." We both laughed a little.

It took us about ten minutes to walk down to the first stop in the tour. Most of the way the passage was wide, but in a few places it narrowed and the ceiling dropped low enough to cause us to stoop. I could feel that these spots made Leonard nervous but he said nothing and kept going. Finally the passage opened up and we arrived at our first destination.

The vast room was dramatic. The cathedral-like ceilings rose above us probably fifty or sixty feet. It was clear why they had likened the room to a church, although I wasn't sure what made it Methodist in denomination. Hanging from the ceiling were thousands and thousands of small white stalactites. They shimmered under the glow of the electric lights. The ranger gave the group a few minutes to take it all in on their own. Then she began with her talk.

"Alvin McDonald began exploring the cave system in 1890. He was only seventeen at the time." A couple of people in the group whispered to each other when she said seventeen. She continued, "I would say that he was a pretty brave and inquisitive young man." The group murmured again in agreement.

Leonard turned to me and said, "I think he was nuts." I smiled but didn't say anything. I didn't want to interrupt the ranger. But I did agree with him completely.

"This is the first of many caves that he discovered. Now, Mr. McDonald explored these caves only by the light of a single candle. To give you better idea of exactly what he experienced, I am going to turn off the electric lights and light just a single candle." A blanket of tension covered the group as soon as she said the "turn off the lights" part. I was a little apprehensive as well. I guess it's just a natural reaction to be afraid of the dark – to be afraid of what you can't see.

Apparently she was used to this response, and before any kind of general panic could set in she said reassuringly, "Wait, wait, folks ... don't worry, it will only be dark for a moment. And I promise that will have my hand on the light switch the whole time."

Leonard observantly said, "Well how in the hell is she going to light a fucking candle with one hand?"

I knew that she couldn't have possibly heard him, but she answered his question, continuing, "Since I only have two hands I will need a volunteer from the group to light a match for me." She had done this routine many times before and she had already picked someone out for the job, "Would you be willing to give me a hand here?" She was talking to a boy of about nine who was in the front row of the group. He beamed and looked at both of his parents for approval. They nodded. He then turned back to the ranger and said enthusiastically, "Sure!"

"Oh, this is just great. I feel like I'm on a plane and the pilot just announced that he's turning the plane over to a kid for a minute."

"Hey, don't worry, Leonard, I'm sure she knows what she's doing."

"I sure fucking hope so, cuz if I go crazy down here I promise it won't be a pleasant experience for anyone."

The kid stepped up and joined the ranger by the light switch. She held a candle in one hand, and with the other, she handed him a box of wooden matches and said, "Okay, now get a match out and get ready to strike it. I'll turn off the lights then tell you when."

"Um, okay ..." The kid tried to sound like he was ready for the big job, but his voice broke a bit. I think that he knew that a lot of people were counting on him. If he fucked up this simple thing they were going to be pissed, really pissed.

"All right, I'm going to turn the lights off on three. Remember, after I turn them off, wait for my sign." The kid nodded nervously. Even from a good fifteen feet away I could see that he was shaking a little. "... One ... twooooo ... three ..." CLICK. The lights went off and it was totally dark – not twilight dark, not camping dark, but dark dark – the kind of dark that exists only in bad dreams and caves. Immediately everyone in the group started oohing and aahing. A couple of people sounded slightly freaked out. One of those people was Leonard. He instinctively grabbed hold of my arm and nearly yelled, "Jesus Christ Mother of Mercy would somebody hit the fucking lights?!"

The ranger had to have heard him, and above the din said, "Okay, now go ahead and light it." Across the room there was a flash as the match caught fire. Given the total darkness it seemed much brighter than I'm sure it actually was.

They lit the candle and the far end of the cave was faintly illuminated in candlelight. Everyone breathed a sigh of relief. "You okay there, Leonard?" I tried to sound serious, but I was half-laughing at his outburst.

"No, I am not fucking okay ... okay? I swear to God if she does that again I'm going to have a spaz attack."

"Well, I wouldn't worry about it too much, I'm sure after your comment she won't."

The ranger went on briefly about the early days of cave exploration before finally turning the lights back on. When she switched them on they glared harshly in comparison to the candle, and it took a few moments for my eyes to adjust to the brightness. As soon as they did, the first thing that I saw was none other than Dieter and Marta standing immediately in front of us smiling excitedly.

Both Leonard and I were a little taken aback. Although earlier we had joked about running into them, neither one of us even remotely thought of it as an actual real possibility. Instantly, they threw themselves at us. Dieter, who was grinning wildly, grabbed my hand and shook it vigorously, while Marta gave Leonard a big hug like he was her long lost brother. Then they switched places. When they were done squeezing and shaking us, Dieter said, "Hello, mein friends!

We thought that it was you but we cannot be sure until they put the lights on again. Is it not good that we meet again? This is a remarkable thing!"

I was less speechless than Leonard was and said, "Yeah, it's good to see you guys again too." I said it like I actually meant it – and I really did mean it.

Dieter was just about to say something else when the ranger interrupted him, "Excuse me ... you folks in the back, could you please keep it down just a bit?"

"I'm sorry, ma'am," I said apologetically. She smiled back pleasantly, apparently understanding the gravity of our reunion.

"It's perfectly all right, it's just that we are in a cave and well ... caves have echoes."

"Sorry, we'll try to be more quiet."

Dieter, who looked somewhat embarrassed that we had broken a rule, leaned over and whispered, "We must talk when the tour is over." I smiled, nodded yes, and motioned his attention back to the ranger.

"Our next stop will be a room called 'The Garden of Eden.' I'm sure that all of you will be very impressed. Please follow me." Dieter and Marta turned to us. They were smiling and nodding enthusiastically. They were as excited as a pair of kids who were on their way to Disneyland. Just as the group was about to leave, the ranger added as an afterthought, "Oh ... and in case anyone was wondering, no, I will not be turning the lights off again." I could almost hear the tension pour out of Leonard as soon as she said it. I think she probably said it for him.

The group was underway again and began to file behind the ranger down the passageway to the next stop. Leonard put his hand on my shoulder, "Hey, hang on here a minute." Dieter and Marta brought up the rear, but were evidently so focused on the next destination that they did not notice that we were not immediately following. We held back from the group until we could still see them, but were far enough away that they couldn't hear us. Leonard motioned, "Okay, let's go." We started walking.

"So Carl."

"Yeah, Leonard?"

"How weird is this?"

"You mean the Dieter and Marta thing?"

"Don't patronize me, Carl, you know what I'm talking about... of course I mean the Dieter and Marta thing, what do you think I'm talking about? This is a big fucking country and we run into those two damn near everywhere we go"

"It's pretty weird, Leonard."

"Pretty weird?! Is that all you have to say is 'pretty weird?' I would say that it's at least too fucking weird."

"Yeah, I would have to agree with you ... it is too fucking weird, but it's always too fucking weird every time we run into those two."

Leonard paused, then said, "No, Carl, it's not even too fucking weird ... it's more than that." He stopped walking. It took me a moment to realize that he had. When I did, I stopped too and turned around. He was just staring at me.

"What?"

"You know what it is, Carl? – It's really, really too fucking weird."

"Yes it is, Leonard, now come on."

We picked up our pace and rejoined the group. Just after we did, the path funneled into an extremely narrow passage. The ranger called back and said, "I know it's a little tight here, but it opens up pretty soon." We wove through about fifty yards of twists and turns, some so small that we had to turn our bodies sideways to slip through. At last, true to the ranger's promise, the passageway did in fact open up. We continued on. The further we went, the more comfortable Leonard seemed to become with the whole cave thing. He was actually relaxed enough to point out to me a few cool formations along the way.

The passageway gradually continued to get wider and wider, until we arrived at our destination, The Garden of Eden. The ranger said nothing more than "Here we are," and made a sweeping motion with her arms. The cavern spoke for itself.

We entered into the room, and the group was left speechless. It was breathtaking. Although not as large as the last room, the walls and ceiling were entirely covered in amber-colored crystals. The whole room seemed alive as they sparkled. I said quietly to Leonard, "Wow, is this beautiful or what?"

He waited for a moment before answering, then simply said, "Yeah, man ... it really is."

Neither one of our comments seemed to really do justice to the room's brilliance, but neither one of us could think of anything more profound to say. I looked over at Dieter and Marta. They were in absolute amazement. Both of them had broad serene smiles on their faces. It made me wonder what they saw in the crystals.

Without looking at her, Dieter said to Marta, "It's so ... so beautiful ... it tempts me ..." Marta kept smiling, nodded, and murmured in agreement.

Leonard apparently overheard Dieter's comment as well. He gave him a what-the-hell-are-you-talking-about look and said impatiently, "Tempts you to do what?" It was an amusing but appropriate question. I was wondering what Dieter was talking about myself. I had to turn away from them to stifle a laugh. Dieter either didn't hear him or didn't want to hear him. Either way, he didn't acknowledge Leonard's remark. He just kept looking around the room in wonder.

After a few minutes the ranger got the group back together and started her speech. "Well, I'm not surprised to see that everyone is pretty impressed with this part of the cave. It is one of my favorites as well. Let me give you a little bit of history and scientific explanation about it." When she said the words "scientific explanation" Dieter and Marta's smiles faded some. Clearly for them there was no need for "scientific explanation."

"Alvin McDonald discovered this part of the cave in 1893, three years after his first venture into the system. I think you might be interested in what his observations were about it." She opened a small booklet that she was carrying. "Here, let me read you an excerpt from the diary that he kept: 'After nearly three years of exploration I have come to a most heavenly place. The splendor of this room only reassures me of the limitless magnificence of God's creation. I shall call it The Garden of Eden ...'" Dieter and Marta were apparently reassured by Alvin's less than scientific observations and they visibly relaxed. Leonard rolled his eyes.

The ranger continued, "Although Mr. McDonald's interpretation is certainly understandable, there *is* an actual scientific explanation for these formations. These crystals are made of a mineral called calcite. It is one of the most common of all the carbonate minerals. They are formed when volcanic rock rising to the surface cools quickly. This rapid cooling process creates an environment that allows the crystals to grow. They are found in many different places throughout the world, and they come in many different colors including red, green, blue, and even black. Calcite is an important economic mineral as well, and is used for a number of industrial applications such as the manufacture of glass, steel and concrete." Dieter and Marta started to tighten up again, like what she had said was sacrilegious. Fortunately she added, "Whatever the "scientific explanation" is for them, she made quotes in the air with her fingers, I must agree with Alvin, they are very, very beautiful." I think that last part saved her.

"We have one last stop on our tour, a room called 'The Pearly Gates.' When we get there I think you'll know why it was named that. Please, follow me." As the group began to follow the ranger down to the next cavern, I leaned over and whispered to Leonard, "I think this is the last stop for a lot of people."

"Not for me, man, I want to be with the interesting folks." We both held back a laugh.

It didn't take us long to arrive at our final destination. Along the way, we walked behind Dieter and Marta, who talked excitedly between each other in German. Neither Leonard nor I could, not surprisingly, understand a word they were saying. Leonard speculated, though, that they were probably discussing what it was going to be like to get a shot at ascension without dying. "This is a good trial run for them," he said.

"God, Leonard, do you always have to be so irreverent about those two?" I was pretty much joking with him, but I was a little serious as well. Leonard picked up on the serious part.

He looked at me without blinking, "Why yes, Carl ... yes I do." He said like it was his job.

When we got there, the ranger held the group up just outside of the cavern. Leonard whispered to me, "Hey, Carl, this is a surprise, I thought Saint Peter was a man." He could hardly say it without laughing.

"Knock it off, Leonard," I whispered back. "You're going to get us into big trouble."

He continued, "I hope that I answer all the questions right ... I didn't have a chance to study." I couldn't even look at him. I knew if I did we both would be in stitches.

The ranger's voice was lowered, "Now, a word of warning before we go into The Pearly Gates. I must ask you not to speak, to stay on the marked path, and please don't touch anything."

"Carl, I just knew this was the way heaven was going to be, uptight, and tons of rules."

"Shhhh ..."

"The formations in this room are called frostwork. They are very, very fragile. Even the vibrations from the sound of a human voice can damage them." Everyone in the group nodded, but no one said anything, like they were practicing for the real thing. "We will only be in the room for five minutes. Please watch me - I will raise my arm like this when it is time for us to leave. If for any reason you need to leave before then, there is a clearly marked exit on the far side of the room. Outside, there is a waiting area. Please wait there for the rest of the group. Does anyone have any questions?" Everyone in the group shook their heads no. "Okay, then, here we go."

The group followed the ranger into the room. Just as she had promised, the cavern was remarkable. The ceiling was completely canopied in a dusting of delicate white ice-like crystals. They twinkled vibrantly. In stark contrast, the walls were of some type of deep black mineral. It shone like incredibly smooth glass, so much so I could see my own reflection in it. At the same time, though, it was difficult to get a true perspective of where it exactly was and where it wasn't. I had the sense that if I had tried to touch it my hand would dissolve into it. I wondered momentarily if this was the real reason that the ranger didn't want anyone to touch anything, but I shrugged it off. I looked back up to the ceiling. I thought to myself, I don't think I would have called this place the pearly gates, but it certainly is an amazing place.

Leonard tapped me on the shoulder. He startled me and I jumped slightly. I turned around to look at him, and when I did, he feigned preparation for a big sneeze. I shook my head, rolled my eyes, and mouthed "asshole." He gave me an impish look and shrugged his shoulders.

Now that Leonard had drawn my attention back to the group, I looked around to see what their reaction was. Everyone was mesmerized as well, but no one more than Dieter and Marta. Their heads were tilted far back and they gazed at the ceiling. I wondered if they had even noticed the walls. They were both in such awe you would have thought that they were looking up at the Sistine Chapel. They appeared to be literally in heaven, or at least at the edge of it ... maybe Leonard's theory wasn't so far off the mark.

A short time later, the ranger gave us the signal that it was time for us to leave. Dieter and Marta were so enthralled with it all that I had to lightly put a hand on Dieter's shoulder to get his attention. He smiled and nodded a thank you. The group filed out of the room and into the foyer where we were to gather before making our ascent to the surface.

The ranger joined us. "Well, judging from everyone's reaction, I guess that everybody was pretty impressed with the cavern. That doesn't surprise me ... it is extraordinary." Although it was now safe to talk, still no one said anything, they just nodded an emphatic yes. "Oh, and I would also like to thank everyone for being as quiet as they were ... especially you, sir." She smiled and looked right at Leonard, "I'm glad that you were able to successfully restrain your sneeze."

Leonard, who was taken a little off guard, said casually, "Uh... no problem."

I leaned over to him and said, "Ooh, busted ..."

Before we started to head up to the surface, the ranger took a quick head count to make sure that everyone was accounted for. When she finished she got a puzzled look on her face and said, "That's odd, I count two more than we started with. That's the first time that's ever happened." I raised my hand to get her attention, "Excuse me, ma'am, that would be us ... we joined the group late." She still looked a bit puzzled, but seemed satisfied with the explanation. Hey, at least she wasn't leaving anyone behind.

The group made its way up the long flight of stairs to the surface. Somehow, going up the one hundred and fifty stairs (I counted them) didn't make me nearly as nervous as going down them, even though I knew they were just as steep. Leonard was pretty darned happy to be heading surfaceward, and appeared more relaxed with each step. On step number one twenty six he said from behind me, "Hey, Carl?"

"Yeah, Leonard?"

"Are you still afraid of heights?"

"Yeah ... why?"

"Remember on the way down when you asked me if they could have made these stairs any steeper, and I said yes they could have?"

"Yeah ..."

"Well, to answer your question, they did ... I wouldn't turn around right now if I were you, buddy." My grip instantly tightened on the railing and although I wanted to turn around and verify my fear, I didn't.

"Why exactly are you telling me this right now, Leonard, couldn't you have waited until we got to the top?"

"Yes I could have, Carl, but like I said on the way down, giving you shit makes me feel better." He poked me in the butt.

"I'm so glad ..."

"Me too."

A couple of minutes later we broke the surface and arrived at the assembly room in the visitor's center. Just as I cleared the last stair I glanced back and looked down the steps. Leonard was right, they were steep as hell. I felt myself get a little dizzy. Going up was one thing, but if I had had to go down them I may not have made it.

The ranger turned to the group and said, "I would like to thank all of you for coming. I hope that everyone enjoyed the tour." A few people said thank you back, the rest nodded.

"If you have any questions I will be happy to answer them. I'll just be over at the information counter." And with that the group broke up.

As soon as everyone dispersed Dieter and Marta came over to us. Leonard leaned over to me and said, "Jesus, here they come ... brace yourself."

"Come on, man, they're not all that bad. And would you quit calling me Jesus."

"Sure, Carl ..." The pair was obviously emotional from the experience.

"Was that not magnificent!"

"Yeah, Dieter, it really was pretty cool."

"Ya, it is hard to say with the words," Marta added. She didn't have to, I could see in her eyes how much it had sincerely moved her.

I again politely agreed with her, "Yeah, I know what you mean ... it really was awfully pretty down there."

Dieter responded excitedly, "The pearly gates - did you see?"

I was about to answer, but Leonard beat me to it and took over, "See what?" I thought to myself, here we go.

"The ceiling ... it was, was ..." a serene and knowing expression washed over his face, then he said reverently, "... like looking into the eye of God." For a moment both Leonard and I were left speechless. For myself, I was wondering how I could tactfully say that I had not seen the eye of God in the ceiling without taking any of the experience from them. Leonard, on the other hand, looked exasperated and, I think, was thinking of how he could effectively fillet them with his answer. I wasn't sure that I wanted him to do that to them.

The pair stared at us innocently, and patiently awaited our response.

Finally, Leonard said, "What?" He sounded exactly as perturbed as I knew he was. I thought it best to step in.

Before Dieter could answer, and the two could get into it, I quickly changed the subject. "So what brings you two here?" Dieter bit on it and turned his attention to me. I was grateful.

"Well, after the Yellowstone we went to the Mount Rushmore to see the faces of the great presidents. It was to be the last place that we were going to see before we go home. But while we were there we met a man who say that this would be good place to come to." He paused, smiled, then added, "I am very glad that we did."

Marta nodded in agreement and added, "Yes, I am so glad that we did not miss seeing this. And we see you again."

Leonard didn't even try to hold himself back and interjected, "You went to Mount Rushmore? That place is such a sham!" Both Dieter and Marta were taken aback. They were, obviously perplexed by Leonard's vehement-sounding comment.

Dieter asked, "What do you mean, sham?"

I again steered the pair away from confrontation and said abruptly, "Forget it, Dieter, you don't want to know." They both still looked pretty confused but following my lead didn't pursue it any further.

Dieter tactfully moved on to an easier topic and asked, "So, where do you camp this evening?"

"Oh, we're up at the Elk Mountain Campground ... heck, I think it's the only place to camp around here."

The pair immediately brightened up, "Ya, that is where we stay this evening!"

Marta immediately added warmly, "You must join us for dinner, we insist."

I looked over at Leonard to see what he thought about it. He just raised a single eyebrow. I guess I was on my own. I turned back to Dieter and Marta and said, "Sure, that sounds great. We're in spot number thirty-three. I don't think that you'll have a hard time finding us though, the place is pretty empty." The pair smiled at our acceptance of their invitation.

"Good then we see you, say ..." He glanced at his watch, "... around seven o'clock?"

"That sounds great ... we'll find each other."

Revelations

We left the visitor's center and headed out toward the van. As soon as we cleared the door, and were out of earshot of Dieter and Marta, I said to Leonard, "So are you okay having dinner with Dieter and Marta? I couldn't read you back there."

"Yeah, I'm fine with it." He didn't sound tremendously excited about it. Then he said, "Why in the hell did you stop me back there, Carl?"

"What, from tearing into those two?"

"Yeah ... why?"

"I guess you have to ask yourself, Leonard, what would be the point?"

He thought about it for a second, then said, "The point would be that their kind of thinking contributed to that," he nodded back towards the visitor's center. I knew he was talking about Custer. "Yeah, I agree with you, Leonard, but I think with those two it's not intentional, they're being sincere, I just don't think they know ... it's a different thing. They have a different point of reference." Leonard looked at me and thought for a moment about what I had said. He nodded slightly, "Yeah ... maybe ..."

We got in the van and drove on back to the campground. Gratefully, after baking for a couple of hours in the hot sun, the buffalo manure hardly smelled, although the van still looked pretty disgusting.

The drive back wasn't nearly as eventful. The buffalo that we had encountered on the way to the cave had moved off into the hills well away from the road. As we passed, I spotted the bull that had charged us earlier. He was standing alone on a ridge above the herd. From afar he looked more magnificent than threatening. I smiled to myself ... I actually felt pretty fortunate to have been attacked by him. For that reason I would never repair the van.

By the time we pulled into our campsite it was early evening. I switched off the van and we got out. In the campground it was quiet and peaceful and the air pleasantly cool. I looked at my watch. It was close to six o'clock. We had about an hour or so before we would get together with Dieter and Marta.

"Hey Leonard ..." I caught him in the middle of a huge stretch.

"Yeah?" He groaned.

"We have a little bit here before we get together for dinner."

Leonard finished his stretch then started to rub his neck with his hand, "Well then, Carl, I think that I'm going to go lay down for a little while." I nodded. He understandably looked tired.

Without looking at me, he slowly walked down to the little clearing in the grove and sat down with his back to me facing the creek. It was obvious that he just wanted to be alone for a bit. I understood and I sat down at the picnic table above. The late low sun lit up the grove and the creek sparkled as the light played off its waters. The filbert trees rustled in the faint breeze. Not far off I heard a hawk, maybe a red-tail. This was a good place.

I sat there and watched Leonard's back rise and fall as he breathed slowly. Soon, I found that quite unconsciously my own breathing mirrored his. I closed my own eyes twice, each time for nearly a minute. Both times when I opened them we were still in perfect cadence with one another.

Maybe ten minutes or so passed like this, and I continued to watch him just sit there quietly in that place. Then ever so gently the wind picked up. It was barely noticeable, just a puff. I looked to the trees to see if they had felt it too. Their leaves shook ever so slightly more. When I turned my gaze back to Leonard, our breathing was out of sync. All of a sudden something flashed through me and I felt helplessly distant from him. It was just for a second, but it was the first time that I had ever felt that way. I didn't know why, and I didn't like it. Even for that brief moment I did not want to feel what it was like to be without his friendship. Almost instinctively, I put my palms on the table and prepared to rise. I felt as if I had to go to him.

I had just stood up when he took one long deep breath and tipped his head back. He held it for a few moments then exhaled. I did not move. Then he stood up slowly, and stretched. When he was done, he turned around to face me. As soon as his crystalline blue eyes met mine I felt another slight puff of wind on my cheek. My feelings of distance evaporated, and I was tremendously relieved.

He smiled up at me and said casually, "Hey, Carl."

"Yeah, Leonard?"

He paused and let me hang on it, "How about a beer?" I was expecting him to say something more profound.

I smiled back at him, "Sounds good, Leonard ... I was just going to get a couple." I went over to the cooler, grabbed two beers, and went down to join him.

We were just finishing our beers when we heard Dieter calling down to us. "Hello ... hello, mein friends." Maybe it was me, but with his accent it almost sounded like he was yodeling.

"I guess that's the dinner bell, Leonard." We both stood up and turned around. Dieter was up by the van. Although we were only about twenty feet away from him, he was waving to us like somehow we wouldn't see him.

"Hey Dieter, it looks like you found us."

"Ya, Marta she makes the dinner now." He was obviously glad that we were coming to dinner, he nearly yelled it.

I waved back to him, trying to be as enthusiastic, "We were just coming up."

Leonard leaned over to me, "Shit, Carl, why do you encourage them, they're nutty enough without it."

"Oh I don't know, Leonard, I think they're kind of fun in their own goofy way."

"Yeah, well I think they're annoying. And you know what else?"

"What?"

"It's pretty hard to take someone seriously when they sound a little bit like Sergeant Shultz."

"Come on, man, let's go. And be good." Leonard took a deep breath, like it was the last one he was going to get for a while, and reluctantly followed me up the path to Dieter. Given Leonard's state of mind, I was beginning to wonder if accepting their dinner offer had been such a good idea.

"Hi, Dieter, how are you doing?" I put my hand out. He grabbed it with both of his, and shook it earnestly.

"I am doing well, my friends." He nodded and smiled to Leonard as well. "Please, come with me, I show you where we camp." By now Leonard was rooting around in the cooler for another beer.

With his hand still in it he said surprisingly politely, "Can we bring anything ... maybe a few beers?"

Dieter shook his head, "No, we have refreshments at our camp ... please come."

Leonard pulled out a beer for himself, "I think I'll take one for the road, how 'bout you, Carl?"

"Yeah, thanks, Leonard." He tossed one to me as he stood up.

We followed Dieter back to their campsite, which was, probably to Leonard's relief, on the opposite side of the campground. Along the way Dieter talked excitedly to us about the many places and things that he and Marta had seen on their trip. I got the distinct impression that not only had the trip been a good one, but that the journey had been tremendously reassuring for them and had fully lived up to their ecclesiastical expectations.

When we arrived at their camp, Marta was laboring happily over the picnic table preparing dinner. She obviously took tremendous pleasure and pride in being a good host. There was a fire going in the fire pit, and a large Dutch oven full of something or other was cooking near the edge of it. Smiling, she stopped what she was doing and waved to us.

She had a fairly large cooking knife in her hand, "Hello – welcome!"

"Hey, Marta, how are you ... dinner smells great." Evidently she wasn't one much for compliments.

She blushed slightly and said modestly, "Ya ... ya it is a chicken. It must cook a while longer." Her reaction was actually rather unassumingly sweet. She scooped up a handful of the potatoes and carrots she had been chopping and added them to the pot.

Dieter motioned us towards a pair of comfortable-looking portable camp chairs and graciously said, "Please, please make yourselves comfortable. May I offer you a refreshment?"

Leonard lifted his can of beer slightly and said, "No, I'm okay right now ... thanks."

"Yeah, me too, but thank you." I sat down. Dieter went over to a shiny stainless steel cooler and got himself a can of iced tea.

"Hmm, looks like I'll be running back to our camp for more beer, Carl. I swear I'm not going to do this evening sober." I nodded in agreement, but inside I wondered where a conversation between Leonard and Dieter might go if aided by the social lubricant of alcohol.

As if to punctuate my point, Leonard tipped his beer back and took a long drink from it, finishing it. He muffled a burp, got up and said, "I'm going to run back and get another beer."

Dieter slightly held up the can in his own hand, trying to mimic Leonard's mannerism, "Would you like the iced tea?"

"Oh, no ... I think I'll stick with beer. I'll be back in just a minute." He was almost suspiciously polite about it.

I took a drink of my beer, then asked, "So Dieter, Marta, tell me more about your trip." He was glad I asked, and I was too. His eyes lit up. I looked over at Marta. Hers did as well. I could tell she wanted to share some of her own experiences and thoughts, but she kindly let Dieter speak first. "Well, it is hard to know what to tell ... there is so much. We have been here almost three weeks. We have been so many places. We have seen so much."

He glanced to Marta for some help. "Ya, we have seen so many ... extraor, extraor ..." She struggled with the word.

"Extraordinary?" I offered.

"Ya, this is the word. We have seen so many extraordinary things. This country, it is truly magnificent." She wasn't making idle conversation, she sincerely meant it.

Dieter took on a pious look and said quietly, but confidently, "Ya, we have found what we came to find."

"I'll bet you did." Leonard added a little tightly. I hadn't seen him come up behind me. He had returned with beer in hand and had overheard the last part of our conversation. "Do you have room in your cooler for these?" He held up a half case of beer minus two we had already drunk and one that he had in his hand.

Dieter hadn't picked up on, or at least he didn't acknowledge, the sarcasm in Leonard's voice, and said helpfully, "We will make room in the cooler." He took the half case from Leonard and one by one started putting them in the icebox. I saw him struggling trying to make room for the last one.

"Hey Dieter, don't worry about fitting that one in ... I'll have another." He seemed grateful that I had so conveniently solved the problem for him. I took the beer from him and opened it, "Thanks."

Dieter sat back down with us. "Ah, where were we?"

"You were telling us about your trip."

"Ah yes, the journey. As I was saying, we have seen so many things. It has made our faith stronger." Marta was apparently done with the dinner preparations and, wiping her hands on a towel, joined us as well. She nodded, "It has." I didn't even have to look at Leonard, I could just feel him tense up.

Dieter continued, "Ya, the mountains, the waters, the trees, the earth ... we have seen Him in everything ... this is truly God's country."

Leonard took a long drink of his beer and set the empty can down beside him. "So ..." he paused for a moment, cleared his throat, and then went on calmly, "... tell me if I have this right ... you came here in search of God." I felt myself tense up. This time there really was no avoiding a direct confrontation.

Dieter smiled pleasantly, "Ya." I could tell though that he was setting himself.

"And, everywhere that you look, you find God, is that right?"

"Ya, everywhere," Dieter replied confidently.

"But ... don't you think if you really, really want to see God, you probably will?"

"Ya ... it is written in the bible." Dieter sounded like he was digging in a little more. "I show you ... excuse me."

Dieter got up and went over to their van. I got up and went over to the cooler, "You want another beer, Leonard?"

"No, thanks, Carl. Not right now." He sounded calm but intense. I grabbed a fresh beer for myself and sat back down. I glanced over at Marta. Like a good host, she was forcing a slight smile but she looked a little guarded as well. I know she sensed confrontation. I tried to be reassuring and smiled pleasantly back at her. I think it helped, but not much.

A few moments later Dieter calmly returned. In his hand was a well-worn leather-bound bible. "Ya, I find it here." He opened the bible and flipped through a couple of pages until he found the place that he was searching for. I took a drink of beer. " Ya, if man search for God then he will find him. Like the wind cave ... it is here in the bible, I read. This is from Kings, nineteen." He took an easy breath then spoke slowly and clearly, "*And then he came thither unto a cave, and lodged there; and, behold, the word of the Lord came unto him, and he said unto him, what doest thou here?*"

After Dieter had savored each word of the passage, he put the bible gently down on the table and looked to us, as if to say "See?" We all sat there silently for a few seconds. And then it happened again. I felt ever so gently a little puff of wind on my cheek, and I heard a rustling like leaves. I looked down at the bible and watched a page quietly flip over.

Leonard broke the silence between us and said to Dieter respectfully, "May I?" He was reaching for the bible.

Dieter smiled at him and gently said, "Of course ..."

Leonard picked up the bible carefully. He cleared his throat, then read from where the page had flipped over, *"And he said, Go forth, and stand upon the mount before the Lord. And, behold, the Lord passed by, and a great and strong wind rent the mountains, and brake in pieces the rocks before the Lord; but the Lord was not in the wind: and after the wind an earthquake; but the Lord was not in the earthquake: And after the earthquake a fire; but the Lord was not in the fire: and after the fire a still small voice."*

Leonard paused for a moment then went on, *"And it was so, when Elijah heard it, that he wrapped his face in his mantle, and went out, and stood in the entering in of the cave. And, behold, there came a voice unto him, and said, What doest thou here, Elijah?"*

Leonard finished the passage and slowly put the bible back down on the table. Both Dieter and Marta stared at Leonard in awe. I did too. Whatever they were expecting, it certainly was not this. Finally Dieter said respectfully, "I did not know you were versed in the bible."

Leonard looked at him seriously and said, "I'm not."

Dieter was obviously confused, and looked at him questioningly, "Then how did you know this passage?"

Leonard paused for a moment and then said simply, "I didn't."

Leonard's answer took both Dieter and Marta by surprise. I was surprised too. They stared at him, astonished. Dieter was just about to speak, but Leonard didn't give him a chance to question him more about it. He went on. "You went into a cave earnestly in search of God and that is what you found. But ... I might ask you, where does Satan live? Had you been looking for Satan, you might have found him there instead. You didn't go to Devil's Tower because of its name. But that's not what God named it – man did that." He took a deep breath, "I suppose the question that you must ask yourself is, did I see it because I wanted to, or did it really come to me?"

He paused again for a moment. He shifted his body and leaned forward, his eyes were intense. He folded his hands and said quietly, almost whispering, "Please understand me, this is not an attack on you. I believe that what you search for, you search for with honesty and with the best of intentions.

But I need to tell you more ... I hope that you understand. There is nothing bad about faith itself, but it is dangerous to blindly dismiss all other ways of knowing and understanding. Spirituality comes in many forms and people who are not careful how, and why they use it can create a wake of misery and ruin.

Once there were two hundred million buffalo here ... in less than thirty years there were only a few hundred left. There used to be rivers that in the fall flowed with more salmon than water. Now in those rivers only a lonely few fish return. Most of the rivers in this country have been dammed. Under the lakes behind those dams are redrock cathedrals greater than anything that man will ever build. Once there were vast prairies, but they were plowed so hard that a hundred million acres were turned to dust, and when the dust blew away the sky turned black. The forests that covered these mountains have but all been felled. Now there are only a few trees left from before ..."

Leonard continued, "Over these hills, less than a hundred miles and less than a hundred years from here is a place where innocent men, women and children were murdered for no other reason than that they did not believe the same and wanted nothing more than to live on this land. Then someone had the audacity to honor the bastards responsible for those atrocities ... and they have named the last beautiful places after them. Such monuments are shrines of intolerance, greed, and ignorance. So it has been, and so it continues to be. That is America's unspoken legacy, and it was done in the name of God. It may very well be God's country ... but what in God's name have they done?"

Both Dieter and Marta were stunned at what he was saying. The usually strong Marta was so upset she looked like she was going to cry. She didn't, though. Instead, they both just sat there and intently listened to him.

Leonard slowly leaned back into his chair. He was finished. He looked exhausted, but he also looked more at peace. For a long while no one said anything. We all just sat there. Dieter started to defend himself, then simply lowered his head and put his face in his hands. Marta gently reached out to him and put her arm around his shoulder. As she did she lowered her head as well. They both stayed that way for few minutes. They were thinking hard. While I watched them I empathetically tried to imagine how such an attack on one's faith must feel, particularly for people of such conviction as Dieter and Marta.

Finally Dieter raised his head up and looked at us. I was really expecting him to ask us to leave. He didn't. He took a deep breath and I could hear that he was shaky. He looked up into the evening sky and began speaking, "I have heard what you have said." He paused. He looked like he was trying to get a hold of himself. Marta held him tightly, letting him know she was with him. He continued, "I believe that what you speak of is true." He bit his lip slightly, and tears came to his eyes. "We came here in search of God, but ... but ... I believe we have been wrong in our journey." Dieter's words trailed off into the still evening air.

He was going to continue on but Leonard put his hand up, stopped him, and said gently, "You did not fail, Dieter, nor you Marta ... you just looked too hard. I know that you both saw God ... but you just didn't know it when you did."

Moments after Leonard spoke, both Dieter and Marta visibly began to relax. They almost appeared to exhale as though they had been holding their breath for a very long, long time. As they calmed, a genuine expression of serenity appeared to wash over both of them. They looked like they believed in something now in a way that they had not believed before. Their evangelical enthusiasm was fading and was being replaced by something more comfortable and more sincere. They said nothing, just nodded and smiled a little.

I reached down, picked up my beer, and took a long pull from it. I felt relieved. I had known that something was going to be said sometime. But, it was a little like dying – you know it will happen, you just don't know when or how.

We just all sat there silently for probably ten minutes or so, letting all of it sink in. Finally, Leonard, who deemed the confrontation over, broke the silence and casually got up and went to the cooler. "I think I'll have that beer now ... how about anyone else? Carl, how are you doing on yours?"

"I'm okay over here, Leonard, but thanks."

Leonard was just closing the cooler when Dieter said, "I think I would like one please, Leonard." Leonard stopped and held the lid half-open. We both looked at Dieter for a second.

Then Marta said, "Ya, and I would like one too ... Leo – nord." She struggled with his name a little more than Dieter had. Both Leonard and I were surprised. Dieter and Marta had never called either one of us by name. Nor had we ever seen either one of them drink alcohol. I guess we both assumed that neither one of them did. On the other hand that would have been pretty hard to believe considering they were German. Leonard reached back into the cooler, took out two more beers, and handed them each one.

"Here you go."

"Thank you."

"Ya, thank you, Leonard." She was better the second time she said it. Leonard smiled at her.

They both opened their cans. Dieter took a drink first. While he did Marta watched him intently, as if she were a bit uncertain of what in fact would happen. Dieter smiled, "Ya, this is good." Apparently seeing that it was safe, Marta took a tentative sip from her own can, said, "Ya ..." smiled, and then took another more intentional drink.

We sat together and quietly enjoyed our beers and the twilight air. The sun was nearly down now and the first few stars of the evening began to appear in the sky. We talked as crickets erupted in a chorus around us. Maybe it was the beer, maybe it was the passing of the conversation that we had had, or maybe it was a combination of both, but everyone relaxed.

Marta got up and went to the fire to check on dinner. She took the lid off of the Dutch oven. Steam poured out of it and immediately the air was filled with a pleasant aroma of roasted chicken and vegetables. As soon as the smell hit me my hunger did too. "Oh man, does that smell good or what?"

She smiled at my remark of approval, and after poking at the chicken with a fork a couple of times, looked up and proclaimed proudly, "It is done."

We quickly finished setting the table. I think everyone was as at least as hungry as I was, and we sat down to our meal. We ate without conversation, with the exception of the occasional comment on the excellence of the dinner. It took us less than fifteen minutes to completely empty the Dutch oven. Even though I was fairly well stuffed I continued to wipe the inside of the pot clean with stray pieces of bread. Satisfied, Leonard leaned back in his chair. "I have not had a meal like that since I don't know when."

"Ya, Marta she is the most excellent cook."

"I would say that's a little bit of an understatement," I added, my mouth half-full of bread. Marta blushed modestly at the compliments. In all honesty, it was probably one of the better meals I had ever eaten.

Leonard saw that I was still at it, moping the remaining gravy off of my plate with a piece of bread, and said, "What exactly are you doing, Carl?"

"I'm doing the dishes, Leonard." Both Dieter and Marta thought my remark was pretty darn funny and started laughing.

"You are a P – I – G." Leonard said it with a southern accent and spelled it out for emphasis.

I purposely moved a large wad of gravy-soaked bread to the front of my mouth and talking through it looked right at him and said, "Yesth, I am." Leonard feigned an overly dramatic wince of complete revulsion. Everyone busted up hysterically.

After we let our dinner settle for a few minutes, we cleaned up the dishes. The sun was totally gone now so Marta lit the lantern and added two more logs to the fire. Our shadows danced off of the trees ringing the campsite. It made everything feel that much more enchanted. I went to the cooler and passed out another round of beer. Dieter took a long drink from what was left of the one he had, finishing it, and opened the next one.

I inched my chair a little closer to the fire, put out my hands out to it, and rubbed them in its warmth. It felt good. There was a chill and crispness to the air. It was the first sign that this summer was inevitably going to come to an end. Everyone else appeared to feel it too.

Dieter took a sip of his fresh beer, made a guttural noise of satisfaction after he swallowed, and set the can down beside his chair. He was feeling the effects of the beer and it loosened him up some. He looked at Leonard and then at me and said, "I mean not to inquire ... but what about you?"

"What do you mean, Dieter?" I answered. I was uncertain of the "what about" he was talking about.

"I refer to your journey ... have you not been on a pilgrimage?" I looked to Leonard. He merely raised an eyebrow and nodded for me to go ahead and answer the question. He was not going to help me out. I turned my attention back to Dieter, who along with Marta, was eagerly awaiting my answer. Evidently not all of their enthusiasm was gone.

I stalled and asked again, "What do you mean by pilgrimage?"

"Well, on your travels have you not seen God?" I again looked to Leonard. He gave me an unreadable blank look. I had the distinct feeling that he *knew* the answer, but he was going to make me to come up with it on my own. I guess that I really hadn't given it much thought, but, I suppose in a sense without knowing it, or intending it, we had in fact been in search of ... something. The answer to Dieter's question suddenly seemed very, very obvious to me.

When it hit me, I paused for a moment and smiled to myself. I turned back to them, still smiling, and said assuredly, "Yes ... I believe we have seen God ..." I thought to myself, "... although I don't think I could tell you *which* God."

Apparently that was enough of an answer for them, just to know. All they did was nod and smile silently. Neither one of them asked anything further. I again looked back at Leonard. He was smiling as well, just a little at the corners of his mouth. He gave me a knowing look and nodded in agreement. It was the right answer.

We stayed up with Dieter and Marta until the beer was gone. Although Dieter had only had three, and Marta only two, they were somewhat tipsy. I looked at my watch. It was just after eleven.

"We should let Dieter and Marta get some sleep here, Leonard."

"Yeah, you're right, Carl." He yawned. "I'm beat too." Dieter and Marta got pensive looks on their faces. I don't think that either of them wanted the evening to end. I didn't either; I was truly enjoying their company.

Then Dieter said sadly, "We must prepare to go back home tomorrow."

Leonard quickly added, "Yeah ... we do too."

Sweetly, Marta got tears in her eyes. She said with a small tremble in her voice, "But please ... please, please, you must say goodbye before you leave."

I reached out and squeezed her hand. "Hey, Marta, don't worry," I tried as best I could to sound casually reassuring, like our parting would be easier than it would be, "we wouldn't dream of leaving without saying goodbye ... really." Although still upset, for the moment she was comforted by my words. It kept an inevitable flood of tears at bay till at least tomorrow. "I'll tell you what, we'll stop by on our way out of here tomorrow, okay?"

"Ya, that would be good. Maybe we can have a coffee together," Dieter said.

"Yeah, that would be nice. Well ... we better get going here. Thank you for a very nice evening and we'll see you tomorrow."

"Ya, and thank you mein friends. We will see you in the morning. God bless you. " For once, Leonard didn't look annoyed.

The Pestilence

Leonard and I headed back to our camp with some difficulty. It was a moonless night and neither one of us had had the forethought earlier to bring a flashlight with us. Along the way I ran into a garbage can, which scared the shit out of both of us.

"Christ, Carl, would you watch where you are going? I nearly had a heart attack."

"Oh, I'm so sorry that I inconvenienced you, Leonard, by racking myself up." I rubbed my leg, which was only slightly bruised.

"Hey, did you hurt yourself?"

"No, but wouldn't you feel badly if I did?"

"Hmmm, can I think about that for a little bit and get back to you?"

"Asshole."

"Friend of asshole."

When we got to our camp I got the flashlight out of the van and switched it on. As soon as the light hit our campsite, there was a moment of furious movement. It happened so quickly that my eyes hadn't had a chance to adjust to the light. I was pretty sure - but not completely certain - that it was mice.

"What the fuck? Did you see that, Carl?"

"Yeah, Leonard, I think that it was just a bunch of field mice." When I said the word "mice," he got a kind of squeamish look on his face. "What's wrong, Leonard?"

"Oooh ..." he pretended to shiver, "I hate fucking rodents. They chew on everything and shit all over the place."

"Oh Jesus, Leonard ... what about Mr. Rat? - You think that he's a good luck idol."

"That's different – he's dead."

"Oh, well, thanks for clarifying that for me. That just makes a ton of sense now, doesn't it."

"Screw you, Carl."

"Well don't be such a weenie. We're in the fucking woods ... that's where mice live. They've probably been at every single campsite that we've been at. We just haven't seen them until now."

Leonard looked at me with horror. "Are you fucking serious?"

"Yeah, I'm fucking serious – are you?"

"Oh, man ..." he put his hand to his belly and rubbed it, "We left the food out and everything. I bet we ate mouse shit and we didn't even know it."

"Well, I have a news flash for ya, buddy, you have probably been eating mouse shit your whole life."

"What?!"

I worked it. "Yeah, haven't you ever heard about all of the stuff that goes into hot dogs? You know the FDA regulates the number of rat hairs and mouse shit that can go into all of that stuff."

"Oh Jesus, Carl, would you please shut the hell up, I do not need to know this."

"Well, hell you asked."

"I do not believe that I did, Carl. And you know what?"

"What?"

"If I get a fucking eating disorder and starve myself to death because you told me about this, it is so fucking on your head."

"Oh, I think I'll live with the risk." I started to laugh.

"Knock it off, Carl, mouse shit is not funny. And don't be such an asshole. Did I laugh at you when you got all paranoid when I was driving over Powder River Pass?"

"Yes, as a matter of fact you did, Leonard."

"Ooh, well maybe that's a bad example ... but I did slow down eventually, ya gotta give me that."

"Yeah, *eventually* ..." I stopped to think about it more, and then figured I'd let up on him some before he really got pissed, "Okay, I'll knock it off. Let's go crash. I'm going to go get some weed out of the van first."

"I'll join you. I think those little fuckers only come out under cover of darkness, and I don't want to be without a light."

We went over to the van. Leonard waited outside with the flashlight while I rooted around in search of the pipe and the weed. "Oh, shit!" Leonard jumped and the light of the flashlight waved crazily around the campground.

"What is your problem?"

"Would you hurry your ass up? I swear I just felt one run over my foot!"

"Okay, God, calm down, I found it." I climbed out of the van with pipe and weed in hand.

We got to the door of the tent and I reached down to the zipper. "What the hell are you doing, Carl?"

I stopped. "Um ... going to bed?"

"Come on man, think. We have to do this carefully or we might get one of these little fuckers in the tent with us."

"And so what do you propose that we do?"

"Okay, I have a plan ... I'll go in first. You cover me with the flashlight and I'll open the tent and jump in. Right before I zip the tent back up you throw me the flashlight."

"Yeah, and what about me? Should I just stand out here all night?"

"No, that's where phase two of the plan comes in. I'll unzip the tent and cover you with the flashlight, then you dive in, and I'll zip it back up. How does that sound?"

"It sounds like you're nuts, but I would like to go to bed so let's get to it."

The plan went off pretty smoothly, except for when my pant leg briefly got snagged in the zipper causing a near panic on Leonard's part. We finally got the tent closed and he proceeded to methodically investigate every inch of it for mice. I loaded the pipe with a little weed.

After a few minutes of careful scrutiny, he was satisfied that we were rodent-free and declared the perimeter secured. "I think we're okay, Carl."

I handed him the pipe and the lighter. "We were okay before, Leonard ... here, calm down."

"Thanks, man." He lit the weed, took a deep drag, and held it.

"Better?"

He nodded his head and said breathlessly, "Better." After holding it for a few seconds, he let out the smoke with a sigh and handed the pipe back to me. I put the flame to the bowl and did the same. "I'll tell you what Carl, just one of those little fuckers tries to get in this tent and there is going to be mousy hell to pay."

I let my drag out and said half laughing, "I don't doubt that, Leonard."

"Are you patronizing me, Carl?" He took another drag.

I pretended to think deeply about it, then said thoughtfully, "Yes ... as a matter of fact I think that I am, Leonard."

He mouthed to me, "asshole," and handed the pipe back to me.

Just as he was letting a breath out we both heard a scurrying across the top of the tent. Leonard immediately grabbed the flashlight and shone the beam up at the ceiling. Silhouetted against the tent was the unmistakable figure of a no more than three-inch field mouse, tail included.

"Get the fuck off of the tent you little rabid bastard!" Leonard tweaked at the silhouette with his middle finger and the mouse instantly disappeared.

"Calm down, Leonard, they're not going to get in here."

"Calm down my ass, don't those things carry the goddamn plague?" He tweaked two more off of the ceiling.

"Well yes, but that was a few hundred years ago on another continent."

"Yeah, well, you just go ahead and be all complacent, Carl. We'll see who's laughing when I visit you on your deathbed. I bet that it's real funny when your freakishly swollen tongue looks like an overcooked bratwurst and your body is covered in weeping pustules."

"Don't you think your being just a tad bit dramatic about this, Leonard?"

"No, I do not, Carl ... Screw you, you four-legged pestilence." He flicked another pair of mice off of the tent – one off the ceiling and one off of the wall. I just shook my head and took another drag off of the pipe. I held it, then exhaled and handed the pipe to Leonard.

"There's one more hit left here."

Leonard took the pipe from me, "Thanks, could you light it for me? I need a free hand here." With one hand, Leonard put the pipe to his lips. I lit it, and he took a big drag all the while scanning the tent for possible intruders with the flashlight.

The combination of the copious amounts of beer that we had drank earlier and the weed that we had just smoked left us hysterically stoned. I couldn't help laughing every time he rocketed another mouse off of the tent. It became contagious, and eventually Leonard thought that it was pretty funny too, especially when I told him that he had animal magnetism. We both were laughing insanely.

"You know, Leonard, this reminds me a little of the movie Willard. Maybe the mice are pissed off with you for making fun of one of their dead brethren."

"Carl, if you don't shut the hell up I am going to slather your body in peanut butter and throw you out of the tent."

"Mmmm ... and let those fastidious little mice tongues lick my naked body clean?! Sounds delicious."

"Carl, there is something so fucking broken inside of you."

"Yes there is, Leonard."

Eventually the parade of mice stopped. Either they were unconscious from being flicked off of the tent or simply had learned that it was not a good place to go. I was actually relieved, since my abdominal muscles were getting pretty sore from laughing. Still, it took us close to ten minutes to recover from our hysterical spasms and calm down enough to even think about getting some shut-eye.

"I don't think that they're going to be back, Leonard. We should probably try to get some sleep here."

"Yeah, you're right, Carl." Leonard switched off the flashlight, and we both hunkered down in our sleeping bags.

"I'll see you in the morning, Leonard."

"Yeah Carl, get some good sleep."

"Thanks, you too." I laid there for a couple of minutes then whispered, "Hey Leonard ... you awake?"

"Yeah, Carl."

"I have to pee."

"Carl?"

"Yeah, Leonard?"

"I would suggest that you wet your pants, because if you go out there I will never let you back in again."

"Never?"

"Never."

"Oh, then I guess I don't have to pee after all."

"I didn't think so."

Goodbye

The next morning I woke up early. The sun was barely up. I really did have to pee, badly. I unzipped the tent and hurriedly went to relieve myself on a tree. I must have stood there for a full five minutes. I was approaching done when Leonard stuck his head outside of the tent. "Jesus Christ, Carl, how much are you going to pee?"

"A lot?"

"Yeah, I guess so ... shit, you woke me up. I thought there was a flash flood or something coming through our camp."

"Yeah, well, how do think I feel? I think I ruined myself," I buttoned up my pants. "So, you want some coffee, or are you going to go back to sleep?"

Leonard yawned, stretched, then said, "Uh, yeah ... what the hell, I'm already awake, I guess I'll get up."

I fired up the stove and put some coffee on while Leonard roused himself. By the time he was actually up, the coffee was ready. I poured us both a cup, and lit a cigarette. "So, were you serious last night about heading back?" Leonard blew across the top of his cup, then took a sip of coffee.

"Yeah, Carl ... hell, we've been gone what, nine, ten days?"

"Yeah, I think it's been eleven, actually."

"And no matter what we do it's going to take us at least three days to get back home." I nodded, took a sip of coffee, and followed it with a drag from my cigarette. I felt a little sad. I didn't want this to end. On the other hand I was missing Althea like crazy, and I would be starting university soon.

"So, which way should we go back?"

"I was thinking that maybe we should head west, Carl."

"Oh, fuck you, Leonard, you know what I mean."

Leonard smiled a little and took another sip of coffee.

"Hey, ya have an extra cigarette there?"

"No, there are only twenty to a pack." He gave me a sarcastic "oh I never heard that one before" look. I reached into my pocket and handed him the pack.

"Thanks." He shook one out, busted the filter off and lit it. "I don't care which way we go, Carl, as long as we don't go through fucking Wyoming again."

"Gee, I'm surprised to hear you say that, Leonard, you seemed so impressed with the state." He took a drag and gave me a "screw you" smile.

"I'll go get the map." I took another sip of coffee, got up, and went to the van.

When I returned, Leonard was topping up our coffee cups. I opened up the atlas to South Dakota and laid it out on the table between us. "So, we're here." I pointed to the southwest corner of the state. Leonard, who had a mouth full of coffee, nodded. "I figure we could just head north on 385 through Deadwood." I traced the route with my finger. "Then we could pick up 85 and keep heading north until ..." I picked up the atlas and flipped back until I found North Dakota, "... we hit Interstate 94. From there it's probably a two-day straight shot back to Mount Vernon."

Leonard studied the route for a moment then said, "Looking good there, Carl ... pretty much one road with no turns. Hell, even Mr. Wrongway Navigator Guy can't fuck that up." I was just about to tell him to fuck himself when he smiled, put up his hand to stop me and said, "I know, I know, screw you asshole."

"Thank you."

"You're welcome ... so where are we going to stay tonight, then?"

I again pointed with my finger, "I was thinking we could set up camp right here at the Theodore Roosevelt National Park. It's in the North Dakota Badlands. It's just a few miles off of Interstate 94. It'll be a pretty long drive, maybe two hundred and fifty miles or so, but we can probably do that in five, or five and a half hours."

Leonard looked at me skeptically.

"What?"

"I seem to remember the last time you said that we rolled into Gillette twelve hours later."

"Okay asshole, then you do the math. How fucking long do you think it's going to take us?" Leonard calmly took another drink of coffee and with his finger made some phantom calculations on the picnic table. "Well?"

"Keep your pants on there, Carl, I'm working on it." I rolled my eyes, took one last drag off of my cigarette, and rubbed the butt out on the table. "Well, by my calculations we should be able to get there in about four hours."

"What?!"

"Yeah ... maybe three and a half if we moderately haul ass."

"Are you kidding me?"

"No, Carl, I am not." Leonard smiled pleasantly.

"Shit, you act like I can't estimate how long it will take us to get anywhere to save my life ..."

"You can't."

"Oh yeah, and then you come up with this obviously lame estimate."

Leonard continued to smile calmly.

"Okay, Mr. Andretti, I'll tell you what we'll do. I'll bet you a night's drinking that we don't make it there in four hours."

Leonard's eyes lit up. "Really?"

"Yes really."

"And do I get to drive?"

"Hell no, you don't get to drive, you'll drive like a maniac and we'll probably both be killed."

"Well, if I don't drive then it's a pretty stupid bet. If you get behind the wheel, Carl, you'll drive like a cotton-head and we'll get there maybe by midnight if we're lucky."

"So I guess you don't want to take me up on the bet then ... chicken."

"Ooooh, Carl, peer pressure."

"Hey, sometimes it works."

"I'll tell you what. I promise that I won't drive like a maniac. I'll keep it at a safe and sane speed."

I thought about it for a minute. Hell, if we were going to have any kind of bet at all one of us was going to have to drive. "Yeah, okay," I said tentatively. "But you have to promise that you will stop if I have to pee."

"How many times?"

"Three."

"Make it two ... deal?" He stuck out his hand to me and raised an eyebrow.

"Yeah ..." I shook his hand, "Deal."

"Okay then, let's get this place cleaned up, say our good-byes to Dieter and Marta, and get on the road."

The night before we had only unpacked the tent, our sleeping bags, and the stove. It didn't take us long to repack. We were both still pretty full from the night before, and agreed that for now we would skip breakfast and maybe get something on the road later. I took one last check around the campground.

"Well, that looks like about it. Ya ready, Leonard?"

"Yep, ready." We climbed in the van and headed over to Dieter and Marta's campsite.

On the way over I looked at my watch. It was only a quarter after seven. "Ya know, Leonard, it's still pretty early. Do you think they're up yet?" Leonard gave me a mischievous look, and suddenly let off of the van's accelerator. The result was an immediate and thundering backfire, which echoed throughout the campground.

"Oh, just a guess, Carl, but I bet they're up." I shook my head.

When we arrived, Dieter and Marta were in fact up, and clearly had been for some time. Marta was back over the stove preparing breakfast. As soon as we pulled in, huge smiles appeared on their faces. Leonard switched off the van and we got out.

"Hey you two. How are you this morning?"

"Ach, we are fine. And you ... did you sleep well?"

"Yes, very well ... that was a great meal last night."

"Yeah, it really was great," Leonard agreed.

"Well, we thought that we would stop by like we promised we would. We have to be going here ... we have a long day of driving ahead of us."

"Please, please you must sit for a moment and have some coffee with us."

"No we really should be ..." My attempt at any further explanation was interrupted when Marta simply thrust a pair of mugs of at each of us. She wasn't going to let us just go. "Well, I suppose that we can stay for a few minutes."

"Just a few, though," Leonard added. The pair grinned.

Neither Leonard nor I sat down. I knew that if we did we would end up having breakfast and probably staying for at least an hour. The sun wasn't up high enough yet to offer any warmth, so we stood by the fire warming ourselves.

"So, you're heading back home."

"Ya, we must go back to Germany. We leave the day after tomorrow. We must drive to Minnesota." He said the state's name almost without an accent. I thought to myself, maybe that's why so many German immigrants wound up there - it was the only state they could pronounce. "That is where we fly from." At the mention of leaving they both looked sad but excited at the same time. "And what about you?"

"Yeah, like I said, we have a pretty long drive ahead of us too."

"We're heading north to the Badlands," Leonard added, "It's on the way home."

Although Leonard put a little extra emphasis on the word "Badlands," neither Dieter nor Marta recoiled. Apparently they really had taken to heart what Leonard had said the night before. They were no longer making snap judgments.

"Speaking of which, we really need to be going."

"Ya ... we understand. We must leave soon also." They both had tears in their eyes. I felt like I was getting some in mine.

"Here, I'll tell you what ... do you have a piece of paper and a pen?"

Marta was on it. "Ya, just a moment. I will get from the van." She hurried over to their vehicle, got a pen and paper from the glove box, and hurried back. "Here."

"Thanks, Marta. So here is my address and phone number. Make sure that you write to me when you get home." I was trying to soften our parting not just for them, but for us as well. I tried to make it sound like our goodbye wasn't a permanent thing, even though I, as well as they, knew that we would probably never see each other again.

"Thank you ... and here is ours," Marta quickly wrote their address and phone number down on another piece of paper and handed it back to me. I took it and put it in my wallet.

"Thank you, Marta. I promise I'll write."

"We need to go, Carl ..."

"Yeah, I know, Leonard ..." I put out my hand out to Marta first, "So, you two take good care of yourselves and have a safe trip." She didn't take my hand, but instead threw her arms around me and hugged me tightly. I could feel through her short irregular breaths that she was very near tears.

After a few moments she whispered to me, "God bless you, Carl," then she really did start crying.

I patted her gently and tried to reassure her, "It'll be okay, Marta ... really, we'll be in touch."

After she calmed some I released my hug, and she did the same. Dieter had just freed Leonard from a similar embrace. He immediately came over to me. He grabbed me and hugged me hard. Marta did the same with Leonard. I could feel that Dieter too was close to crying. After a couple of minutes he relaxed his embrace, stepped back, and took my hand in both of his. He looked at me with watery eyes and said, "You have been good friends ..." He paused and chewed his lower lip, then continued, "... Thank you."

"But Dieter, you have nothing to ..."

He stopped me mid-sentence, "Please, Carl, nothing more ... just thank you."

I nodded. I turned to Leonard. Marta was just finishing whispering something to him. I couldn't hear, but I suspected that she was saying the same thing to him that she had said to me. Leonard patted her gently, and whispered something back. Although she still had tears in her eyes, she smiled. Then he turned to me.

"Well, Carl?" His voice was a little shaky.

"Yeah, let's get going, Leonard."

Leonard reached into his pocket for the van keys. "I'm driving, right?"

"Yeah ..." We headed to van and got in.

Dieter and Marta stood a few feet in front of the van. They were holding hands and tears were on both of their cheeks. Leonard put the key in the ignition and was just about ready to fire it up. "Hang on for a second, Leonard," I opened the passenger's window, "Hey ... take good care, you two ... We'll write each other soon." My voice was shaky as well. Dieter nodded and closed his eyes hard. Marta inched closer to him.

Leonard started the van and we backed out of the parking spot. When we were onto the road, he opened his side window as well. He put the van in first and we started to drive off. Both of us waved goodbye to Dieter and Marta, who had walked out to the road behind us. They waved back. When we were about a hundred feet away, Dieter called something to us, but I couldn't hear him over the motor. I put my hand to my ear and leaning out the window yelled, "I couldn't hear you, Dieter." He started to say whatever he had said again, but we rounded a corner in the road and they disappeared from our view behind a wall of trees.

North Dakota

After a bit, we both calmed down from our emotional goodbye with Dieter and Marta. I knew I could speak now without my voice wavering, and I shared a personal observation with Leonard. "You know ... I think you actually did something very nice for those two there." He looked at me with a somewhat bewildered look on his face. "Yeah, I know, maybe that wasn't your intention, but I seriously think that's what you did. And you know what else?"

"What's that?"

"I think that makes you a prophet." I said it as convincingly and seriously as I could.

He smiled a little, and then looked right at me and said, "Fuck thyself, Carl."

Roughly ten minutes later, we got to the junction with the highway that would take us north. Leonard pulled the van over, stopped, and said, "So, do we start timing this now?" In the midst of our emotional goodbye with Dieter and Marta, I had almost forgotten the bet.

"Oh ... yeah ..." I said a little surprised. I glanced at my watch to get a start time, "... it's exactly eight o ..." I didn't get a chance to finish. Leonard punched the accelerator hard, sending the van momentarily into a tire-squealing fishtail. When the tires found traction we began to rocket down the highway. I instinctively grabbed the "oh shit" handle on the passenger side of the dashboard.

"Jesus Christ, Leonard, you promised that you wouldn't drive like a maniac!"

He grinned at me diabolically and said, "I lied, Carl, there's just too much at stake here."

I figured that since he had the wheel, the best I could do at this point was to try and meet him part way. "Well, at least try to keep it at a dull roar."

He kept grinning maniacally and said, "Sure, Carl ... sure ..." I hoped that I wouldn't have to pee for the next four hours.

We shot north on 385 through the Black Hills National Forest. Although Leonard was flying, the road was good and only twice did I reach out for the "oh shit" handle and tell him to cool it. It was nearly sixty miles to the town of Lead. We did it in just forty-five minutes.

"What time is it, Carl?"

"It's eight fifty one."

"Oooh, I'm making good time, aren't I?"

"Yeah, I suppose you are."

"Mmmm ... I can just taste that beer now."

"Oh, shut up."

"Carl, could you please keep an eye out for a sporting goods store for me?"

I could smell a trap, but I asked anyway, "Why, Leonard?" I said it deadpan.

"I need to get a pair of ski gloves."

"What ... why?"

"Yeah, cuz the beer that you will be buying me is going to be just that cold."

"Oh, screw you." We both started laughing.

Five minutes later we left the National Forest, hit Interstate 90, and headed west. As soon as we did, there was a vigorous renewal of the Wall Drug signage. After we started keeping track, Leonard and I would count at least twenty-seven Wall Drug signs in the one hundred and ten miles until we reached the North Dakota border. Apparently the sensibly minded North Dakotans took a dim view of their southerly neighbor's garish advertising practices and the signs would end there. I was happy about that.

At Spearfish, we left 90 and picked up U.S. Route 85. From here on out there would be no turns or junctions til we would come to the Badlands. We were just outside of Belle Fourche when a familiar sensation came knocking at my lower abdomen. I could feel my bladder filling. The diuretic effect of the massive amounts of caffeine that I had consumed earlier was no help.

We had made a two pee-stop deal when we initially made our bet. But Leonard had welshed on the maniac driving part already, and I wasn't sure that he wouldn't do the same with this part of it as well. It was entirely possible that during Leonard's run for the gold I would have to pee out the window. On the other hand, I knew that at some point we would have to stop for fuel. The van only held eleven gallons, and at eighteen miles to the gallon there was no way we were going to make it the whole way. I hoped that I could hold it till then.

"Hey, Leonard."

"Yeah, Carl?"

"So, I'm wondering about that pee stop thing."

"What about it?"

"Well, I'm wondering if that's something that's going to happen anytime soon."

Leonard looked over at me, "Are you sure that you want to squander one of your pee stops already?"

"No, no, you don't have to stop right now, I'm just trying to get a feeling for where we're at with that."

He gave me the squinty eye. "Oh ... so let me get this straight. You're wondering if I'm going to go back on our little deal here." I felt my bladder fill a little more. I winced. I was starting to feel uncomfortable.

"Ah, yeah ... that's basically it, Leonard."

"Well, to tell you the truth, Carl, I was not going to go back on our deal, but ..."

"But what?"

"Well, I guess that I'm just a little bit hurt. Maybe I won't stop after all." He was doing the wounded lover routine thing again.

"Shit, I hate it when you do that, Leonard."

"Do what?"

"You know, that fucked-up no matter what I say it's the wrong answer, and I'm going to turn everything around so that it looks like you're an asshole girlfriend imitation."

"I have no idea what you are talking about, Carl. I'll tell you what, though, I think that you are being extraordinarily insensitive with my feelings right now."

"Yeah, well, my bladder thinks that you're being pretty insensitive too."

"I thought that you didn't have to pee right now."

"Well, my bladder changed its mind, okay?"

"I'm not going to talk to you if you raise your voice like that."

Every time that we did this I knew it was a joke. It was a game that we frequently played. It was always a challenge to see how long one or the other of us could go without completely snapping. Leonard was better at it than I was. I don't know, maybe he had more patience ... or maybe more experience with it. Still, although it was funny, there was a part of me that got moderately pissed off every time. It must have been some instinctual thing.

I took a deep breath, then said in a lowered voice, "Okay ... Leonard, could you please pull over whenever it's convenient for you so that I can void before my bladder ruptures?"

Leonard looked at me smiling, "That didn't sound very sincere, Carl."

I looked back at him and said through somewhat clenched teeth, "Oh, but it was, Leonard ... really." I gave him a syrupy fake smile.

"Well ..." he put on the turn indicator and began to slow down, as if he were going to pull over. I felt a wave of relief in sight. Then he switched the turn indicator off and sped up again. "No, I still don't think that you were sincere about it. I think you just said that so that I would pull over."

I was determined to win this time. I stayed calm, "Oh, gosh, Leonard, I'm so sorry that you feel like that. Will you ever forgive me?" My bladder was aching now.

"Well ... maybe." He pretended to pout.

"Oh, I so hope so ..."

Like a light switch, Leonard stopped pouting and began to laugh. I had evidently won this round. "Oh man, Carl, I'll tell you what, that was good ... very, very good. You are really refining your groveling abilities."

"Gee, thanks, Leonard, what a compliment. Now do you think that you could find a place to pull over?"

"Do you really have to pee?"

"Fuck yes, I really have to pee!" He looked at me smiling. "Okay man, so it's only a partial win, is that what you want to hear? Just fucking pull over."

"Can you hold it for another couple of miles?" He sounded more serious.

"Maybe ... why?"

"Because I saw a sign back there that said 'Geographic Center of the U.S. - two miles.' '

"If I say yes will you pull over when we get there?" I waited a few seconds for his answer. "Well?"

"Calm down, Carl, I was going to pull over anyway. I have to pee too."

About a minute later we came to a sign with an arrow pointing to the left. It said, "Welcome to The Geographic Center of the United States."

"Here it is, Leonard, turn, man."

"Yeah ... I see it." We went about a hundred yards down the road to a small blacktop parking lot. There was no one else there. "I guess this isn't considered a vacation destination."

"No, apparently not," I said somewhat distractedly. I was more concerned with the urgency of urination.

Not far away, up a path, there was a bronze plaque stuck in the ground near a tree - apparently the marker. Nearby there was a self-serve interpretive center, complete with restrooms. Leonard pulled in and parked. As soon as he stopped I leapt out and made a beeline for the restroom. I slightly wet my pants the moment I got to the urinal, but I did make it.

As I stood there relieving myself I thought about a couple of similar episodes I had experienced in the past. I wasn't sure what the physiology, or maybe more appropriately, psychology, was behind it, but it was always the same. No matter what your destination was, if you really had to pee, you were nearly wetting your pants the second you got to the place where you could. It was a bizarre phenomenon. I finished up. I was much more relaxed.

When I came back, Leonard was peeing on the marker. "What the fuck are you doing, Leonard?"

"What the fuck does it look like I'm doing?"

"It looks like you're peeing on the geographic center of the United States."

"That's right, Carl ... that is exactly what I am doing. It's an experiment. I'm seeing which direction my urine runs."

I corrected him, "I think that's what you're supposed to do when you're on the continental divide."

"Oh ... oops, my mistake." He didn't sound very concerned about it. He smiled and buttoned up his pants.

"So, what would you call this - central fucking nowhere?"

I looked around. There was literally nothing as far as the eye could see. "No, Leonard, I think I would call this outer central fucking nowhere."

"Well, seeing how it's the Geographic Center of the United fucking States, you would have thought that they would have made a little bigger deal out of it."

I took out a cigarette and lit it, "Yeah, you would have thought so." I took a drag. "Any suggestions, Leonard?"

"I'm so glad that you asked, Carl ... hey, can I have one of those?" I flipped one out of the pack and handed him the lighter. He busted off the filter, lit it, and said pensively, "I was thinking maybe something Disneylandish ..." he motioned with his hand, "maybe a few rides over here, some carnie games over there, a few folks in bubble-headed cartoon character outfits walking around ..."

I interrupted, "Oh, and don't forget the gift shop."

"Hey, I was getting to that ..."

Suddenly he lost the enthusiasm of his sarcasm and his voice trailed off. I think the reality that somebody might actually consider doing something like that set in. He took another drag off of his cigarette. We both stood there and stared off to the endless prairie watching the golden tall grass flow back and forth. It was utterly quiet except for the wind. Neither one of us made any more comments.

I finished my cigarette and butted it on the blacktop. "Come on, man, we should get going here."

Leonard did the same. "Yeah, let's go." We got back in the van. Leonard fired it up, backed part way out of the parking spot, put it in first, and punched it. The van roared. He left two long black ribbons of probably five hundred miles worth of rubber behind us on the asphalt. This time he looked serious when he did it, and I didn't admonish him for it. I knew that it didn't have a thing to do with trying to get to the Badlands in four hours.

We continued north on Route 85 past the towns, if you could call them that, of Redig and Buffalo. The highway was flat, straight, and the loneliest stretch of road that we had been on so far. I suspected that it might very well have been one of the loneliest stretches of road in the lower forty-eight.

Leonard took advantage of it. Since there was nothing but grassland as far as the eye could see, there was no way to determine, by just looking out the window, how fast we were going. That is except for Mr. Rat, who was waving back and forth frantically in the slipstream. We could have been doing forty, or we could have been doing a hundred. I glanced over at the speedometer. Leonard was doing a little over eighty. The speedometer in the van only went to ninety.

We stopped briefly to fill up at the town of Ludlow. I didn't have to, but I took the opportunity to pee again. Once we were back on the road, Leonard asked, "What time have you got there, Carl?"

I looked at my watch, "It's ten forty-two."

"And how much farther do we have to go?" I pulled the map off the floor of the van and opened it to South Dakota.

"We should be reaching the border any time now ... maybe another five miles."

"And how far after we hit the border?"

"Hang on here for a second." I turned a few pages of the atlas until I found North Dakota. I added up the miles on the mileage markers, "Hmmm ... twenty-four, and twenty-four, and nine, and twenty-six, and fifteen ... Looks like we have about a hundred miles to go."

"No, Carl, we have exactly ninety-eight miles to go."

"I said *about,* Mr. Math-hole."

"When did you pickup a speech impediment, Carl?"

"Fuck off, Leonard. If I were you I'd start to haul ass. You have exactly eighty-four minutes to go ninety-eight miles. Mmm, mmm ... I sure can taste that beer. And you know something else? I think they taste better when they're free."

Leonard ignored my last comment about the beer. "What!? Give me that map."

"You heard me ... ninety-eight miles in eighty-four minutes, look for yourself." I handed the map to him. "You better fly there, partner." Leonard laid the map across the steering wheel of the van. While he was driving he did a few quick calculations. "And you know what else, Leonard?"

"What?" He looked up briefly to keep his bearing on the road. "You owe me another wee wee break. Factor that in too."

He ignored me and kept tallying numbers in his head. Finally he threw the atlas down on the floor at my feet and said, "Hell if I owe you a wee wee break. Shit, you are so math-challenged it's pathetic. I added those numbers up and it's two hundred and eighty-two miles total."

"Yeah, and so what?"

"So you said it was two hundred and fifty miles."

"No, Leonard, that's not what I said ... I said that it was two hundred and fifty miles *or so*. Besides, my ability to read a map correctly was not a stipulation of the bet."

Leonard rolled his eyes. "So is that how you've been navigating the whole trip?"

"Yes, as a matter of fact that is exactly what I have been doing."

"Well, I guess that explains quite a bit now, doesn't it?"

"Hey, you were the one who threw the itinerary out the window back in Oregon."

"Yeah, well, that wasn't doing us any good either now, was it." He had a good point.

Our banter was going nowhere. I attempted to get us back on track. "So, I guess the bet is off then."

"No, Carl," Leonard said calmly and succinctly, "the bet is not off ... the bet is modified."

"How so?"

"I *know* that I can still get us there in four hours, but ..."

"But what?"

"But you get no tinkle break." I didn't even have to think about it. I was more than willing to pee out the window if necessary to keep the bet going.

"Okay, pal," I pretended to sound tough, "I can handle that."

We were in North Dakota now and Leonard was giving the van everything it had. Just a few miles outside of Amidon, we passed a North Dakota state patrol car parked on the shoulder of the highway.

"Oh shit," Leonard said after we passed him. I looked down at the speedometer. We were doing just over eighty-five. Leonard powered down the van to a moderate sixty in preparation for the inevitable pullover. "Here we go, our first ticket." We both kept looking in the rearview mirror waiting for him to pursue us. He didn't. I theorized that he probably thought that it was impossible for a V.W. van to go that fast, and attributed whatever numbers he saw on his speed gun to equipment failure. After he was out of sight Leonard brought the van back up to speed again.

"So what time do we have, Carl?"

"It's eleven twenty-four. You want me to take a look at the map and see how much farther we have to go?" I tried to say it as sarcastically cheerfully as I could.

"Uh, no, Carl. Why don't you just hand me the map." I picked it up off the floor and handed it to him. He glanced at it for a second, pitched it back to the floor and said happily, "Oh, I so have your ass ... we only have forty-one miles left and we have, what time is it again?"

I looked at my watch, "Eleven twenty-six." "... And I have thirty-nine minutes to do it ... piece of cake. So Carl ..."

"Yeah?"

"Could you go aft and get me a Coke please?"

"Sure." I got up and started to head for the cooler.

"Hey, and while you're back there, why don't you get one for yourself." He smiled.

"Ah, I don't think so, Leonard, I'm feeling a little full already."

"Good, Carl, all the more reason for you to get one for yourself. I really want to see you pee out the window."

"That ain't going to happen, Leonard."

"We'll see," he said confidently.

It didn't. I held it.

I had to admit that barring any unforeseen natural disaster or catastrophic mechanical failure, it was seriously looking like Leonard was going to make it and win the bet. I also thought, though, that he was being just a little too smug about it. So, I tried to make that impending taste of victory a little less sweet for him.

"So Leonard, let's just hypothetically say that you win the bet."

"Hypothetically?! Are you kidding me, Carl? Hell, of course I'm going to win the bet ... mmm, free beer good."

"Okay, so you win. I have to buy you a night of free beer, right?"

"Free beer good," Leonard repeated like he was in a trance.

"Yes Leonard, we have established that free beer does in fact taste better. But, the bet does not specify what kind of beer ... does it?"

Leonard looked at me flatly, "Don't even, Carl ..."

"Don't even what?" I said innocently.

"Don't even think that you are going to try to settle this bet with me with some warm cheap-ass swill beer."

"Well, we didn't really stipulate that now, did we." I smiled at him pleasantly.

"I'll tell you what we'll do, Carl ... whatever beer you buy me to settle this bet you have to drink it too. Sound fair?" I hedged for a few seconds trying to think of how I could outmaneuver him on this. Leonard pressed me for an answer and repeated more emphatically, "Okay?" It was clear that he had pulled a clean reversal on me and there was no graceful way out of it.

I hesitantly acquiesced, "Yeah, yeah, yeah ... okay."

Leonard smiled and said again, "Free beer ..."

I cut him off and finished the sentence for him, "... good."

Finally we arrived at the town of Medora, the entrance to the Theodore Roosevelt National Park and the Badlands. Leonard said smugly, "Excuse me, Carl, what time is it?"

I looked at my watch, "It's exactly eleven fifty-three, Leonard."

"Why, thank you, Carl. And could you remind me again please what time did we need to be here by?"

"That would be twelve o'six, Leonard."

"Oh yes, that's right ..."

"Hey pal, we're not in the Badlands yet ... that was the deal." Leonard had a smirk on his face. He raised an eyebrow. "Remember what Minnesota Fats said, 'It ain't over 'til ya squeeze the tomatoes.'"

"Sure, Carl ... whatever."

Through the town, we followed the signs toward the park entrance. Medora appeared to be an opportunistic little place with no reason for existing other than that the national park was right there. They, like the restaurant in Gillette, had gone with the rough-rider western theme. No matter how old or new the buildings were, they all had the appearance of being built in the late eighteen hundreds, but with air conditioners and double paned windows.

The whole town was such a ridiculous sham of an imitation that I thought that it was actually pretty funny. I was sure that Leonard was not amused by it. The western facade thing universally offended him, so much so that he refused to even see the humor in it. The only comment that he made was that they should have named the town Medusa. He claimed that it would have been far more accurate. Beyond that, he said nothing about it. I think that he was far too elated by his imminent victory to let anything get him down.

At the end of the main street we came to a brown sign with an arrow pointing to the right that said, "Park Entrance

Five Hundred Feet." Leonard put on the turn indicator and prepared to execute the turn.

"What are you doing, Leonard? We're supposed to make a left here."

Leonard shook his head and said, "Oh dear God, Carl, please... that's just pathetic." He turned right.

We rounded the corner and were almost immediately confronted by a line of a half dozen cars waiting to get into the park. At the head of the line there was a forty-foot Winnebago Adventurer RV with Florida plates. On the back of it was an outline map of the United States.

I had seen these before on other RV's. It was a giant sticker, with each state color-coded. As you made your way around the country you would add sticker states to the map as you visited them. I guess that it was some kind of retiree's badge of honor to fill the thing up. It probably made you just that much more extra cool when you rolled your land yacht into the old RV park. On this one only Hawaii and Arkansas were missing. I understood the Hawaii one, with the ocean and all, but the lack of the Arkansas sticker left me wondering why they hadn't made it there. Maybe they just forgot that the state existed. Heck, I think everyone else in the nation tried to.

"Shit!" Leonard moderately yelled as he banged his hand against the steering wheel and pulled the van into a spot at the end of the line. I glanced at my watch – it was eleven fifty-seven. "What time is it, Carl?"

"It's eleven fifty-seven," I said cheerfully.

"Shit!" He banged the palm of his hand against the steering wheel again. "Fuck. I'll bet, I'll just fucking bet that there are a pair of cotton-heads up there in that RV." He looked at me. "It's always the cotton-heads." I was having a hard time not laughing. I put my feet up on the dashboard and pulled out my pack of cigarettes.

"Want one, Leonard?"

He glared at me. "No, I don't fucking want a cigarette... I want this fucking line to fucking move ... and quit fucking gloating, Carl."

Through a smile, I lit my cigarette and said as sincerely as I possibly could, "Sorry, Leonard." I wasn't sorry at all, and he knew I wasn't. It pissed him off even more.

We sat there for a couple more minutes before Leonard impatiently said, "Oh dear Lord, what is going on up there?"

As if she heard his question, an elderly white-haired woman popped her head out the passenger window and called back to the line sweetly, "I'm so sorry, folks, Grandpa can't find his wallet just yet. Thank you so much for being patient."

I leaned out the window, waved, and called back to her, "No problem, ma'am, take your time."

Leonard shot me a look and said, "Oh Christ, Carl, what did I tell you - cotton-heads! I am *not* going to lose this fucking bet sitting in line. I'm going to go pay for them myself." He stormed out of the van and headed up to the ranger's booth.

After a brief, and from what I could tell, a surprisingly civil conversation with the ranger and the elderly gentleman in the RV, he stormed back to the van. "Well, Leonard?"

"No I am *not* going to pay for it myself ... it's eighteen fucking bucks to haul that thing in here."

Leonard and I stared at the RV for the next few minutes, both waiting for something to happen. The more time that went by, the more agitated Leonard became, and he vented his frustration with various creative expletives.

Finally, the old man put his arm out the window and handed the ranger some cash. Apparently he had found his wallet. The ranger handed him back his change and receipt, and the RV started up and slowly rolled on into the park.

At last the line moved. "Oh my God - it's about time!" Leonard sounded like he was on the verge of a stroke. I looked at my watch. It was twelve o' nine.

"Speaking of time, Leonard, do you want to know what time it is now?" He looked at me. I smiled back at him calmly. He could read it on my face. He had lost the bet.

"No Carl, I do not want to know what time it is."

I badgered him. "But I know what time it is, Leonard," I said cheerfully.

"I'm sure you do, Carl," he said through tight lips.

"Are you sure you don't want to know?"

"Yes, I am extremely fucking sure."

I then tried to sound philosophical about it, "Yep, it's just like so many things in life ... it's those little things that get ya." Leonard glared at me. I kept smiling, but I thought it best shut the hell up. I even managed to restrain myself from repeating the "free beer good" mantra.

The rest of the line moved pretty quickly, and we reached the ranger's booth less than five minutes later. By the time we got there, Leonard had accepted his loss and was trying to let the whole bet thing go.

We pulled up and a friendly-looking ranger who seemed like he might have been retired himself greeted us. "Oh, hi, it's you," he said with a pronounced North Dakota accent. "Say, that was pretty darn nice of you to offer to pay for those folks. Even though they were too proud to take any money from you, I know that they sure appreciated the gesture. Kindness like that don't go unrecognized." Leonard looked a bit self-conscious. He didn't say anything; he just quietly let the compliment go. "So, how long are you fellas staying?"

"Just for the evening," I answered.

"Well, I'd normally say that that would be six-fifty, but let's just forget it, okay? Like I said, kindness like that don't go unrecognized."

"That's darned nice of you," I said, "Thanks." The ranger smiled at us and handed Leonard the park pass and the map.

"Hey, before you fellas take off here I just have to ask you, what the hell is that?" He pointed at Mr. Rat.

"I believe that it's a petrified rat," Leonard answered.

"And why exactly is it on your antenna?" the ranger inquired, stifling a laugh.

Leonard said seriously, "It is part of our navigational gear, sir. He tells us the wind direction."

The ranger chuckled, and rolled his eyes, "I'm sure he does ... Your park pass is good through tomorrow. There is a campground about five miles up the road. You'll see the sign for it. You fellas have a nice stay."

"Thanks," Leonard said, and fired up the van. I thanked him again as well and waved as we drove off.

The Prophet

We followed the winding road through the painted hills of the North Dakota Badlands toward the campground. The landscape was breathtaking and somewhat unexpected, after driving for hundreds of miles across the nearly flat prairie. As we drove, we were surrounded by an undulating geography of striated hills colored in layers of red, yellow, gray, and light brown. Dotting their sides were a variety of grasses, sagebrush, and junipers. In the valleys, where small seasonal creeks flowed, there were groves of willows and other smaller shrubs. The air through the open windows of the van blew with the fragrant aroma of blooming sage. There seemed to be a meaningful pattern to all of this, but I was unable to translate it. Still ... I could feel it was there.

As I took it all in, I thought about my family. My mother had grown up in a small town a couple hundred miles from here. That association hadn't occurred to me when Leonard and I had made the decision to come through North Dakota and to the Badlands. I was reminded of the stories that she had told me about how my grandfather used to come here to hunt deer and grouse. He loved the place dearly. I realized that, although I had never been here before, I had a history here. It made me feel all the more connected.

"Wow, Leonard, is this cool or what?"

I could tell that he was taken with it as well. "Yeah, Carl ... *very* cool."

"Did I ever tell you that my mom is from around here?"

He looked over at me somewhat surprised, and said, "No, man, I didn't know that."

"Yeah, I guess my grandfather used to come here all the time to hunt deer and grouse. She said that it was one of his favorite places." Leonard nodded.

"You know, I really loved my grandfather. I only met him once when we came out to visit when I was about five years old. I don't remember too much of that trip. I do remember though that he used to tousle my hair every so often. It made me feel loved." I stopped for a moment. It bothered me that I didn't remember more. I went on, "He was a pretty neat man. I remember that he had this big vegetable garden, at least that's what he called it, a garden. I think that it was more like an acre or so. He found out that I wanted to have a vegetable garden too. My mom must have told him. Anyway, he would send me these huge boxes wrapped in about a half a roll of filament tape. I think that he didn't trust the postal service. Inside he would pack different things that he had grown, squash, potatoes, carrots, peas, corn ... whatever was in season. He would also send me seeds for my own garden with specific instructions and diagrams of how to plant everything. His handwriting was pretty shaky ... he was already an old man by then. I remember one time he even sent me a coffee can full of chicken shit... he said that it was the best fertilizer." Both Leonard and I laughed a little at that before I continued on.

"After I had gotten everything out of the box, I would have to go through the straw that he had packed it all in. He hid silver dollars in there for me ... he called them 'pocket pieces' ..." I stopped and looked out the window of the van. I had not expected any of this.

We rounded the corner and started to head down the hill. Off in the distance I could see the campground in the valley. Leonard said gently but emphatically, "It sounds like your grandfather loved you very much, Carl."

"Yeah ..." When he said it I immediately felt a twinge in my heart. "... My father was a bastard, Leonard, but my grandfather was very good to me ... I wish that I had been able to spend more time with him. "

"Maybe you will," Leonard said, with an odd tone of certainty in his voice. I was a little confused by his comment, but I let it drop.

A couple of minutes later, we arrived at the Cottonwood Campground. Leonard immediately and jokingly nicknamed it the "Cotton-Head campground." When he had first used the term, despite my own tendency for irreverence, I had thought it more than slightly disrespectful. After some insight, though, of how he had been so kind to the elderly couple in the RV, I understood his use of the term to be nothing more than harmless fun.

This was the last place that we would be camping on our trip. Tomorrow we would be in Missoula, and, after a hellishly long drive, in a hotel. It was a good last place. The campground was situated in a stand of cottonwoods and elms right along the Little Missouri River. It wasn't a big campground - maybe thirty campsites at most. Only a half a dozen of those sites were occupied, one of them by the couple with the RV who had held us up at the park's entrance.

We drove twice around the horseshoe-shaped road running through the campground, finally picking out a nice little secluded place near a couple of large cottonwoods. Although our campsite was nicely shaded, we had an unobstructed view of the painted hills surrounding the valley. It was just before one o'clock. We had made good time and had most of the afternoon.

Leonard parked the van and we proceeded to set up camp. Putting up the tent was now a snap, and we could do it in less than five minutes. That is, as long as we didn't indulge ourselves in anything that might inhibit our spatial relations ability beforehand.

I got out the lantern and set up the stove while Leonard went back to the van to check out our food supply. We intentionally hadn't stopped to replenish it, knowing that we would only be cooking for one, maybe two, more meals. Also, both of us were starting to run out of money. We deemed that what cash we had left would be best spent later on a hotel and a meal cooked by someone else.

Leonard came back and announced that dinner was going to again be a south-of-the-border affair, consisting of a couple of cans of Dennison chili, some tortillas, rice, and a few limpish-looking two week old carrots. For dessert we could have the stale, crumbled remains of the cookies that Althea had baked for us. More importantly, he had checked the cooler ... we only had four beers left.

"Well, that looks like about it. I think we're pretty well set up. So what do you want to do with the afternoon, Leonard?"

He looked at me and simply said, "Sleep."

"Are you serious? This is beautiful county out here. We should take off and maybe go for a hike or something. Shit, we've been cooped up in the van most of the day. It would be good to move around a little bit."

"Yeah, later, Carl, right now I gotta take a nap. I'm fried from that insane marathon driving thing. Maybe you should take off for a while on your own. Hell, I'll still be here." He did look pretty tired, and I knew that we had a huge driving day ahead of us tomorrow. He would need to be fresh for that.

"Yeah, maybe you're right ... I think that maybe I will take off for a while."

Leonard sat down next to the bigger of the two cottonwoods and leaned his back up against it. "Hey, before you take off here, could you be a friend and leave me a couple of cigarettes and get me a Coke?"

"We have any left?"

"Yeah, one ... you want it?"

"No, just asking."

In the short time it took me to get the Coke from the van and return, Leonard already had his eyes closed and was snoring quietly. Without waking him, I gently laid the Coke, a pair of cigarettes and my lighter on the grass next to him. Before I left, I stood there silently and watched him sleep for a minute or so.

Leonard was a true companion, a very, very good friend ... I was fortunate. But in the time we had spent together on this trip I had seen something else in him, something that didn't have anything to do with our friendship... something inherently spiritual. And part of Leonard's greatness was that he wholly rejected it. I stood there watching him, and then with complete clarity it came to me ... he *was* a reluctant prophet. The offhand joking comment that I had made back in South Dakota was in reality no joke. That fact seemed very obvious to me. It made sense. As if he were confirming my thought, Leonard let out a snore and rolled over in the grass.

Shadows

I left Leonard and headed out alone. Within a short time, I was outside of the campground area and the shade of the grove of trees there. Before me lay the vast and beautiful rolling hills of the Badlands. I stopped for a moment to take it all in. The afternoon sun was high in the sky, and the wind blew just ever so slightly, offering a comforting breeze. Although I was a stranger to this country, I somehow felt completely comfortable wandering into its wilderness.

I picked up a well-worn path and followed it along the bottom of the valley. As I wandered along, every so often I could feel the waist-high prairie grass brush lightly against my legs, as if to tell me that I was not alone.

After a quarter of a mile or so, the trail nudged to the left and meandered down to the banks of the Little Missouri. At its edge I found a place where the grass had been laid flat, most likely by animals who had bedded down a night or two before. I sat down there, as they had, to rest for a moment. In late summer with nothing to feed it other than occasional rain, the river was low. I could have, without difficulty, walked to its other bank without getting my pants wet above the knee. Still, with what little water flowed, the river patiently continued its course.

I lay down on my back into the soft grass and stared up at the sky. Above me, I watched a single small cloud dancing lazily. It slowly twisted and grew and shrank and changed shapes over and over again, as if to try out all the things that it could be. It had the sky to itself and it seemed to delight in that. I watched it for a few minutes until it finally tumbled its way over a nearby hill and out of my sight. I thought it was a sign that I too should be going.

I put my hands down in the grass to prop myself up and prepare to rise. When I did, I noticed that under my left palm something felt different and soft. I took my hand away to look. In the place where I had lain down, there was a small clump of walnut brown fur. I picked it up. Buffalo ... I wasn't sure how I knew that, but I did and I was sure. I rubbed the fur gently between my fingers, and before putting it in my pocket, I put it to my nose and smelled it. It didn't just smell like bison ... it smelled like sage and grass and rivers and meadowlarks and thunderstorms. It smelled like the earth. I thought of my grandfather and knew that he had probably thought the same. I felt a slight breath of wind and the fur that I held between my fingers ruffled.

I picked up the trail again and continued on. The path followed the river for roughly another hundred yards, until at a bend it veered away and headed off back through the valley. I followed it. Maybe twenty minutes later, I walked out of the dry golden tall grass onto a plain of lush green pasture.

Almost as soon as I emerged, I spotted not far off a small herd of perhaps a half-dozen horses. I thought to myself that this trail probably led to someone's ranch. I felt a rising twinge of disappointment that this might be the case, and the end of my walk. No matter, the horses were beautiful, and I figured that if someone wanted me off of their land they would let me know it.

I started to walk over to the horses for a closer look. As I walked toward them I looked for signs that I was trespassing - a house, a road, a fence. I could see nothing to indicate that I was. As I moved closer, the horses shifted on their feet, signaling that they were aware of my presence. Slowly I kept walking. Finally, when I was a couple of hundred feet away, one of the horses separated from the herd and positioned himself between the group and me.

He was the largest of the group, a strong and rugged-looking horse, the stallion. His coat was an amazing steel blue-gray color. It was a color that I had never seen on a horse. His mane and tail were black. He raised his head, nodded it, shook his mane, and whinnied. This was as close as he was going to let me come. I respected that and stopped. As soon as I did, he appeared to relax some, and without moving away, went back to grazing. He did keep an eye on me, though.

I knelt down on my haunches in order to make myself less threatening to them, and watched. I noticed that it wasn't just the stallion that was of remarkable stock. All of the horses had markings and colorings of a breed that I was not familiar with. There was one that was a chestnut color, with a light tan mane and tail. Another had chocolate legs that gradually faded into a body of light tan dappled with small white spots. And yet another was pure white except for a gray muzzle. Then it struck me ... these were not domestic horses-they were wild.

Aside from the stallion that had separated himself, the rest of the horses were crowded together in a rough circle. I looked harder and saw why - in the center there were two foals, one maybe three weeks old and the other just slightly older. The younger of the two dipped its head under its mother's belly and nuzzled her for milk. The mare obliged, lifted one her hind legs, and the foal began to nurse.

I watched the horses for probably another fifteen minutes. Gradually, they finished grazing over this spot of pasture and slowly began to move off. The stallion, though, stayed behind and stood watching me. When the herd was near the far end of the plain, the stallion again nodded his head and whinnied, as if to bid me goodbye. He then reared up and swung around in a single graceful motion, and galloped off to join the herd.

After he was gone, I got up to leave, and for a moment felt slightly dizzy. I must have stood up too fast. Through my faint haze, out of the corner of my eye I sensed a movement. I turned, and just for a brief second I thought that I saw the ephemeral image of a person. It made me tingle. As my vision returned to normal I scanned the plain – yet there was no one else there, just the horses and me. Then I felt the wind ... ever so gently, it picked up and I felt my hair tousle in the breeze. I thought of my grandfather and smiled.

I went back in what I thought was the direction I came from in search of the trail. I looked for a while, but could not find it. It was almost as if it had never been there. Unafraid of becoming lost, I decided to set off on my own; I felt as if I knew the way.

I started across the plain and headed for a line of trees that snaked up a narrow valley between the buttes. I don't know why I chose this course, but it seemed like the right way to go.

The trees were farther off than I had anticipated. I was finding that distance was hard to judge in this country. I was also finding that it was impossible to tell what the landscape had to offer in between. Three times I had to scramble my way up and down deep arroyos that had been carved in the earth by seasonal flash floods. I had seen no evidence that they existed when I had chosen my course.

Eventually, though, I did reach the trees. Most were willows, but there were a few cottonwoods as well. I was refreshed by the coolness of their shade. I was also pleased to discover that they had grown there because of water that a spring farther up the hill provided. In a shallow gully nestled under their canopy a small rivulet ran. Every few feet or so it rested on its downhill journey and pooled.

I walked down to one of those pools, knelt down in the grass, and put my hands in the water. It was surprisingly cold and clear for being so late in summer. As soon as I did, though, a voice in my head that didn't sound like my own said, "Don't drink." I paused, and said out loud, "I wasn't going to ... I'm just cooling off." In cupped hands, I brought the cold clear water to my face and washed in it. It tingled on my skin as if it had effervescence.

I dipped my hands several more times, running the water over my neck and forearms, until I felt rejuvenated. I was just about to rise and continue on, when I was startled by a loud noise just up the grove. Its tone was a harsh "gawlk" and it had enough volume to resound for a second or two back and forth in the trees. I listened and looked intently from the direction that it came, trying to spot the creature had made the noise. I could see nothing except for a dense thicket of underbrush.

I sat there for a couple more minutes quietly, so quietly that my light breathing began to sound like a roar to me. Finally, I heard the noise again. This time it was closer, and I could see the underbrush move slightly less than twenty feet away. I squinted my eyes to try to make out a form, but was unable to. I decided to investigate. Slowly, and still kneeling, I inched forward in an attempt to discover the source. I felt my every sense alive searching for a clue.

I had made my way about ten feet when all of a sudden there was an explosion of sound and movement. Out of surprise and instinct, I reeled backwards onto the grass. As I did, I caught the fleeting form of two very large birds bursting out of the brush. I lay there on the grass recovering from my start, and began laughing at my own reaction.

When I finally composed myself, I got up and exited the thicket in the direction the creatures went. I knew they were birds, but in the brief glance that I had gotten of them, I had no idea what kind.

Outside of the thicket it was open uplands again, and I stood there in the waist-high buffalo grass searching for the birds. I stared, as I had in the grove, for any kind of noise or movement that might reveal their place. This time, though, I knew what I was looking for. My eyes scanned the hillside, but I could see nothing. After a couple of minutes I quit looking and relaxed, figuring that they had flown further away.

I started walking up the narrow valley, following along the edge of the line of trees. I hadn't gone more than a few feet when I spotted a feather in the grass. I stopped, reached down, and picked it up. It was about ten inches long and strikingly beautiful. It was iridescent bronze, with metallic golden stripes that shimmered as I moved it in the sunlight. I had never seen anything like it before. No doubt, though, it belonged to whatever I had flushed from the brush. I held onto the feather and walked on, pondering over the possibilities.

I only went another ten feet before I spotted another feather. This one was caught in a sagebrush. I again reached down and picked it up. It was of similar size, color, and beauty as the other feather, but instead of the golden stripes, there was a single broad band of blue across the tip of it. I examined it for a bit, and then added it to the other in my hand.

I began to walk on through the grass, but this time I was stopped after only a couple of steps. Again, there was a feather at my feet, and again I reached down to pick it up. This time though, when I did, I came across another, and still another. Each feather that revealed itself in the grass led me to another, until I had a handful of at least twenty. I smiled excitedly to myself as I examined them. Each feather was of a different size and color, yet clearly belonged to the same type of bird.

As I was delighting in my bounty, I heard the call again, and looked up in the direction it came from. Just ahead of me, in a downed cottonwood tree, there were five large birds. Although they looked extraordinarily familiar, for a moment I was unable to put a name to them. Then it came to me ... they were wild turkeys. I knew that wild turkeys were somewhat rare and elusive birds, and I immediately felt a tremendous wave of good fortune seeing them here.

I slowly sat down in the grass, so as not to spook them, and watched them for a few minutes. They moved up and down the limbs of the dead cottonwood, stopping every so often to pick at something in the bark - probably insects and grubs. As they worked their way around in the tree, I observed that they were not nearly as large as domestic turkeys, nor were they as clumsy. Every so often one of them would spread their beautiful iridescent wings, take to the air, gracefully light on another branch, and continue feeding.

I sat there in grass for probably ten minutes or so, until I decided that it was time to move on. I stood up as slowly and as quietly as I could, but still I startled them and they exploded in flight from the tree. The group soared low over the grass and sage, finally disappearing behind the contour of the hillside.

Once the turkeys were out of sight, I took my fistful of feathers and tried to put them in my pocket as carefully as possible so as not to damage them. As I fumbled with them, I all of a sudden I got the sense that someone was watching me.

I quickly turned around, and again, as I had on the plain, briefly caught what I thought to be the ephemeral image of a man out of the corner of my eye. I stood there and scanned the landscape. I searched for any sign of movement in the tall grass, the stand of trees, and the surrounding hills. I saw nothing. I shook off the sensation, and finished up putting the feathers in my pocket.

Just as I was trying to find a good place for the last and smallest of the feathers, the wind picked up and lightly snatched it from my fingers. I watched it as it lofted high into the air and then floated up the slope of the hill. When it was almost out of sight, the wind stopped as quickly as it had started, and it drifted back down to earth, landing somewhere in a rock outcropping near the top of the hill. I started hiking up the slope after the feather.

Initially the grade wasn't too bad, but it soon steepened and I found my pace slowing. The hot mid-afternoon sun beat down on the barren slope and I was sweating profusely. When I reached a slight flat spot, I stopped briefly to catch my breath. I reached over to a nearby sagebrush, broke off some leaves, and crushed them in my palm. I put my hand to my nose and took in their wonderfully intoxicating fragrance. It seemed to clear my head some. I looked up the hill and tried to get a bearing on how much further I had to go. It was difficult to determine exactly how far away I was, since the rolling contours of the landscape prevented me from seeing any further than about two hundred feet further up the hill. I dropped the crushed sage, and continued on.

Apparently I was closer to my goal than I thought. Only a few minutes later the slope flattened out to a large grassy landing, and I found myself at the base of the rocks.

The entire rock field was only forty feet high or so. The boulders were made of some type of grayish wind-smoothed sandstone. Their amorphous shapes made them seem like a kind of modern sculpture.

After again catching my breath for a couple of minutes, I set out to explore the rocks. Initially the climb was easy. There was a clear animal path that wove its way up, and the boulders offered plenty of handholds. I followed it. After rounding the first traverse in the path I came to a flat stone that jutted out from a crevice. On it were four small piles of grass. I knelt down, and without disturbing them, took a closer look. They appeared to have been intentionally laid out, as if by some tiny farmer, to dry in the sun. Probably some critter preparing supplies for the long hard winter ahead. I got up and continued on.

As I reached the top, the path gradually faded out, and I began picking my own way up through the rocks. This last bit was fairly steep and I carefully chose my hand and footholds. Finally I came to a large boulder. I couldn't see over the top of it, and I was a little nervous about blindly putting my hand up there. Although I hadn't seen any, this was rattlesnake country, and these rocks offered a perfect home for them. I looked around to see if there was another route up, but there wasn't. If I was to go on, this was the only way. Tentatively, I put my right hand up on the lip of the boulder, ready to take it back immediately at the slightest threat of a snake. I listened hard, but heard nothing. I grabbed on with my other hand, and cautiously pulled myself up. Slowly I peeked up over the lip.

There was no snake there, but the wide flat rock was covered in little piles of grasses like the ones I had seen further down the slope. Tucked neatly into one of those piles was the feather. I hauled myself up and onto the rock. I started to reach down to pick up the feather, but changed my mind and stopped. Whatever critter had found it probably was going to needed it more than I did. It would make good bedding.

Suddenly, I was startled by the sound of a scurrying movement. I jumped a little, and instinctively scanned the rock – no snakes. I determined that the sound had come from a foot-wide cave-like crevice that went back into the hill near the edge of the rock. I had probably startled the animal that was responsible for the little grass piles. Carefully, I looked back into the crevice to see if I could spy what had made the noise. When I looked in I saw a small rodent-like creature with large round eyes peering out at me from only a couple of feet away. It was maybe a foot in length, and had somewhat longish tawny fur that covered its six-inch tail as well. It was a peaceful and sweet-looking creature. Although I surely had surprised it when I first climbed up on the rock, it now appeared to be completely unafraid of me.

We both just sat there and stared at each other for a few minutes. I didn't move. Then, ever so slowly, it began to walk toward me. Finally, when it was less than an inch from my foot, it sat down, looked up at me, and sniffed. It was apparently satisfied that I was not a threat. Then it got up again and walked over to the pile of grain that had the feather in it. It looked at me, then gently picked up the feather with its forepaws, put it in its mouth, and made its way back toward its cave. When it got to the entrance it stopped, turned around, and looked at me one last time, and then disappeared into the cave. I smiled after it, and said in a whisper, "Have a good winter, little guy ... I hope that feather keeps you warm." I was glad no one was listening.

It was time to move on. I stood up, stretched, and looked around to see where to continue my hike. I was near the top of the butte, and although I had a pretty good view of the valley below, there were two higher buttes on either side of me and I could not see the campground where I had come from.

"I suppose," I said to myself aloud, "I'm lost." I said it, but inside it really did not feel like I was. Then I thought about what Leonard had said, "Not all who wander are lost." It made me laugh.

Determined to go onward rather than try to retrace my steps, I figured that probably the best thing to do was to hike to the top of one of the two higher buttes to see if I could get a better view. Without giving it any more consideration, I chose the one to my left and began walking.

I had only gone a few feet when a strong breeze came up from my right. I stopped and turned into it to take advantage of it and cool off. As I stood there with my arms out and the wind blowing over me, I looked out to the butte that I had not chosen. I studied the beautiful gradients of the colors in the hill, starting with a golden grasslands at the base, fading to green juniper, and finally ending with a crown of red baked clay - scoria.

Just as my eyes reached the crest, I saw a man walk up and over the top, then disappear from sight. I looked hard to see if I could catch another sight of him, but he did not reappear. Figuring that he must have been on a trail, I set off in a new direction and headed for that butte instead.

For most of the way I walked easily through more tall grass, gently gaining altitude. By the time that I reached the junipers, the way steepened again. Fortunately, the tough evergreens offered good hand and footholds and I kept moving without difficulty. When I reached the red scoria, though, it was different. I found that it was hard to get a good purchase on the broken terra cotta-like surface, especially wearing cowboy boots. A couple of times I found that I was slipping so badly that I resigned myself to crawling up the steep slope on hands and knees.

Finally, I did make it to the top. As soon as I crested the hill, I stopped and stood panting for breath. From the vista I had a sweeping view of the surrounding landscape. Ahead of me, in the distance, less than a mile away, I could clearly see our campground.

Before I started my descent down the hill and back to the campground, I turned around to take one last look back at valley where I had come from. When I did, I froze at what I saw. Down below me maybe three hundred yards away, there stood out in the grass an aged gentleman. I looked as hard as I could to try and make him out better. He was a big man, maybe six feet tall. He was dressed for hunting, yet his clothes were for a colder season, maybe late fall. He wore a red and black plaid wool mackinaw, and calf-high leather boots. Slung over his shoulder was a rifle.

He just stood there, the deep grass waving around him, looking up at me. Then he raised his arm and he waved. I waved back. He started to walk off then stopped, turned and called out, "It was good to see you, Carl ..." His words echoed off of the hills. When they faded away, he waved again, then turned and continued to walk on out into the Badlands until I could see him no longer.

I was stunned, speechless, and tears rolled down my cheeks. He had been with me the whole time, and I had felt him there all along. He had showed me this, these things that he had loved, and I had loved them too.

For a long while I could not move. I just stood there looking out over the hills and valleys taking all of this in. As I stood there, I began to realize that it was precisely because I wasn't looking that I had found someone very dear to me. My grandfather had always been with me ... I just hadn't let myself see him.

I don't know how long I stood there on the butte, but it was quite some time. The sun had dropped lower in the sky. It was that time of day that you could call either late afternoon or early evening. I looked at my watch - it was nearly five o'clock. I had been gone for almost four hours. I could see in the distance that Leonard was up from his nap. It looked like he was beginning to prepare dinner. It was time for me to be heading back.

I took one last long look at the place where my grandfather and I had spent the afternoon together. I knelt down, put my palm to the earth, and thought, "Goodbye ... I'll be back soon."

It didn't take long to get back to the campground, maybe a half an hour at most. It gave me time, though, to begin to make the transition between leaving one world and entering another. It was an odd feeling, and it left me melancholy. I wondered if, in some way, it might be possible for me to live somewhere between the two. I would work on that.

When I walked into our campground Leonard was in fact beginning to prepare dinner. He looked up from the stove, smiled, and said, "Hey, Carl, good timing, man ... I was just getting dinner together." I didn't say anything. I just nodded. I was still transitioning.

"So did you have a good hike?" He turned his attention back to the stove. I paused for a moment trying to think exactly what to say.

Finally, quietly and a little hoarsely I said, "Yeah." Talking felt strange.

He stirred the chili a bit more, and turned over the pair of tortillas on the griddle. Then he stopped what he was doing, looked at me intensely, and hit me with it point blank, "Did you see your grandfather?" We stared directly into each other's eyes. I felt a flash of energy between us.

I wavered for a few seconds before answering, then simply said, "Yes."

Leonard looked pleased. Immediately, a knowing smile drew across his face, then he said casually, "Yeah, I thought you probably were going to." He went back to his stirring. "So, how do you feel?"

"What do you mean, Leonard?" He didn't reply, and he didn't look up ... he just waited for my answer. "I feel, feel... a little weird, to be honest."

He nodded. He knew exactly what I was talking about. "I know, Carl ... it does feel odd, doesn't it?" I nodded.

Since neither one of us had really had any lunch, we were starving. With a minimum of conversation we ate our last camp dinner. After trying one bite of an ancient carrot, Leonard deemed that the rest of them were best left in the brush for the critters. I didn't have to try one to agree with him. They looked pretty bad.

After we finished, we polished off the powdered remnants of the cookies that Althea had baked for us while we quickly cleaned up and packed away the kitchen stuff. We left out the stove and the coffee, which we would need in the morning. We wouldn't need anything else for the rest of the trip, and cleaning it up now would save us precious travel minutes tomorrow morning.

When we were done, Leonard went over to the cooler to grab a beer.

"You want one, Carl?"

"Man, we only have two apiece ... are you sure you want to squander one now?"

Leonard gave me a look like "don't be an idiot," and said, "What do you think, that they're an investment commodity? Like if you hang onto your beer it's going to be worth more tomorrow?"

"Yeah, yeah, yeah ... give me one already." He tossed it to me.

We took our beers and went and sat down on the grass underneath the cottonwood tree in the same spot where Leonard had taken his nap earlier. The grass was soft and comfortable, and we had a good view of the surrounding country. As we sat there watching the sun disappear below the hills and drinking our beer, I briefly thought about telling Leonard what had happened on my hike that afternoon. But it didn't seem right. It was something that was just between my grandfather and me ... something intensely personal. I think that Leonard understood that before I did, and asked me nothing more about it.

"So, Carl, I guess we're headed out to Missoula tomorrow."

"Yeah, we have a hell of a drive ahead of us. I'm almost not sure that we can make that many miles in a day."

Leonard looked at me and said half-smiling, "You want to bet? Double or nothing." His comment struck me as funnier than it probably was. I was in the middle of a sip of beer, and when I tried to hold back a laugh I nearly ejected it out of my nose.

When I recovered myself and was able to swallow I said, "Goddamn it, Leonard, don't do that to me. Man, you almost made me nose-hurl beer."

"Really?" He sounded extremely pleased with himself.

"Yeah, really ... we only have two apiece and I would really like to enjoy mine if I can." Leonard shrugged and took a sip of his own beer. Seeing an opportunity, I quickly tried to think of something witty to say to see if I could get him to have a nose-hurl experience of his own, but nothing came to me.

Not long after the sun had vanished, the sky began to light up in a bold display of color. Gradually it turned from a soft pink afterglow to an extravagant show of streaks of bright magenta that were reflected off of the wisps of clouds.

Leonard got up and went to the cooler for another beer, "You want another, Carl?"

"Yeah, that would be great ... thanks. Hey, on your way back why don't you get the weed out of the van."

"You were reading my mind, Carl."

When he got back he handed me my last beer, sat down, and proceeded to fill the pipe with the last of the Wiccan weed. "Well, it looks like that's about it for the pagan smoke."

"Man, that lasted us just about the whole trip. And you know, Leonard, I have to say that it's just a little bit better quality than that stuff you grew in your closet."

Leonard ignored my comment, lit the bowl, and drew in a deep drag. He savored it and held it for a good long time before exhaling. When he finally did exhale, hardly any smoke passed his lips. He then handed the pipe and the lighter to me, and I did the same. Even before I exhaled I could feel the weed begin to take effect.

We passed the pipe back and forth probably a half a dozen times before we finished it. Maybe it was the angle of the light or maybe the effects of the weed made me appreciate it more, but with each successive pass the sunset appeared more and more brilliant. We both sat there on the grass in awe.

"Man, Leonard, I don't know if I've ever seen a sunset like this. This is amazing."

"Yeah, it really is Carl ... it really is."

"You know, Leonard, it's kind of ironic ..." The moment I said the word, it reminded me of Dieter and Marta. They would have loved this.

"What's that, Carl?"

"Well, that they call this place the Badlands. I think that this is one of the most beautiful places that I've ever been to."

"Yeah, it is ironic. I suppose that it's all in your perspective, Carl."

"Yeah ... perspective," I said pensively. "I suppose that's what it's all about, isn't it ... perspective."

"Yep ..."

"Ya know, Leonard, I think I would call these the Goodlands."

Leonard looked at me and said, "Then I think you should, Carl."

Slowly the sunset faded and was replaced by darkness. A thick ribbon of stars filled the sky above. Leonard and I lay on our backs and looked up at them. Every so often one of us would point out a shooting star to the other. The evening air was warm and there was a light refreshing breeze. The night animals had come out. Off from the direction of the Little Missouri a chorus of frogs sang. In a nearby tree an owl hooted. I could hear in the surrounding underbrush the scurrying of tiny critters - probably field mice. I thought it best not to point them out to Leonard.

We lay there for probably an hour or so. It was peaceful; I didn't want the evening to end. Finally, though, Leonard asked, "Hey Carl, what time is it?"

Without rising I looked at my watch and said, "It's just after eleven."

"We should probably crash soon ... We need to get up early. We have a hell of a long drive ahead of us tomorrow. We're going to need our sleep."

"Yeah, I suppose you're right," I said reluctantly. Neither one of us made an immediate move to go to bed.

A few minutes later Leonard took the initiative, got up, and said, "Come on, man ... sleep calleth."

"Yeah ... okay." I rose as well. Just as I stood up, I saw in the sky to south, behind the hills, a flash, and then another and another.

"Do you see that, Leonard?"

"What?" He turned around and looked in the direction that I was looking. There were four more big flashes from behind the hills. "Yeah ..."

"What the hell is it?"

"Thunder storm, Carl," he said calmly.

"But I don't hear any thunder."

"It's a long, long way away." There were two more flashes followed by a very one large one that lit up a good portion of the horizon.

"Man, that must be some thunder storm. How far away do you think it is?"

"Could be a couple of hundred miles. It's pretty flat out here."

The sky lit up again with a rapid succession of flashes. "What's out that direction?"

Leonard looked at me and said, "Devil's Tower." We both smiled at each other.

"Come on man, let's crash."

"Yeah ..."

That night I slept hard and well, except for waking up about an hour before sunrise. I'm not certain why I woke up, I just did. I unzipped the tent and poked my head outside. There was light on the horizon, and only a few of the brightest stars were left in the sky. The air was completely still and there wasn't a sound ... not a single sound. I had never experienced such a thing before – complete quiet.

As I lay there, I thought to myself how never before in my life had I felt so clear ... so grounded ... so connected. Something in me had changed on this journey with Leonard. It was something that I had not been looking for nor had it been something that I had expected, at least consciously. I had found a spirituality inside myself - it was good. I smiled to myself – I was at peace.

I slid back down into my sleeping bag and zipped the tent back up. As I did, the silence was broken by the howl of a single coyote somewhere far off up in the hills. I listened to him. He howled one more time, and then there was silence again. I rolled over in my sleeping bag and went back to sleep.

Montana

For a change, Leonard had gotten up before I did. He had just finished making a pot of coffee, and decided that it was time that I got up too. He called from outside the tent, "Hey, Sleeping Beauty, time to get up." I heard him walk away.

I called after him, "Hey, if I'm Sleeping Beauty, don't I get a kiss?" I opened the tent.

He was standing near the picnic table pouring a cup of coffee for himself. He looked at me and said simply, "Ah, no, Carl ... and quit being a tease."

I reluctantly got up and joined him. I was hardly awake. It was daylight, but just barely. The sun wasn't even over the hills yet. Leonard handed me a cup of coffee. "Here you go, Carl, this ought to help get you going."

"Thanks." I took a sip and promptly burned my lower lip a little on the rim of the tin mug. "Shit! I so wish I would stop doing that." I set the mug back down on the table to let it cool.

"Hey, but at least you're awake now ... didn't I tell you it would help?"

I gave Leonard a "screw you" look, then said, "So what the hell time is it anyway?"

Leonard blew on his own coffee to cool it, carefully took a sip, and when he was done said, "I don't know. You tell me, you're the one with the watch. My guess is that it's really early."

"Well, I guess we're setting the tone for the day now, aren't we, Leonard?" I looked at my watch, "Jesus, it's five fifteen!"

"Shhh, Carl, you'll wake the other campers."

"Screw the other campers, what the hell are we doing up at five fifteen in the morning?" Leonard calmly took another sip of coffee. I picked mine up to give it another try. It was still hot, but this time I didn't burn my lips.

"Well, Mr. Navigationally Challenged Guy, yesterday I took the liberty of taking a serious look at the map. Missoula is, to use a Carl-ism, '*about* six hundred miles from here.' I figure that if we absolutely haul ass ..." He took another drink of coffee, then continued, "... and we have a tail wind, and the gods are with us, we might make it there in ten hours."

I took sip of my own coffee then said meekly, "Oh ... I was figuring more like five ..."

Leonard stared at me, "Oh, you are so full of shit, Carl. Man, not even you are that fucked up."

"Yes I am, Leonard." We both started laughing. We quickly shut up when somebody from a neighboring campsite called over to us, "Would you guys be quiet, it's five o'clock in the morning!" I mouthed an "oops" to Leonard, who apparently didn't feel as apologetic.

He called back, "No, it's five fifteen." We both had to fight hard to keep from seriously busting up aloud and making things worse. When we regained our composure, Leonard poured us both another cup of coffee. "Well Carl, there's no sense in hanging out around here. We should get things packed up and get a move on."

"Yeah, I suppose you're right, especially since we pissed off the neighbors. You know, before we leave, I should give Althea a call. I keep promising her that I will, and then I don't."

"You know that she's gonna to be pissed."

"Maybe, but I figure at least I'm telling her that I'm coming home. That should help some."

"Well if anything, she's going to be pissed at you for calling her at four thirty in the morning." I gave him a puzzled look, then realized, "Oh yeah ... we're on Mountain Time."

"Duh, Carl."

I ignored his last comment. "I'll tell you what, why don't you pack up and get us ready to leave and I'll go and call Althea from the pay phone over by the restrooms. When you're finished up, just come over and pick me up."

"Sounds like a plan, Carl."

I topped up my coffee, checked my pocket to make sure I had change, and went off to call Althea. As I headed over to the phone booth, Leonard was already getting on to the business of packing.

When I got to the phone booth I pulled the change out of my pocket, separated the quarters and dimes, and stacked them atop the phone. I had two dollars and ten cents total. It would have to be a moderately short call. I pulled a cigarette out, lit it, dropped a dollar fifty in the phone, and dialed.

The phone only rang twice before Althea picked it up. I'm sure that I caught her in a dead sleep. It took her a second to answer, but finally she said with a croaky morning voice, "Hello?" As soon as I heard her, a flood of homesickness and missing her hit me.

"Hey Althea, it's me!" There was a pause on the other end of the line, and I could hear the covers rustling. She was getting up.

A moment later she said, with more enthusiasm than anyone else would have had at four thirty in the morning, "Carl - where are you?!" Her voice was still a bit croaky.

"We're out in the Badlands."

"Where?"

"The Badlands ... they're out in North Dakota."

"Oh ..." I was expecting her to be angry, but her voice sounded soft and disappointed. I felt like a jerk for not having called her sooner.

"Hey, don't sound so sad, Althea ..." I could hear the covers rustle some more. I continued, "Cheer up, I wanted to let you know that I'm on my way home. I'm going to be there late tomorrow."

As soon as I said that I was coming home she exploded, "Oh my God, Carl, are you serious ... you're going to be home tomorrow?!"

"Yes I'm serious, we're driving to Missoula today, and..." I didn't get a chance to finish. She pulled the phone away from her mouth to save my ear and let out a loud whoop. I started smiling.

She came back on. She was totally awake, and was so excited she was falling over her words, "Oh Carl, I've missed you so badly ... I can't wait til you get here!"

"I know, I can't wait to see you too."

"So when do you think that you'll be here?"

"Oh, sometime late. I think that it's about a six or seven hour drive from Missoula."

"I'll make dinner ... you have to be here for dinner – promise me."

"Hey, I promise."

"Say the mantra, Carl." Her tone was serious. I knew that she was going to make me say it.

"Okay, okay ... Hare Krishna, Hare Krishna, Krishna Krishna, Hare Hare, Hare Rama, Hare Rama, Rama Rama, Hare Hare." In her mind, the chant sealed my coming home in stone. When I finished, Althea let out another whoop. Back from the direction of our campsite I heard Leonard start the van. "Hey Althea, I can't talk long."

"What?" She sounded a little disappointed.

"I just heard Leonard fire up the van. He'll be over to get me here any minute. We're going to get on the road." The line clicked and we were interrupted by a recorded message informing us that we only had another minute left on the call. When the message was over and line cleared, I added, "Besides, I only have sixty more cents."

She seemed more reassured by the fact that the sooner that we got off the phone the sooner I would get home. "Okay, Carl, hurry back ... I love you so much, I can't wait to see you."

"I know, Althea, I love you too." I could hear Leonard approaching in the van. "I'll see you tomorrow ... I'll get there as soon as I can – promise."

"Okay Carl, I love ..." The line abruptly went dead. We had run out of time.

I knew that Althea and I were pretty much done with our conversation when the line went dead, but it seemed rude to cut us off one word from the end. As I hung up the phone I briefly cursed the phone company for its insensitivity. I thought to myself, "I wonder how many other people have been cut off in the middle of conversations with their girlfriends?" Shit, I wonder how many relationships have ended because folks couldn't get out that one last important word.

"Bastards," I said aloud.

I was collecting my sixty cents off the top of the phone when Leonard pulled up. He turned off the van and got out. "Well, how did it go, Carl?"

"It went well, except that the friggin' phone company cut us off when we were saying goodbye."

Leonard looked surprised. "Are you serious? She wasn't pissed at you for not calling?"

"Nope, and she wasn't pissed that I called her at four thirty in the morning either. She was just happy to hear that I'm coming home."

"Well, good, I'm glad it went well. Sometimes you two just sweat the small stuff way too much. You should knock that off, you're good for each other."

"Yeah I'm glad too ... I can't wait to see her." Saying it brought on another twinge of homesickness. I wanted to get moving. I changed subjects, "So do you want me to take first shift at the wheel there, partner?"

"Whatever you want to do ... there's plenty of road out there and we're both going to be driving a ton today."

I pulled my keys out. "Yeah, I'll take the first shift, I'm kind of in the mood."

We climbed in and I started the van. We were off. We wound our way out of the campground and back out to main road. I felt a tremendous sadness in leaving, and wished that I could have stayed longer. I knew, though, that we needed to be heading back. As I looked in the rearview mirror at the valley behind us, I felt my throat tighten and tears start to come. I said to myself, "I'll be back ... soon."

I stopped looking and tried to get my mind back to the task at hand. I said to Leonard, "So how far were you saying we have to go, Leonard?" Leonard ignored my question. He must have heard the waver in my voice.

"You okay, Carl?"

"Yeah, I'm fine ..."

He paused then said, "Hey man, don't worry, you'll come back."

"Yeah ... I know."

Leonard picked up the map and studied it for a minute. "To answer your question, we have a little less than six hundred miles to go."

"How much less?"

"A *little* less."

"Whew, that's some drive."

"Yeah, but like I was saying last night, we should be able to make that in ten hours at worst. Just so long as we don't fuck around, and we stick to driving."

"What about food?"

"What about it?"

"Well, hell, we're not going to drive for ten hours without eating, are we?"

"No."

"So maybe we should drive for a while and then stop." I looked down at the gas gauge. It read a third of a tank. "We're going to need fuel soon anyways."

Leonard nodded and then flipped through the road atlas until he got to Montana. "Well, in about a hundred miles there's a town called Glendive. How much gas do we have?"

"Eh, probably four gallons or so. We should be able to make a hundred miles no problem."

"Good, we'll stop there, fuel up, and get some chow. But no sit-down breakfast or anything like that, we gotta keep moving."

"Roger," I said in agreement.

A few minutes later we passed by the ranger station. It was too early for anyone to be there, but I waved out the window and said goodbye anyway as we left the Badlands behind.

Once out of the park, we followed the signs toward the interstate. Gratefully, we did not have to go back through

Medora to get there. After a quarter of a mile or so we spotted a big blue sign for the on ramp. It said, "Interstate 94 West – Glendive."

"Here we go, Leonard ... we're headed home."

As I drove onto the freeway and got the van up to speed, Leonard pointed his finger at the road ahead and said boldly, "Go west, young man ... go west."

It was good to be back on a freeway. Although not nearly as scenic as the highways and backroads that we had been on for most of the trip, the road was three lanes wide, and built for speed. We would have no problem making good time. It was a beautiful clear day, and a landscape of easy rolling hills meant that we could see for miles in any direction. It was early enough in the morning that we were the only vehicle on the road, and soon I had the van doing eighty.

In no time we passed by the town of Beach. Leonard looked over at me and said with raised eyebrows, "And the beach would be … where?"

"I think it's just optimistic thinking on their part, Leonard. Maybe they really want a beach."

"Yeah ... well I would call it delusional, Carl."

Soon after, we reached the border between North Dakota and Montana. At the side of the road there was a large sign in the shape of a buffalo. It said, "Thank you for visiting North Dakota – Discover the Spirit." I immediately smiled and thought to myself, "I did."

Leonard commented, "Well, that's just a little prophetic now, isn't it."

I nodded, "Yeah, I would say so."

A couple hundred yards later we came to another sign. It was in the shape of the state of Montana - "Welcome to Montana – Big Sky Country."

"I think it should say 'Welcome to Montana – Big Drive Country.'"

"Speaking of driving, Carl, you know what I just realized?"

"What's that, Leonard?"

"I don't think that they have a speed limit in Montana."

I looked at him, "Are you serious?"

"That's what I've heard."

"Yeah well, maybe that's what you've heard, but is it fact?"

Leonard shrugged, "I guess there's one way to find out."

"How's that?"

"Keep doing eighty and see if we get pulled over."

"You know, we could ask someone instead."

"Sure we could, Carl, but really, where's the fun in that?" He had a point. I kept the van at full power and a half an hour later we had eaten up the thirty-eight miles to Glendive.

"Hey man, we're here."

"Damn, Carl, we keep this up and we'll be in Missoula in no time."

"Yeah, relatively no time."

I pulled off the freeway and into the town. "So, any clues on eats and gas?"

"Not a one, Carl, but I bet that if we just drive on through we'll find something." I nodded.

I followed what was apparently the main street in search of food and fuel. Glendive was neat, tidy and exuded friendliness. The rolling hills and proliferation of large trees and other greenery in town made it feel like we were out of the Great Plains and back in the West again.

"You know, Leonard, this is kind of a cute little town."

"Cute?" Leonard repeated. "Man, you keep saying that."

"Yeah, cute ... see, I'm comfortable enough with my manhood to call something cute."

"Well I'm so happy for you, Carl ... I'm not. I do have to agree with you though, this is a pretty nice town ... if that's what you mean by cute."

We had only driven about three blocks when we spotted a Stinker brand gas station, with its trademark fifteen-foot high smiling skunk logo. I had always thought that their trademark was refreshingly appropriate considering their product. Right next door there was a takeout restaurant, Glenda's. Out front there was a presumably life-sized, yet somewhat dysmorphic dinosaur made out of concrete. Underneath it there was a large sign that identified it as a "Glendasaurus."

"Hey, over there, Carl."

"Yeah, I see it ... you want to stop there?"

"No, Carl," Leonard said sarcastically, "I'm just pointing out one of the big tourist highlights of Glendive."

"Hey, I'm just asking ..." I put on the turn indicator and pulled into the gas station.

I filled up the van and Leonard went over to investigate the menu at Glenda's. I was returning to the van after paying for the ten and a half gallons of fuel, six-pack of Coke, and pack of cigarettes when Leonard waved to me from across the parking lot.

"This'll work, Carl ... park it over here."

"Cool," I hollered back.

I got the van moved, and joined Leonard at the takeout window of the restaurant. It was exclusively a breakfast and lunch joint, with an extensive Americana menu. Judging from the fare, their primary customers were truckers who filled up at the gas station next door.

Their breakfasts included any combination, as well as any amount, of meat, potatoes, eggs, and pancakes, including my personal favorite, chicken-fried steak. Above the menu there was a large notation that said, "Any of the items below may be ordered to go 'On a Stick.'" The idea seemed bizarre, yet at the same time functional. I leaned over to Leonard and said, "My God, these guys have everything you could possibly want."

"Yes they do, as long as you're not a vegetarian."

"I think that I'm going to go with the chicken-fried steak and eggs."

"Are you serious, Carl? How in the hell do you propose that you're going to eat a chicken-fried steak and eggs while you're driving?"

"Hey, man, read the sign ... they put it on a stick."

Leonard looked to where I was pointing above the menu. He got a screwed up look on his face and said, "Oh, there is just something so wrong about that."

"What?" I tried to sound sincere and innocent.

"Because, Carl, only corn dogs live on sticks."

"Why?"

"Would you please shut the hell up? The whole idea of putting different shit on sticks is making me queasy."

I was just going to point out to Leonard that shit on a stick was in fact a possibility when a woman appeared at the window. "Morning, fellas."

"Morning," we both replied in near-unison.

"Sorry to keep you waiting, my help didn't show up this morning and I'm runnin' the show on my own." She smiled. She didn't look too upset about it. She was a pleasant and somewhat roundish woman, probably in her late thirties or early forties. She looked like she thoroughly enjoyed her work. "So what can I get for ya?"

I went first. "Well, I think I'll have the chicken fried steak with hash browns and two eggs."

She jotted the order down on a pad. "You want gravy with that?"

I looked at her, "Is there any other way?"

She smiled at my comment and said, "Not in my mind, there ain't." She turned to Leonard, "And what'll you have?"

Leonard, who was still looking at the menu, stalled for a moment then said, "Can I get something on the lunch menu?"

"Course you can," she said cheerfully.

"Then I think I'll get a cheeseburger and a large order of fries."

While she was jotting his order down I leaned over to Leonard and said, "Man, I don't think it's proper etiquette to have a burger before ten o'clock."

Leonard gave me a "fuck you" look and said, "Yeah, well it's ten o'clock somewhere."

The woman overheard us and laughed slightly at one or both of our remarks. "So will this be for here or to go?"

"We'll have it to go away."

"I'll only be able to do the eggs hardboiled on a to-go order ... that going to be okay?" Leonard winced at her comment.

"That'll be fine, ma'am," I said, "What do I owe you?"

She quickly punched our order into the register. "That'll be nine twelve." Leonard started to reach for his wallet.

"Forget it, Leonard, I've got this one."

"Thanks, man."

"Don't worry about it, I'll get you back when you buy me dinner and beers tonight." I pulled a twenty out of my wallet, handed it to her, and said, "That's a damned good deal."

She smiled, "That's what Glenda's is about ... good food, good price." She handed me my change back. "It's going to be a minute. If you want, you fellas can make yourselves comfortable at one of the tables out on the patio." She motioned with her hand off to the side of the building.

"Thanks, we'll do that." She disappeared back into the kitchen.

On the way out to the patio I asked Leonard, "So you think that's Glenda?"

"Duh, Carl ..."

Then I said in my best Wizard of Oz imitation, "Oooh I'm not a bad witch, Dorothy, I'm a good witch."

Leonard looked at me like I was an idiot and said, "You know, Carl, it's not just distance that's going to make today's drive long."

Leonard and I made ourselves comfortable at one of the tables out back. We had barely finished our cigarettes when Glenda hollered from up front, "Your orders are ready."

When we got up there to pick them up, Glenda had them sitting on the counter. "The burger and fries are in the bag, the chicken-fried steak's in the box."

"Thanks, smells good."

"You fellas want ketchup or Tabasco?"

"I wouldn't mind a little ketchup with my fries," Leonard said.

As she was grabbing a fistful of packets from a box behind her, I said, "Mind if I ask you a question?"

She turned around with ketchup in hand. "Shoot."

"So what's the deal with the dinosaur out front?"

"Do you like it?" She looked past us at it. She was beaming that we had noticed it.

"Yeah, as a matter of fact I do." She stuck the packets in Leonard's bag.

"My husband made that a few years back. Took him three summers to build it. He says it's a monument to his love for me. " She smiled proudly.

I turned around, looked again at the dinosaur, and said, "Judging from the size of that thing, he must love you quite a bit."

"Yes, he does ... and you know what else?" She leaned on the counter, with her cheek in her hand. She had a dreamy schoolgirl look in her eye.

"What?"

"I love him just about that much too."

I nodded and smiled. "Well, I sure thank you for the food. We gotta be going here, got a long drive ahead of us."

"Well, you are surely welcome. You fellas take good care."

"Thank you, we will."

On the way back to the van, I said to Leonard, "That's kind of a sweet story, in kind of a goofy sort of way, don't you think?"

He finished chewing a fry then said, "Yeah, it really is, Carl ... it's amazing what people will do to show their love."

"Yeah, it really is ..." I thought of Althea.

Leonard was already halfway through his cheeseburger when I hit the on ramp to the freeway. "My God, Leonard, are ya hungry enough over there?"

"Hey man," Leonard said through a mouthful of burger, "I want to finish this before you start in on that chicken-fried thing. I'm afraid that I might lose my appetite watching you."

I shook my head, "Oh, shit, it's not that bad, Leonard."

"You haven't opened the box yet."

When I got the van into fourth, and would no longer have to be encumbered with the task of shifting, I opened the box and put it on the dashboard in front of me. Leonard was just stuffing the last of his cheeseburger into his mouth. After he swallowed he said dramatically, "Whew, made it ... that was close."

Just as advertised, everything in the box was neatly impaled on a stick. There were three of them, one with the chicken-fried steak, another with the hash browns, and finally another with the two hard-boiled eggs. In the corner there were two large containers filled with gravy.

Leonard stared at the open box with disgust, "Oh Carl... no, no, no ..."

"What? I think it looks good." In reality I thought that it looked kind of weird myself, but I sure as hell wasn't going to let on to Leonard that I thought so.

I opened a container of gravy and picked up the chicken-fried steak-on-a-stick. I dipped the end of it in the gravy and took a bite. Leonard stared at me with horror, "Oh my God, I can't believe that you just ate that."

"Believe it, buddy," I pretended to relish it. In reality it was only moderately good. I dipped the steak-on-a stick in the gravy again, deeply, and took another bite, this time I looked right at Leonard when I did it. "Mmmmmm."

"Okay, Carl, *that* was unnecessary."

"So don't look."

"I can't help it man, it's too freaky. I have to watch."

I gave him a little bit of a break and traded the steak for the hash browns. He seemed relieved. "You know, Carl, have you ever thought about what the hell chicken-fried steak really is?" I think he was trying to make me not pick it up again. I swallowed my mouthful of hash browns.

"As a matter of fact, I have, Leonard. I think that it's a combination of both chicken and steak ... yet at the same time it's really ... neither. I like to think of it as one of nature's wonder foods."

"You are broken, Carl." He was half-laughing.

"You want some gravy for your fries, Leonard?"

"I'll pretend that you didn't just ask me what I thought you did."

"Okay, then I'll keep pretending that this is food." We both busted up.

I ate all of the hash browns, half of the steak, and one of the eggs before finally calling it quits. Leonard's constant editorial while I was eating was taking effect, and my loss of appetite was more intellectual than physical. Surprisingly, it was the eggs that freaked me out the most. When I told Leonard that, he said that it was probably some Freudian association on my part and I should get help.

Done with breakfast, or lunch, or whatever the hell the meal we had just had was called, I was now able to fully concentrate on driving. We passed by the towns of Marsh and Terry, and before we knew it we had eaten up the seventy miles between Glendive and Miles City.

"Man, we're making great time here - it's only eight-thirty."

Leonard was unimpressed. He picked up the map, did a few calculations and announced, "Good, we're right on schedule ... only four hundred and eighty-four miles to go."

"Well, you could at least sound a little excited about it ... maybe some words of encouragement. How about ... 'Gee Carl, you sure are doing a great job driving.'" I smiled insincerely at him.

Leonard stared at me blankly for a minute then said, "How about these for words of encouragement, Carl ... the faster that you get there, the more time that you will have to drink free beer."

I looked at him, "Yeah, that works too." I put my foot into the accelerator.

We continued to make good time but having the van near-floored was having a devastating effect on our gas mileage. Just after the town of Forsythe, I happened to glance down at the gas gauge. We had about a third of a tank left. The towns out in eastern Montana seemed to be pretty well spread out, and I started to think if I didn't pay attention to the fuel gauge we could very well run out of gas in the middle of nowhere.

"Hey, Leonard."

"Yeah, Carl?"

"What's the next big town coming up?"

He quickly glanced at the map. "Billings, why?"

"Cuz we've got a little over a quarter of a tank of gas, that's why."

"Well shit, we sure aren't going to make it to Billings on a third of a tank of gas." He picked up the map again. "There's another town coming up in about twenty miles or so, Hysham. Let's stop there and fuel up."

"Right."

Fifteen minutes later we rolled into Hysham. Fortunately they did have a gas station, and fortunately it was open. Later, on the road to Billings we spotted only two gas stations. We wouldn't have made it to either one of them. We quickly filled up, jettisoned the remaining chicken-fried steak - whose smell was making us both slightly nauseous - and were back on the road.

The van had taken just over eight gallons. Leonard did some quick math and announced that we were getting just over seventeen miles to the gallon. "Hey, performance has its price, pal," I said back.

Leonard rolled his eyes. "Whatever, Carl."

We arrived in Billings just an hour later. It was the first true, although certainly small, city that we had been through for days. I found that I was actually kind of intimidated to be back in traffic again.

"Man, I'm not used to this."

"What?"

"The traffic ... I actually have to pay attention to other cars."

"Hey, it's my theory that if you're going faster than everyone else, then everyone has to look out for you. Your problem, my friend, is that you just aren't going fast enough."

"Yeah, well, I don't feel like getting pulled over either."

"By what? Hell, we've driven for two hundred and fifty miles and haven't seen a single cop ... punch it."

As a matter of record, we didn't see any highway patrol on the entire six hundred and some-ought miles of Montana interstate that we drove on. Later I would suggest to Leonard that maybe troopers were an endangered species. His response was that maybe they approached traffic laws the Darwinian way. If anyone wanted to drive themselves to oblivion in the middle of nowhere they were welcome to – they were just weeding out the gene pool. That seemed plausible.

Billings wasn't a beautiful city, but it wasn't an awful one either. Judging from what we could see from the freeway, it existed primarily as an agricultural and transportation hub for eastern Montana. It was functional. I think that the deep foothills and the appearance of pine trees helped its appearance. We were clearly off of the prairie now. It made me feel like we were making real progress west.

About halfway through Billings, Interstate 94 became Interstate 90. We didn't turn, we didn't merge, we didn't anything, it just happened. I wouldn't have known it, except for a sign above the freeway that said, "I-90 West – Missoula." This was the road that would take us home.

"Hey Leonard, did you see that?"

"What?"

"The sign to Missoula – that's the first one we've seen. This is good."

"Yes it is ... how are we doing on fuel there?"

"We have about a half a tank ... we can go for a while." Leonard nodded, then leaned his head against the passenger door and closed his eyes for a nap.

"You going to rack there, Leonard?"

"Yeah," he said without opening his eyes, "Wake me up when we stop for fuel, and I'll take over."

After we got past Billings, the frequency of towns increased dramatically. We were no longer traveling though the edge of nowhere. Consequently, obsessively watching the gas gauge and spotting for gas stations was no longer necessary. I could put my full concentration to eating up as many miles as possible as quickly as possible.

I kept the van at a good speed and while Leonard napped we passed through Laurel, Park City, Columbus, and Reedpoint. When we got to Big Timber, we were down to under a quarter of a tank. I pulled off the freeway and into the first gas station – another Stinker. I didn't have to wake Leonard. As soon as I switched off the motor he opened his eyes and said drowsily, "Are we there yet?"

"Yeah, Leonard, that's pretty much it." He glared at me, but I think was still too sleepy to give me any severe shit back.

"Why don't you make yourself useful, Carl, and get us a couple of Cokes from in back while I fuel up."

Eight and a half gallons later, we were back on the road. Leonard was now at the wheel, and judging from the frantic undulations of Mr. Rat in the slipstream, he was doing around eighty. I picked the road atlas up off of the floor to see where we were at in our marathon drive. Leonard noticed that I was looking at the map and said smiling, "No matter what you tell me, Carl, I am not going to listen to you. This time I know we're heading in the right direction."

"Oh, screw you, I was seeing how much farther we have to go. It looks like we're over halfway there already." I looked at my watch. "Man, it's just before noon ... we keep this up and we're going to make Missoula before five easy."

"Yeah, well, remember what you told me back at the Badlands ... it ain't over til rabid vermin infest your trousers."

I started laughing. "Um, I don't think that's really what I said."

"Yeah, well, I thought that the other saying was dumb so I changed it a little. I think my proverb sounds better." He started laughing with me.

Leonard ate up miles, and before we knew it we were on the outskirts of Bozeman. By now the country had clearly changed. Although the freeway ran through the foothills and the driving was still easy, just to the north and south huge peaks rose up. We were in the Rocky Mountains.

Bozeman was considerably different from Billings. Even from the freeway, the city exuded a certain hipness. The downtown was neat, clean, and had been aesthetically laid out by architects. When we passed a shopping center, I could see that it was filled with swanky stores with catchy names like "The Mountain Zone Ski Shoppe," "Native Pottery," and "Whole Earth Foods." It didn't look like anyone who lived there had a thing to do with agriculture, ranching, or anything else that might get one's hands dirty. It looked like folks had money, and probably a lot of it.

"Hey, Leonard, isn't this where all the beautiful people live?"

"Yeah, I think so. It's where all the rich folks from California come to to get back to the land. You know, kind of roughing it."

"Hmm ... that would explain why I don't live here."

"How's that?"

"Well, I'm just not beautiful enough."

"Oh sure, we're beautiful enough, we just don't *choose* to live here – we're that cool."

"No, I don't think that's it, Leonard ... I really don't think that I'm beautiful enough."

Leonard paused as if to think about it for a moment, then said, "Well ... on second thought, maybe you're right, Carl, maybe you're not. But, you know what? I know that I sure am." Then Leonard put his hand on my shoulder condescendingly, as if to comfort me, and said earnestly, "It's okay, Carl ... *I* think you're beautiful."

I pretended to try and get a hold myself, "Thanks, man..." then sniffed back a few fake tears. We both busted up.

As if to punctuate his beautiful people point, a yellow Porsche with a stunningly attractive blonde at the wheel passed us like we were standing still.

"I guess that answers your question about a speed limit in Montana, Carl."

"Yeah, maybe ... but on the other hand she might just be too good looking to pull over."

"That's possible too ... good thing I'm driving."

After Bozeman, the terrain continued to change, and more quickly now. By the time we reached the town of Three Forks, we were clearly in mountain country. Although the terrain was beautiful, the monotony of the drive chiseled away at us. I found myself staring silently out of the passenger window, drifting in and out of an interstate-induced trance.

As I sat there with my head against my rolled-up jacket, I watched the foothills of the Rockies race by. Even though it was mid-afternoon the sun hung lower in the sky and the shadows were beginning to get longer. There was a change of seasons in the air. Fall was coming. This was a time of year that I had always loved. It was a time of transitions. And, although I loved it, it always made me just a little bit melancholy – like I was saying goodbye.

Hail Mary

Apparently I had fallen asleep, and when we stopped at Butte for fuel Leonard woke me up. As he was getting out to gas up the van, he shook me gently on the shoulder, "Hey Carl, time to get up ... your turn to drive. Oh, and you might want to brace yourself." The last part of his comment seemed strange, and as I was just waking up I wasn't even sure if I had heard him right. When I opened my eyes I realized that no matter what Leonard had said to me I wouldn't have been prepared for it.

I roused myself from my nap position in the passenger's seat. Outside of the front window directly in front of me, I stared into the side of a large mountain. Covering most of the side of that mountain was a gigantic earth-red scar – a vast pit. Inside of that pit tiny machines moved around, plumes of smoke billowing behind them. I heard a dull, deep "thud" and a larger plume of black and red smoke rose up from inside the pit. I felt like I was looking into a scene out of Dante's *Inferno.* I blinked hard and with my hands rubbed the sleep from my eyes, as if somehow my perspective was errant. The view didn't change.

I got out of the van and was immediately assaulted by a gritty fine dust that filled the hot air. I turned to Leonard, who was still at the pump. "Where the hell did you drive us to, purgatory?"

"Well, sort of ... I drove us to Butte." Neither one of us laughed.

"Do you have any idea what the fuck that is on the side of that mountain?" Just then a thicker cloud of dust blew through. Both of us turned our backs to it to avoid choking on it. When the wind subsided, we again faced each other and Leonard was able to answer my question.

"I saw a sign when we were coming into Butte. It's the Anaconda copper mine."

"Well, it looks more like hell to me. Jesus Christ, how in the fuck can they get away with doing something like that?"

"Good question, Carl ... maybe nobody ever told them that they couldn't."

I looked back up at the mine, "Man, I'm never going to look at a penny the same way again." As soon as I said it, Leonard started whistling "Pennies From Heaven." Given the context the song sounded tremendously sad. I turned back to him, "You know, I bet the folks who are sentenced to work in that hellhole don't whistle that."

"I bet you're right, Carl," he said solemnly, "... but I bet the bastard who owns it sure does." Again, neither one of us laughed.

Leonard finished topping up the tank and headed in to pay. I called after him, "Hey Leonard, I'm going to step on over there and have a cigarette while you do that."

He nodded, "I'll find you."

I walked away from the pumps and over to the side of the station. I pulled a cigarette out of my pocket, lit it, and stared up to the mountainside. From the side of the station I had an even better view of the horrific scene. As I stood there smoking my cigarette and looking up into the maw, I noticed something ... it was odd and out of place.

High up above on a peak at the upper edge of the pit was a pure white statue. It must have been close to a couple hundred feet tall, but at the same time it seemed small, dwarfed but the enormity of the pit. I squinted and put my hand above my brow to shield my eyes from sun's glare. I stared harder to try to make it out. The statue of whatever it was wore a long flowing robe. Its arms were outstretched a little above waist level, and its hands were open – palms up. From a distance I couldn't make out the face, but I could tell by the head, slightly tipped to the left, that it gazed down into the mine.

A minute or two later I heard footsteps approaching from across the parking lot. I turned. It was Leonard. When he was close enough, I pointed up to the hill and said, "Mother of Mercy, what the heck is that up above that pit ... you see that, that statue up there?"

"Good guess, Carl. I saw it too when I was going in to pay," Leonard said evenly. "I asked at the register. The woman in there said that it's a statue of Mary, Mother of Jesus. They call it Our Lady of the Rockies." I looked at Leonard to see if he was joking. He stared back at me. His jaw was set tight. I hadn't heard it in his voice, but he looked angry - very angry. He wasn't joking. I felt my own rage of indignation rise inside of me like a fire set to consume the slander. My own jaw tightened. I threw my cigarette butt to the ground and crushed it with my boot.

"Man, that ain't religion ... that's something else." My voice was shaking. Leonard put his hand lightly on my shoulder. I looked at him, and our eyes met.

"You sound like me, Carl." He was smiling just a bit. He was right.

"Yeah, I guess I do, Leonard ... let's get going."

It was my shift at the wheel. We got back in the van. I fired it up, and headed off toward the interstate.

"Do you have any idea how in the hell we get out of here, Leonard?"

"Yeah, make a right up here. The freeway is a couple of blocks away." The light had just turned yellow. Instead of stopping, I punched the accelerator hard and fishtailed the van through the intersection. Leonard looked at me with a wry smile.

"Leonard, I just want to get out of here."

"Hey, did I say anything, Carl?"

"No, but you were thinking it."

"Why yes, I was."

Two blocks later we were back on the freeway and on the way out of Butte. Neither one of us said anything else until we were clear of the city. We didn't have to. The rest of the town, which consisted of a smattering of dust-encrusted developments and strip malls, looked like it had been built on the leavings of the mine. There wasn't a single tree or bush or plant of any kind. I don't think that it was that all of the people who lived there kept the landscape denuded intentionally. Rather, I think that everything that was planted there just lost the will to live. As I watched it all pass by the van's windows, I felt a deep sadness for the folks who either couldn't or wouldn't move away.

Just outside of Butte the freeway took a climb up and over a long hill. As we reached the top of it, I glanced in the rearview mirror one more time back at the abomination. The mine was no longer visible, but I did catch a glimpse of the statue of Mary on the top of the mountain before it all disappeared from sight.

Happy Trails

The whole Butte experience had been a traumatic one, and it took me ten or fifteen minutes to get myself back together. When I did, I tried to normalize the conversation and get our focus back to the mundane task of driving.

"So Leonard, about how much farther do we have to go?"

Leonard looked at the map briefly. "It looks like about a hundred and twenty miles til Missoula - maybe a couple of hours."

I looked at my watch. It was just after two thirty. "We ought to be there by four thirty or so ... this is good. I can't wait to get the hell out of this van. I'm starting to go road nuts."

"This is not a particularly reassuring thing to hear, Carl. Especially since you have the wheel right now. I mean, are you trying to say that you're just getting bored or is it something maybe more serious?"

"Oh, I'm okay, Leonard ..." I tried to sound a matter of fact about it, "... just a few delusions now and then, you know the stuff."

"Actually, no, I don't know, Carl, could you please be more specific?"

"Well, like that group of possums back there by the side of the road."

Leonard pretended to take me seriously. He said delicately, "Carl ..."

"Yeah?"

"There weren't any possums by the side of the road back there."

"Oh, I know that, Leonard, why do you think that I'm driving so fast? I'm trying to get away from them. Every time that I see them they tell me to do things."

"What kind of things, Carl?"

"Naughty things ..." I gave Leonard a look like I was completely mad. "... I mean I know that they're bad things, but sometimes they kind of make sense ... that's when I drive really fast."

"I think that you have a good plan there, Carl ... you just keep driving." We both started laughing.

By now we were fully into the Rockies. The freeway twisted and turned through the steep mountains that rose up along both sides of us. Still, it was moderately easy driving. Although I had to slow down some through the passes, I still managed to keep the van at a respectable sixty-five to seventy miles an hour.

Apparently this was mining country. Nearly every town that we passed had some reference in its name to the mining industry. Fortunately none of them even approached the apocalyptic magnitude of Butte. I was grateful for that.

We were both really beginning to feel the effects of having been on the road for over nine hours. Neither one of us said much of anything. By the time we reached the town of Phosphate, Leonard had dozed off again. It was three thirty, and maybe another hour or so til Missoula. I was alone with the road and my thoughts.

As I drove my mind wandered. For a while I thought of Althea. I thought of love. This was the first time in my life that I had actually felt what I believed to be real love. After having been away on this trip, and having some distance from her, I was convinced that what we had wasn't completely infatuation, although at times we maybe behaved like it. It was something deeper; something that I know that neither one of us had ever experienced before. It was rare, intense, and new ground for both of us. That intensity combined with the unknown was, at times, for lack of a better word, frightening. I wondered if when I got back I would be able to rise above that fear and as Althea had said, "be holding hands when we were eighty."

Just after passing the town of Bearmouth, I spotted a sign – "Missoula 43 Miles." I almost wanted to wake Leonard and let him know that we were nearly there. He was peacefully fast asleep, though, and I restrained myself.

The afternoon sun was low enough now that its light rhythmically flashed as I drove in and out of the shadows of the tall pines. I tried to keep my mind on driving, but the intermittent and erratic glint of light became more and more hypnotizing. I found myself alternating between watching the road and watching the sunlight play off of the icons on the dashboard. I started to play a little game with myself. With each flash of light, I tried to look at a different icon. The more I looked, the more they began to not look like separate entities anymore, but more like different representations of exactly the same thing. It all seemed so simply clear to me. Something profoundly complex effortlessly unraveled into understanding.

My deeply philosophical road trance was abruptly broken when I felt the van drive over the safety ridges at the shoulder of the road. I braked hard and steered the van away from the guardrail and back into the lane of the freeway. The maneuver woke Leonard up.

"Jesus Christ, Carl, what the hell are you doing?" Leonard looked out of the passenger's window and down into the deep gorge just beyond the guardrail. "You're not listening to the road possums, are you?"

"No, sorry, man ... I just spaced out for a minute there."

"Good Lord, Carl, I can't leave you alone for a minute, can I?"

"No."

Leonard straightened himself in the seat, "Hey, where are we at anyway?"

"We're coming up on Missoula in maybe another half hour. Go ahead and go back to sleep if you want. I'll wake you up when we get there."

"Are you kidding? I want to get there alive."

Fifteen minutes later we rounded a curve and broke out of the mountains. Ahead, in the valley, was Missoula. "Right on, man, we made it."

"Yeah ... finally," Leonard stretched and yawned. "What time have you got there?"

"It's a quarter to five."

"Gee, and it only took us eleven hours ..." Leonard said sarcastically. "My God, I am so ready for a beer."

"Yeah, me too, and you know what? You're buying." I grinned at him.

"That's right, Carl, I am. And you know what else, Carl?"

"What's that?"

"We're not going to stop drinking until I say we stop ... even if you beg me."

"I feel sorry for Missoula."

"So do I."

"So where do you think we should pull off, Leonard?"

"How in the hell should I know? I've never been here before."

"Woah buddy ... just asking."

"Hey man, all that I want to do is get the hell out of this fucking van." He started clawing at the passenger's window like a caged animal.

"Hmm ... I'll just take the next exit."

Leonard was now pretending to gnaw on his arm. He stopped long enough to say, "Good idea, Carl."

As soon as we got off the freeway we spotted a sign that said "University of Montana."

"Hang a left here, Carl. I bet if we get over towards the university we'll run into somewhere to stay."

"Good plan." We crossed under the interstate and followed the signs for six or seven blocks. Missoula seemed like a damned nice place. It was green, it was in the mountains, and there wasn't a strip mine.

As we got closer to the university the neighborhood became more hip. We had found where the students hung out. There were a number of coffee shops, bookstores, and natural food groceries. Leonard pointed out a brewery on the corner,

The Glacier Brewing Company. "Wherever we stay, we need to be within walking distance of that."

"I think we can do that."

A half a block later we came to a Super 8.

"Here we go Carl ... this'll work."

I kept driving.

"What are you doing, man? There was a Super 8 back there."

"Yeah, I know, but there's a Best Western just down the street."

"So ... the Super 8 is probably cheaper, turn around."

"Nah, it's our last night out, Leonard, let's splurge and stay somewhere nice. Besides, Daryl probably put out an APB on us at every Super 8 in the country after our stay in Gillette."

Leonard raised one eyebrow and nodded, "You might be right, Carl ... the Best Western it is."

I pulled into the parking lot and shut off the van. As soon as we were stopped, Leonard leapt out, dropped to his knees, and kissed the asphalt. I glanced over at the doorway of the hotel to see if anyone else saw him. The doorman was staring at him like he was insane.

"Don't you think you're being a little over-dramatic, Leonard?"

He got up and said, "No I do not, Carl, that was a hellish drive."

"Well, do you think that you can at least contain yourself until we get a room?"

He rolled his eyes up to the sky as if he were seriously considering it. Finally he said, "Best I can do on that is *maybe,* Carl."

"Well, try hard, we need a place to stay."

We grabbed our bags out of the van and headed on in to the hotel. As we approached, the doorman opened and held the door for us. He seemed to be pretty much over his surprise at Leonard falling prostrate in the parking lot. "Good afternoon, how are you today?" His voice sounded a little muffled.

I smiled and said, "Hey thanks, how ya doin'?"

Before he could answer my question, Leonard added, "I'm better now ... thanks for asking."

We approached the front desk and were greeted by a polite fellow in his late twenties. He had close-cropped dark brown hair and wire-rimmed glasses. He looked more the part of a graduate student, probably political science, than a concierge at a hotel.

"Good afternoon, fellas, are you after a room today? " His voice had the same muffled quality that the doorman's had. On top of it, I noticed a slight overall ringing in my ears.

"Good afternoon ... yes, as a matter of fact that's exactly what we're after."

"And would that be for one night?"

I leaned forward some. "I'm sorry, I didn't hear that last part. "

"Is that for one night?" he said more loudly. This time I heard him, but his voice still sounded muffled.

"Yeah, just one night." The desk guy nodded and looked through his book to see what was available.

Leonard touched me on the shoulder, "What did he say?"

"He asked if we are just staying one night." Even though we were only a couple of feet apart, I could tell that Leonard was straining to hear me.

"Oh, tell him yeah."

"I did."

"What?"

"I did," I said more loudly.

"Oh ..."

Apparently after spending hours in the van, the full-throttle echo of the motor had had detrimental effects on our hearing. I had experienced it before, but never this badly … but then again I had never driven in the van for eleven hours straight. Leonard suffered it worse than I did, and I had to repeatedly practically yell everything that the fellow behind the counter said to us.

Finally after a series of "whats," and "could you repeat thats," we got our key and headed up to our room. As we walked toward the elevator, I noticed the other guests in the lobby furtively staring at us with pity. Leonard noticed it too.

Once we were in the elevator, he said, "What the fuck were they all looking at?"

I yelled back at him, "We're deaf from driving in the van ... we've been yelling at each other. I think they felt sorry for us."

"Oh ..." A light bulb of understanding popped on in Leonard's mind. "I was wondering what the hell was going on... I feel like I've been to a Molly Hatchet concert. Do you think we're ruined for good?" He was sincere about that last part.

"Nah, our hearing will probably come back in an hour or so." Then I thought to myself, "I hope."

Once in the room I laid down on one of the beds. After being hunched over a steering wheel for hours, it felt good to stretch out. I gave Leonard first crack at the shower. I figured that the hot water and steam might be therapeutic to his cilia, and would help him recover his hearing more quickly.

I was spacing out, staring at the ceiling, when Leonard emerged twenty minutes later, still drying his hair with a towel. "Oh shit, did that feel good." He wasn't talking nearly as loudly as he had been before the shower. Maybe my theory had been correct.

"Yeah, you sound better too ... how's the hearing?"

"Better. I think the shower helped. Now I only feel like I've been at a Lynard Skynard concert."

"I don't know if that's better or not." I rose from the bed. "You save any hot water for me?"

"No, I used all the hot water for the entire hotel ... sorry."

"Asshole." Leonard smiled insincerely back at me as he grabbed the TV remote and lay down on the other bed.

"I'll be out whenever."

"Enjoy."

Leonard was right, the shower felt great. I stayed under the water for at least fifteen minutes. When I was done I was severely pruned. Afterwards I shaved, which also felt great. I had let my beard go for a few days and it had been at the stage of itching like crazy.

Finally I emerged, refreshed. Leonard was lying on the bed watching a rerun of "Voyage to the Bottom of the Sea." Apparently a giant jellyfish had taken hold of the submarine and everyone inside was being thrown around. In the control room, Chief Sharkey was screaming frantically into a radio set, "Kowalski! Kowalski!" The camera panned outside of the sub to Kowalski in a scuba suit. He was desperately trying to peel a jellyfish tentacle from around his throat. It didn't look good for him.

"What, no televangelist?"

"Ah ... no, Carl." Leonard switched off the TV.

"Hey man, don't turn it off, I want to see what happens."

"Don't worry, he lives." Leonard put down the remote. "I'm just about starving here, Carl. As a matter of fact I believe that my stomach just ate part of my liver."

"That's disgusting, Leonard."

"You're right, it is, so let's get going."

The Glacier Brewing Company was only about three and a half blocks from the hotel. We walked. It felt good to stretch our legs. By the time we got there it was a quarter to seven – plenty of time to have dinner and get stupendously drunk.

The brewery was fairly well packed with college-age folks. Evidently we had made a good choice. Inside, the brewery was one large room. In the back, there was a wall with huge doors that opened to a deck outside. A refreshing breeze blew through. Although the building was new, it was constructed entirely with raw logs. It was definitely Western in flavor, but well done ... really more artistic than anything else.

As soon as we walked in, a friendly rugged young guy wearing faded Levi's, a Glacier Brewing Company tee shirt, and beat-up cowboy boots greeted us. "Hey guys, how ya doin' this evening? You here for food or beer?" His voice sounded only slightly muffled. I was recovering.

"Both," Leonard said.

"Great, follow me, man."

He seated us at a table right next to the open doors. It was a good table. After we sat down, he handed us the menus. "You guys been here before?"

"Nope, we're new in town."

"Well, you're in for a treat ... great eats, great beer. No matter what you get, I recommend the Cajun sweet potato fries – they're killer. Your waitress will be over in a minute."

"Hey, thanks, man."

"No problem."

Neither one of us had eaten anything but a couple of bags of chips and a few Cokes since Glendive. We were both famished and immediately descended on the menus.

"Man he's not kidding ... they've got good chow here." Leonard, who was engrossed in making a food decision, sort of grunted and nodded.

A couple of minutes later our waitress arrived. "Hi, fellas, how ya doing?"

"Good, thanks."

"Can I get you anything to drink?"

She was an attractive young hippie girl with short blond hair. Except for the hair, she reminded me a little of Althea. Looking at her, I felt another wave of homesickness come over me.

"What do you recommend for beer?"

"My personal favorite is the Glacier Mountain Lager."

"Sold," Leonard said, "We'll take a pitcher of that."

"And have you decided on any food?"

"Yeah, I think that I'm ready, how about you, Carl?"

"Yeah, I think that I'd like the ribs."

"Good choice." She smiled approvingly, then turned to Leonard.

"Make that two," he folded up the menu, "and could you give us a large order of sweet potato fries."

"Will do, I'll be back with your beer in a minute." She said breezily and went back towards the bar. A couple of minutes later she was back with our pitcher. "Here you are ... your food will be up in not too long."

"Hey, thanks."

Leonard immediately poured both of us a couple of beers. "Here's to a trip, Carl."

"Yeah ..." We both took a long pull from our glasses. The ice-cold beer tasted good, and I took another short drink before setting my glass back down on the table. On an empty stomach, I could almost follow the beer's path to my head. After the long drive, the relaxation was welcome.

"Ya know, Leonard, I wasn't really going to hold you to this bet thing, it was more of just an entertainment deal."

"Bullshit, Carl. I have every intention on making good on our wager." He took another drink off of his beer. "If it makes you feel any better, Carl, if you had lost the bet I would have been training for this moment." I thought to myself that I sort of doubted he would have held me to it. He would have been more than satisfied enough with just winning.

"Yeah, I guess I do feel better," I lied, "Thanks for alleviating my guilt." I took another long pull, finishing my glass.

"You are so welcome, Carl." Leonard refilled both of our glasses.

We were more than halfway through our second beers when the waitress came with our food. "Here ya go, guys." I quickly cleared off a spot on the table. She set the plates down along with a mountain of napkins. I stared down at a half rack of fat ribs smothered in barbecue sauce, an ear of corn, and a massive slice of cornbread. On the table between Leonard and I there was an additional platter of curly orange sweet potato fries.

"Man, this looks great."

"Yeah, I don't think you're going to go away from here hungry."

"No, I don't think that's going to be an issue."

"Can I get anything else for you?"

"Yeah," Leonard said, "could you get us another pitcher of beer when you have a second."

"Be happy to." She topped up our glasses with what remained in the pitcher. "I'll be back in a minute ... enjoy."

Leonard and I quickly set to work on devouring the ribs. I slowly savored the first few bites, but then fell into a quicker pace. Leonard did the same. The ferocity at which we attacked them reminded me a little of a National Geographic that I had seen on hyenas. As I ate, I started to growl and make guttural noises. Leonard looked up at me and said through a mouthful of ribs, "Are you okay over there, Carl?"

"Meat good."

"Sometimes, Carl, you frighten me."

"Meat good," I repeated.

Leonard shook his head, threw down a spent bone, and picked up another. "My God, you are strange."

In spite of the massive amount of food, it didn't take us more than fifteen minutes to completely clear our plates. There were still some fries left, and although we were both stuffed, we slowly kept working on them between sips of beer.

Finally even the fries were gone, and Leonard and I reclined in our chairs to let our food settle. The waitress returned. She glanced down at the bones and spent corncobs on our plates. "So, maybe this is a dumb question, but how was everything?"

Leonard smiled, "Man, I'll tell you what, those ribs were murder."

"Yeah, hands down the best I've ever had," I added, "and those fries ..."

"Good aren't they?"

"Killer ..."

"Well I'm glad that you enjoyed everything. Can I get you another pitcher of beer?"

"Yes, please, that would be great." She smiled, picked up our dishes and was gone.

We sat there and slowly sipped our beers, waiting for the next pitcher. I noticed across the room a woman coming in with a guitar. She was probably in her late fifties. She was a folksy-looking woman wearing a dark red gingham skirt, denim shirt and cowboy boots. She had shoulder-length wavy graying hair. She walked over to a small stage at the far end of the room, put her guitar down and began setting up. "Looks like we have music tonight, Leonard."

He turned around to see where I was looking. He studied her for a minute then said, "Cool."

The woman was tuning up her guitar when our waitress returned with our third pitcher. "Here you go."

"Thanks ... Say, who's the music this evening?"

"Oh boy, are you in for a treat. That's Patsy Statler, probably one of the best folk singers in all of Montana, maybe in the whole country. She's from Libby, comes on down here only a couple of times a year. She could go national but she likes that quiet country life. Doesn't play much in public."

"Hey thanks, it sounds like it's going to be good."

"It will be," she smiled.

I was just finishing topping up our beers when, without introduction, she started playing. Her first song was something that I hadn't heard before, but since it was about Libby I guessed it was her own. The waitress was right, she wasn't just good, she was damn good. After she finished the song I leaned across to Leonard and said, "Is she something or what?"

"Yeah, man, she's amazing." Without pausing for applause, she immediately broke into her next song, a Patsy Cline cover, "Crazy." It wasn't exactly the same as the original, but it was beautiful. It was apparent that she had lived these lyrics. As she was singing I wondered if, while she was still in the womb, her mother had had a vision that when her daughter grew up she would be a great musician. She had named her after Ms. Cline.

When she finished, she stopped for a moment to tune her guitar again. During the brief pause the tavern went wild. Leonard leaned over to me and said something. I nodded, but I couldn't hear him over the applause.

She sang without stopping for about two hours. The whole time, everyone in the tavern was silently mesmerized. About half of the songs were her own. The rest were, from what I could tell, exclusively Hank Williams, Patsy Cline, and John Prine covers, with one notable exception – a slow folk/blues version of "Happy Trails," which she closed with at the end of the evening. I personally thought that it was an appropriate song for us to be ending our trip to. When she finished her closing song, everyone was quiet for a moment, as if catching their breath before applauding. There wasn't a dry eye in the house.

She was done playing for the evening. She stood up and said simply, modestly, and sincerely, "I would like to thank you for coming and listening to me ... I'm Patsy Statler, I hope you enjoyed my music." The tavern went crazy.

When she was finally packed up and off the stage it was around about midnight. Leonard drained the last of our fifth pitcher of beer into our glasses. Just as he was setting the empty pitcher back down on the table, our waitress came by our table and asked pleasantly, "Can I get your tab?" I half drunkenly looked up at her. From my angle she was standing right in front of a single stage light that had been left on. It made a ring of light around her head.

Leonard and I were pretty tight by now, not sloppily so, but we were definitely headed in that direction. Even in my inebriated state I picked up on her gentle suggestion that we maybe quit while we were ahead and avoid a crushing hangover in the morning.

I looked over to Leonard and said, "What do ya think there, partner? We have a pretty long drive ahead of us again tomorrow. I'd rather not do it with a raging hangover."

In spite of his earlier threat, Leonard didn't argue a bit, "Yeah... you're probably right, Carl. I'm pretty gassed anyhow... any more beer would probably be just a waste."

We paid our tab. In spite of Leonard's earlier insistence that he hold good on the bet, I convinced him that splitting it was something that I wanted to do. He accepted that.

We wove our way half-drunkenly back to the hotel. It was a beautiful, warm, starlit night, our last night. We took our time. By the time we arrived at the hotel the night air had cleared our heads some. Still, we were both exhausted. We headed up to our room and went straight to bed.

"Good night, Leonard."

"Good night, Carl."

I paused for a moment then added, "This has been good, hasn't it."

He sighed deeply. He was almost asleep, "Yes it has, Carl ... Yes it has."

I curled up under the cool crisp covers of the fresh hotel sheets. There in the darkness, just before sleep overtook me, my mind raced through all that I had experienced over the last two weeks. Gradually my mind slowed and my thoughts turned to Althea. Tomorrow I would fall asleep next to her. I smiled to myself and drifted off.

Infidels and Crusaders

The next morning I woke up to the sound of the shower. Leonard was already up. I lazily rolled over in bed. In those few minutes between sleep and awake, I checked myself for evidence of a hangover. As far as I could tell, I had none. I pulled my arm up from under the covers and looked at my watch. I heard the shower shut off. It was just after eight. I got myself up and put on my jeans. Leonard emerged from the bathroom with a towel around his waist. There was another one wrapped around his head. It made him look like a Sikh.

"Well, mornin' there, sunshine." He was wide-awake and smiling.

"Hey, Leonard." I croaked, still half-asleep. "Did ya get any sleep last night?"

He undid the towel around his head and began to dry his hair. "Yeah, I slept like a baby ... not even a trace of a hangover. How about you?"

"Yeah, I'm feelin' pretty darn good myself."

"Hey, I'm done in there." He motioned towards the bathroom, "If you want to, take a shower."

"In a minute here, I'm still waking up." He threw the pair of towels down on the bed and put on his jeans.

"Well, don't screw around too much, we got another big drive ahead of us."

"Yeah ..." I got up and headed in for a shower. "You save any hot water for me?"

"Nope," he smiled, "used it all again ... God, I'm an asshole."

"You took the words right out of my mouth."

"I know I did."

Ten minutes later I came out of the shower refreshed. I skipped shaving. Leonard had already packed up our stuff and was ready to go.

"Hey, thanks, man."

"No problem there, Carl, just being the helpful kind of guy that I am." I finished dressing and after a quick check of the room we were off.

Down in the lobby I went over to the desk and checked us out while Leonard worked over the continental breakfast for road supplies. He wasn't even remotely subtle about it. He filled at least four napkins with food – a half dozen croissants, a dozen or so strips of bacon, and enough slices of cantaloupe to make an entire melon. He also got us two large cups of coffee. I could see the desk guy looking past me at him. He seemed more fascinated than anything else.

When Leonard was done he cheerfully joined me and said brazenly, "That ought to hold us for a while ... are you just about done here?"

"Yeah, I was just finishing up." I turned back to the desk guy, "Hey thanks again, and the room was great."

"You're welcome. You fellas have a good trip, okay?" He was sincere about it.

"Thanks, we did ..."

Leonard took first shift at the wheel. Before hitting the freeway, we stopped briefly to top up the tank, and were quickly back on the road. After Leonard had the van up to speed I laid out our breakfast on the floor of the van between the passenger and driver's seats.

"May I interest you in a croissant, sir?" I asked an affected accent.

"Oh, why certainly."

"Concorde grape jelly or marmalade, sir?"

"Damn, did I grab marmalade?" Leonard said in his normal voice, "I hate that shit ... bunch of ground up fucking orange peels."

"Yeah, there's a couple here."

"Gimme the grape." I split a pair of croissants with my pocketknife and slathered them both with jelly. I handed one to Leonard. "Thanks, man."

Before starting in on mine, I grabbed the road atlas and opened it up to Montana.

"Well?"

"It looks like we have about an hour and a half left of Montana."

"How many miles?" I took a bite of my croissant while I did some mental calculations.

"Uh, it looks like about ninety miles."

"About?"

"Okay, Mr. I'm-So-Anal I-Have-To-Know-The-Exact-Number-Of-Miles-Guy, its *exactly* ninety-six miles."

"Why, thank you, Carl," Leonard said sarcastically, then took another bite of his croissant. "And what comes after that?"

"Idaho."

"What?!" he whipped around and looked at me with an overly dramatic expression, like I had told him that we were going to enter the land of predator monkeys. "Oh Christ – I fucking forgot about Idaho!" He pounded the steering wheel.

"Well, at least we're going through the skinny part of it. If you punch it we'll only have to be in Idaho for an hour."

"That's far too long, Carl ..." he narrowed his eyes, "Is there any other way that we can get home without going through Idaho?" I flipped the pages of the atlas back to Montana.

"Well, I suppose we could head north on ..."

Leonard cut me off, "Oh dear God, Carl don't be such a freakin' knob ... I'm just going to pretend that you thought that I was kidding – I'll haul ass."

"Hey ... it's early."

"It's not that early."

When we hit the Idaho border it was ten twenty.

"Hey, pretty good time, Leonard, you picked up ten minutes."

"Yeah, well that ain't nuthin' - hold on ... we're entering Idaho." As he shoved down on the accelerator, we shot passed a "Welcome to Idaho" sign with Spuddy Buddy, the anthropomorphic potato guy, on it.

"Hi, Mr. Spuddy," I waved as we flew passed him.

"Hey, knock it off, Carl, this Northern Idaho deal is serious stuff." I looked out the window at the rugged mountains.

"Oh, I don't know. Leonard, I think this northern part isn't half bad ... it's kind of pretty up here."

"Yeah, well, don't let the scenery fool you. It's beautiful country all right, but these woods are crawling with pockets of white supremacist Aryan Nazi fuck-head cross-burning bastards."

"I feel like you're holding your true feelings back from me again, Leonard."

"Hey, Carl, this is serious fucking stuff ... if it's one thing I hate, it's ignorance and intolerance. And you know what else? People like that, they don't like us too much. We're infidels and they're on a crusade."

We wound our way along the freeway through the mountains. We passed by Wallace and Osburn, Silverton and Pinehurst. None of the towns looked particularly threatening, and actually most of them looked kind of pleasant. Still, I heeded the seriousness of Leonard's warning and kept an eye out for signs of trouble.

By the time we passed Rose Lake we had begun to come down out of the mountains. I again looked at the map, "Hey, we're getting there, Leonard, a few more miles and we're in Coeur d'Alene. A few miles after that and we're in Washington."

"Good," Leonard said simply. He sounded like he couldn't wait. All of a sudden he added, "Oh shit, here we go."

"Here we go what?" I pitched the atlas back onto the floor and turned to him. He was looking in the rearview mirror.

"Behind us, coming up fast, Nazi fuck-heads."

I was about to turn around and see what he was looking at when a pair of skinheads in an International Harvester pickup truck spray-painted barbecue flat black pulled up next to us on the right. The pair looked over and gave us the eye. I looked back at them, and as tough as I could kind of half-smiled. They did not smile back. They looked like they wanted to kill us, but for what I don't know.

"For right now, just ignore them, Carl."

"What do you mean, 'for right now'?"

Leonard ignored my question and continued, "Those fuckers are probably packing Lugers or World War Two German-made machine pistols ... fucking sissies." I didn't comment. From the looks of them, I believed him.

Leonard gave the van all it had, and where the road permitted, we were doing close to ninety. For about fifteen minutes the pair dogged us - sometimes following behind, and sometimes pulling up next to us. During that time, neither Leonard nor I said anything to each other - we just kept a close watch on where the truck was.

Finally we reached Coeur d'Alene, the big city. Although they were still with us, I started to feel a little relieved. Just after passing a sign for the Hayden Lake exit, Leonard said, "Good."

"Good what?"

"Good, they're taking the exit." As we approached the exit they pulled up along side and glared knives at us one last time. It was still beyond my comprehension why they hated us so much. Then they dropped back and started to pull off.

As soon as they were committed to the off-ramp, Leonard said, "Here, Carl, take over for a second." Without waiting for me to take the wheel, Leonard hoisted himself half out of the window. I quickly grabbed the wheel. He leaned out and gave them both the finger. They were still watching us, and as soon as they saw him do it they slammed on their brakes, sending their pickup into a smoking four-wheel lockup. They apparently didn't see the semi that was following behind them. It too did a full lock-up. Fortunately, the semi driver managed to steer his rig toward the shoulder of the road, and instead of a full-on blow, just took off the rear quarter panel of the pickup. As the rig skidded to a shrieking stop, it jackknifed, blocking the off-ramp.

Leonard climbed back in, sat down, and took over at the wheel. "There ... that ought to put the fear of God into 'em

– narrow-minded little fucks." Then he added, "I suppose that Jesus told 'em to act like that."

During the course of our trip both of us had developed a healthy aversion to hypocritical dogma. Leonard's aversion on the other hand, had been transformed into action. Leonard was apparently quickly willing to do battle with anyone, or anything that manifested that kind of thinking.

Twenty minutes later, we crossed into Washington and were just outside of Spokane. I was still a little shaky from the adrenaline rush of our experience back in Coeur d'Alene. Leonard looked down at the gas gauge. "We're going to need fuel here, Carl."

"There's a station coming up here at the next exit."

"I see it."

"I can take over at the wheel, too. You've been driving all morning."

"Yeah, I could use a break."

Leonard pulled the van into the station. I got out and started to fill up. Leonard got out, stretched off some tension, and joined me. I had already put nine gallons in.

"So, what the fuck was those guys' big problem back there?"

"Their problem is, Carl, is that they think that they're the only ones who are right. "

I topped up the tank and put the gas cap back on. "Don't you think that it's a little ironic that somebody who thinks that they're so fucking right could be so fucking wrong?"

"Yeah, just a little, Carl, but it seems to be the way of the world ... come on, let's get going."

As I was getting in the van I walked past Mr. Rat. I reached over and rubbed him on the nose. Leonard climbed into the passenger's seat next to me. "Man, Carl, I've never seen you touch Mr. Rat before."

"Yeah, it's a first for me. It was a little rough, but I figure a little more luck can't hurt."

Once we were under way, Leonard promptly rolled up his jacket for a pillow, leaned against the passenger door, and took a nap. I figured that he was at least as exhausted as I was by our Idaho experience.

The Last Leg

The drive between Spokane and Moses Lake was an uneventful one, but I managed to make good time across the flat channeled scablands of Eastern Washington. Just after we passed out of the city limits Leonard woke up.

"Hey, good morning ... you have a nice nap there?"

"Yeah ..." Leonard said groggily. He yawned and looked out the window. "Where the hell are we, Carl?"

"We just passed Moses Lake. We're about forty miles from the Gorge."

Leonard squinted out at the desert landscape. "Jesus, if Moses had delivered the Israelites here I think they would have been pretty pissed at him." We both started laughing.

A little over a half an hour later we came to the Columbia River. This was familiar country for both of us, and after we crossed the river I felt like we were really on our way home. "Man, Leonard, we're really getting there. We're only about two and a half hours out of Seattle. Another hour after that and we're home."

"Yeah, if we don't hit traffic."

"What time is it?"

"It's two."

"So we ought to be there by dinner time."

"Got an extra cigarette there, Carl?"

With my free hand I pulled the pack from my shirt pocket, "Well ..."

"Don't even start with me, give me a fucking cigarette." I handed him the pack. He shook one out, busted the filter off, and handed the pack back to me. "How about a match?" I took the pack from him and started smirking. "And if you say 'my butt and your face' I will personally come over there and pound you."

"I wasn't going to," I said innocently. I handed him my lighter.

"Oh, but I think you were." He lit his cigarette. I shook one out for myself and lit it before returning the pack to my pocket.

Leonard took another drag and stared out the window. "So what are you going to do when you get home, Carl?"

"I'm gonna make sweet, sweet love to my baby all – night – long." I kind of sung it.

Leonard turned away from the window and looked at me seriously.

"Sorry, man." I got serious too.

"I was thinking about more long term, Carl."

"Well, school starts here pretty soon. I'm going to have to get ready to move down to Seattle." We stared at each other silently for a few seconds. Then Leonard turned away and looked out the window again.

He took another drag off of his cigarette and said quietly, "Yeah, I suppose so." He wasn't happy, and all of a sudden I wasn't either.

"You know, Leonard, even after I move we're still going to be getting together. Hey, Althea's still up in the valley. I'll be up there all the time. And hell, you can come down and visit, Seattle's only an hour away." I tried to sound reassuring. I took a drag off of my cigarette.

Leonard looked back at me again and forced a smile, "Yeah, I know, Carl." We both knew it was a lie. Life was changing. Neither one of us said anything for the next few minutes. There wasn't anything to say. Leonard was the best friend that I had ever had, and the thought of not being around him constantly anymore was not something that I wanted to accept. The transition was going to be, to say the least, hard. To add to it, we had both grown even closer on the trip. When you share things that change your life forever with somebody, they're part of it. You can't help but become closer.

Not much later I spotted a sign that said "Ellensburg – one mile." I glanced down at the gas gauge. We needed to fill up before crossing the pass. A little food would probably do us good too.

"Hey, Leonard."

"Yeah, Carl?"

"We need fuel again. Why don't we stop at Ellensburg, fill up and get some chow."

"Sounds good." We were both still subdued.

As we approached Ellensburg I noticed that there was a fog lying over the town. "Man, that's weird."

"What?"

"Look, it's afternoon and the fog still hasn't burned off."

Leonard looked out the front window, studying the weather anomaly. "Yeah, that is weird," he said suspiciously.

Just as we got to the exit we hit the "fog." "Oh, dear God!" Leonard immediately put his hand over his nose and mouth. The stench was overwhelming. As we drove off of the freeway, I saw that just to the right of us there was a massive feed lot with maybe a couple of thousand head of cattle. "That's not fog, Carl, that's methane."

I put my own hand over my nose and mouth. "Yeah, that's pretty bad alright."

"Pretty bad? Good Lord, what an understatement. Hey, I have an idea, let's get back on the freeway and get gas at the next town."

"We won't make it, we're nearly on empty and the next town is Cle Elum about twenty miles away."

"Shit."

"Literally."

"Oh, shut up and find us a gas station."

We drove a couple of blocks down the main strip and quickly found a Texaco station with a burger joint next door. "Here we go." I pulled the van in, "I'll fill up and you go grab us a couple of burgers next door." I switched off the van. Leonard didn't move from the passenger's seat. He just stared at me like I was insane.

"What? A burger is not exactly what popped into my mind when we drove into cow hell here. My God, Carl, have a little sensitivity, this place is enough to make a Hindu cry."

"Then go get us a couple of nice bean burritos from that stand across the street." Without another word, Leonard hopped out of the van and went across the street. He still had his hand over his mouth and nose. I did too.

I quickly filled the van and then drove across the street and joined Leonard, who was still waiting for our order.

"How ya doin' there, partner?"

"God, I wish these guys would hurry up."

"So, let's think about this ... how does smell work?"

"I don't know, Carl, but I bet you have a theory."

"That I do, my friend." Leonard stared at me blankly. "Now I believe that the sensation of smell is generated by molecules bonding to smell receptors in one's nose. In this case that would be cow poop molecules."

"Goddamn it, Carl, would you please shut the hell up."

I was near laughing, "Hey, just trying to offer a scientific explanation," I said innocently. Just then our order came up.

Leonard grabbed the bag off the counter, "Well, stuff your empirical theory and let's get out of here before I hurl."

Five miles outside of Ellensburg, we tentatively took our hands away from our mouths and noses. I took mine away first.

"Is it safe?" I sniffed, then took a deep breath.

"Yeah, we're okay now." Leonard took his hand away and sniffed.

"Thank God. Man, that was rough."

"Yeah, very rough."

Leonard reached into the bag and said sarcastically, "You want your burrito now, Carl?"

"Uh, no, I think I'll wait on it a little."

"Yeah, I thought so ... me too." He opened the side window, stuck his head out, and let the fresh air blow over him. Even though we were both hungry, it took us another ten miles before either one of us had recovered enough to consider eating.

Just east of Cle Elum, we passed by the rest stop where we had first met Dieter and Marta.

"Hey, Leonard."

"Yeah Carl?"

"The rest stop," I pointed across the freeway, "Remember? Dieter and Marta."

Leonard smiled and nodded, "Yeah ... I wonder what they're up to now." He took another bite of his burrito.

"They're home," I said simply. "You know, Leonard, I really miss those guys. I wonder if we'll ever talk to 'em again."

"Yeah, maybe ... but if we don't, just remember the good stuff. That's what it's all about, Carl, remembering the good stuff in folks."

"Yeah..."

We were in the mountains again - the Cascades - and we were approaching Snoqualmie pass. Once over the pass, it was maybe an hour to Seattle. I started to think hard about Althea. I couldn't wait to see her. I wondered if she could feel that I was just a couple of hours away now ... probably she could.

I had finished my burrito, but Leonard, who was affected more adversely by the smell back in Ellensburg, was still working on his.

"So, Leonard, what about Gwendolyn?"

"What about her?" he said casually, then stuffed the remains of his burrito in his mouth.

"You haven't said anything about her for a few days now. You forget about her?"

He looked straight at me, finished chewing, then said, "Nope," and smiled.

"So you still think you're going to try and look her up when we get back?" Leonard looked at me for a second. I think he was trying to determine if I was giving him a hard time again about Gwendolyn.

"Hey, I'm really not giving you shit or anything, Leonard ... I'm just asking."

Satisfied with my answer, he looked out the window and said, "Yeah, like I said before, Carl, she and I are meant to be ... we *will* find each other." He smiled, continued to look out the window, and just left it that. I didn't press him any further. I was pretty sure that they would find each other.

Once over the pass, the freeway opened up and we flew down the mountain. The road was familiar now, and I felt confident in boldly shattering all traffic laws. Before we knew it, we had passed North Bend and Preston and were just entering Issaquah.

"Uh, navigator to pilot?"

"Roger, navigator, over."

"Ship speed eighty five – speed limit, fifty-five. Suggest slow down – speed trap."

As soon as Leonard reminded me, I immediately stood on the brakes and began, as quickly as I could, to drop the van down to exactly fifty-five. I had forgotten the nefarious Issaquah visitor tax. The police in this California-like suburb of Seattle were famous for ticketing drivers for as little as two miles an hour over the speed limit. Catching us on a radar gun doing eighty-five would have been a trooper's wet dream, and would have meant a ticket that would have required that I take out another student loan in the fall.

Our brake lights were still on when we in fact did pass a state patrol hidden behind an overpass pillar. He saw our brake lights for sure. He glared at us as we drove by him in the fast lane.

"Did he get us, Carl?" I looked down at the speedometer. We were doing exactly fifty-four.

"Nope, not this time."

Leonard turned around in the passenger seat, looked back at him, and broke into a James Cagney imitation, "You dirty copper ... you ain't got nothin' on me, see." Although he hadn't witnessed us breaking any laws, the trooper pulled out and began to tail us.

"I think he heard you, Leonard."

"Shit." Leonard turned back around in his seat. We both sat there innocently. The officer followed us for about a mile or so. Just before taking the next exit, he pulled up alongside us and did a 'tsk, tsk," with his index finger. It was his way of letting us know that we had been lucky this time.

Soon we were out of the suburbs and rolling into Seattle. Without ceremony, Interstate 90 ended and we turned north on Interstate 5. Gratefully, traffic wasn't at a complete standstill, but it was still horrendously congested. As we passed through downtown, Leonard said, "You know Carl, I can't deal with the city ... too much stimulation. How in fuck are you going to live here?"

"Well, for one, I have to. I suppose that I'll get used to it."

"Yeah, well, people get used to warts, too."

"Hey, man, I'll probably come back to the valley when I'm done with school."

"I hope so, Carl ..." He said it like he didn't believe that I would.

Soon we were out of the city and well on our way north. With each passing mile I felt more and more excited. In minutes, not hours, I would see Althea. We had been gone just short of two weeks, but it felt like an eternity.

Just after passing Everett, and even through my excitement, I noticed that we were nearly running on empty. We briefly discussed taking a chance and pushing on, then determined that it would be a bummer to run out of gas only miles from home. Reluctantly we pulled off at Marysville. I didn't waste time filling the tank, and quickly put only three gallons in - easily enough to get us home.

Within minutes we were back on the road. After all of the miles that we had traveled on our trip, the thirty miles to Mount Vernon should have seemed like nothing. It didn't. My mind was filled with both the passionate desire to see Althea and thoughts of Leonard and everything that we had been through on the trip together. In a way I couldn't wait to get home, and in another I never wanted this trip to end ... only a few more precious miles. I looked over at Leonard, who was staring out passenger's window. He looked sad. I didn't have to ask, I knew he felt the same way.

Home

Finally the freeway dropped down and into the valley. The air was fresh, clean and familiar. Home. Just outside of town, I watched a lone farmer harvest the last of his corn. It was the end of this summer. It was the end of this season.

We pulled up in front of my apartment. Althea had been watching for us. I had barely turned off the van and gotten out when she came bounding down the stairs. She had a huge smile on her face and was so happy to see me that she was crying a little. She threw her arms around me and we hugged each other tightly. I could feel her shaking. Then she put her lips to my ear and said softly, "I love you Carl, I love you so much."

"I love you too, Althea."

After a couple of minutes, I whispered to her, "Leonard." We pulled ourselves apart. Leonard was patiently standing by the van watching us. His bags were beside him. He already had gotten his things out of the van.

Althea and I walked over to him, and before I could say anything to him Althea threw her arms around him, kissed him on the cheek and said, "It's so good to see you Leonard. Thank you for bringing him back home safe."

Leonard kissed her on the cheek back, smiled at her, and said, "You're welcome, Althea."

Then he turned to me, "I guess this is it, and Carl ... I should get home myself."

I nodded, "Yeah ..." I felt like I was going to cry. Something about this felt like saying goodbye. We put our arms around each other and hugged hard. After a couple of minutes we eased our embrace. Leonard stepped back and we looked deeply into each other's eyes.

I smiled. "It's been a trip, hasn't it ..."

"Yes it has, Carl ... it's been a trip." He smiled too.

Then he picked up his bags. "I'll be talking with you soon, Carl, okay?"

"Yeah." As he started to walk away, I said, "Hey man, I can drive you."

He turned around. "No, Carl," he said quietly, "I think I'd rather walk for while." I nodded – I knew what he meant.

Epilogue

I suppose that all of us at one time in our lives must go on a pilgrimage – wherever, or however it may be. As I look back on that prophetic summer, I realize that - without knowing it - Leonard and I were in search of something. And we found it ... we found a deeper meaning within ourselves, and in the world. I suppose you could say that we found spirituality together. That revelation of spirituality has stayed with me. I also do believe that some of us really are prophets, even if only for brief periods of our lives. Leonard was one of those people. I know that in the years that I was close to him I was close to a very great man.

I hang on tightly to these memories, although sometimes the distance makes it hard to remember what was real and what was not. But I do know some things that are fact.

Shortly after the trip, I moved to Seattle and began school. That transition changed the course of my life.

Althea and I are no longer together. We broke up about six months after the trip. One evening when I was up visiting in the valley, she threw an entire stack of dishes onto the floor, shattering them to pieces, and then left in a rage. It was a metaphor for the end of our relationship. She wanted to get married, and I had tried to put her off, yet again. She'd had enough and wanted no more of the excuses.

Sometimes, looking back, I think I probably should have married her. As trite as it might sound, I was young and I really didn't know how good I had it at the time. Now, about once a year I run into her – usually in the late summer at the outdoor farmer's market. That it's always that time of year when I see her seems ironic to me. She's married now and has two lovely children. And, although I think about her from time to time, I no longer feel her presence on the planet.

I miss that feeling, and I miss her.

I did hear from Dieter and Marta a couple of times following our trip. I wrote back, too. But the longer that they were away from the States, the worse their English became. Finally, either the writing became too difficult for them or they didn't know how to get a hold of me. Eventually I heard from them no more. In Dieter's last letter, he told me that he and Marta had decided to become Buddhists. I hope that worked for them.

I miss them.

I haven't seen Leonard for a long, long time, although I know we are still close friends. About a year after the trip we just sort of began to drift apart. It really started after Althea and I broke up, and I stopped coming up to valley with any frequency. It was nothing bad between Leonard and I ... it was just two friends in separate places, going in separate directions. I guess that happens. Eventually, when our long-distance conversations got more and more awkward we just stopped talking altogether. I think it was easier to just let it go that way.

A few years after finishing up my degree I moved back to the valley for a teaching job. I tried hard, but unsuccessfully, to find Leonard. He must have moved. I like to think that he finally found Gwendolyn and they are blissfully happy together. In reality, though, I have no idea where he is or what he is doing now, but I think about him from time to time, and I wish him well.

I miss him most of all.